FIRE & SMOKE

THE RED MASQUES SERIES - BOOK 4

M. SINCLAIR

Copyright © 2019 M. Sinclair
Published by M. Sinclair
In the USA

All rights reserved.
All rights reserved. No part of this publication may be reproduced/transmitted/distributed in any form. No part of this publication shall be shared by any means including photocopying, recording, or any electronic/mechanical method, or the Internet, without the prior written consent of the author. Cases of brief quotations embodied in critical reviews and certain other non-commercial uses permitted by copyright law are the exception. The unauthorized reproduction/transmitting of this work is illegal. This book is a work of fiction and any resemblance to persons, living or dead, or places, events or locales is purely coincidental. The characters are products of the author's imagination and used fictitiously.

Formatted By: Kassie Morse

The Union of Love & Madness

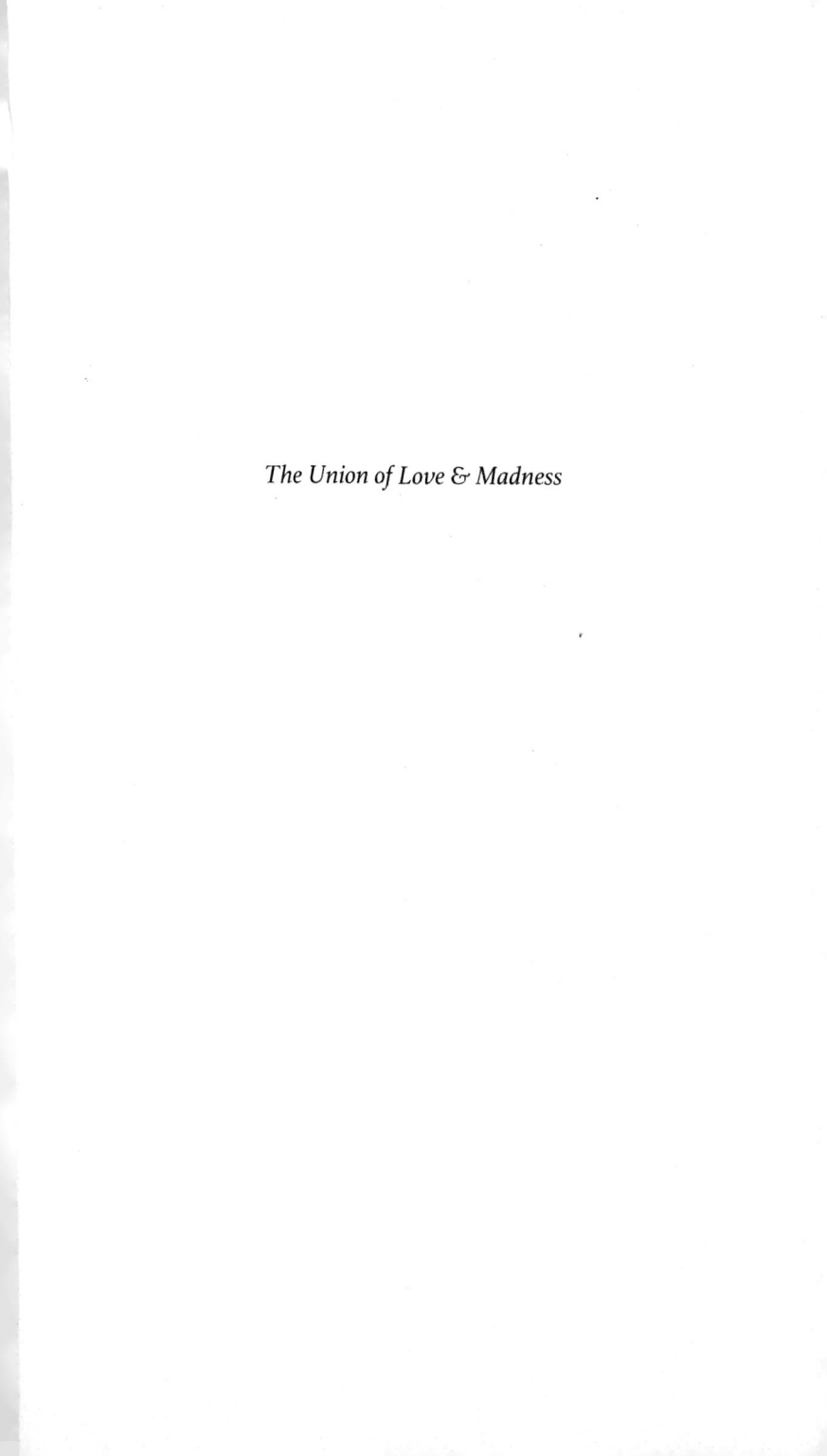

CONTENTS

Description — vii

Part I
THE EARTH REALM

1. Vegas — 3
2. Vegas — 30
3. Vegas — 52
4. Vegas — 63
5. Vegas — 84
6. Vegas — 110
7. Vegas — 137
8. Vegas — 153
9. Grover — 179
10. Vegas — 183
11. Vegas — 217
12. Vegas — 228
13. Vegas — 249
14. Rocket — 261
15. Vegas — 279
16. Bandit — 304

Part II
THE DARK FAE

17. Kodiak — 327
18. Vegas — 341
19. Vegas — 354
20. Vegas — 358

Epilogue — 378

M. Sinclair 381
Also by M. Sinclair 383
Stalk me... really, I'm into it 387

DESCRIPTION

Tick. Toc. Tick. Toc.

Do you hear that? Yeah. That is the sound of a countdown. What countdown you ask? The one where everything goes to shit. Everything had been silent for a week. A week filled with rest and change. A week we needed. Thanksgiving is today and a feeling of apprehension has me brimming with nerves. I know something big is about to happen and I have no idea what.

Well, not exactly.

Will there be a clash between my stalker and I? How the hell are we going to make this relationship of eleven work? What about Gray, my totally badass sister, finding out about our relationship? Or the things we have been neglecting as a Red Masques team? Oh, and let's not forget the war with the crazy Dark Fae king!

Oh, no.

But what if it is even larger than that?

At least we have Thanksgiving to look forward to, right? Hadn't I said something about living until the holidays?

I mean, what's the worst that can happen...

This 100k fourth installment of the Red Masques series (A paranormal urban fantasy RH) is filled with fantasy, adventure, and a ton of steamy steam. Get your fans and water bottles ready because this is going to be a hot one! Not to mention the substantial blood, violence, and swearing that we've come to love! Be ready for this fast-paced and exciting continuation with Vegas and her boys!

A note to readers of both the Red Masques & Vengeance:
There will be spoilers!!! The plotlines intertwine so I am releasing both books at the same time. Feel free to pick either release but I just wanted to give you a heads up! Enjoy!

Also, don't forget to follow my FB group Sinclair's Ravens for new updates!!!

I

THE EARTH REALM

1

VEGAS

Excess, thy name is Byron.

"We can't accept this," Blue muttered softly in disbelief. His voice betrayed his growing eager excitement. I leaned against the doorway that led from the back hall to the massive showroom sized garage that had clearly been an addition to this classic home. I was placing my bet now that the Horde property didn't have one of these babies. Then again, it had magic...

...so I was willing to excuse what it lacked in modern luxuries.

Edwin stood behind me, his shadows wrapping around my ankles, as his smoky red wine scent surrounded me like a warm blanket. Mind you, I hadn't confirmed visually that it was him but I was nearly positive. I may have been bothered enough to check if I hadn't been absolutely bamboozled by whatever the fuck was occurring in front of me.

Yes. I did use that word. Deal with it.

"You can," Byron spoke confidently with his large tan hands shoved in the pockets of his tailored dress pants. "And you will. It's an inconvenience and a safety concern for all of you to be limited to one car. Additionally, you can't respond to threats if you have to wait for someone to pick you up. Imagine if Vegas was in trouble and the car wasn't here. You could be putting her life at risk."

Oh! Our poor SUV and sedan, Byron had done his homework. Aced it. Proceeded to get a PhD and was now manipulating my boys to accept these outrageous cars. I had to admit, he was fucking good at this. I should have been taking notes.

Originally, I had been concerned about all of the designer shit I had ordered to replace what we lost in the fire. Then Byron had persuaded the boys to see "reason" in that the purchase wasn't a personal expense but, rather, a team one. His analogy was something along the lines of "if an employee had an accident at work their medical bills would be covered by the company." It was complete bullshit but, hey, I wasn't complaining. The boys and I had always been comfortable financially, even when Vivian had passed away. She had set aside a trust in our names for when we turned eighteen, but I was starting to suspect that somehow the money had come from the Horde.

These magical bastards were sneaky.

I mean, we couldn't afford to be prideful considering we had almost nothing left from the old house. These cars though? Well, these weren't designer clothes and they were definitely not a *need*. This was a whole new level of excess.

"I get that," Blue stated as I watched the boys' expressions ranging from shocked to confused. They reminded me briefly of the young boys I had known in high school. *Ah, boys getting toys.* Never really changes with age, does it?

"It's just. I mean. Do they have to be… well, fuck, Byron, these are all worth over a hundred grand easily," Blue stated in a pathetic and truly poor attempt to dissuade him from this gift.

FIRE & SMOKE

Come on baby, you aren't even trying...

I wouldn't either but I was still going to give him shit about it. You know, on principle alone. The man needs to know who's calling the shots around here.

The dramatic psychopath Vegas. Always the dramatic psychopath. Stupid question.

"I already had them and they serve our current purpose because of how fast they are," Byron stated.

Liar. I'm sure he already had them after he customized and ordered them to the house as convenient gifts.

I finally straightened myself up and spoke. "Boys, just accept the gift. It's fucking awesome and everyone needs a way to get around without depending on our current vehicles."

Yep, that was all they needed.

Each of them took the key fobs that Byron had handed out and the garage exploded in excited deep voices as they each found their designated car. I chuckled as Byron looked back at me with a pair of crackling lava eyes made of a deep chocolate mixed with crimson. Despite the glamour, I donned and the brother's hidden blood ink form, they just seemed a tad different than before our Horde trip. Or maybe I was just more focused on them.

In honor of Thanksgiving, Byron had worn a bright red quarter-zip sweater and dress pants. We had tried to explain to the two of them that the holiday was for consuming mass quantities of food and football, but I don't think they were really getting it. Silly magical asshats.

They would, though. Oh, they would.

It was still early in the day, around 10 a.m., and the Macy's parade could be heard from the kitchen. Bandit hadn't begun cooking yet unless you count putting the turkey in the massive commercial-sized oven that resided in the Ivanov's kitchen. I was finding it far easier to adjust to this home than I would have assumed. I know. Surprising. I mean you would have thought it would have been more difficult to adjust to such excessive wealth.

Nope. It fit me just like a motherfucking jewel-encrusted glove. Or something that rich people would wear. You feel me?

"See? That worked great," Byron offered while mussing his white-blonde hair with his left hand. Ever since mentioning that I liked his hair messy the other day, he had stopped styling it and I wasn't about to bring it up in fear of him reverting back.

I smiled my teeth pressing down on my lip slightly. "And how long until they notice the custom interiors, model year, and license plates?"

Byron narrowed his eyes with a sexy smirk. "The license plates are numbered."

"Yes," I grinned feeling a curl of desire tingle through me at his narrowed gaze. "In order of when each came into my life. You don't think that's convenient for someone who just had them 'sitting around'?"

Byron chuckled as his eyes sparkled. "Fuck, doll, you notice everything. Don't you?"

"I think this was really sweet of you," I commented softly with a more serious expression. There was a slight vulnerability to his tanned face as he offered me a shy smile that was so different from his sexy smirk. Before he could respond Decimus walked up. I bit back a laugh as Deci ran a hand through his thick hair and rubbed the back of his neck.

"Listen, I already have a motorcycle. I can't accept..."

Byron turned. "The motorcycle was a birthday present from all of us. This is a necessity. How are you supposed to transport more than one person on that thing? Also, do you want Vegas riding on a motorcycle? That sounds dangerous to me."

I scowled.

I would have liked to point out that the ridiculously expensive cars barely fit two people if that. But still, the bastard had thought of every conceivable argument. Decimus swore and took off towards his car. Byron grinned. I had to give him credit. The man was a genius. I'd have to keep an eye out for his tricks. I'd fallen for a few even in the past week. Hence the closet filled with insanity upstairs. I let him pass through the door as he offered me a wink. I couldn't deny the heat that flashed through my body at that.

Honestly, though, the heated desire didn't surprise me.

Despite everyone's exhaustion this past week, something had been turned on inside of me. And no, not just my fucking hormones. Those were a bitch though because every single day I was resisting the urge to fuck like a bunny. Christ. Maybe this was because I'd gone so long without sex, now I was constantly turned on. Oh, well. *I hope the boys can deal.*

I nearly grinned at that. Oh, I bet they would be able to deal.

"You know, *dolcezza*," Edwin spoke softly from behind me. "He has a car for you as well."

Normally, his random appearances would have made me jump. Instead, I looked up at him and found his beautiful eyes staring down at me. They were framed in thick dark lashes that highlighted the amber color that brightened to pumpkin orange. It was a unique color and one I had started to really like. Much like Byron, Edwin had put on dress pants and a sweater, because that is truly dressing down for him. Sometimes Edwin struck me as so relaxed and other times he was a fucking lunatic. A well dressed lunatic, of course. It was a fifty-fifty chance every morning. I resisted the urge to twirl my finger through his thick black curls that rested lose and down to his shoulders.

The man was just beautiful. No denying it.

I shook my head. "I can't accept it."

"You haven't seen it." His lip twitched. "Go, check it out. Remember, Vegas, Byron really only knows how to show his affection through what he's used to. Money has been constant since birth, so buying presents for the people he cares about seems right to him."

Ah. Fuckity fuck. When you put it that way...

A key fob slipped into my hand as his lips grazed my temple before walking away. Besides one or two passing kisses in the past few days, we hadn't had much time alone. It didn't seem purposeful, we just were busy. I was really hoping for some alone time though because the quick kisses weren't enough. I was very greedy and wanted more now that I had admitted my frustrating attraction and affection toward the magical asshat.

And, yes. I would still be calling him that from time to time.

Since coming back from the Horde, the group of us had been busy and not the bad type of busy. Because I may or may not have gone full out on purchasing festive fall decor and preparing for Christmas. They just had so much space to cover, I mean what could a girl do *except* decorate every square inch of it.

When Edwin had suggested hiring someone to do it, I had been furious. I hadn't talked to him all day and it confused the shit out of him until Grover explained the problem and my wounded pride. Eventually, I compromised agreeing a professional could do Christmas lights but that was only because I didn't want my boys, including them, going up that high. Byron had made a quip about "caring about them" and I didn't correct him. Instead I fixed him with a look and a hitched brow daring him to laugh about my affection towards them some more. I think he and Edwin had been shocked about my lack of sarcasm.

That's just how I was though, once I cared... I cared a whole fucking lot. So they would need to get used to that and get used to being part of 'my boys.' It also convinced Edwin to have the Horde house decorated as well, which was fucking awesome since they didn't celebrate Earth realm holidays. With the two of them having returned into the massive house, I smiled and skipped down the stairs to see the shiny new toys.

"Oh, wow," I chuckled at my first stop.

Grover looked down at me from where he stood, his arms crossed over his muscular chest. The guy was a dream boat. Today, like a normal person, he wore sweatpants and a black shirt. Even our comfy clothes were designer and well made. It was fucked up.

I couldn't even start to tell you about my wardrobe. I'd deal with that later. *Extensively.*

Grover's hair was mussed, the rich auburn color darker than normal, and almost matched his warm chocolate brown eyes. The thin silver ring circling his pupil had been a permanent change and it transformed his face from classically handsome to something else. Something less human and more ethereal. He hadn't shaved yet so his jawline had a slightly dark shadow that was absolutely yummy. Then again it could be that I was intoxicated by his delicious scent which smelt like *my* fucking body wash. I swear to god, one of these days I would say something.

"What is this?" I asked with curiosity.

He chuckled with a nearly overwhelmed and disbelieving expression, "this? This is an Aston Martin DBS Superleggera Coupe, Angel."

"I have no idea what you said, but it looks fancy," I smirked playfully. It was a beautiful car with a sleek crimson shape that seemed very Grover-ish. Attention grabbing and a bit sporty. Then again, did I really know what classifies a car as 'sporty?' Hell, no.

If it goes fast then it's sporty to me. *Vroom. Vroom.*

Grover shook his head, smiling at me affectionately, and kissed my cheek before approaching the vehicle. I walked towards Cosimo and his brightly lit crystalline eyes. Out of everyone, besides me, Cosimo got into the spirit of American holidays the most. Today he wore a sweater with a massive turkey on it and pajama pants, because he would no doubt fall asleep at some point. His tall lean form looked more muscular than usual but his midnight messy asymmetrical hair was still 100% him. He also had a black hoop in for his lip ring and a small crystal stud in his eyebrow. My attention had a hard time straying from the lip ring though. I wanted that lip ring against my lips...badly.

The man was just sexy.

"What'd you get?" I asked curiously as he wrapped his arms around me along with his soft expense aftershave. Can we say 'edible?'

"I have to be honest," he smiled. "I know nothing about cars, but *mierda*. It's cool as fuck."

It was and I reluctantly separated from him to examine it. The car itself was bold, unique, and slightly eccentric with a low profile in electric blue. The back of the car was black and created two C-line curves behind the doors. It was absolutely visually captivating like its owner. I snapped my head up to see how Cosimo looked standing near it.

Oh. Byron was good.

The car matched his dark midnight hair and bright blue eyes. I opened the door and pulled out the information on it. "It says it's a Bugatti Chiron."

Cosimo whistled and got into the driver's seat. I kissed his soft lips in a light peck that had him making a soft low sound in his throat. I winked and moved out of the car, traveling onwards to my next lover.

"Rocket," I sang as my mad scientist peeked his tousled platinum and blonde waves from his car. A car that was very much Rocket. I knew this car though. It was a Mercedes-Benz S class in silver. How did I know that? Because Rocket had only *wanted it* since it came out. I'd latched onto that small nugget about him, since it wasn't often he expressed a preference, and somehow Byron had found it out as well. The car had a powerful yet classic style to it.

"Do you see this, sugar?" He grinned and I think the sky broke open as a choir of angels descended. It wasn't often that Rocket smiled and when he did it was beautiful. Although, I had to admit to seeing a lot more smiles lately. Like a fuck ton.

His birthday two days ago? Yeah, that didn't hurt.

As I've mentioned, Rocket always prefers to do something interesting that will further his knowledge base on his birthday. So, of course I expected something with magic. Instead the fucker did something way more romantic that nearly had me sobbing like a baby. On November 21st I had gone to sleep and when I'd awoken? I was in Alabama on a jet with just Rocket and Booker.

Yes. That was as delicious as it sounds.

Well, almost. Unfortunately for me, we still haven't had the chance to sleep together. I know. They were freakin' gorgeous and I was alone with them. Talk about perfect timing! But they resisted while I pranced around the hotel in Alabama wearing a pair of leggings and a fitted top. I may have worn a pair that was just a little tighter than normal and it took all of five minutes before Rocket was trying to change my outfit.

I only did it because it was his birthday. Just for the record.

But really, who is actually comfortable in a half top? Not this girl.

Anyway, the reason for our trip was actually very cool. For his birthday, Rocket had asked Edwin and Byron to go visit his family home with Booker and me. Of course, the first had already seen it. For me, the massive white mansion shone like a diamond as I stood before the huge home that was technically Rocket's when he turned twenty-five. While his father and Booker's lost their respective fortunes, they had done something right by creating trusts for both boys. Rocket's included this luxurious monster of a house. I shook my head remembering exactly what it was like being there.

"Rocket," I whispered as he looked down at me. We had just walked through the first level of the estate and were looking over the extensive land that stretched as far as I could see. The property, despite no one living on it, was well maintained and retained employees. You know normal stuff, like a person to take care of your pure-bred horses and wash your diamond chandelier. Normal shit.

"It's just money," he assured gently.

"You've been keeping tabs on this place the entire time?" I frowned while trying to ignore how out of place my Vans were on this stunning southern porch. A slight chill, reminiscent of Boston, hung in the air.

"Yes," he sighed and then looked around. "I may sell it when I take official ownership."

"Why?"

His thumb drifted to my chin and he was quiet for a bit. "It is a beautiful house. Yet all I can think about is my father and I don't want to think about that. To think about him."

My arms wrapped around his as he kissed my forehead gently. I understood that. After Vivi's murder, the house in Ohio had just felt different. I hadn't slept well until we had officially moved into our house here.

Booker and I never confirmed why he'd wanted to go back to his family home, especially now. Something told me it was a goodbye. While there were no tears or big emotional breakdowns, I felt as though he was trying to release a part of his old life. I'd come back to Boston feeling as though I'd grown even closer to both of them.

I think Rocket felt the same because the bastard was blinding me with smiles.

His skin was slightly paler than normal due to the season but he still had a glowing southern tan that never seemed to fade. His dark brows matched the shorter sides of his hair and created a contrast to his metallic silver eyes. Somehow, maybe due to magic, they had truly become a metallic silver. I loved it.

"Sugar?" I blushed at his nickname and slight southern drawl. "Do you love it?"

He scooped me up and pressed me into his hoodie covered muscular form. I know! Rocket in a hoodie! We took this holiday relaxation thing very seriously. His mint scent surrounded me as he placed a very surprising and enthusiastic kiss on my lips.

Oh, shit. He really was happy.

"Wow," I breathed looking up at him as he nipped my nose with a low growl and went back to his new baby. It was rare for Rocket to get this worked up over something and I loved it. I mean, damn. The boy was just so fucking beautiful. I shook my head to claim back my brain and walked in a daze towards the next car in the line up.

"Wowza," I breathed as Booker nodded while studying the car in front of him.

So, it went without saying that Booker was the artist of our family. The man constantly smelled like paint and fresh laundry. The car in front of us was truly a work of art and I wasn't even positive this type of car was on the market for sale. I think they called them concept cars? I wasn't positive but I *was* in love.

"What is this?" I asked in a hushed tone.

"This is a Koenigsegg Jesko," he whispered. "It's so fucking cool, kitty."

I shivered at his term of endearment and examined the white car. Although, it was many colors if I was being honest and very unique in its angles. The bottom of the front was curved and came out in a black shelf resting under the white frame. It had a bold electric green streak down the center that matched the green in other places on the car's structure. The place where you put your foot had a blue and yellow coloring to it. It shouldn't have been pretty but somehow it was.

"Yeah, it is," I nodded before squeezing his hand. Booker was dressed in jeans and a hoodie that was made to look like *Nympheas*. The painting that featured water lilies was by Claude Monet, an impressionist artist that Booker all but worshiped. His golden hair was pulled back in one of those man buns I loved and his tan skin seemed to be lit up from within like his diamond earrings. Yeah. That had been an upgrade as well. I met those soft velvet gray eyes and smiled, pulling him into a hug. It was totally an excuse to feel the rippling muscles that he always hid underneath bulky designer clothes.

Couldn't we have a 'walk around shirtless' rule?

Decimus's car was next and caused me to let out a brilliant laugh because I totally understood why he had felt bad about having two vehicles. First, I'd like to note that his motorcycle, a present from all of us, had been crazy expensive. We had, of course, each given him a small gift of our own and planned a special day for him. Byron though had insisted on giving the motorcycle as a group gift.

This year I had made an extra effort to make his day special due to the craziness of our life lately. Just because we now had magic, we couldn't forget about family. We had gone out for dinner the night before at a local Greek restaurant, just the two of us per his request, and spent most of the night curled up in a booth talking. Very romantic and unexpected. It was super sweet. We had, of course, taken a short intermission from classic romanticism to fuck in the car like teenagers before heading home.

What? Like I wasn't supposed to take advantage of time alone with him? The man is sinful. Plus, it had totally fulfilled a fantasy I'd had since highschool of him and me.

On the morning of his birthday we had surprised him with red velvet cake and explained that we were all staying home to have a movie day with pizza. I think he had expected us to throw something bigger at him and I could see the relief paired with true happiness at the concept.

After we had exchanged a few small gifts, we had brought out the big guns. I had waited to give him his present until we walked into the garage. He frowned in confusion at the black matte helmet I had handed him until we revealed his new Ducati Desmosedici, or something that sounded close to that, at least. It was in a special order black matte and unlike we predicted, he instantly fucking accepted it. He had known how to ride forever and had never had the funds to get a bike like this.

Before leaving for a test drive, I had whispered for him to check the inside back of the helmet. When he had seen the inscription *"for my dark knight,"* the bad boy had turned ten shades of red and yanked me into a kiss so hard that Blue whistled. He wouldn't tell anyone why but I felt as though I had very much done well this birthday.

Metaphorical pat on the back for me and all that jazz.

Decimus was a broody snarling bastard and I was absolutely in love with him because just underneath the surface was a totally romantic sweetheart that was extremely loyal to his family. However, none of this took away from the fact that he was a fucking leather wearing badass who could fuck you up five ways from Sunday. Decimus could be pretty fucking scary when he wanted to be. Not in the "I will cut you open" way like Blue, but in the "I'm going to beat you bloody" way.

It was why this car was so fucking perfect for him. This car was as *bad* as they come.

"I don't think I can drive this." He looked at me with large amber eyes. They were lighter than normal and surrounded by thick onyx colored lashes that matched his dark messy hair. Despite his efforts against it, the man was stunning and it was in part due to the contrast of his stark white complexion against his dark hair. I could have stared at him all day. Sometimes I did and I am positive that if he didn't already love me, he would find it creepy.

"Yes, you can," I encouraged. I breathed in his sea salt scent before noting the leather scent in the air from all the new cars.

"This is a Lamborghini Aventador SVJ Roadster,

princess," he whispered while wrapping his arms around me and placing his lips against my neck. "I'm scared I will break it."

I snorted and shook my head looking over the dark purple car with yellow accents. It was so fucking badass and so very him. I turned to look at him and grasped his face moving in close, nose to nose. "Deci, you better not repeat this because I will light your ass on fire... but you are the best driver in this household. You will be perfectly fine."

His eyes went wide in surprise and then a small smile tilted the corner of his lips as a dark glint filled his eyes. "Princess, that opinion would cause some very big fights if anyone heard that."

"Don't you dare," I threatened knowing he loved shit like that.

"What will you do? I'm pretty sure an elemental mage can handle fire," His cocky smile was addicting.

I narrowed my eyes. "No sex."

Anyone else and I would have wondered if it was too soon to make that joke. Instead, Decimus let out a deep laugh that caused everyone to look over. He yanked me closer and tugged on my lower lip gently. "That, Princess, is a very naughty thing to say and a punishment for both of us."

I groaned softly because he was right.

"Now, go on," He pulled back leaving me with a wink. "I'll keep your secret."

"You're an idiot," I huffed and walked toward Bandit.

"Your idiot," Decimus offered after me in an amused voice. He was. This was true. I was his princess, though I hadn't even needed to make that damn agreement. The minute his tattoo went on the urge to smoke went away. Byron said it was unusual because he thought Deci would be leaning more towards fire but I knew he was far more like water. A constant force that could symbolize strength and depth or a destructive force of nature.

Yeah. He's way more like water than fire. Plus, I totally called dibs on that shit. Unintentional dibs, but still dibs.

"Oh, my god!" I bounced on my toes and jumped on Bandit. I loved his car. Like, I would be driving it. He grinned at me and tilted his head down to kiss my brow gently.

Much like his car, Bandit was somewhat a mystery and very complex. The silver-haired man in front of me could be fucking adorable at times, like when he got a haircut because I did or how he wore an apron when he cooked. Other times? Well, the man was a methodical killer and possibly... maybe... slightly... a sociopath.

Oh, well! If he was a sociopath then he was *my* sociopath.

I'm so glad I didn't have a mother because these were the exact type of boys she would have warned me about. Good thing they were already Vivi approved.

His spring green eyes were bright while looking at the car and matched his electric, fresh cut grass smell. Today, he wore a hoodie that matched my own and joggers. We both were in all black with cute matching socks that had turkeys on them.

What? It's fucking adorable.

"You can borrow it," he winked. I noticed he had all his black gauges in today. I looked over at the Rolls Royce Phantom and shook my head. Byron even got the color right. It was black and only added to its sleek, deadly, and quiet nature. God. I literally loved this car.

"Beautiful," Blue whined dramatically. I kissed Bandit's nose and ran straight into Blue.

He swung me onto his back so that I was looking at the new car over his shoulder. I inhaled his cinnamon scent and felt slight moisture from his freshly washed crimson hair. He had chosen to wear jeans today but had a long sleeve henley on that totally hid his lean muscles. *I should take it off him.*

Blue turned his head to look at me with those denim baby blues and offered me his dimpled smile. I had spent so much time looking at Blue that I could tell you how many freckles he had. Was that sorta creepy?

"Do you like it?" I asked him. Blue's car made so much sense and was so completely him I was starting to wonder if I hadn't picked out these cars instead of Byron.

"I love it," he sighed. "But I am contemplating calling him on the fact that they are personalized."

I smiled and moved to stand in front of him, not surprised that he had noticed. I clasped his jaw with my palms and talked quietly. "I don't think you should say anything."

"Beautiful...". He offered me a look.

"This was a big deal for Byron," I commented in a whisper while remembering his shy smile. "More than that. Edwin brought up a good point. Not everyone shows affection like we do. I think this is the way Byron shows it."

Those eyes flashed with understanding and I sometimes wondered how he had a psychotic unhinged side to him as well. He seemed so grounded. Blue nodded and chuckled. "Man, Vegas. This is going to take some getting used to though and I don't like relying on them. It feels wrong. And we've always been independent. Just the nine of us and Lucida."

I frowned and then spoke aloud what I'd been thinking. "Even if you don't think of it as a job related benefit, I think that they rely on us equally, Blue. Sure. We don't have this type of money, even with everything we've saved up, but they don't have this type of family. I mean, Christ, the past few Thanksgivings? They just ordered take out and sat around this massive house by themselves. The crazy bastards didn't celebrate Thanksgiving! They didn't even eat mashed potatoes, Blue! Mashed potatoes!"

Blue groaned and nuzzled into my neck. "When did you get so fucking smart, Vegas?"

"I've always been this smart, you ass!" I exclaimed as his eyes flashed with a dangerous heat. Before I knew it, the back of my legs were hitting the front of his white and black BMW i8 Coupe. The car had been something Blue had always commented on liking and it suited his personality in a way that you would only understand if you knew all of him. The car has classic smooth lines that showcased its luxury while the carbon fiber electric blue lining added just a splash of color. You know, like the *not* so small splash of insanity in his head.

God. These cars were really becoming a psychoanalytic exercise.

"I'm sorry, Vegas." He pressed me down onto the car as he caged me in with his muscular arms. "I didn't hear what you called me. Would you mind repeating it?" Bandit, the bastard, laughed from his driver's seat a few feet away.

"I called you an ass," I grinned because a slightly aggressive Blue was hot as fuck.

"Yeah, that's what I thought." He sighed in mock disappointment. "Now, that isn't very nice at all, beautiful. I'm thinking you should be punished for that."

I blushed as Kodiak's head shot up and a predatory smile crawled onto his face. I shook my head as he walked over and leaned against Blue's car. "What's this about punishment?"

Blue's eyes sparked. "Well, I mean she called me an ass. So, I just think..."

I slipped away from Blue with a laugh of victory then cried out in shocked horror as Kodiak caught my waist and picked me up. He chuckled at my sad attempt to run away. My legs wrapped around his muscular waist as Blue shook his head. "Beautiful, you should be expecting a punishment later. I want you to think about that all day."

The bastard. I groaned as my body heated up and Kodiak carried me towards his truck. I offered a smile to my grizzly bear turned wolf. The weird magic animal inside him pissed me off because he was my grizzly bear, not my wolf. Apparently, I didn't get a choice in shit like that. His familiar forest scent hadn't changed, though. I breathed in the pine that always seemed to follow him around. I wasn't positive what type of truck we were sitting on but it was big and fit Kodiak perfectly. It was a solid black with massive wheels and a huge open back flatbed that he could put camping shit in or pull an RV.

"What type of truck is this?" I asked with a flirty voice as Kodiak's brows raised behind his dark framed glasses. Those dark green eyes dilated and a lock of his messy chocolate brown hair flopped over. I was happy to announce that for once he wasn't wearing boots and instead wore slippers and comfy clothes. Thanksgiving was turning everyone into a lazy bum for the day.

Vegas: 1

Productivity: 0

"I'm still on this punishment thing," he warned. He smoothed his massive tanned hand along my jaw and neck in a soft hold. I let out a soft sound as he kissed my lips gently but with an undercurrent of possessiveness that was getting me all hot and bothered.

He pulled away with an excited glint to his eyes. "But it's a Ford King Ranch 450, with a towing capacity I don't need but could be helpful down the road."

"It's big," I pointed out.

Kodiak chuckled. "Well, I'm a big man."

He was and the car fit him because it was dominant, a little scary, but you would no doubt feel very safe while driving it or as a passenger.

... I would like a test drive of my own.

I bit my lip and locked my ankles behind him so he had to step closer. "Yeah? How big?"

A low rumble came from his chest as he shook his head. "Nope, you are still getting punished."

"Damn you," I cried. He put me down and smacked my ass.

"Kodi!" I jumped and offered him wide eyes.

"Vegas!" he mocked in a high voice with a dangerous mirth on his face.

I shook my head scowling because I knew he wanted a reaction. I turned in a huff and looked at the following cars. I saw a BMW Sedan that I had seen Edwin driving, along with Byron's black matte Ferrari. That made a lot of sense because as far as the eye could see were nothing but designer cars. So, cars were Byron's thing? Cool. I could work with that. Or maybe it wasn't cars and he just liked collecting pretty things? Anyway, it didn't surprise me that Edwin had a classic BMW and I would bet he didn't even like driving all that much.

He didn't try to be very human. As I've mentioned, I will not be dissuaded from the belief that he was part of the Knights of the Round Table.

I saw our sad looking SUV and sedan. Then I tilted my head because next to Byron's car, in front of our old cars, were two beautiful Escalades that were clearly meant to replace the others in the case we wanted to travel together. Smart man. Smart, magical, not so ass-hat. He was very sweet actually. Completely unstable but sweet.

So, exactly my type.

But, I mean who does this type of thing? It wasn't even about the price either as it was very clear that he loved cars and had taken a considerable amount of time planning this out. It was very thoughtful. He purchased exactly what they wanted even if they themselves hadn't known what they desired. It spoke to an empathetic streak I hadn't assumed from Byron. I was impressed.

In some ways, if we were to continue on this deep pattern of thinking, I would say this entire week had symbolized us starting our new life. We were off from school with only finals left. We were living in a new house with luxury items that we had never even thought of. We had magic. We were somehow making our relationship work. It was a new chapter for us. It was like we had gotten a system update or an upgrade.

Don't even get me started on the physical changes either! Remember when I had mentioned Gray's men being larger than life? Well, it seems whatever magic nonsense made Edwin and Byron so perfect had begun to affect my other boys. They had always been handsome but now there was this *other* quality to them. Even Cosimo had grown one or two inches and I promise you that Bandit had not been *that* muscular before. I mean I wasn't complaining but I noticed everything so it was fairly shocking. It was a slight change but it made them just that extra boost of scary that they had been missing as humans.

Because we weren't human anymore. I shook my head. I mean really, what the heck was my life?

I had also undergone some physical changes that were just freaking me out a bit. If someone had told me that the key to having toned muscle was magic, I would have laughed. *Turns out -- it is!* I had slowly started to notice the physical change as any fat, albeit wasn't much before since I'd always been thin and awkward most of my life, disappeared and was replaced by lean and long muscles like a ballerina. Unfortunately, I hadn't gotten Gray's killer curves but my skin had become slightly more luminescent and even with my glamour on, my hair seemed longer and thicker. Did I mention my eyes were very much undeniably purple now? Oh yeah. So that was fun to explain to people. I wasn't positive they bought the contact lie. I wondered how Rocket got away with his silver eyes, but I was afraid to hear his response. Usually when people questioned Rocket, it didn't seem to end well.

My favorite part? My short nails were now slightly longer and had an opal like texture to them. Can we hear it for never painting my nails again? Pair that with the silver tattoo running down my chest and I began struggling to look human. Note, this is all before I have even mentioned our magic.

The magic that had somehow made us more agile, graceful, faster, and stronger. I was starting to think that the vampire mythos really was connected to the Horde. I would need to watch *Twilight* for research.

Right, Vegas... research. Alright, I would watch *Interview with a Vampire* to even it out.

Edwin had said we would slowly start to develop our powers over time. However, even he had to admit they seemed more advanced than normal and seemed to "blame" it on me. I suppose with the issues occurring in the Horde that wasn't a bad turn of events. I mean who really knew what the fuck was going to happen next.

I was just hoping that my powers were strong enough to kill my bastard stalker. The one who had been oddly quiet the past week which never bodes well.

Now, you are probably thinking *"Wow, Vegas, I bet your boys have been totally responsible with this new awesome magic shit."*

Well, don't. Don't think that because the fuckers have been causing problems left and right. Decimus made a pipe burst during an argument. Blue licked a drop of blood off my finger. I mean it had been a small kitchen knife cut and he had said it was only "to kiss it and make it better." That didn't explain why he had let his tooth nick it just a tad more.

Ugh. Vampires! It isn't like having a vampire boyfriend was my fantasy or anything…

Speaking of vampires! Byron had only drank my blood once in the time we'd come home and it had been in a rush to go help with something regarding Tamara and her men. Apparently, they were outside of the city a bit and attempting to block my stalker from moving through dimensions so it would be easier to track him. But yeah, he had run off and I had been left all hot and bothered. Very unfair. In fact, the orgasm train has been somewhat slowed this past week between decorating for the holidays and finally just using the bed for some good, old-fashioned sleep.

Not completely slowed though. I shivered thinking about how Blue had woken me up this morning in the shower.

"Vegas," Blue chided softly, interrupting my delicious memory. "You are putting off the inevitable."

I looked up at him because I faced away from the car that I knew was mine based on the beeping my key fob caused. I really, really didn't want to look at it. The other boys started making their way toward the car and me.

"Stop making those expressions!" I cried at the unadulterated shock on their collective faces.

"You need to look," Booker said softly with excitement.

I cringed at all of the *excess*... I almost fell to the floor when I saw my car. Oh, sweet jesus.

"That's a two mil-" Grover had started but someone hit him. Too late. I knew. God. I already knew how expensive this car was because it had been my eye candy for so long. I didn't "do" cars but I knew this one and on top of all the money Byron spent it wasn't technically street legal. Not that he would care because he could just magic his way out of a problem with the cops. Still, I think I was suffering from shock because who in their goddamn right mind gets someone a McLaren Speed Rail in robin's egg metallic blue.

I couldn't even properly describe this car, you just need to see it.

"What's wrong with her?" someone asked as I knelt at the altar that was my car. No, really. I was on the garage floor, which was surprisingly clean, with my arms wrapped around the front of it. I couldn't even try to deny his gift because it would be like saying no to the gods themselves.

"Do you like it?" Byron asked softly.

I hadn't realized they had joined us. I spoke muffled against the car. "I think I'm in love with this car. I'm going to wife this bitch up. Go to Cannes, France and have a million babies with it."

Silence.

"Shit! I'm suddenly jealous of a car," Decimus exclaimed and stormed away.

A murmur of agreements and laughs sounded. Byron seemed satisfied because I heard him laughing. When Rocket's mint scent and Edwin's shadow moved over me, I looked up but continued to hug my car possessively.

"Have you ever been to Cannes? I'm not really a fan," Edwin said softly with curiosity.

Rocket tilted his head. "Let me get this straight. You will have babies with this car but not me?"

Edwin laughed at that.

I hugged the car tighter, worried Rocket might try to take it away in the heat of jealousy. I smiled coyly. "I'll make a deal, Rocket. We can have babies, but I'm marrying the car."

Edwin shook his head. "No can do, *dolcezza*. If you like it you better put a ring on it."

My mouth popped open as I let go of the car. "Did you just make a fucking Beyonce reference?"

The mage shrugged and laughed while he walked off. I looked up at Rocket who was still staring at the car with interest. I went back to hugging it protectively as he squatted down to level me with a hungry look. I squirmed slightly.

"How many babies?"

Christ.

I would like to state that this is what happens when a brilliant man with obsessive tendencies gets stuck on an idea. I swear he was possessed by the concept of me having his baby.

No. That was not flattering at all.

Lies.

"Oh, my god!" I exclaimed. "You are crazy! We can't have babies right now."

I mean we could. Technically. We were all working our

way towards our mid-twenties and individuals far younger than ourselves had created children...but, still.

No.

Rocket frowned. "But after all this?"

I laughed softly. "Yes, Rocket. I will have your babies one day."

He smiled brilliantly and kissed my forehead with a primal rumble. "Thanks, sugar."

As he left, leaving me in shock once again, Byron sat down on the floor with me. I smiled at him softly and may have rubbed my cheek against the paint of my baby.

"Do you like it?" he asked softly with slight hesitancy.

I let go of the car, crawled forward, and wrapped my arms around his neck. I didn't want him to feel hesitant around me. His smoky bonfire scent that was probably more like a funeral pyre, wrapped around me. Despite our new relationship, our emotions had sorta exploded after last week. I think I had always known Byron would be one of those relationships where everything moved at lightspeed.

His massive tan hand pressed against my lower back as he trailed his nose against my neck. I could feel his desire as he groaned before pulling back. He was a very touchy person and I couldn't lie. I loved it.

"I love it." I sat back and looked up at him. "Thank you so much."

He flashed a toothpaste white smile. "I'm glad, doll."

"How did you know?" I asked as we both stood up, his hand in mine to help.

Byron offered a hesitant look. "If I said I looked through your private Pinterest boards..."

"I would say that it is a huge invasion of privacy and completely expected from you boys, but resulted in a fantastic outcome," I quipped as he chuckled.

"Check out the license plate," he tugged my hand.

On it the plate read: VE.

I looked up at the man who I had only recently discovered had known me since essentially birth. Ve was my birth name and the gesture was extremely representative. My arms wrapped around Byron as I offered him a tight hug. When I pulled back his eyes were filled with emotion he didn't seem to know how to handle. I tried to lighten up the situation because now was not the moment to delve into the complexity of Byron.

"Is it legal to drive?"

"Is it legal to have magic?" he responded with a grin as the intensity relaxed slightly. "Come on. Let's go for a test drive."

Abso-fucking-lutely.

2

VEGAS

*L*ucida was right. I wasn't cut out for this Martha Stewart bullshit.

Instead, knowing my place in life, I sat on the kitchen counter in the far corner while eating some mashed potatoes that I was "sampling" for quality assurance. Bandit knew my game and was on the same team. We had gotten home from our little luxury drive about three hours ago... which in case you were wondering, was good. Thank you for asking about the mind-blowing experience, which oddly had nothing to do with sex, that I had this morning.

Moving on.

"You know," I mumbled with a spoon in my mouth as Bandit stirred something. He moved a large bowl into the buffet line. "We are sort of 'couple goals,' Bandit. Like, I bet we could be one of those Instagram couples. The famous ones that get sponsored and paid for being cute."

Bandit looked up at me with an amused glint in his eye and a small smile.

"No," Kodiak called from the living room. The kitchen had a smaller door that led to the foyer and then two very large French doors that led to a family lounge. The lounge had leather couches and a huge fireplace that my magical asshats had requested be lit for me. I always felt better with some type of flame around me, candle or bigger.

No Vegas, that doesn't sound like you're a pyromaniac at all, sweetie.

"Why not?" I asked grinning at the back of my overprotective grizzly bear. Damn it, I mean my overprotective wolf. Honestly, I'm a tad pissed about the wolf thing like am I just supposed to change my mental definition of Kodiak's protective nature? I mean cut a girl some slack. I ignored Edwin's lip twitching my thoughts. *Mind-reading bastard.*

Kodi turned and gave me an "are you joking" look. I batted my eyes innocently as he spoke. "Baby, I want you to just guess how I feel about you posting pictures online for the world to see."

I chuckled because he wasn't even the reason I didn't have social media. I actually wasn't a fan of it, but it sure was fun to mess with Kodi.

"You're okay with it because Bandit and I are super adorable with our turkey socks? I mean he even changed out one of his earrings with a hoop that has a "V" on it, Kodi. We are so cute. In fact, how about we just do an Insta profile featuring all of us. It will be a new take on alternative living and I'll bet you the entire Ivanov fortune that we would get offers for a TV show. It would be like *19 Kids and Counting* but instead *Vegas and Her Super Hot Magical Boyfriends.* Think *Queen of the Damned* vibes mixed with a hint of *Sabrina the Teenage Witch,* a bit of *Underworld,* and a dash of *Dracula.* The newer one, of course, with the hot guy with dark, long hair. And no, Edwin, don't let that go to your head, although I will admit you are far hotter than Gary Oldman. Plus he had a weird mustache in that. On second thought, this may be way too scary for tv. We should just make a movie."

Silence sounded as all nine heads turned from the game at the end of my rambling. Then it broke.

More like shattered.

"You think we're hot?"

"That's a lot of money."

"She didn't include our personal assets, we're good."

"That's a horrible name."

"That is an odd combination of shows and movies."

It went on and Kodi rolled his eyes. Bandit walked over and kissed my nose before continuing his work on the delicious food that would soon take residence in my stomach. I jumped down and stretched out before running and sliding towards the living room on the fancy floors. Edwin watched me with amusement as I glanced at the game for a mere second.

For the record, if you thought our lives were always action-packed adventure and fantastic sex, I would like to point out that we most definitely have completely normal moments. In fact, it was nice to be able to complain about my boyfriend watching sports while we are together. Well, boyfriends, but still.

There was an odd feeling to the house though, now that my boys had magic. While they had messed around with it a bit, the last week had been mostly devoted to detoxing and taking some time off. Even Edwin, our workaholic, had spent most of his time with us watching movies. Mind you he was in a suit. It was progress though. While this time off had been needed, the energy was quickly becoming overwhelming and I knew it would reach a point where the boys would need to use it. Honestly, I was starting to feel pretty tense now that the exhaustion had subsided. I felt the need to use the energy brimming right under the surface but was a tad afraid of doing it in a non-controlled environment.

I really liked this house and didn't want to accidentally burn anything.

"The party has arrived!" Luci shouted from the front door. I grinned and turned to see her and Miranda come into the foyer. I realized it was their first time here because the two of them had just returned from their anniversary trip to Colorado. They had been only given a small summary of our past week.

"Dude," Miranda stated, looking around. "This house is beautiful."

Luci leveled a stare my way and waved her hands. "When were you going to let me know that you lived in a mansion? I'm just waiting for a very charming Dracula to pop out here."

See! She understands my vibe.

Miranda snorted. "Oh, yes! So you can what? Tell him to stick his misogynistic attitudes up his ass?"

I was in the middle of hugging Miranda when I snorted out my own laugh.

I took the bottle of sparkling wine from her and backed up into the kitchen, motioning for them to join me. Once through the French doors, I sighed. "It's a lot, isn't it?"

Luci hugged Bandit in greeting as Miranda helped me grab some champagne glasses. Both of them had worn the required comfy clothes that they somehow had managed to make cute. Miranda was dressed in light pink silk pj's with her red hair done up in curls and held back by a pink ribbon. Luci had dyed her hair a pastel blue, smooth and hitting her shoulders, and wore matching pj's. Both of them wore slippers and seemed very relaxed. Vacation looked good on them.

"That is an understatement," Miranda whispered smiling as the three of us sat down at the kitchen island. With our champagne glasses filled we fell into easy conversation as I caught them up on everything that had happened since we returned home.

Unfortunately for Luci, Miranda hadn't given up asking her about the magic comment so she was now in the loop. I had already updated them on Horde-related events before Colorado and they were in the process of deciding if they wanted to move forward with the blood ink tattoo process as a couple. I think Luci had been surprised by how methodical and logical Miranda was being about all of it but I wasn't. Miranda played *Dungeons and Dragons*. It was a logical next step for her.

As we sat in the kitchen sampling the food and drinking cheap wine, my boys made excuses to walk past and somehow interact with me. I tried to ignore it as I further explained in more detail what I had learned about my past in the Horde, my interactions with Gray and how I was keeping secrets from her, and our plan moving forward. I even explained to her all of the stuff going on around our house including the cars and Deci's birthday. I would have included gossip about my orgasm express but she saw them as brothers so would probably punch me or puke. I think it hit Luci the reality of our relationship when Grover came up behind me and nuzzled my neck while Blue was still twirling my hair from where he stood talking to Bandit.

It was funny because she'd always been supportive about my not-so-secret crush. When I felt like a total weirdo in highschool, she'd once looked at me with a frown before saying something that eased my heart. She reminded me that a lot of children grew up together in the same neighborhood and fell in love. She didn't see the difference if they lived in the same house. Especially since we had all been part of the foster care system. That was my sister though, able to rationalize everything.

"What?" I asked Luci as Miranda smiled knowingly.

Luci smiled while shaking her head. "It's just so weird."

My forehead furrowed and she continued. "I've literally *never* seen them date anyone and now... well, shit, Ve! This is just crazy. It seems so normal to all of you already."

Grover chuckled softly and walked away as a smoky scent drifted around me. Edwin gently massaged my scalp with one large hand as he placed a bottle of expensive champagne down to replace our sparkling wine. Blue made a discontent sound at him touching my hair to which Edwin offered a knowing smirk. I felt like the two of them were going to spend the rest of our lives bickering like old ladies.

Oh, shit. The rest of our lives? What freaking kool-aid are you drinking?

The love flavored, I guess.

Gross.

I leaned back into him and listened to Miranda finish her story. I was half-tuned out but I knew Luci was watching everything going on. I knew it was probably odd to her how easily we all gravitate around one another and my theory on that was two-fold. First, our family had never suffered from physical boundaries. Except for maybe Rocket and Booker the boys were extremely comfortable around one another. The amount of times that we had all fallen asleep in a big old pile like puppies happened more often than not. If you add into that the memories of many years together and even my previously forgotten memories now returned, you've got a comfortable atmosphere. Secondly, even if we didn't have that I think we would still be very close. The connection like the tattoo running down my sternum was a part of me, just like they were. I could tell you where they were in the house and the ten of them were usually pretty clued into me as well as each other. It was very useful.

So, yeah. Despite the emotional boundaries that existed for some of our family, namely the two new members, we were pretty comfortable. I think I had fully adopted the "rolling with it" concept because trying to sort this all out in my head would have been painful.

"Oh!" I jumped up and caused Edwin to swear. I shot him a grin knowing he had been surprised by my not-so-human quickness. "I need to show you both something disgusting upstairs." Booker and Byron both shot me a scowl at that, I grinned all the more.

The girls followed me upstairs and I tried to not succumb to dizziness entering my room. The Nathan experience was still fresh in my mind. I had decided to keep it from Luci and Miranda as well as a few other choice events that could incriminate them, or make them feel guilty. The version I had offered them had been the PG-13 one. I also didn't want to make Lucida feel weird that every time I saw a door handle I got all *twitchy*. I mean I'm sure I was suffering from a tad bit of PTSD, but that's life.

"So after the house burnt down..." I drawled.

Luci gathered me in a hug and her bubblegum scent surrounded me. I smiled at the woman who was my sister and hugged her back. "What was that for?"

Her amber eyes were sad but she offered me a small smile. "I've missed hanging out and your house burnt down, which is sad."

Miranda grinned. "Well put, honey."

Luci shot her a smile as I walked them over to the closet door of my bedroom. The room suited the Victorian nature of the house and was a near replica of the one in the Horde.

Edwin had mentioned the room had been mine when I lived there with Byron and him. The gesture was sweet and left me feeling warm inside despite the oddness of having forgotten my own childhood.

I couldn't deny that the brothers still confused me. In a way, I understood Byron better than Edwin. He was outspoken and unhinged with a ton of emotional baggage. Edwin, though? I felt as though I never knew what he was thinking. I wondered if I could see in his head like he saw in mine. Yes, it was decided. I would need to test that later. I always felt like we were on the cusp of things but he continued to skim above the surface and I wasn't sure why. I just chalked it up to him being tired for the first few days back but now I was just frustrated. As most of my boys knew, I didn't like shit kept secret so if you've got a problem, issue, concern? For the *love of fae,* just talk about it!

The carpet underneath our feet was cream colored and the walls a soft yellow. French doors led to a balcony that overlooked the gardens and contrasted against the brick fireplace on the other side of the room. It seemed to always be lit which was very much due to Edwin's direction, I'm sure. I'd also noticed Byron having fresh flowers placed in my room after I mentioned loving the ones in the living room. Honestly, the two of them were growing on me like mold, albeit attractive sexy mold.

I'm such a freakin' weirdo.

"Sweet room," Miranda commented.

I smiled my thanks before putting my back against the closet door and offered a serious expression. "I would like to state for the record that I never asked for this and that it was forced on me as compensation for my hard work."

Not at all. Byron had made sure to impress upon me that

it was a gift. Evil bastard. He knew I wouldn't be able to reject a gift from him.

Lucida smirked. "It must be really bad."

It was. My reaction when I had first realized the extent of the madness had been worse.

I squirmed under Bandit's body as he lightly nibbled my collarbone. "This is why we don't take naps."

He offered me a lazy smile and began to kiss up my neck with electric pecks as I gasped, nearly moaning at his touch. "Bandit..."

"If you offer me an authentic reason to leave this bed, I'll consider it," he whispered as his energy made my body buzz. In the past few days, I hadn't had nearly enough time alone with my boys so I really didn't want to move.

"Chinese is here!" Decimus yelled.

Both Bandit and I paused. He finally spoke, "Well, I can't fucking argue and win with food being downstairs."

I put my hand on his nice muscular pec and offered him an understanding smile. "But Bandit, this is one of the many reasons why I love you. We have similar values and tastes. You like food... I like food."

Bandit chuckled and rolled us out of bed. I went towards my closet door to grab a hoodie and paused upon entering. That was when my brain broke.

"Bandit!" I squeaked as he appeared behind me. "What in the ever living fuck is this?"

He wrapped an arm around me and pulled me back. "Shit. Maybe it's like Narnia. If we leave, it will go away."

"Fantastic idea," I whispered as we closed the door and offered each other dark concerned looks. My back was pressed against his chest as we both stared at the offending doors.

"No one can wear that many different items of clothing," he admitted softly after a moment.

"Why are you two..." Grover paused at seeing us looking scared.

"What's wrong?" he demanded.

I scooted back with Bandit from the door and pointed. "Go look at it, Grover. Someone or something insidious was here."

"What the hell?" He frowned and tossed open the door.
Silence.

"Fucking, Christ!" He slammed it shut and looked at me. "Whose idea was this?!"

"I know!" I exclaimed as Decimus strolled in looking pissed.

"What are you doing up here? The food is getting cold." He petered off as all three of us just kept looking at the closet door.

"It's a portal of some kind," I announced. "To a department store."

Decimus pulled open the closet door and stumbled back. He let out a curse in Greek and stormed from the room. I heard yells from downstairs as feet pounded up the way.

"Oh," Booker smiled confidently upon realizing the source of the discord. "You finally saw it."

Byron sighed while adjusting his suit. "Took her long enough."

The other boys were confused so I yanked open the door and motioned to the horrid monstrosity that was my closet.

Rocket frowned looking in and spoke. "Oh. Well, you would need to wear a different outfit nearly everyday for the next..."

I blocked out the numbers because frankly I did not want to know.

"No one needs that many clothes," Kodiak said with his eyes wide. I also could see him looking over the clothes probably wondering where to place the trackers. My not-so-little stalker. The good kind though, not the bastard we hated. No. Kodiak was the type of stalker I wanted in my bed.

Wow. Okay Vegas. Crazy train leaving the station. Choo, choo!

Cosimo looked at Booker. "How did you even decide on that many things?"

"Half of the stuff was delivered by designers." He shrugged.

Edwin walked in with Blue. "What's wrong?"

I pointed at the closet and Blue's expression had me in tears. He stepped hesitantly into the room and then stepped back. "Beautiful, this isn't funny. Someone has taken over your closet."

Isn't it funny how life works out? We are scared of a fucking closet. Out of everything we've faced, a closet would be our downfall.

"Maybe I should switch rooms," I offered.

Byron snorted. "Leave it. Time for dinner."

Bossy.

I looked back at the closet one last time and began plotting it's demise. Booker offered me a dry look and wrapped his arms around me.

"Kitty, you burn down that closet and I will personally punish you."

A shiver went up my spine as I looked back at him.

"What I'm hearing, then, is incentive to burn it down." I grinned as Booker chuckled.

I groaned and opened the door to a closet that belonged to someone that was not the little Vegas from Ohio. Both women cursed as they stepped into the massive space. Apparently, it had once been a guest room. To make matters worse? Byron had told me he'd ensured that this closet and the one in the Horde were filled. I think he'd had help from Booker picking out my clothes because they had been perfectly chosen.

The two of them were trouble. Expensive. Handsome. Male modelesque. Generous. Trouble.

"Is that a shoe wall?!" Luci growled motioning to an entire wall of shoes. Now, you are probably thinking that it's lined with impractical footwear, right? No. Like I said, someone knew my style well, making it difficult to disagree with any of it. The bottom quarter of the shelf was lined with boots of various styles ranging from Timberlands to over-the-knee leather stiletto boots, which were totally kick-ass! Very *Buffy the Vampire Slayer*. The middle section was filled with sneakers that were an array of neutral tones in shades of black to white. I had never seen a "fancy" gym shoe before I had this closet and it was truly a life changing experience. The top portion was made up of heels and were all very gothic and pointy looking. Dangerous. Like me. I smirked at that.

Ignore me boosting my ego over here in my fancy closet.

I hated to admit that I loved all of this. I also loved the handbags and every other fucking thing in here. So, naturally I felt guilty about how much money it was. I mean, shit. My t-shirts, my motherfucking t-shirts, were even a better quality. Don't even get me started on the lingerie! Man, our family was starting to look like those rich people with labelless dark clothes.

It made me want to fuck shit up. Spill something on it or wash it wrong. Yeah. I have the maturity of a twelve year old. Sue me.

"So, yeah," I mumbled running a hand through my hair, "this is it."

Miranda looked at me and grinned. "This is fucking crazy. You know that, right?"

I nodded as Luci climbed up the rolling ladder that went around the room to reach the customized shelves. Yeah, I know. Fucking ridiculous. Add in a plush carpet and ottoman to make me feel like a real princess, why don't you?

I had said that to Byron as a joke. He didn't take it as one.

"I think I may need to move in," Luci determined and looked at Miranda.

Her girlfriend shook her head. "Honey, we are not making the magic decision off the obvious material benefits."

Luci scowled. "Miranda. She has a Gucci bag. The woman doesn't even use a purse!"

I let out a hoot and laughed as I laid in the ottoman. They began to argue in a teasing tone as I caught my reflection from where I sat. My hair had grown along with my other physical changes and it rested near my hip in soft waves that complimented my bangs. My skin shimmered just slightly and I could see that my natural lip color had darkened. I swear to god this was *Twilight*. Didn't the vampires become super good looking? I heard the two girls raising their voices and swore, remembering why I hadn't seen them all week.

"I forgot to give you an anniversary present!" I exclaimed.

Miranda offered me a "forget about it" look and Luci smirked. "You're right, you did. To think, I could have remembered to text you if I just had that extra finger."

I snorted and flipped her off with a smile. "Fuck you. But seriously, pick something out from the shoes, purses, clothes. I don't care. It will be my gift."

Luci didn't hesitate to climb up and grab a black purse lined in yellow. It made me laugh because I almost wondered if they had placed it there for this purpose, it didn't fit the other purses at all. Miranda shook her head because both of us were needling her with a look.

"Pick something," I demanded and stretched out further on the comfy surface.

She offered me a final "I give up" look and grabbed a

pair of killer heels with light pink bottoms. I stood up and moved toward the door, shutting off the light as I passed. The three of us began to make our way downstairs when Luci asked the question I knew she had wanted to in the kitchen.

"So, when did the two magical asshats become part of your harem?"

The nickname had caught on!

Miranda chuckled as I scrunched my nose. "Not harem. It's a relationship... with ten men."

"Mages," Miranda corrected with a smile.

"Accurate," I chirped.

"You didn't answer," Lucida pressed. This was why she was a private investigator. Bitch noticed everything. I wondered if the Horde had anything similar so her hard work and talent could have an opportunity to grow. Did they even have police? I would need to check for her. Although, she hadn't mentioned being upset about leaving her current human job nor did she seem stuck up on school.

I shrugged. "Something just changed. Even before I realized I had grown up with them. That was the cherry on top, I suppose." I had already explained how we were all connected through magic so I wasn't going to attempt to rehash that because, as Edwin explained, unless you have magic it is hard to understand it.

"Time to eat," Grover called out as we jogged down the stairs.

As mentioned, our Thanksgivings were casual. All of us grabbed either beer or wine. Edwin upgraded us to Dom Perignon as we migrated to the family lounge. When I tried to put mine into a red Solo cup the magical asshat had scolded me. Come on! The cup had turkeys on it that

Booker drew by hand! It was art! And it was fucking adorable.

Honestly, though? I sorta liked when Edwin scolded me because it could lead to a fight. Fighting with Edwin was sexy. Both of us got along most of the time but then one of us would start antagonizing the other and it would always get physical. Neither of us would back down and it always made me feel like I needed to shake some sense into him. So, yeah. I liked fighting with him.

The game was now blasting on the screen and I wiggled my way between Edwin and Blue. I placed my legs across Edwin's lap while I sat on an angle with my back pressed to Blue. For once, I finally felt my age: very happy, goofy, and a bit cozy. This was how a twenty-one year old should feel but, as we know, I'm not just any twenty-one year old.

"Comfy?" Edwin asked in amusement.

I looked at my legs and then up at him. "I should have asked, shouldn't I?"

He shook his head while smiling and placed a hand on my leg while resting his plate there. I felt Blue kiss the top of my head as I relaxed into the comfort of my family.

"You guys are the best, I'm so thankful for all of you," I admitted feeling all sentimental and shit.

Lucida turned, narrowing her eyes at me. "Bitch, I'm going to get all emotional if you pull that. I have food to focus on."

I chuckled and put up my hands in defense. I felt a warmth fill my chest because of my family.

That was what this was. Family and, damn, was I so fucking thankful for them. We had needed some downtime and this was like the grand finale. So, logically, I probably should have realized that it wouldn't last. I should have realized that this week wasn't a break but simply the eye of the storm. The fates were cruel. Halfway through the football game the doorbell rang. Edwin frowned and I stood up as Kodiak followed. I wasn't positive who else came along but I was very curious who knew where we were living.

My mind considered that it was someone Edwin or Byron knew, but that didn't make much sense. Unless, it was someone they had dated before visiting them for the holidays? Oh, man. I was not good with this jealousy thing and I totally hadn't considered their previous experience. Edwin made a soft discontent sound as I looked at him with narrowed eyes.

"Get out of my head."

"You're projecting, dolcezza. For the record, I have never officially dated anyone."

My lips crooked into a slight smile as I looked back at him.

What about Byron?

He didn't answer. I shook my head ignoring the weirdness that was our mental connection. I knew. I knew it was going to suck when everyone was clued into our bond. It was bound to happen if they got stronger, which they would.

Deciding to mess with Kodiak, I shot him a grin and jogged ahead to the door. I was about a step away before he growled and pulled me back, not liking the idea of me being exposed to danger. I chuckled and stood behind Edwin as the door opened. After receiving his magic, Kodiak had dropped the pretense of not being animalistic and was just outright overprotective, territorial, and possessive. He was constantly touching me and when he wasn't I could feel his eyes on me, like a predator tracking its prey.

It was totally sexy.

Edwin opened the door and chuckled softly, but it was his scary laugh. Like the one that puts your hair on edge.

Suddenly, and similar to how my boys had their darker side, my body stilled and my smile faded. I opened up my senses and caught the scent of driftwood and cologne. I placed a hand on Edwin's shoulder as he opened the door to offer me a view of... Levi?

Kodiak grunted and the three of us stepped out onto the porch to face the kid we had saved from the Letters. I could tell Kodiak was pissed I was on the porch, but with me tucked between them I was very safe. Plus, this was Levi. The kid who had tried to bomb the school. The kid who looked far too pale, thin, and exhausted to be alright.

"Levi?" I frowned. "What are you doing here?"

He seemed slightly twitchy as he met my gaze. "Vegas. You. Wow, you look great."

The guy ran a hand through his stringy hair as I frowned slightly. I tried to ignore the deep rumble that came from Kodiak's chest. I really should have been out here with some of my other boys. It wasn't like Edwin and Kodiak were the most understanding people when it came to other men.

"Thank you?" I asked softly, "You seem sorta off, Levi. What's going on?"

I mean the guy was always fucking weird but this seemed almost sick.

He grunted and looked up. "You still do Ravens' business, right?"

Kodiak spoke for me. "Yes."

Levi swallowed. "There's this party being held tonight."

"So?" Kodiak asked. "We aren't here to bust up underage drinking on campus. You know we only get involved in special cases."

"You should be there to monitor," he rasped out, his eyes darting away. "I heard that there was going to be this drug dealer there. He's from New York."

My back stiffened slightly at the tone of his voice. "How did you hear about this?"

He swallowed and looked at me with large eyes. "I bought from one of his dealers in the area. His name is Gabriel."

Rocket let out a low sound from behind me as he joined us. I leaned back into him as he whispered something to Kodiak that stilled my wolf. He looked back up at Levi.

"Is his product clean?" Kodiak asked quietly. I knew he didn't really want to get involved and frankly I would rather enjoy my Thanksgiving. Let me repeat just for clarity. I *do not* want to go to a college party. The last time we went to a party besides at our house, it had been awful. I felt like I had bodyguards and I honestly couldn't tell you one person that had attended. Something that Rocket said to Kodiak made him almost seem resigned though, as if we had to go. I was curious to know what it was.

Levi licked his dry lips. "Mine wasn't. I'm hooked on some pretty bad shit and trying to detox."

I frowned because something was off about what he was saying and I knew each boy felt it as well.

Edwin spoke then and Levi looked slightly scared of him. "May I suggest you go to a hospital for treatment, your heart rate is fairly irregular."

I almost rolled my eyes. Edwin was not even pretending to be human.

"How did you..."

"I can see your pulse," He responded mildly. I wondered how he got away with his astute observations as a doctor. It was probably why he was so liked at the hospital. I still couldn't believe he was an actual doctor. Edwin's lip twitched at that.

Damn it. I needed to work on my mental block.

Levi frowned and his gaze darted back to me. "Will you go tonight? I don't want anyone else ending up how I am right now."

Kodiak grunted and I looked down at the porch where my cute turkey socks stood in stark contrast to the dark stained wood. The house was a beautiful maroon color and had all the architectural elements that you would associate with a true victorian. I needed to ask how old this home was, I would bet it had some solid years behind it.

"What time?" I asked giving in.

Levi offered me hopeful eyes. "They said around six because they are also showing part of the game. The house is on South street. Jamie Lang's."

We didn't know him well but that wouldn't be a problem. People didn't make a habit out of not letting us into parties. It resulted in negative consequences.

Kodiak frowned as Rocket rubbed my back gently. I spoke. "Fine. We will be there."

He smiled. "Thank you so much, Vegas."

Then he was stumbling back down the stairs and jogging towards a black car parked in the driveway. The four of us watched him leave as the cold Boston wind hinted at the harsh December to come. My eyes followed him until he left.

"So, what gives?" I asked looking at Rocket and Kodi. "Why are we going?"

Rocket met my gaze for a minute before he called Cosimo's name. I felt my brow dip as my Spaniard jogged outside and frowned at my expression, mirroring it before standing behind me. He wrapped his arms around me before speaking. "What's up?"

"Tell them what you told me about, Gabriel," Rocket said with an easy drawl.

Cosimo grunted and I widened my eyes as he spoke. "So, I blame myself in part. For being so distracted lately with all of, whatever this is."

"Magic," Edwin commented as I snorted.

"Anyway," Cosimo sighed, "on campus. The day of Halloween. Do you remember the asshole we bumped into?"

I snarled. "Yeah, and then he was there later. At the party. Such a dick."

Rocket cursed as Cosimo swore, turning me into him. "He was at the party?"

"Yeah," I frowned. "But so was half the school, and then Luci came back..."

"Gabriel Mathers," Rocket explained, "is the local drug dealer and the same asshole that bumped into you. His profile isn't terribly messy but this past semester his grades have dropped to failing and he has yet to return any social media messages or texts."

I didn't even want to know how he knew all of that.

"Okay," I frowned. "So, he's some drugged-out asshole."

"We think he might be your stalker," Cosimo mumbled so quietly that I barely heard it. But Kodi did.

"What the fuck?" Kodi growled stepping forward. "How long have you two been looking into this?"

I shook my head immediately. "No way. I've been around this guy twice and he is magic-free."

Edwin went to open his mouth but Kodi continued. "Cosimo, how fucking long?"

I felt Cosimo bristle as a low sound came from his throat, Rocket's face blanked. I could see Kodi's temper building and I knew this would end bad, which we couldn't afford because we needed to be on our "A" game.

"Since we returned from the Horde," Cosimo clipped.

"Is that a fucking joke?!" Kodiak's jaw clenched as Cosimo's arms tightened around me slightly.

"Do not yell at him," I snapped as he flinched slightly at my tone. "Seriously Kodi, I saw him twice and didn't suspect a goddamn thing so don't go blaming Cosimo. It wouldn't have done any good for them to tell all of us when they were still looking into it."

"We could have handled it!" he argued, his eyes burning. If it was anyone else, I would have probably moved away at his tone but I felt like I couldn't afford to do that with him. There were limits and my hard one had to do with my boys. I didn't want him attacking Cosimo for something that wasn't his fault just because he was frustrated.

"What are you going to do? Waltz in there and demand he stop?"

Kodiak grunted as I shook my head. "Don't be a jerk Kodi, just be glad they noticed it now."

The man grunted again and went silent. I sighed. "Besides, he has no magic. It's not him."

Edwin spoke and I jumped, forgetting he was there because of Kodi's outburst. "I agree it's not him but his proximity is odd to this circumstance. He may be part of the problem but I can assure you that you would know if someone with that much power came within ten feet of you."

"So, we need to keep tabs," Rocket concluded, looking tense from the yelling.

"We need to do a location check. I don't trust Levi," Kodiak stated.

Edwin spoke. "Let's plan on doing that in the next thirty minutes, and then the rest of us can join whoever is on watch. I want to make sure we catch anything unusual."

I nodded and Kodiak pulled me from Cosimo for a brief

hug as he muttered apologies and went back into the house. I chuckled inwardly because the fucker said "sorry." Cosimo kissed my cheek as everyone but Edwin went in. I sighed and leaned into his touch that grazed my back. For just a moment I allowed myself to be a baby. I wanted to eat more mashed potatoes and cuddle.

But that wasn't my fucking life. So, I womaned-up and strode into the house toward the family lounge. I muted the T.V. as the boys and girls offered me confused looks.

"Six o'clock. Jamie Lang's house on South Street. New York drug dealer is visiting and selling laced product. The tip is from Levi so we need a few people to go ahead and scout out the location. Rocket and Cosimo also want us to keep eyes on a Gabriel Mathers, who may be part of my current stalker issue."

Silence.

I knew they had processed my words, considered being babies as I had, and then accepted their fate because, suddenly, everyone was moving in ten million different directions. Blue was telling others what to do as Miranda and Luci approached me.

I offered a weak smile. "Sorry guys, you are more than welcome to stay here."

Luci frowned and flicked my forehead.

"Ow," I complained. Kodiak growled softly, making Miranda jump. Luci offered him an eyeroll. He went back to talking to Cosimo and it seemed their small spat was resolved. Good.

"We are going, so let's put that closet to use." Luci announced.

Oh, dear.

3

VEGAS

Unfortunately for my scheduled date with a bowl of mashed potatoes, it turned out that Levi was not lying about the party or the location. I grimaced as I remembered just how oddly people tended to react to our group. I figured it would only be intensified now by the odd energy that we put off. It was similar to how I had always sensed there was something unusual about Byron and Edwin. Humans wouldn't be able to understand the difference but it would affect them. As our new Escalades pulled up in the empty circular driveway, I realized someone must have told them we were coming.

How sweet.

A thrill of energy pulsed through me at the thought of returning to Raven business. I would never toot my own horn or anything but when it came to Raven stuff, I was a total badass. I could admit to feeling out of my league when it came to magic but dealing with college kids? I could do that with ease. I assumed it was the mixture of growing up with a group of boys that didn't take shit from anyone, Luci's signature "fuck you" attitude, and Vivi's strong opinions. In any event, despite my softness around my family, I tended to harden and grow colder in situations like the one at hand. The shift helped me feel in control despite the rest of our lives.

Honestly, college kids annoyed the fuck out of me. I mean, come on. Shouldn't these guys be home with family or relaxing on the couch with food? It's motherfucking Thanksgiving! A party like this just seemed unnecessary. The other half of my attitude problem came not from my bitterness over my holiday being interrupted but my instinctive hatred of people trying to fuck other people over.

We had enough problems to deal with in this fucking world besides screwing one another over.

I hadn't been bullshitting when I had mentioned being the unofficial leader of the Ravens. I could feel that persona growing the closer we drew to the front door and I found it interesting that the Ivanov brothers seemed to recognize the shift and assimilate with ease. I fought my grin.

Good to know they were so damned adaptable.

Edwin chuckled and shook his head, drawing my attention away from the heated debate between Kodiak and Rocket regarding my outfit. A conversation that was amusing Miranda and Lucida greatly. Frankly, I was done with that particular conversation because, as I told Kodiak, a hoodie wasn't very intimidating.

Plus, now I looked like a total badass.

The two other women had continued their matching theme of the holiday. Despite their very different styles, Luci had managed to make it work. Both had donned a pair of high-waisted, black ripped jeans that showcased fishnets through the split material. Miranda, her stature slightly taller and leaner than Luci, sported a feminine style highlighted by a vintage floral crop top. She had exchanged out her pink bow for two top knots that kept her thick red hair from her face. On the opposite end of the spectrum, Luci wore a neon tube top and a bright white baseball cap. As I stated, somehow she made it look cute. I would have probably opted for the sweatshirt vibe if it wasn't for her. No need to tell Kodi that, though.

So, what type of outfit had the boys panicking?

Well, Luci had put me in a pair of pants that were a silky material in bright green with a white label running down the side with black text, referencing a brand that I had never heard of. The pants were actually fairly loose but they hit my lower waist and showcased my pale, toned stomach. My shoes were black with silver and white accents that matched the very small black bralette I wore. It was daring but very sporty chic. Because I knew what that was, right? My hair was pulled up in a sleek ponytail and my tattoo on full display. I felt fantastic and I could tell that the boys thought so as well, despite their possessiveness.

Still, I knew Kodiak had brought a hoodie for me and was just waiting to spring it on me.

As we walked through the massive front door of the mega mansion, I offered a mental thanks to Luci for the lack of clothing. It was hot as fuck in here. The room was thick with people and as we made a not-so-discreet entrance, the crowd parted for us. I would like to tell you that we had tried to be nice about it, but that would be a lie. In fact, I would imagine that we looked fairly intimidating and that notion was only supported by the widening of eyes and paling of faces.

My ten boys split in half, five on either side of me in a slightly protective formation that easily pushed through the crowds and sweaty bodies. Edwin and Blue stood on either side of me and I could feel that Kodiak and Byron were at the back. All of them, as usual for this type of business, had worn black tonight but there were small, differing aspects that made them unique, from the type of shoes they wore to individual piercings. It didn't take away from the effect of unity though.

Luci and Miranda were behind me. I could hear the latter whispering about how weird it felt to have everyone looking at us. Which they very much were. Stared, really. I met every eye we passed as our easy gait took us towards the massive living room. While the music continued, everyone's conversation seemed to lull as people noticed us. I felt a small smirk hook the corners of my lips.

"Blue! Vegas," A large man, Jamie Lang, greeted us. I could see he was tense. I would guess that Mr. Lang didn't like us at his party. Everyone resumed their conversations but kept their respective distance.

Maybe, just maybe, this was why I had issues with dating before.

I nearly chuckled as Edwin's eyes darkened and a low rumble came from his chest at my thoughts. I looked down trying to contain my grin.

"Jamie," Blue greeted quietly before the man met my gaze with guarded caution.

"What are you guys doing here?" he asked in a *sotto voce* tone, eyes darting between us. I knew he was purposely avoiding talking to me. Half because he was scared Blue would snap at him about it and the other half I'd like to think was due to my scary badass nature.

Or because of your ten massive boyfriends, Vegas.

"What do you think we are doing here, Jamie?" I asked softly with a knowing look. "We've got a tip about a dealer that is in town from New York selling laced product. Do you know anything about that?"

His face paled and Edwin chuckled softly. Jamie looked at him and frowned momentarily. "Who's this?"

"Not of your concern." I felt a slight growl bubble under my words as Edwin's lip twitched. All right. So, I was a tad protective over the fucker. I blamed my magic. The bitch was psycho.

"Aren't you too old to be here?" Jamie sneered. Edwin's eyes sparked with mirth. It was that dangerous glint I was always glad to not be on the receiving end of. Although, that could be a lot of fun, I thought guiltily.

Edwin's eyes shot to me for a moment, heating, before he stepped closer to Jamie.

"Aren't you too young to die?"

Oh, shit.

Blue chuckled softly as Jamie backed down and looked at me with slight desperation. "I don't know anything, Vegas. I heard a rumor that he was going to be here from Levi, but so far I haven't seen anyone I don't know."

"You will let us know when you do." Blue didn't ask but instead trailed a hot hand along the soft skin of my lower back. I held in a moan at how good his touch felt.

Jamie nodded and scuttled off as I groaned in annoyance. Blue flashed Edwin a smile. "That was good."

Edwin chuckled as I rolled my eyes. Good to know that their odd sense of brotherhood formed through getting off on scaring people. At least it wasn't as bad as Blue's bonding with Byron over blood. Those two were on their way to becoming serial killer besties and it was a tad worrisome. Then again, we had brought Tamara and her demons into our life, so was anything really scary anymore? They seemed to make anything less than their crazy pale in comparison.

The thirteen of us moved toward the back corner that

had a dark stone back wall and leather couches. It allowed us an entire view of the room and was slightly higher in elevation than the rest. I moved to sit down and everyone spread out around us. My eyes roved the crowd with interest as I attempted to catalog what I was seeing. I felt confidence surge through me.

I was good at this.

I was really fucking good at noticing shit. Everyone stared at us but even the bravest of individuals didn't approach, each for different reasons. The men because, well, that would just be stupid. The women because I would likely bite their heads off.

Yikes. My magic had gotten possessive.

Good excuse, Vegas.

"Does everyone usually stare this much?" Miranda asked softly, her cheeks flushed. Luci was positioned slightly in front of her in a protective and shielding gesture. It was fucking cute as hell. Both of them sat in a chair near me.

"Yes," Luci nodded as her eyes scanned the room, she absently played with Miranda's hair. I could tell something had changed between the two of them and I wasn't positive what that *thing* was. It almost seemed as if they had grown impossibly more in sync. Maybe it was from the additional time they'd been spending together?

I shrugged and tried to refocus. "Well, the boys are scary."

"And Vegas is beautiful! So they look."

Miranda nodded to Luci. She seemed to accept it for now. I sighed and looked back over the crowd, resting my elbows on my knees. It was true, everyone did look at us, and right now I was noticing it more than usual. The men didn't bother me as much because I had experienced that, but the women? The looks were downright hostile. Shit, man. What'd I do to them?

Oh, wait. I've got this! I did absolutely nothing.

There was nothing I hated more than shaming other women. Didn't we have enough problems in this world? Even if you are suffering with insecurities or jealousy, as most of us do from time to time, the answer is not to put other women down! How fucking hard is it to build yourself up *and* the women around you? It is not mutually exclusive, folks. I mean shit, if we took all of the moments we spent talking shit about other women and used them for positive change, we would have had the first female president ages ago.

All right. All right. Rant over.

"Are you okay?" Cosimo asked, noting my tense body position. I looked up at him and nodded as he pressed an impatient kiss to my lips that surprised me. I tried to deepen it and he made a low appreciative rumble before pulling back. I scowled and he offered me a roguish smile, making me want to nip at that lip ring.

"Unless you want to have public sex..." he teased.

I cocked an eyebrow and moved closer. "Maybe I do."

Cosimo bit his lip in humor before kissing my temple gently. I noticed a few girls sneering and as Blue walked up to me it only got worse. They had probably heard the rumors about the nine of us, all of which hadn't held true until a month ago. I felt a small smile creep onto my face as my hand closed on the material of his shirt in a light tug.

"Beautiful?"

His lips melted into mine as I pressed into his hard, hot body enthusiastically. Blue responded immediately, his hand grasping my pony tail as he grew hard against me in record time. I'd found Blue liked a little aggressiveness.

My breathing hitched as his other hand held my jaw and tilted my head up so that he had full access to my lips. Fuck. I could get lost in a kiss with Blue but forced myself to pull back as his eyes darted over my shoulder with curiosity. A big grin split his face, with dimples, as I scowled at him.

"Being possessive, are we?" he chuckled softly against my ear. "I wonder how that feels."

I scoffed, my cheeks tinting. "I don't know what you are talking about."

Blue kissed my neck as some of the women and men looked on with a mix of blatant curiosity, anger, and a myriad of other emotions I didn't want to analyze. "Don't worry, beautiful. I think it's hot."

I growled as he nipped my neck and walked away. Still, I couldn't stop the smile I shot to everyone watching. As I mentioned before, the hardest part about this relationship would be the human Earth realm aspect of it. The Horde, not so much. So, how would I handle it? Be brazen about it. I had nothing to hide. Ever since our connection had been completed, my emotions had been more intense and extreme. I think it was just the nature of being Fae.

I had never been ashamed about my family nor our somewhat unique relationship. It had been like this since high school, but it didn't help that we were such a diverse group of individuals. We had never been "cool" but we weren't "uncool." We just were unapproachable. An island.

My right hand, chipped nail polish and all, gripped the red Solo cup as I let out an annoyed sound at someone nearly bumping into me. I really hadn't wanted to attend this party, but Kodiak, Grover, and Decimus were all on the football team and it was homecoming weekend. I couldn't say no, could I? By this time in my high school career, I had come to long resent high school football in the midwest. It wasn't nearly as fun as shows like Friday Night Lights made it out to be.

I turned from the keg and my face hit right into the front of a smelly jersey. Really? That is what you wear to a party? I am all for school spirit but hygiene takes precedence. I winced and looked up as my long hair fell from the hood of my sweatshirt. I was so glad I'd dressed comfortably tonight. I wasn't a fan of some of the eyes on me tonight so a pair of boyfriend jeans and a sweatshirt made me feel comfortable and somewhat shielded. I wasn't hiding exactly, but I feel like every girl could relate to how being somewhat invisible was beneficial around certain groups. In this case? Horny, drunk highschool football players.

"Vegas, right?" *a massive guy, nearly double my size, asked with a bright grin.*

"That's me," *I responded to the man I knew to be our senior quarterback. He was a cute guy in that all-American way that I didn't find particularly attractive. Unfortunately, I did know what I found attractive and I tried to not think about why. I tried to convince myself that my aesthetic love for tattoos, piercings, and dark clothes had nothing to do with the group of men across the room. You know, the ones with their eyes on me at every moment of the freaking day? Yeah. Those are mine. My boys.*

Jeez! Possessive much?

"I've wanted to talk to you for a bit now," *he confessed while rubbing a hand through his brown hair.* "I just couldn't seem to ever get you alone."

I nearly snorted at that. Same, dude. Same. I didn't understand the notion of alone time any longer. In fact, I could practically feel the eyes on me from across the room. I hoped they wouldn't interfere though, I could handle myself and we had recently had a chat about boundaries because certain people - cough, Kodi - were overbearing.

"Well," *I offered an awkward smile.* "Here I am."

He chuckled softly, looking semi-uncomfortable. "Listen, I heard you don't have a homecoming date."

Seriously?

No.

The dance was tomorrow. Who asks this fucking late?

I had to say "no" on principal.

"I wasn't planning on going," I stated. *The reason? None of my boys had asked me. Apparently, "dances were a waste of time." Not my words. Real cool, Deci.*

I'm not bitter though. Nope. Not at all.

"Well," *he nodded with a slight blush,* "if you don't have plans."

Just then some asshole bounced into us causing me to grunt, as his arm hit my shoulder. Our quarterback grasped my waist as the drunk bastard just chuckled and looked at the two of us. I could feel the eyes nailing into the back of my head as the man chose to not release my side. Fuckity fuck. I had to handle this pronto.

"Oh, it's her," *the drunk guy laughed.* "Good to see you're talking to her, Jason!"

I cringed. Jason shook his head. "Freddy, you seem really drunk, dude."

"She's always with those freaks," *he chuckled and nudged me suggestively.* "Why is everyone so afraid of those guys, anyway? I don't see anything worth being scared of over there."

All right. I was about done with this.

"That is my family you're talking about," I stated easily as I detached from Jason. "I would appreciate it if you stopped."

Freddy rolled his eyes. "'I would appreciate it if you stopped,'" *he mocked and then smiled.*

"I mean, come on, girl. My boy Jason here is way better than those foster brothers of yours." *He grinned and leaned in.* "I have *to ask though, is it true you are fucking all of them? I can't believe it, but maybe you're slutty like that."*

My first collided with Freddy's nose.

I didn't have a temper, except when it came to my family.

Jason cursed as Freddy fell onto the ground and started cursing, his nose bleeding. "What a fucking bitch."

I looked at Jason. "Sorry, J. I don't think this is going to work out. You seem nice but the company you keep is disgusting."

I turned and walked toward my boys. All of them were watching in unfiltered shock as I jumped up onto the counter in the kitchen and began examining my bruised knuckles.

"Beautiful," Blue chuckled, "what the hell was that?"

Cosimo was already applying a wet paper towel to clean off Freddy's blood.

I looked him dead in the eye. "Jason was asking me to homecoming and Freddy started talking shit about you guys. I asked him to stop. He asked me if I was fucking all of you and if I was slutty, so I punched him."

My boys were silent for a minute before they lost it. Kodiak was the only one who didn't really laugh. His eyes focused on a concerned Jason and an angry Freddy. Yeah. No matter how much my boys were laughing now, I had a feeling those other boys would be in pain later. Well, at least Freddy. Jason was undetermined.

My eyes trailed to Blue.

Okay, possibly Jason also.

4

VEGAS

*A*s the latter part of the second hour passed, I began feeling frustrated. Levi hadn't shown yet and I wasn't positive who we were looking for besides him or Gabriel. Add on the fact that the women crowding our area were offering me scathing looks and my temper began to simmer under the surface. Hadn't I said we would reach a boiling point from a lack of release? I had a feeling this wouldn't be the fun type of release either. Well, for them at least.

When a familiar pair of eyes caught mine from across the room, my jaw clenched so hard my teeth felt like they would break. This fucking asshole. The audacity. I hated being right and the image in front of me almost solidified that we had been right on the fucking money about Gabriel.

"Edwin?" I called out.

"Yes, *dolcezza*?" He stepped towards me and I watched as something hit his senses. Those stunning eyes snapped immediately to where I was going to point. They darkened and the soft shadows that constantly surrounded him began to darken in response to the power I was feeling.

"That's what I thought," I cursed under my breath and looked back at Gabriel.

"It's not him," Edwin spoke quietly, his voice hesitant. "At least, not physically."

My eyes were on him from across the room, his smirk confident and the power levels insane. I recognized the power levels but I knew that Gabriel's body wasn't the original owner of that power.

"He's using him as a vessel," I muttered and looked to Edwin. "Which means Levi is also working with them or somehow was convinced to do this."

Luci moved closer. "What's happening?"

"You remember your captor's voice, right?" Edwin asked curiously. The pieces were starting to fit together and my bet was that whoever my stalker was, they had been using Gabriel as a puppet for a bit of time now.

She nodded and I looked back up at Edwin. "How?"

Edwin looked back over and seemed stuck in thought. Finally, he spoke. "If he was a vessel, it would explain how he was able to go unnoticed by anyone looking for someone with magic and get past the wards without problem."

He grimaced. "On the other hand, in order to possess someone as a vessel...well, I hope that isn't the case. That takes a lot of raw power."

Oh, good. There is nothing I love more than to have an extremely powerful stalker enemy.

"But why now?" I asked quietly.

All this time in secrecy, all these games, and invading my dreams to show up here? I suppose the pussy wasn't actually showing himself, but it was still very blunt. Also sort of fucking annoying because we could have done this ages ago.

I recognized the power inside of him and could tell it wasn't part of Gabriel's real aura. Call it instinctual. Most humans, like Levi and the green-eyed asshole, carried a signature that was soft like a pastel color. I could feel it and remember it. Like a taste. It was something I hadn't fully realized until leaving the Horde. My magic was more free now and it was breathing knowledge into me that seemed almost ancient and primordial in nature.

So, when I tell you that green-eyed douche was being used by my stalker, I fucking knew it. I could feel that same magic from my dream rolling through the room like a sudden tidal wave. I looked around making sure that the fucker knew I felt him. Which I did. I very much felt as though he was in the room, looking at me. The green-eyed asshole looked at me with interest and something jolted him, his eyes turning a midnight black.

Here we go.

"The humans," Edwin whispered and looked at me. "He wants to talk but doesn't want a fight. He's using the humans as a buffer."

Motherfucker. I looked around the room. He was smart because if these humans weren't here I would rip this place apart trying to find the creep.

"We need to talk to him, then."

Edwin nodded and began to talk to the other men. I knew the boys would freak out, but I was caught in a motherfucking staring match right now and, damn it, I would not lose. Despite it not actually being him, I felt as though I was meeting my stalker's gaze head on. When Edwin came up behind me and made a motion with his hand, the green-eyed asshole and his band of jerks walked over. I noticed all of them had the same dark eyes that were completely unnatural. Levi walked with them but his eyes were normal despite the terrible health of his body. I stood watching as this massive bastard walked forward.

"You," I hissed with heat rolling through my body like a wave. I was angry but no longer scared. My entire focus was on Gabriel and the man using him. The four other men and Levi faded from my focus. Levi, who I wanted to punch before I smacked myself for falling for his well-orchestrated attempt to get us all in the same room.

"My little flame," the man purred with unrestrained heat in a voice that was far silkier than what I remembered Gabriel's to be. "Now, don't blame the messenger. He's been such a good vessel. It is so good to see you finally figured it out, though. I knew we were connected enough that you would know when we were in the same room."

My nostrils flared. "Then why don't you face me yourself? Instead of using some human?"

"Well, isn't it obvious?" He opened his massive arms. "I wanted a place to talk to you outside your dreams and this seemed to work. It was either that or show up at Mr. Ivanov's home. As for using this human meat sack, I figured it was better than incinerating everyone here. I have no urge to fight you currently and I can tell you are a bit trigger-happy. It seems those men of yours aren't helping you foster your powers."

Edwin stiffened beside me. I felt his worry at the acknowledgment of his name.

I tried to calm myself down as I spoke in a soft detached voice. "I don't know who you are, nor do I care. I can't imagine what you want to talk about but if you haven't gotten the hint by now, I am not interested."

"Victor," he supplied the introduction. Byron muttered a curse as the man continued. "Heir to the Kingdom of the Dark Fae."

"What?" I felt my brain still. There had been many

words that I'd expected him to say. That phrase was not one of them.

"Yes, little flame, but don't let my royal status intimidate you. Once we are together it won't matter." I could hear the softness in the fucker's voice, as if he was authentically concerned I would be intimidated.

I couldn't even respond to him at first. I felt a bunch of details click into place as I briefly thought of Gray and how this would affect her.

I spoke carefully as if I didn't care. "My thoughts on the matter are the same. I don't want you. I don't even fucking know you. Nor does your status matter to me at fucking all. You're telling me you don't have better shit to do than possess a human and stalk a new mage?"

His eyes filled with darkness before he caught himself and laughed. I could hear one of the boys talking to Luci and I hoped this wasn't causing a massive panic attack. I should have thought about that, dammit. I was just so fucking angry and it was causing me to not think through how it might have affected her.

It was odd hearing this voice coming from Gabriel's mouth. It was so obvious why I had continued to run into this guy. He had been a vessel for some time and I hadn't realized it. I hated that we hadn't guessed he would be powerful enough to do that.

"You know," Victor drawled casually. "When my father assigned me the responsibility of searching for you, I didn't really understand his purpose. He had heard rumor of a woman made of magic and I thought he had lost his fucking mind. Turns out he hadn't."

Shit. He knew a lot. Way more than he should. Levi seemed to be shaking even more and I realized that he was being subjected to a few looks. Glares. Murderous glares from my boys. I hoped the kid could run fast because I was about done saving his ass from them.

"Then, I saw you," he groaned almost as if he was talking to himself. It was creepy and I felt like we were experiencing private insight into my stalker's mind. I have to admit, honestly, after everything that happened, I was just creeped out. Creeped out and concerned. Very concerned.

I didn't like the fact that I wouldn't be able to recognize this guy when we did come face to face and I hoped my knowledge of his power signature would be enough to give me a heads up. It seemed that the spell Edwin had implemented had kept him from my dreamscapes recently, but every so often I felt him pushing at my barriers. I refocused as he continued to spew madness.

A sneer took over his face. "But you were with them! Something that only derailed me momentarily, my little flame. It took very little time to decide that instead of delivering you to my father for enslavement, I would simply keep you for myself."

Oh. Well, then. That's totally different. Thanks, buddy, for not wanting me dead.

It concerned me that Edwin didn't toss me a mental chuckle at my sarcasm. This situation was far too fucking serious. Don't bad guys take the holidays off? No? Well, I would. You can't be evil one hundred percent of the time or else you'd run out of steam.

Right?

When he stepped forward my predatory instincts, new and unfamiliar, rose. I let out a dark sound and responded.

"You don't get to keep me," I said in a soft menacing voice. "You don't get to keep anyone. I'm not a fucking collectable, you creep."

I wasn't entirely positive that I was choosing these words.

It felt as though my magic had created its own entity and was talking through me. I didn't feel out of control or anything but it felt... odd.

It was pretty badass, actually.

Victor's nostrils flared as anger passed over his face once again. "Now, Vegas, that's a rude name, don't you think?"

"Screw. You."

I was completely digging this thread of badass confidence. I lumped some of the blame on Gray and 99.9% on the magic that shaped me. You could just tell my magic was a leather-wearing badass straining to be released. I had a feeling we wouldn't have to wait long.

I was going to need popcorn for this shit.

"You will need me in order to save them," Victor warned and stepped forward.

Kodiak let out a low growl. The mage looked up and quickly surveyed all of the boys behind me. Something dawned in his fathomless eyes and he gripped my arm, his eyes searching my skin and landing on the tattoo. He did it all so quickly no one reacted to stop his touch.

Except me.

Before he could comment or my boys could lose their shit, I let loose my power. I didn't like how close he was to my boys and I felt myself act instinctually. My skin began to glow and Gabriel/Victor cried out, letting go of my hand as his skin smoked from his burn. Now, that was a neat trick. Served him right. I felt a hint of remorse because the human would be left with the ramifications but it was clear by the sound of the cry that the stalker felt my magic as well.

My stalker who was the prince of my sister the queen's archenemy. Cool. Wonderful. That was all I needed. Bright side? I have a fucking name! Victor the Douche Bag. Victor the Crazy and not the fun kind. For the record, I do very much love the fun kind.

"You even think about touching me again and I will kill you," I hissed against the vessel's ear. "If you touch any of them ever, I will do worse than kill you."

"You fucking bonded with them?" he nearly yelled. I wasn't completely positive what he meant but sure? I mean shit, I'm not sure how much closer all of us could get at this point. Edwin's mental chuckle had me smirking.

Oh, true.

I suppose there was a fun way for me to get closer to all of them.

"Stop assuming anything I do is your business," I growled out. Why wasn't he fighting back? I could feel the power coming off Gabriel's form. I knew he was strong enough. I could feel his sick energy filling the room. Unlike the unremarkable scent that Gabriel had when we'd first bumped into him, this creature inside of him put off a putrid, almost rotten smell. His magic felt sick. Not like dark magic either. It was as though his magic was somehow infected.

"I will not hurt you, Vegas. You will come to me when Mario is knocking at your door," he promised while removing my hands from him. "Or I will take you by force."

I let out a snarl. "Don't talk to me about what you're going to do when you can't even show your fucking face! I won't play this stupid game with you."

"This isn't a game!" he roared as the atmosphere in the room thickened and became suffocating. Except, strangely, I found it didn't bother me. Instead I became ignited as someone let out a curse behind me.

I felt something peek out from behind my normal consciousness and it shone in my eyes. The vessel froze and those eyes expanded out to absorb the whites so that they were like cosmic skies. I grabbed his shirt and met them, wanting to look straight into the eyes of whoever the fuck this Victor guy was. I mean, shit, I didn't even know who this green-eyed bastard was. I sorta felt bad about him getting involved.

Not completely, though, because he was a local drug dealer.

His eyes didn't leave my face and the power he held so strongly wavered slightly. I felt almost as if I was in a dream as the flame inside of me broke loose and filled my eyes. I could feel something dark and primal shimmering underneath my skin. I was taking a back seat to my power and happily so. This type of scary was all new to me. In fact, the intensity of my emotions, powers, and sex drive were very close to overwhelming me. Everything seemed intensified and extreme. I worried what would happen if I just couldn't deal with something.

I suppose, after everything I'd been through, it would have to be rather shocking.

The show of dominance that was occuring had little to do with our physical bodies. Our magic was so vastly different. His sick, unhealthy one and my white hot one were battling. I could feel my energy growing and expanding out like a wildfire. The creature inside of me was not okay with his attempt at dominance. There were only a few men she excused to behave like that and she did that because they were her men. Our men? That hurt my head a bit. Somehow my power had claimed each of theirs and it was like two sets of people in my head. I could feel the urge to merge with my magic completely bubbling under my skin but something was blocking my ability to do so. It didn't make me any less powerful but I felt dissatisfied at the lack of union. I could feel my boys' powers rise up in response to her, wanting to break free. I realized in that moment why they seemed to be growing so quickly in skill. My magic fueled their own. It would be shocking to see what would happen when we actually started training.

"Let's make something clear," I hissed softly my magic speaking through me. "I am well aware this is not a game, Victor. You would never survive a game with me. So, be a good boy and stay out of my fucking way. I'm not scared of you anymore. You fucked up and now I know exactly who you are. The suspense is gone. The fear is gone, and now you've just made me fucking pissed. You are simply a creepy stalker who won't leave me alone. *Just. Like. Nathan.*"

He lunged for me and in a movement so fast I was impressed, I turned out of the way and elbowed him in the stomach. It was a pure instinctual movement that made him grunt and curse. I walked around him as my skin began to glow just slightly.

"*That wasn't very nice, little flame,*" I mocked before he stood up and backed away. "Now, get the fuck out of here and take Levi with you. I can't promise your vessel's safety nor Levi's once you leave them. It would be best if both of them left town or they really will disappear."

"I don't care for them because they were a means to an end. Just as this little game is. When he comes for you, which he will, you will find me," Victor warned with serious eyes. "I won't let him have you. I will take you before that even happens. I will kill you before that happens. We know just how well your powers work compared to mine when we are in the dreamscape. It will be far worse in person. This was me acting civil and you would do best to remember that after I've discarded this human form."

I snarled as they turned and walked away.
Well, shit.

Normally, I would have thought I'd be exhausted. Instead, I felt restless and furious. I wanted more of a fight. I could feel when my stalker left because all of the power snapped out of the room, only leaving mine which I retracted and pulled into me. My breathing heaved roughly as if that alone had been a full exercise.

"It's the new power," Edwin spoke softly explaining my exhaustion. "It's like two entities in one body. It will be like that, I imagine, until you work with it on a more intimate level. Although, with the amount of power you have, it may never completely merge. I do wonder what would have happened if you'd never had your powers blocked. I have to assume that the second part formed because of the separation."

I grew distracted as he got lost in thought. I turned back towards the boys as Edwin kissed my temple gently. I snorted. Fuck, those were some great expressions. Blue stared blankly at me. Kodiak's mouth hung slightly open, his brow furrowed. Booker looked wide-eyed and Rocket, curious. Grover looked impressed and Decimus proud, an expression echoed by a teary-eyed Luci. That made me feel guilty. Miranda seemed completely focused on her girlfriend. Bandit still watched the retreating figures as if he hadn't expected anything less from me. Cosimo offered me a goofy grin like I was the coolest person ever.

This felt good. I felt good. I gave a mental pat to my power as she rolled her eyes. Maybe this magic shit wouldn't be too bad after all!

I smiled at Kodiak. "How close were you to losing your shit, Kodi?"

My grizzly bear grunted and yanked me close before wrapping his arms around me. "Not as much as I would have assumed. You were pretty intense. I'm still pissed you put yourself in possible danger."

I grinned. That was pretty high praise from the overprotective bastard.

Byron caught my eye as he watched me carefully. "How are you feeling?"

I rolled my shoulders back and looked toward the rest of the room that seemed fairly oblivious of the magical happenings. "Restless and like I want to kick Victor's ass."

I moved forward then as my arm slung around Luci's waist. "I'm sorry, hun, I wasn't thinking."

She shook her head and put on a brave smile. "No. really. I'm glad I saw that. It made him seem less..."

"Scary," I provided. "Yeah. I mean, I'm sure the motherfucker is scarier in person, but come on. The guy's name is Victor."

"Sorta anticlimactic," she quipped as I saw my sister return to her normal state.

Byron grunted. "Scary is an understatement, doll. The power he is packing? Well, that isn't anything to joke around about."

I looked at him with false hope. "So, it's not over?"

"Oh, it's not over either way," Blue sang softly. "Cain promised me a hunt and I want that guy. Well, first I want Levi, then I want the stalker. Maybe, even the green-eyed asshole. Scratch that. Definitely him. He was a dick to you."

"Let me know when he's in the basement," Bandit stated and Rocket nodded thoughtfully. Probably thinking about all the sharp tools he has down in the basement. Probably thinking about all the terrible things he wants to do to the three of them. I shivered thinking about the body preserved right beneath our feet everyday. Honestly, though? I wasn't scared just cautious because that shit was intense.

"What?" Miranda asked.

Booker looked at her and squeezed her shoulder. "Trust me. Better not to know."

Yeah. He was probably right. Did I get to select the "not know" option?

No, I fucking didn't.

"I'm going to grab a beer," I announced as I walked toward the makeshift bar. Blue motioned for Decimus and Cosimo to go along. I was all keyed up and Decimus chuckled, trying to calm me down by sliding his arms possessively around my bare waist from behind. I barely noticed everyone was looking at us and probably should have considered the ramifications of walking into the general population.

"Guys," I whined quietly as energy flooded my system. "Now I want to fight something."

Or fuck.

I solemnly swear I'm not normally this violent.

Cosimo chuckled softly as we approached the bar. "There are other ways to handle that frustration, *mi tesoro*."

See? This guy understood me.

I winked and kissed him lightly as Decimus slid his hand into the back pocket of my pants. We began grabbing beers when I started to notice things, to hear things, that I should have just tuned out. Then again, as I warned, I was very keyed-up.

"With all of them? Fucking slut."

"It's like a gangbang," some asshole said.

"Maybe she's just easy."

I turned and looked at the offending parties. The one girl and three guys stopped their conversation. I offered a dark look as the girl smiled. She was very human and I tried to restrain myself as she sneered. "What the fuck are you looking at, slut?"

Wow.

So, I just want to point out again that I hate slut shaming. It is unacceptable. Honestly, I was even willing to let this girl apologize but then she just had been rude directly to my face. I had literally done nothing to her and her little boyfriends. Noting all that, I was not about to *not* stand up for myself.

I felt Decimus stiffen as the area around us quieted. I placed my beer down and for a solid minute I considered not responding. And then I was irresponsible. I honestly think I was making up for not being able to hurt my actual stalker.

God. I fucking hated that guy.

"I'm sorry," I purred my voice and energy dangerously close to magic as all the men near by stiffened. The woman, who looked slightly older than me, stood up and her eyes darkened even further. Ah, we've got a bold one! See, this was the problem with being a powerful woman. There was always someone trying to dethrone you. A lot of women in college assumed I was only acting the way I did because of my boys and while that made me feel more confident, I could totally kick ass. I mean I'm not athletic but Decimus wasn't about to let me go to college without being able to defend myself. I had to admit my fighting ability wasn't trained or pretty, it was more of a rough and dirty type of fighting.

Like sex, but not nearly as satisfying. Although, this instance might be an exception.

I released a long breath. "I was just giving you an opportunity to talk shit directly to my face."

The woman swallowed, but to her credit didn't back

down, "I have no problem calling you a fucking slut to your face. Who the hell fucks ten guys?"

I grinned because this was so fucking funny. Like, really? I've dealt with human trafficking, demons, finding out I'm made of magic, and now some college bitch was going to try to bully me? I finally understood the confidence of the Ivanov brothers in that moment. It was just like living on a different level. You had much more perspective and your power was far more potent than anyone that was human. However, with that being said, I considered defending my actions to her regarding my boys. Explaining myself.

Nope. Fuck that.

I stepped into her space and spoke. "Me."

Yeah. She didn't expect that.

"Whore!" She spat and it landed right on my cheek. An impressive feat since she was slightly taller than me. Come on, though. Not only was that unoriginal but so unsanitary, says the girl who was bathing in blood a week or so ago. In my defense, that was different because it was pixie blood and fantastic for the skin, but not necessarily for the pixies. Poor pixies. Although, Edwin said they sucked and I'm inclined to believe him. The mage is pretty fucking smart.

My hand flashed out and I grabbed her hair in a tight hold, tilting her head back. The woman let out a cry and her knees broke so that she fell to the ground. I twisted my grip and looked down at her as the entire room quieted to watch. I bet she had been expecting a punch.

For the record, I was totally having a Queen of Hearts "off with their heads" moment. After my tussle with my stalker I realized the confidence came form knowing exactly who I was now and partly being fed up with whatever the fuck this was. Also, because I was totally becoming a badass.

I mean if I was going to be Gray's weapon, I had to be cool, right?

"Don't fucking touch her," Decimus snarled as I snapped my head to the man right near me. His eyes darkened and nostrils flared. Fuck you, buddy. My little friend tried to move and I tightened the grip making her scream. Oops! Did I pull some hair out? Sorry, babe.

"Get your fucking whore in check," the man spit. Once again, it landed on me.

Dude. So fucking gross. Like, I'm going to get checked after this or some shit. I mean really it's almost as bad as finding a used condom. *Okay.* Not really, but still. I have no idea where the fuck your mouth has been.

I looked down for a brief millisecond only to look back up, and see a fist colliding with the guy's pudgy face. I felt my mouth pop open at a seething Cosimo, assumingly because of the "whore" comment. Holy fuck. Cosimo had broken his nose. Cosimo's jaw clenched and he stood at the man's eye level, his eyes darkening. Oh, shit.

Now, that was just sexy.

That about did it for my boys, unfortunately for everyone else. Absolute chaos erupted because if Cosimo was throwing punches it was a worthy cause. I shoved the bitch away from me and the entire room turned into a massive brawl.

Ah. Humanity. Shit, when did I start thinking like that?

I turned, wanting to go to the uplifted living room space and watch but then I felt someone grab my ponytail. In that moment I knew I wouldn't be leaving this place with any pent up energy. I turned and used my elbow to hit one of the girls from earlier in the gut.

I could feel a small smile lift on my lips. Don't fuck with my hair, lady.

"Now, what did we learn children?" Edwin quipped from his place near the kitchen counter. He was completely unharmed and drinking a glass of amber liquid. Asshole. Sexy asshole. His eyes heated on me as I moved slightly in my seat trying to not be affected.

"That Vegas is a badass?" Grover grinned, his teeth still stained with blood as Miranda helped patch him up. Unfortunately, physical affection healing only works one way or else I would have been the first one to suggest all of us having sex.

Joking.

But not really.

It seemed Grover had really gone for it because his left side was all bruised and his upper lip busted. The fucker was still pretty.

"That Vegas has an unexpected new sense of bloodlust and badassery?" Decimus offered with a bag of ice against his eye. I scowled.

I'd always been a badass.

"That it is way more fun to fight with Vegas by our side?" Blue offered while applying multiple bandages to his bare torso and wrapping a few of his fingers. Yeah. We were going to be real pretty tomorrow. I tried to not focus on his lean, cut, lickable abs.

Lust. Bloodlust. It was a fine line.

"That Vegas can defend herself." Kodiak mumbled softly, looking like he'd just taken an afternoon stroll.

"What was that?" I tilted my ear toward the big bear while Luci massaged my pulled hair. Blue was furious about that little injustice. I iced my jaw. It would heal later, most likely. My boys' injuries would take a bit longer. I didn't feel that terrible about it though because Edwin had mentioned that they would heal faster than humans even without my magic healing shit.

"Nothing," Kodiak smirked.

"That Cosimo fights," Booker pointed out as the guys all laughed and clapped. Cosimo was healing because of his magic but still appeared pretty beat up, his tanned skin purple and blue. My boys would find this an accomplishment. My poor pacifist.

Doesn't take away from the fact that I found it sexy. He was totally defending my honor. Can we say swoon-worthy?

"That humans are fucking crazy," Byron chirped. Everynone nodded.

"It was difficult to hold back so that I didn't accidentally kill anyone," Rocket noted curiously. Edwin was drinking and he nodded in agreement.

Bandit came over and wrapped his arms around me. I leaned back into him and looked up to meet his slight dark green gaze. It was filled with a smooth, eerie darkness that didn't bode well for my stalker.

Oh, yeah. Him. Almost forgot about that pesky bugger.

"We need to tell Gray about the connection regarding Victor and we need to call off Tamara and her men," I commented more to myself. Byron nodded, however, and began making the calls. He really was very good at getting stuff done, wasn't he? So organized and productive. That was sort of sexy though completely at odds with his personality.

"Alright," Miranda groaned. "You're all patched up."

Luci smiled and stretched. "Time to go home, sweetheart?"

Miranda nodded and Edwin spoke to both of them.

"There is a car waiting for you. I don't want you driving after everything tonight."

Surprisingly, both sleepy girls agreed and offered hugs before wandering off. I grinned as Luci tugged Edwin into an awkward hug that had him grunting. Miranda shook her head in amusement. I was glad to have spent some more time with Miranda. I knew a divide would be coming soon as we spent more time in the magic-filled universe. It was selfish, but I was hoping they joined us. I didn't want to lose my sister.

My boys all offered me sleepy kisses or hugs and began to trail upstairs an assortment of pain medicine, water bottles, and snacks in tow. I closed my eyes and put my head down on the cool counter as Bandit left as well. I knew Edwin was still in the room and as he sat down next to me. I turned my head so that my cheek pressed against the cool granite. My eyes focused on his tired expression.

The guy needed a nap.

"Well," he commented with entertainment. "That was by far the most eventful Thanksgiving I've experienced."

I started laughing and couldn't stop, tears welling in my eyes as Byron entered the room. He looked completely perplexed which made me laugh even more.

"You broke her," he whispered to Edwin in mock horror. The older magical asshat rolled his eyes and leaned forward to press a kiss to my forehead. I tried to not analyze why I was upset it wasn't my lips as he walked out. I finally managed to calm my breathing down enough to focus on Byron.

"I've got a new nickname for you," Byron announced, picking me up by the waist and setting me on the counter. I shouldn't have liked how easily he moved me but my body reacted instinctively as I snuggled into his massive warm chest. The man made me feel so small and dainty.

Ew. What the hell are these thoughts in my head?

"What is it?" I asked.

"Trouble," he announced.

I couldn't help the stupid smile on my lips that formed at his announcement. "I like that way more than doll."

I really did. Something about doll always made me feel like he thought I was, well, doll-like. Plastic and perfect. Two things I am not. I felt in some way this was humanizing me and making him see me as fallible. I mean *I am* fucking perfect, but not actually. It was in more of a "I fucking rock" vibe. Does that make sense?

"What did Tamara say?" I asked softly.

"They are heading to the Horde to help Gray." He sighed and became serious. "Edwin has been considering that option for us as well. With Mario starting this war with Gray, it may not be safe for us in Earth realm and I don't trust your stalker to not pull something now that we know how directly related he is."

"And school?" I asked clutching at the straws of normalcy.

He offered me a knowing look. "You all are doing great. So, if you feel comfortable with it, we can just manipulate the school records to say that you finished the semester and your finals."

My mouth dropped open as I leaned forward. "You can do that? Do it! Like now!"

It wasn't that I disliked school. I really did enjoy it but you would be shocked by the things that took a back seat once magic and massive realm wars entered your radar.

Byron laughed and shook his messy white blonde hair.

"I love the things that impress you, Trouble. Come on. Let's get you to bed."

I slid down from the counter. As we made our way upstairs, I realized that this Thanksgiving had been sorta fucking awesome. It seemed that the calm had officially ended, though.

Eh.

I had been getting bored anyway. I couldn't imagine what the new day would bring.

5

VEGAS

Unfortunately for my sleep schedule and healing body, the new day began at four in the morning. I awoke, shooting upright up in bed and causing Kodi to grunt and roll over on top of me. I winced at the impact on my bruised body but didn't say anything for fear of him having a panic attack over causing me minor pain. I slipped past some of my boys and wrapped a robe around myself, feeling as though something was slightly off. I began walking down the long, carpeted hallway as the shadows level with the floorboards wrapped around my feet and ankles, causing me to feel comfort rather than fear. I knew they were a by-product of Edwin and that alone comforted me.

I frowned in thought.

The two of us really needed to talk before I attacked him due to my sexual frustration. I was also hoping, praying that Byron would need to use magic soon because I was a very willing participant in his need for blood. My weight made the floorboards creak very lightly as a shadow moved across the foyer. The grandfather clock chimed, barely visible by the light of the gray dawn skies.

"Deci?" I whispered as a pair of burning eyes met mine. They were so dark in this light that you could barely see the amber streaks that resided in them. His sea salt scent surrounded me as he grew closer and my hands grabbed his leather jacket. I let out a sigh, feeling better, as his grip tightened on my hips. I could feel the tension in his touch and I wished I could see his face better in this light because I knew something was wrong.

"I'm just going for a walk princess," He whispered in his raspy voice. "You should get back to bed." My brow dipped. No. His voice didn't seem completely right. He was lying. Why would he lie?

"Where are you really going?" I demanded as my eyes tracked the way his jaw clenched.

"On a walk," he barely mumbled. I pulled back and moved my hands onto his covered abdomen but really wanting to touch his skin. He stilled my hands and brushed a rough palm to my cheek.

"Don't lie to me." I swallowed hard, my heart hurting. What would he want to hide from me? A million possibilities lit up in my head but only one or two seemed to resonate. He shook his head looking away as realization hit me and I grasped his jaw.

I let my face grow serious. "Don't you dare, Decimus."

His nostrils flared as he shook his head. "I don't know what you are talking about."

"I'm talking about going to see Gabriel. He's just a fucking puppet in all of this and going alone would be even more dangerous," I whispered as my hand brushed the cold metal of the gun at his hip. It didn't surprise me because I'd figured Grover had made sure some of his weapons were in a vault in storage. Still. I didn't like it. I tensed and he continued to look me in the eye. Panic flooded me at the thought of him doing this alone.

"Promise me, Deci, that this will be just a walk," I whispered as his eyes flashed down to my lips. I knew the man was stubborn as sin but his promises were good. They always had been. He yanked me close and a wave of pleasure washed over me as our mouths clashed. I groaned and he growled against my mouth, pulling back as his breathing ebbed from rough to calmer.

"I promise, Vegas," he managed as if in pain.

"Come back to bed," I whispered, still sensing unrest.

He lifted a thumb to my lip as he touched a small split. I saw the flames of anger flare in his eyes at the thought of the party earlier. His hands tightened on my one side as he nodded, hope filling my chest.

"I will be back to bed soon," he mumbled, kissing me softly this time. "I just need to clear my head. Keep the bed warm for me?"

I nodded and stepped back while his eyes tracked my steps backwards. I finally turned around but not before I spoke softly. "I love you Deci."

"I love you so much, Princess," he whispered looking like he was suffering. "We will make this all okay, I promise."

I knew that this situation made him feel out of control and I couldn't blame him for his need to fix it. It wasn't on him though. It was bigger than just him. I nodded and climbed the steps. The door shut and I stepped back out of the shadows of the steps to stand on the landing. I had a sickening feeling in my gut and I prayed he would decide to be safe.

He promised me.

He wouldn't lie to me.

Right?

"Trouble," Byron's silky voice wrapped around me as my head whipped to look at him. His eyes were nearly crimson in the gray light. His impressive muscular body was clothed only in a pair of flannel pants. My hand snaked out to his forearm as he curled me closer to him, my fingers playing softly along his old scars.

We were still trying to figure out a way to replace his need to cut himself for the creation of potions. He hadn't needed it yet and any magic for large spells that he used could be supplemented by drinking from me. I was concerned about the first element, though. I could never tolerate him hurting himself again. I hoped, I prayed that we had pushed past that barrier and I felt good knowing that Byron seemed authentically happy lately.

"Why are you looking at the door like that?" he whispered against my ear as my body tightened and a shiver broke across my skin.

"I just," I sighed starting again, "I just hope Decimus keeps his promise."

Instead of answering, Byron kissed my temple. "If Decimus told you something, I'm sure he meant it. I'd never known him to be a liar."

"He might if he thought the good outweighed the bad," I whispered expressing my fear.

"*Dolcezza*," Edwin spoke from behind me as well. "You should be in bed."

I turned towards both of them and let out a breath. I spoke quietly with a head shake. "I won't be able to sleep until he gets back."

Byron looked at Edwin and after sharing a look, the blood mage jogged past me and I heard him go into the kitchen. I took Edwin's offered hand as he led me towards the family room. I smiled at the lit fireplace as I curled into the leather couch. I sighed contently as a cup of tea was pressed into my hands and Edwin turned on a classic noir film in French. Sometimes, in moments with just the two of them, it was easy to forget that we had such a spotty past of time spent together.

Everything about the three of us felt natural. Even if I wanted to kick Edwin's ass sometimes.

"How concerned do we need to be about Mario's son?" I asked softly. "What type of power are we talking about?"

Edwin grunted and spoke quietly. "He's an Heir to the entire Dark Fae realm, Vegas."

I swallowed hard because Gray was a True Heir and her power was insane. I had to imagine that a normal heir, elected by succession of birth, would be powerful as well. I wondered if the dark fae had True Heirs like the Horde. I would have to ask Gray.

Byron smoothed my hair gently and I felt as though both boys were holding back their opinions on my stalker. If the Ivanov brothers were being quiet it meant it was a really bad fucking situation. My blood mage drew my legs across him as my head rested against Edwin's lap, a pillow and blanket tucked around me and surrounding the three of us. I felt peace invade my soul and despite my concern about Decimus, the boys were right.

He wouldn't lie to me.

I wasn't positive when I'd fallen asleep, but when I awoke I was sad to find that I was alone. I could feel a few of the boys on the property but it felt as though they were in the training room, gym, or outside. It was fascinating watching them train and workout most days. Well, less fascinating and more sexy but I expected once they began working with their powers more it would become very interesting. Their powers were each so unique.

Some of them had powers that required less physicality and more mental. For example, Rocket and Bandit both spent a lot of time in meditation and thought exercises led by Edwin. Apparently, Nicholas had offered him an extensive collection of knowledge on the training of each type of mage. The two of them were at a standstill until they could truly release their powers fully. Then you had more physical mages such as Grover, Decimus, and Kodiak who practiced mostly with their preferred tool, from animals to metal, and fine tuned their physicality. Mage powers such as Cosimo or Booker required a specific skill set. The two of them could be found either reading up on healing potions and herbs or in Booker's case practicing with pencil the runes that would create a new reality with ink.

Then you had Blue.

There wasn't much he needed to train on besides his overall physicality which was already pretty lethal. All of my boys were far better fighters than I ever realized and I wondered if something instinctively had told them they needed to be ready one day. Ready for the madness.

Anyway, the biggest struggle for most blood mages was the concept of drinking blood in large amounts. Something he hadn't done yet but didn't seem opposed to. At all. Byron had offered him a ton of texts on blood magic and potions. It was sort of hot watching Blue read in the library. I know it made no fucking sense. I think I just found him sexy no matter what he did.

The morning light stung my eyes as I wrapped the blanket around me and stumbled upstairs. Most of my injuries were healed but fuck if I didn't feel like shit still. I almost felt hungover. Maybe it was from the use of power? My throat closed up as I attempted to draw on Decimus power but it seemed he wasn't on the property.

That didn't mean he hadn't come back inside, right? I mean for all I knew he was out with Grover or something. I hoped.

My bedroom was empty but the sheets were messed up and no doubt smelled like my boys. I slipped off my robe and walked towards my closet, pulling on a pair of joggers underneath my oversized sleep shirt. I added a hoodie and some cute socks before leaving the room after brushing my teeth in my attached bathroom.

I should have put more effort into getting ready but this wasn't really my "getting ready" for the day. I was just in the weird stage between getting up and looking like a presentable individual. That could be translated into a lack of coffee as well. As I walked into the kitchen, fixing myself a cup of coffee... I realized it was nearly two in the afternoon. *Shit.* My eyes focused on the icy gray skies knowing somehow that it would rain.

When my phone rang, I frowned. Who the fuck was calling me? No one ever called me. I slipped the smooth material into my palm and placed it on speaker.

"Hello?" I asked curiously.

"Princess?" Decimus spoke in a gruff voice that spelled trouble. My breath exhaled in relief that he was alive but my eyes closed in preparation for the trouble I knew was coming.

"Where are you, Deci?" I asked in a barely-there voice.

He grunted. "Local station. Brought in for trespassing."

"I'll be there in five," I whispered as fury broke through my system and made my skin prickle. Decimus muttered something but I hung up. *Motherfucker.*

I was boiling with anger. I didn't even care about him being arrested. It was *why* he'd been arrested. I knew it had to do with Gabriel. I tossed on boots and grabbed the SUV keys from the garage. My jaw clicked as I got in and blasted the heat. I took the Escalade and peeled out of the driveway as icy rain began to hit my windshield. I could feel the anger and hurt mounting inside of me. It's one fucking thing to not tell me something, if I don't ask. It's another thing to promise me one thing and do another, literally right away.

He promised he wouldn't go. He lied to me. Fuck that hurt like a bitch. I pushed the gas down harder as I neared the local jail, not giving a fuck that two cops hung out under the archway.

"Came in pretty fast there, miss," the younger man with a slight accent, stated. I realized I was still in my oversized hoodie and leggings. I probably looked pretty young. Except, when I didn't say anything back, just looked at both of them for a moment, they both looked at each other in confusion. It was enough for me to get through the doors. I was barely restraining myself and I wondered if the humans could recognize my power levels as they continued to shift.

"I'm here to provide bail for Decimus Petrov," I muttered to the tired looking front desk officer. He nodded and took my ID as well as the cash from my wallet. The number was lower than expected and I was suddenly glad that Edwin had put cash in my wallet when I wasn't looking. I'd have to thank him later if I didn't get sent to prison for murder.

"Are you his wife?" he asked, noticing our same name. "Or his sister?"

This was why we never used our last name. Vivi had

been able to formally adopt us around our junior year. Well, that was what we were told. Now, I'm just thinking she used her last name because it was easier. Did any of us actually have a last name? God, why the fuck didn't I question shit like that back then? It seemed magic was able to turn a lot of curiosity away from us.

I frowned, feeling annoyed with my answer. "Wife."
I should divorce his ass.

I then proceeded to get pissed that we weren't married so I *could* divorce him.

The officer nodded but began typing as he ordered one of the young men from outside to go grab Deci. I leaned my head on the counter, so pissed that I worried about burning the place down briefly but figured they had insurance. I'm sure the boys were going to be livid when they realized I'd just left the house in weather like this. Especially alone. I'd also left my phone in the car which would have them panicking.

Ask me how many fucks I gave right now though?

"You should be glad you have such a forgiving wife, son," the older cop stated as I met Decimus's eyes. He winced at my expression as they uncuffed him and I got my ID back.

"You're good to go, but don't let me catch you trespassing again," he stated in a gruff voice before patting Decimus's back. I was already walking out toward the car. Decimus said something to him and jogged after me, our bond shimmering with my rage. I'm sure the other boys could feel it. I tried to shut it down but as I climbed into the seat, Decimus stopped me with a hand on my arm.

"Princess," he said softly. "You shouldn't drive."

I slipped into the car and closed the door with a resounding bang. No! Fuck him. I was worried about him getting hurt when he went 'spying' and now he doesn't want me driving? No way. No way, no how. Asshole.

He got into the other side and I could see the tension riding his body. There was a tick in his jaw and his wet hair dripped into troubled, nearly black eyes. I cursed mentally because the weather seemed to be getting worse and I had to wonder if it was because of us.

That would be some fucking shit.

Our ride was silent and he didn't say anything, trying to keep his temper in check and not ignite mine any further. It was very rare that the two of us got into a real fight instead of just being snarky to one another. I could feel this building though as every second passed in silence and had a feeling it would be rather explosive once we got home.

I parked in the driveway, turned off the ignition, and was jogging up to the house before he could say a word. Instantly, I knew that most of the boys were home now. Probably concerned about us and the rage simmering through the bond. I kicked off my shoes and turned toward the kitchen to get a goddamn glass of wine. I was taking the day off, officially.

This was my Thanksgiving re-do. Now where were those leftovers?

"Vegas," Decimus attempted to demand my attention.

"Don't you dare," I shot back at him.

"Princess," he measured out calmly, his fists clenching, "You need to-"

I lost it.

"I need to fucking what, Decimus?!" I snarled looking at him. "I need to lie to your face minutes before I do something? I need to make false promises?"

Decimus closed his eyes attempting to breath through his nose while gripping the counter. "You don't understand."

Oh, I understood perfectly well. I knew that he figured his concern and need for control in this situation outweighed his promise. He acted impulsively and emotionally.

"I understand fucking plenty!" My voice in a tone I never used. "What *you* don't seem to understand is how fucked up this is. What if something had happened to you? This was a selfish and impatient choice!"

"Vegas?" a deep voice questioned as Kodiak walked into the room. I ignored him, as well as some of the other boys that slipped in. I took a sip of my wine and continued to glare at Decimus. The Greek shook his head and looked out the window with frustration. Kodiak tried to approach me and I met his eyes. He stopped then and pursed his lips before backing up to lean on the counter.

"I shouldn't have lied," Decimus stated softly.

"No fuck," I snapped.

"What the hell did you do?" Kodiak looked at him with more shock than anything else.

"Oh, what did he do?" I drawled sarcastically. "He lied and made me a false promise. One that he broke minutes later. Minutes! Deci! What the fuck is wrong with you?"

Decimus lost it. "What's fucking wrong is that this guy is still around! What's fucking wrong is that we are doing jack shit as he continues to fuck with us!"

Oh, good. Now, we were both yelling. I didn't feel as bad.

"What the hell were you going to do if you found him? You had no backup! We don't even do Raven shit without backup and this guy is on nearly the same level as Gray! Deci you could have fucking died!"

Decimus was trembling with frustration as Kodiak just watched us with a blank face. I shook my head and poured another glass. Kodiak made a noise in his throat. I didn't give a fuck. Plus, I had to give props to Edwin. This was some damn good angry wine.

I had never been one to have a temper but the flame inside of me was furious. It felt wronged and I could feel it building. I didn't even take the time to see who else was in the room with us. No, instead I decided to leave. I needed out of this room before I really lost it.

I avoided Deci walking past and when his hand snapped out to grab my arm, I growled ferally. "Let me go!"

"Not until we fucking talk about this!" His voice raised as Kodiak seemed to vibrate behind me with concern. I also recognized Bandit's bond near Booker's off to the right nearby. I felt bad for yelling because of Booker but I just was so furious right now. It removed any other concern I may have had, which wasn't healthy but probably something to explore *later.*

"I don't fucking want to talk about it," I hissed meeting him head on. "I don't want to talk to you right now, so let me the fuck go."

"No," his stubborn ass replied as his grip tightened.

"Now!" I tugged my arm back.

I was up and over his shoulder, as my wine glass shattered on the floor. I struggled to get away from him but he pushed through the kitchen door and I briefly caught some of the boys in passing. At the stairs, I raised my energy just a bit to sear Decimus's hand. He swore and I was able to push out of his arms. He tried to step forward and I moved back with a swift step.

"Princess, we are talking right now," he ordered, his breathing harder than before.

"I'm not your princess," I snapped. "Princes don't break fucking promises!"

Good one, Vegas.

They probably did, actually. I'd have to ask the brothers. It didn't escape my notice that everyone was watching us. Did I care? No. The other bonds were silent and I could sense the authentic surprise through them. Decimus and I had never had a blow out like this.

"God damn it, Vegas!" Decimus roared, "It's one fucking lie and it was about your goddamn safety anyway!"

I poked a finger into his chest as I continued to yell in his face, "Don't talk to me about safety! I had you promise. You fucking promised you weren't going over there! Then you get caught and I have to bail your ass out of jail? Like, really?! We are talking about my safety?"

I turned on my heel toward the stairs and when his hand touched mine the power in the room exploded. A power surge hit the house as thunder lit up outside. Several lights shattered throughout the house. I heard Blue swear but I just yanked my hand from Deci in the dark, sprinting up the stairs with an energy and speed I had never possessed before.

I felt overwhelmed. Angry. Pissed. I moved toward my bedroom and slammed the door shut, the sound echoing through the now silent home. Then, for the first time ever, I locked my door.

DECIMUS

My back hit the wall across from her door as I focused on the damn barrier I had been pounding at for nearly an hour along with some of the other guys. Yet, she was silent. We knew she was in there but the silence was cold. No one dared to remove the door forcefully, worried it would cause bigger issues. I scoffed. Could it get bigger than this? I had fucked up. What the hell had I been thinking?

You were thinking about protecting the woman you love.

"Anything?" Grover asked softly, his eyes dark. It had been an hour and I could tell the other men were feeling a mixture of shock, confusion, and frustration with me. I didn't answer and put my head down on my knees. I could hear him walking away after a small shoulder squeeze and was thankful because this was fucking depressing. I didn't want to face any of them right now.

Blue had given me a frustrated, nearly reprimanding look that made me want to punch him. Kodiak had just seemed genuinely shocked with her yelling because, normally, she really didn't have much of a temper. Although, I think everyone had noticed the change in intensity that had occurred in all of us. Edwin had explained that she would most likely have more extreme reactions now that she was being constantly flooded with our emotions as well as her magic. Byron had walked past several times looking at the door with a confused and slightly lost expression. I wasn't completely positive if the man could survive without Vegas, now. They had seemed to have formed a fairly dependent, close relationship within a matter of days.

It would have been funny if I wasn't positive I looked like a fucking lost pup also.

Booker had been silent since she started yelling and it was as concerning, if not more, than Rocket's complete shut down. He had changed so much recently and now he was back downstairs working on whatever the hell it was he did. I felt terrible and guilty, what type of fucking family member was I?

I swallowed hard thinking of how my own family had left me. I would be lying if I said there wasn't a part of me that wasn't terrified that wouldn't happen again. Grover had been understanding and Cosimo had offered me a shoulder squeeze in support. It didn't make me feel better at all. Possibly even worse.

Then there was Bandit.

Bandit who had no temper, usually. I could feel his seething anger at the situation though as the bond shimmered with frustration. I was going to give him a wide berth until this was fixed. I had a feeling being on his bad side if he lost it would be bad. Sorry, not *if* he ever lost it but *when* he lost it. Mark my words that day would come and probably sooner than later.

Not that I was planning to leave this spot. No. I'd sit here all fucking night. Maybe into the next year. I looked to the end of the hall where the icy hail continued to fall behind the stained glass window. This fucking day. My chest hurt and my body felt cold.

"Vegas," I knocked on her door again not even bothering to stand. "Please let me in."

She didn't. Three hours later, she still hadn't.

My stomach was clenched in stress and Cosimo had attempted to bring me dinner, but I couldn't. I couldn't do anything but sit here and stare at her door. I had long ago shed my jacket and continued to run my hand through my hair again and again. My eyes hadn't closed since the night before last and I could feel my 5 o'clock shadow growing thicker. I would end up looking like a fucking mountain man if she didn't come out soon.

"She needs to eat," Kodiak mumbled having walked up the stairs. I was confused in some ways about his reaction the most. Kodi was always aggressive and protective, yet right now he just seemed confused. I think that he was having issues being mad because the situation was an internal one and not external.

I thought about what he was saying regarding dinner.

She did need to eat. I was fucking that up. I couldn't leave though. God, I always fucked shit up, didn't I? It didn't surprise me that my family had left me. I was feeling more like a fuck up with every minute that passed. My stomach clenched in pain at the feeling of rejection that washed through me.

Vegas had never locked her door.

"Vegas!" I called out in a near beg, hitting my head against the wall. "Just talk to me for five minutes! Please, sweetheart."

My eyes rounded in shock as her door opened to reveal a pair of lilac eyes, dark with worry and shadows. I hadn't expected her to open it and now that she had, I didn't know what to say.

"What?" she asked her voice raw and eyes rimmed red. Fuck I'd made her cry. That hurt far more than the rejection, I leaned forward slightly and looked up at her.

"Can I come in?" I asked softly.

She crossed her arms and offered a slight head shake. "If you have to say something, say it."

I stood up my legs feeling tight as I stepped forward into her space. Vegas didn't move but I saw her breathing heighten as anger flooded our bond. Shit, she had been blocking this entire time.

"I shouldn't have gone," I started out bracing my arms on the door frame above me.

"Damn right, you shouldn't have," she snapped as tears brimmed her eyes and she began shaking. "You lied to me. You promised me, said it right to my face, and then went to do that exact fucking thing."

I inhaled with pain. "Vegas, we need to figure out a-"

Her door began closing, but I blocked it with my foot and walked in closing the door behind me.

Vegas hissed. "Get out!"

"No." Something sparked in my chest. The insecurities from before pushed aside by desperation. I wasn't going to let her go. My family left when I was gone from the house, so if I never left her alone she couldn't leave.

Rational, dude.

Something raw and ingrained had me panicking at her distance. She was mine. Vegas was mine and if I lost her, I would have nothing else. Nothing. My jaw clenched as tears pricked my eyes at this fucking situation. I knew this wasn't about my night in jail. No, she was authentically hurt that I lied to her and broke my promise. Authenticity and honesty were trademark qualities that Vegas deemed necessary in a relationship. I was such a dumbass. She would have been less mad at me if I'd just told her I was going anyway. Except then she may have tried to come with. My hands twitched to pick her up and hold her to me until she relented and forgave me. She'd have to give in eventually, right? The woman could be more stubborn than myself so I wasn't sure.

"Decimus, I swear to god, you will leave this room right now or else," she growled.

"What else do you want me to say?" I exclaimed, throwing my hands out. Literally. Whatever it was. I would do it. I would beg. I would kiss the fucking ground this woman walked on.

Vegas turned around her hair fanning out in a silver wave. "How about you start with a fucking apology?"

Oh, shit. Yeah. I was an idiot.

"Of course, I'm sorry Vegas," I whispered feeling my throat tightening. "I have no idea what I was thinking. I just can't stand the thought of this asshole walking around being able to hurt you. I should have told you and I shouldn't have

FIRE & SMOKE

lied or promised something I wouldn't be able to keep. I don't regret trying though, princess. I am always going to try to keep the bad guys away from you."

My words stilled her. Big tears spilled from her thick dark lashes and I could see the raw hurt past the anger. It hit me like a shot to the chest. I had never felt more like a piece of shit.

"How am I supposed to trust your promises?" she asked her voice raw but gaining strength. "Also, did you ever consider what could have happened to you? How you could have gotten hurt? No of course you didn't. Because you are fucking stubborn!"

Her comment about trust was crushing me. I felt like I couldn't breath.

"You don't trust me anymore?" I asked in a strangled voice that was so rough and low it was barely audible. I felt any façade of who I was break away as my emotions laid bare across my face.

Her eyes softened before she looked away in frustration. "I asked you, not the other way around. How am I supposed to trust your promises?"

"Princess," I stepped toward her as she sat down on the edge of her bed, looking exhausted. I noticed that her little fuzzy socks were slipping down her feet and her legging was pushed up to her knee, knowing it had moved like that from the way she slept on her side. I felt determination filter through me. I knew Vegas, really fucking well, she needed me. I would make her see that.

"Answer," she responded without looking at me.

Without prelude, I moved between her legs kneeling and wrapping my arms around her waist. She looked down at me and her hands twitched where she kept them on the bed. I wanted them strung through my hair like when we watched movies together.

"Vegas," I started quietly. "I've never been more sorry about an action I've taken than this one. I have no excuse. I had already been heading out and I hoped you would be still sleeping by the time I got back. I didn't want you worrying about me. It's no excuse though, I should have never lied and broke my promise. But, sweetheart? Please don't stop trusting me because of this. I fucked up and I will spend the rest of our lives proving you can trust my promises, but please don't shut me out like that again. You've never locked your door before."

She swallowed hard as her eyes filled with tears, her long fingers grasping my jaw lightly. Her eyes searched my face and she took a shuddering breath. "I can deal with a lot in this fucking crazy world we are part of. But one of you lying to me or purposefully breaking a promise? I can't do that."

I nodded and swallowed. "Vegas, I am so sorry."

Her lips curled up slightly as she shimmied off the bed to sink to the carpeted floor with me. I pulled her body against mine as I held her like I would never let her go. God, nearly five hours fucked me up in the head. I nuzzled her hair as she took a deep breath and looked up at me. What the fuck would happen to me if I ever was separated from her longer than that?

I wanted to kiss her. I needed to kiss her. I'd never been one for panicking. My temper usually overrode that. Right now, though? I could feel my chest releasing the anxiety that had built up. She was touching me. She wouldn't be touching me if she didn't want me, right? If I was even half rational right now I'd call myself out for being a bitch, but I didn't even care at this point.

"I need to know things are okay between us," I said softly, my eyes trailing her face. I tried to ignore the hot desire traveling through my body but it was impossible. Everything inside of me was urging me to claim her and to make sure she was connected to me. Make sure she wouldn't leave me. I needed to know she wouldn't.

I was starting to see Rocket's point about starting a family. I knew it wasn't the time, nor was my reasoning solid in the heat of the moment. Yet, I still understood it. Vegas pulled my jaw down and kissed me lightly. I couldn't keep it light, though, and my hand gripped the back of her neck as I picked the two of us up. She moaned lightly as her center pressed against my jean covered erection.

"Deci," she spoke quietly. I laid her down on the bed and crawled over her, my chest aching and the need to make her forgive me growing.

"Please," I openly begged. "I need you Vegas. I need to know you still love me."

Vegas stilled as she frowned, pain marring her face. "Deci, of course I love you. I would never not love you for something like this. I may be really fucking angry, but my love? It's unconditional and has been since the day I first met you."

"Don't leave me. Don't block me out." I whispered while placing my forehead against hers.

Vegas's breath hitched as she kissed me. "Never."

I could feel the abandonment issues from my family leaving me in America flushing through my veins. I deepened the kiss as her nails bit into my shoulders. I couldn't deny how good it felt to have her marking me.

"Let me make you feel good, princess," I murmured as her body shivered under me. "Please?"

"Okay," she whispered as I thanked the gods.

My hands began to peel up her large sweater and I groaned to find her breasts free. Those pink tight nipples were hard and I followed her blush that expanded from her chest to her cheeks. I leaned in to take one taut nipple between my teeth as she hissed, arching off the bed. I soothed it in my mouth gently feeling something dark building inside my chest.

"Princess," I whispered softly while praising her body, "you taste so good."

I pulled off her sweater completely as I looked down at her hooded gaze. With an easy movement, I peeled down her leggings to find a small black thong. I groaned as I tightened my hold on her thighs, opening them up in front of me. I wanted to fucking tie her legs to each post of the bed and keep her exposed to me all night. It didn't escape me that it would also stop her from leaving me, a concept I was very caught up on currently.

"Deci," she wiggled, her breathing tight and rushed.

I tightened my hold. "I want to make you feel good. I want to embed myself in you, until you forgive me. I need to know you trust me. Do you trust me?"

Her eyes widened as she nodded. I peeled off her panties and leaned down to run my tongue over her wet, pink pussy. I didn't hold back the moan of ecstasy from her taste. I could feel her pleasure rocketing as I devoured her center. I swore as she practically jumped off the bed as I sucked on her tiny clit. Fuck. Maybe I'd just keep my head between her legs from now on.

I knew my need for control was resurfacing, though, as she drew closer to her orgasm. My short scruff rubbed against her thighs and I loved the red marks it left. I groaned into her center as she exploded on me, her taste flooding my tongue. Oh, fuck. I held onto her hips as she whimpered and moved against me, getting off on my face.

"Hands up, princess," I hissed as my dark need rushed forward. I think she saw the change because her eyes widened and she became even wetter against my fingers. I nearly smiled because I knew exactly what my little princess needed and right now it wasn't soft and romantic. I loved giving her that. I loved that she was the only one to make me want to do cute shit like buy flowers and cuddle her perfect body while watching her favorite movies.

But right now? Right now she needed to be fucked into the next day.

"Up," I demanded as her arms lifted above her head and wrapped around the headboard iron bars. I grinned at her increased breathing as I peeled off my shirt with ease. I wasn't going to be able to take my time with this. No, I needed to fuck her and fuck her good until I was positive any anger between us was gone.

Sometimes, I thought I was a bigger control freak than even Kodiak. Then again, the fucker was far more into controlling Vegas's punishments and pain. I couldn't wait until she realized what she was really in for with him. Then maybe we'd both take her, I would love to slide inside her tight little ass while he fucked her. She moaned as I shifted her legs open further, loving how wet she was for me. All for me.

I unbuckled my jeans and her eyes watched as my impossibly hard cock bounced out from the restraint of my dark jeans. I was glad now that I'd gone commando, at the time it was because I'd been rushing out of the house but now it meant I got into her faster.

"Decimus!" she cried out as I slid, balls deep, right into

her. The tightness of her walls had me nearly passing out. Fuck.

She was going to kill me. Hell, I would love to fucking die this way.

"Princess," I groaned against her neck before kissing her soft skin, "are you always going to be this tight? I might pass out because of how fucking good you feel. I think we need to break you in more, what do you think? It may take everyday but I feel like you're up for the challenge."

"Yes," she mewled as I bit down on her neck to calm her wiggling down. Instantly she stopped and her breathing turned quicker. I licked the bite, tasting copper, as I began to slowly move my length in and out of her tightness.

"Faster," she pleaded.

My eyes flashed up as I offered her a dark smirk. "No. You aren't in control here. Who is in control, princess?"

"You!" She gasped as I felt her contract around me as I began to move in and out of her. Out and then fully back into the hilt. The mixture of our skin coming together and her moans was erotic. I could feel the sweat breaking out across our bodies as I continued to go at a punishing pace. Her body was shaking and I could see that she was close to coming, so I let her.

I slammed home again and bit her nipple, causing her to scream out her release. Her fingers released the bed post as I chuckled and quickened my pace. Normally, I'd spank her ass for letting go but as her nails bit into my back and drew blood, I was glad I hadn't. She locked her legs around me and I rolled her.

My eyes followed the curve of her body as she began to slide up and down my dick. I felt a small cocky grin slip onto my face at the obvious desire on her face. Her body was flushed and she was extremely wet, her nipples hard like diamonds. I was close to coming. Really fucking close but watching her take control was fucking hot, it was like she was using my dick.

"Princess," I hissed as she ground out against me, our pelvises connecting.

"I'm so close," she whined.

I slipped an arm around her, locking her against my chest as I began to pump into her earnestly. She screamed as I demanded her orgasm, my dick easily slipping in and out of her extreme tightness because of how wet she was. I felt her pleasure explode on my cock as I bit down my roar on her collarbone and the lights in the room exploded. Not metaphorically. The lamps shattered completely. My orgasm had both of us crying out as thunder sounded outside and my powers wrapped around us.

Oh, fucking shit. I tried to catch my breath as she laid on top of me in the silence. I didn't even try to remove myself from her because I was still hard and this felt amazing.

"Shit, Deci," she muttered as she smiled her normal infuriating smile against my chest. "That was some explosive sex."

An authentic chuckle left my mouth. I kissed her and pulled her into my chest so that her body was wrapped protectively against my own. I loved this fucking woman and her dorky jokes. A sense of peace hit me because I knew that somehow we were okay now. Maybe even better in some ways.

"Everything okay in there?" Grover's amused voice asked.

"Better than okay," Vegas mumbled out as Grover laughed.

For a moment, I just held her and when she spoke I

knew we were better. "So, did you find anything out about the bastard?"

My fierce princess. I spoke. "No. I hadn't stepped more than a foot onto his property, the address I'd gotten from Rocket's files, before the police were there. He must have seen me walking down the block or maybe they just have tabs on us."

She scowled and I smiled at her as the lights came back on. I smoothed her white hair out of the way and spoke.

"I want him gone, sweetheart. I want these threats gone. It's so fucking furstrating. I want to do something. Anything. At first our excuse was a lack of magic but now I just feel like we are playing a waiting game. We are sitting ducks."

"We will," she promised softly. "We know who he is and we know that there is something bigger at play here. Byron mentioned going back to the Horde."

My chest relaxed at that thought. "I think that's a good idea."

"I already handled the school files," Byron opened the door with a pointed look. "Congratulations you all ended the semester with A's. Except you, Deci. You got an A- in your lab."

"Fuck you," I chuckled as Byron grinned and walked out. Vegas was smiling contentedly as she wrapped herself up in covers. I offered her my t-shirt which she slipped on.

Bandit spoke from the door as well. "You okay, Ve?"

Vegas looked up at him and smiled. "Yeah, I am."

Bandit looked at me, his eyes alight with something that was no longer angry and more amused. He offered me a head nod and walked out closing the door. So, he's not mad then? Odd. I had expected more of them to demand our attention right now.

Oh.

I peeled her shirt back off her as Vegas began to protest while looking at the door. "Trust me, princess, no one is coming in here tonight, so I want you naked."

She frowned and I took that opportunity to pin her to the bed as she let out a soft laugh. I nuzzled her neck. "Do you know what that means?"

"What?" she whimpered, her voice soft with desire.

"You're all mine."

6

VEGAS

"Jerk," I grunted as I barely avoided another jab. My body was still sore from Thanksgiving but now that it was Saturday morning I felt a tad better. The boys were also looking far less like rotten apples with their bruises and cuts healing.

"It's not nice to call names, angel," Grover shot out as I avoided his skilled movement, rolling onto my shoulder to avoid him.

It goes without saying that I have never and will never use the gym. However my handy dandy powers had increased my strength and agility. The downside? The boys having decided training for self-defense and fighting is a necessary evil for me. That is why folks, I was currently attempting to not get hit by Grover's frustrating jabs.

The most annoying, frustrating jabs on the planet.

"Hah!" I moved quickly but groaned as he lightly hit my knee and I fell to the mat. Sweat crowded my face and certain parts of my body were still sore from Decimus's delicious treatment of it throughout the entire night. As in every other hour. My increased sex drive had really just gone off the charts after last night and it felt as though it had been a pivot point. Unfortunately, being in bed alone with someone meant that some of my boys like Kodiak didn't get a good night's sleep. He was napping now, but I knew that later he would need some quality sleep time wrapped around me like a snake.

I really made a lot of animal references when describing him.

"Why are you being so mean?" I groaned as I rolled over flat on my back. My oversized shirt stuck to my sweaty body and the spandex shorts I wore rolled up my thighs slightly. I had no idea how Grover had this much energy in the morning before coffee.

He hadn't let me have any before training and spoke some cruel words of reason. "We can't have coffee until after training because it will dehydrate you.'

Bitch. I won't be able to train if I'm half asleep. Well, clearly that wasn't true. But still.

Grover grinned and helped me up. "Because, angel, the way I see it we have two options. I can treat you like the fucking stunning angel you are and keep you shielded from all this shit, possibly risking your safety if something breaks through us. Or I can train you to become a little force to be reckoned with, but it means I have to be a tad hard on your body."

Hard on my body? I love the sound of that.

The man was so charming, his smile full force and those warm eyes amused. I wanted to lick the sweat off his shirtless body. Seriously? How was I turned on right now? It was like a constant hum and I found myself wet more often than not.

If it was between either fighting or fucking, I'd pick the latter because the other had the ability to burn down the house I was falling in love with. I wonder if a fire extinguisher would work on me.

"Aren't there other ways to train for endurance?" I smirked as he leaned closer.

"What did you have in mind?" he asked, his voice deeper as a dangerous glint darkened those warm happy eyes.

"I'll show you but you have to agree to no more training today," I smirked and ran a nail up his impressive shirtless sweaty body.

"I'll make you a deal." He leaned closer his lips right near mine. "If you can knock my ass to the ground, you can decide what we do for the next hour of training."

Fucking deal.

Without agreeing, I moved swiftly and used the move he showed me to knock his legs out. Unfortunately, I wasn't watching for when he grabbed my waist and pulled me down with him. I let out a laugh as he rolled up and looked down at me from where he straddled my hips. That didn't work out nearly as well as I had hoped. He was now a trained mage with increased strength and agility. I was screwed.

Couldn't I go against a human instead? They weren't as fast.

"Good try," he commended. His massive coiled arms fell to either side of me in a cage as his sudden erection caused me to shift with need.

"Let me try again," I whispered and ignored the urge to pull him down for a kiss.

He offered me a cocky grin and spoke in a darker voice. "I sort of like you like this though, remember I get to choose now what we do for the next hour."

I liked the sound of that.

"Aren't we training?" I asked coyly because I was totally

getting what I wanted. Well, hopefully. He grinded against me slightly before grasping my hands and pulling them above my head so I was laid out for him. He let out a low rumble and nibbled my ear.

"Well, angel, now that I've got you like this, all I can think about is how you sounded when Decimus was fucking your tight little pussy last night. I couldn't stop touching my cock and imagining you on top of me, my entire length buried deep inside of you."

I involuntarily moaned at his words and the charming bastard grinned. He continued. "You know what else I thought about last night as I listened to your moans?"

I felt my breathing quicken. "What?"

"I thought about fucking you in front of them." He nibbled my jaw as my head and back arched desperate for his attention. "All of them. I thought about spreading you out on the kitchen counter and fucking you so that everyone could see how fucking sexy you are and how good I make you feel."

My body clenched as he smirked at the shiver running through me. I had never seen this side of Grover and let me tell you, I. Was. Not. Complaining.

"Do you like the idea of being watched, angel? Knowing that any of us would kill to be inside of that tight little hole? I bet we will fight over who wants to be inside you first everyday for the rest of our lives, as everyone else watches your beautiful fucking body come. How would you feel about everyone paying attention to you like that? I know I want to fuck you on every surface in this house, with or without an audience. Can you imagine what's going through everyone else's minds?"

I cried out as his fingers slipped down my spandex shorts and he groaned at my obvious wetness. I whimpered as he drew his rough large hand up my shirt and left me in just a sports bra and spandex shorts.

"These have been teasing me all morning," he grumbled while peeling them off and sliding down my sports bra to let lose my heavy and taut breasts. The cold gym air washed against my sweaty skin as he took a nipple in my mouth and tugged slightly.

I wiggled against him and he ground into me, so that the two of us were grinding against one another like fucking teeneagers. He left small bite marks down my body. I hissed in pleasure as his fingers slipped into me fully. He flicked his tongue over my clit and I cried out his name, my orgasm approaching.

"I want you to come for me Vegas," he whispered against my heat. "I want to train your little body to come on demand. I want your taste on my lips throughout training today."

Shit. I loved his dirty mouth.

Prince charming with a filthy mind and mouth.

Also, this type of training sounded far more fun.

"Grover!" I cried out as he devoured me and brought me to a beautiful, muscle clenching orgasm that had everything in my body awakening with pleasure. I felt like sugar had been poured on my body and I turned into a gooey, wet mess of desire.

"Well, fuck," a rough nearly sleepy voice stated. "I was wondering where you went after your shower and now I know."

Grover continued to lick me up, seemingly content between my legs, as I met Decimus's heated and amused gaze. I closed my eyes blushing as he moved closer. There was no hiding how laid out I was. Rather than feeling embarrassed, I felt like I was boiling with desire.

"No need to be embarrassed, princess. I happen to like this version of training," he growled as Grover pulled up my spandex shorts and lightly slapped my center. I cried out as a mini orgasm rolled through me that had him groaning in delight.

"However," Decimus sucked on an abused nipple while adjusting my sports bra, "everyone is about to come train and while I'm not opposed to group sex, I should warn you that if you are naked when they come down here I can't control what happens."

My brain flashed with the idea of being with multiple of my boys.

Oh, sweet god, I needed coffee!

The door opened so I scrambled up to pull on my oversized shirt and remove myself from the beautiful fucking men around me. I moved toward the French doors to walk out on the patio, needing a moment alone. I controlled my breathing as I heard the boys' voices echoing throughout the room. I'm sure everything smelled like sex and sweat.

A large hand wrapped around my center, as Blue's cinnamon scent invaded my senses. "Beautiful."

"Blue," I grinned and looked up while leaning against his chest. He offered me a simmering look, his dimples dangerous as a possessive gaze narrowed on my lips. I would be lying if I said I hadn't missed them in bed last night. Edwin was right about the bigger bed concept. Maybe we could have a custom one made for eleven.

"You smell edible," he growled lightly, his hand playing with the edge of my spandex shorts. I whimpered as his lip twitched dangerously. I knew exactly what he was talking about.

"And you seem in a rather good mood considering

yesterday and the night before that," I whispered suspiciously as his eyes darkened from their denim blue.

"I *am* in a good mood," he whispered. "Do you know why?"

No, but fuck if I didn't want to know. Blue usually was only this happy when it came to fucking and killing. Since we hadn't had sex yesterday...

"Why?" I asked pushing against him slightly as he looked down, unashamed of how hard he was against me.

"The more we learn about this guy," he whispered, "the sooner I get to kill him."

I groaned as his nose skimmed my throat. It didn't surprise me that his head was on blood right now. Specifically, I knew he and Cain had talked twice about their future "hunting" trips. I *so* didn't want to be part of that.

"Blue!" I exclaimed in shock as his tooth nicked my neck. He chuckled and his tongue soothed over it causing me to feel all sorts of delicious sensations.

"I really do hate constantly interrupting," Booker said with a calm smile, "but we are waiting for the two of you to start."

I narrowed my eyes playfully at Booker as his ears turned pink but he kept his velvet grey eyes on me. "Wouldn't it be more fun out here with us, Booker? Do we really want to work out?"

Booker grinned as Blue licked my skin again. Then Grover called out something that made my face turn pink. "Angel, if you don't get in here, what I explained earlier will come to fruition sooner than you think."

My mouth opened with snark. "You say that like it's a punishment."

"That sounds a lot like a challenge," Decimus goaded

and Kodiak expressed interest from where he was setting something up. Too much interest.

"Coffee," Cosimo offered me one and I instantly was curling into his chest ignoring Blue's complaints about my distance.

"You're my favorite," I goaded the other men as Cosimo let his hand around my waist slide down to slightly squeeze my ass. I blushed and if the music hadn't started in the other room, I'd be upstairs already. I needed more time alone with this man. Soon.

"Come on, Ve," Bandit called out in a relaxed amused drawl. "You're going to cause a fight."

I snickered and walked over to Bandit and Rocket, both of them watching me with interesting and dark looks. Rocket didn't reach for me and after winking at Bandit, his eyes flashing with a feral glint, I wrapped myself around our good doctor. He instantly had me up in his arms, my butt resting on his crossed forearms as I met his gaze head on. It was mostly blank.

"I'm sorry," I whispered knowing he wouldn't ask for it or expect it. I also knew how much fighting upset him and I didn't want those walls I bulldozed down to start forming once more.

He continued to look into my eyes for another moment until a small rumble broke from his chest and he pulled me close in a vise grip. I nuzzled his neck and he began playing with my hair, causing Blue to growl from across the room.

So possessive.

"I love you," Rocket whispered in my ear so quietly that maybe only Bandit heard.

"I love you more," I teased as his lip twitched. I wanted to kiss him but the two of us couldn't kiss without practically ripping our clothes off of one another... so yeah maybe I should kiss him. No training for me!

Edwin jogged down the stairs and looked over the nine of us as Byron followed him. I wiggled down Rocket's body but that was as far as he let me get. I scowled as he winked and my heart stuttered. No. He was not allowed to wink.

Christ.

He wiggled his eyebrow and used his other hand to close my mouth that had popped open.

Edwin started speaking. "Alright. So, I think we need to leave Earth realm for a time. Byron has closed out the semester for all of you with passing grades and until this threat passes, I think we are more prepared in the Horde."

No one argued.

"With that being said, I think we need to leave tomorrow and that means upping your training. So, today I want you solely working on that, as well, please, be mindful that there is one of us here that is connected to all ten of us. So, try to not shatter any lamps."

Decimus smirked. "That didn't just happen when we were fighting."

I shot him a wink as Rocket rumbled against me, gripping me harder at the insinuation. Edwin ignored him. "Everyone split off. I am going to be working with Vegas today out on the patio. I don't suggest stepping outside unless you want to get burned."

I grimaced as Kodiak chuckled at my disgruntled expression. I adjusted my sweaty shirt and his eyes flashed down to my necklace and arm, the bastard smiling at what I am positive he considered his brand. Don't even get me started on the tattoo down my chest. He had randomly been stroking the one part associated with being a naturalistic mage. The bastard had somehow, impossibly, become more territorial. I totally loved it.

"Dolcezza," Edwin sang as he smirked at my thoughts. I scowled and followed after him. I shivered once we were outside but not nearly as bad before my magic was released. I faced the bastard and his pumpkin eyes were lit up with dangerous mirth.

It goes without saying that seeing my boys in casual athletic wear wasn't unusual. It wasn't even odd to see it on Byron, but Edwin? This shit was odd. I narrowed my eyes and moved forward without permission, looking at his gym shoes and joggers with a normal shirt. All black of course and labelless.

His hair was messy today though and I didn't hide the fact that I was checking him out as I met his heated gaze. All the eccentric bullshit was gone and a raw desire was there. I could feel my blood heating as Edwin's jaw clenched, his hands twitching to reach out for me. A boldness I didn't expect went through me as I stepped right up against him, chest to chest.

"Vegas," he spoke softly with warning.

"What?"

I licked my bottom lip just a bit as his eyes turned molten and his hand finally reached up to grip my chin. I felt victory surge through me just as his eyes softened. I could feel his desire but aside from that there was something intense and cautious.

"Edwin," I spoke softly as his eyes met mine and he had a brief almost fearful look flash through his gaze. I knew he'd step back before he did.

My temper flashed through our bond as he looked away with slight frustration. What the heck was his problem? Was he regretting our kiss from before? Did he think I was too forward? Was this about Mario and the Horde? I shut down our mental block as I turned and walked a few feet away from him. I turned back to see his face filled with something I didn't understand.

"Vegas," he spoke my name again with concern.

"Let's do this," I stated blankly. His eyes darkened at my tone and I could nearly feel his magic reacting to my demand. That was happening more often than not lately, I realized that it was this entity that made the Horde citizens so intense and deadly. I held his gaze and neither of us looked away as a burning sensation grew in my chest. My emotions were like roaring waves instead of soft suggestions. I was losing control of it. Edwin's caution was making me furious.

Why?

Because I was almost fucking positive that I was falling for the bastard and that was a problem if he didn't fall as well.

EDWIN

I was such an asshole.

I could feel the pain through our bond and hear her thoughts clear as day. I couldn't bring myself to talk to her just yet. I mean, god fucking damn it. How did I explain the dilemma I was facing?

"Let's do this," she growled and everything inside of me lit up like a fucking firework show. That tone made me want to bend her over and show her just exactly how I wanted to *do this*.

I hated that my temper was sparking in reaction to hers. I was trying really hard to not be antagonistic because that seemed to be our two extremes, physically distant or fighting. I suppose fucking would have solved both of those, wouldn't it? I nearly bit out a groan at the imagery of how she would look bent over, her back arched, and perfect ass pressed against my pelvis as I buried myself completely inside of her.

We hadn't been training with our magic recently because I knew they had been worn down after our visit to the Horde. That downtime was no longer an option anymore. I'd felt how tense everyone was growing so this seemed like the perfect time to work through the initial troubles that new mages faced. I needed them to be focused when we entered into the Horde. While I didn't express it, I was impressed by the skill level they were performing at already. I knew if Vegas was able to get rid of the power block in her head then she'd give their magic a boost as well. Plus, she would feel far more connected to her magic.

When I had originally left Vegas with Vivi, the spell I had cast to contain her powers was only breakable through the union of Gray's magic. While the original work was blown to pieces, it seemed her magic had built up its own defenses over time and that wasn't going to get us anywhere positive. I needed to push her.

My eyes stayed on hers as I called up my magic without giving her direction.

Unlike most magic, where training and hard work were traditionally effective, hers was very instinctual and tended to make an appearance when there was direct trouble. In fact, more often than not it wasn't the threat of her being in trouble but rather the people she cared about. It was a fatal flaw built into her because of her purpose with Gray. I knew she could overcome that though and I needed her to in order to protect herself as well as others. Thanksgiving night had shown me it was possible for her to fight a battle for herself, even if it was just with a human.

"What are you doing?" she demanded as my shadows rolled over the pavement towards her. I didn't bother with responding to her. I knew if I spoke, I'd either reassure her or confess something she wasn't ready to hear at this moment. How did I explain to her how the fuck I felt about her? It would have her running out of my arms for good because it even sounded crazy to me, which was saying something.

My shadows loved Vegas and I watched as they gravitated towards her. No. That wasn't a metaphor. They specifically were very attracted to her. Always had been even when I was a child. They circled her and the ones behind her built up to reach out and touch her pale, beautiful skin. The savage inside of me had a momentary feral urge to wrap her up in the darkness so that I would be the only one that could reach her. Only one that could touch her.

She would be mine. Completely mine.

I was possessive by nature when it came to her and I couldn't afford to dwell on those primal thoughts for too long. That kiss had broken something in me though and I could no longer view her as a concept or ideal. She was fucking real and I wanted her. All of her. It wasn't rational and I worried that if I gave into it, I would kill anyone outside of her ten that touched her. Either that or I would officially snap, which could be fairly disastrous.

I needed to know she was strong enough to fight the madness she brought out in others. I needed her to be strong enough to be ours completely. I never wanted her to lose who she was because of how the ten of us acted. I needed her to show me that she could be strong enough for this new world that they had entered.

There was not a doubt in my mind that she was. I just needed to see it and for that I needed her to realize it. The first step to that process? Unifying her magic and her. I grunted as I tried to focus on the situation at hand instead of being distracted by the way her breathing grew tight in response to the power shift around her. She was distracted and didn't see my magic reaching out.

When the shadows finally touched her she hissed in realization and I felt her aurora pulsate. It wasn't enough though, that flame inside her chest shining like a small flickering candle. I walked forward and kept my eyes on her as my shadows began crawling up her legs and arms.

"Damn it, Edwin," she growled trying to break out as they held her still. They knew her body as well as I did probably, having studied every tiny piece of her. She didn't realize it but there were constant eyes on her. My shadows were always there. They were simply an extension of myself and every touch was one I felt. It kept me up at night, often.

"Dolcezza," I purred. "If you want out of it, then you better fight for it."

"You're an ass," she hissed and I could hear her power talking. I felt bad for her because I knew that Vegas was dealing with a massive power source attempting to expand out through her tiny body. Her calm façade had another side to it. An explosive one, and I could see those purple eyes turning darker with frustration and anger.

Maybe if I tied her to a bed she'd work out all this aggression in time... or she'd burn down the room. Something that shouldn't have had my cock hardening.

She breathed, her chest pattering an uneven beat. "How do I fight it?"

"You know how to," I spoke circling around her as my shadows caressed her gently.

A flash of desire pulsated from her at their touch and I fought the urge to play with her power. There were a lot of things that my shadows could do and I practically growled at the thought of her spread across my bed with them caressing her skin.

"You have light inside of you," I whispered against her ear biting down slightly. "Use it to get rid of the shadows."

I needed this. I needed her to come into power. I needed to know that she could fight them. Could fight me. I didn't trust myself to not consume her and lock her away. I thought I had better control over my animalistic instincts. It's clear that I'd been wrong in that notion. More so, I knew how powerful I was and I needed to know that she could hold her own against someone like me or stronger.

It kept me up at night thinking of how much danger she was in.

"This is stupid," she spit.

My lips twitched. "You're only saying that because you can't do it."

A real growl came from those pouty lips and my dick grew harder in my sweatpants, drawing her attention slightly. Fuck, if I'd known these types of clothes would have her looking at me like she had moments ago, I would have gotten rid of all of my suits. Not really. Still, I'd make more of an effort to dress casually.

"Screw you," she muttered and her flame expanded out slightly.

Anger. That would have to do for now. Either anger or sex. Gods. This was so not the time to be thinking about how quickly I'd be able to strip those clothes from her body. I closed my eyes and focused back on the present situation. Now, what would really piss her off?

Mind reading bastard.

That concept would do.

"You know," I drew out in a taunting voice, "that dream you had last night was interesting."

And fucking hot.

She stilled as her fire began spreading out like molten heat through her body in a quick yet graceful pattern. I would have been worried if we were inside but we weren't and watching her power expand was hypnotic.

"What did you say?" she hissed out with venom.

I stepped up close to her and traced her lips with my eyes, "I said that your dream last night was interesting."

"Stay out of my dreams," she growled, her face turning light pink. "Those are mine for a reason."

My lip twitched. "I disagree, your dream very much involved all of us."

I loved being able to see her thoughts through our connection, and dreams could end up being an entire errotic experience on their own. This element of the connection had only recently made an appearance and I was loving it. I wasn't going to ignore her thoughts and dreams when she was broadcasting them, I wasn't that strong.

I could feel the tension building and I knew she needed to get it out. That had happened the morning before receiving their tattoos. If I needed to fight with her magic to achieve our goal I would. My magic loved the concept and I was positive that I was the only one able to stand against her power even in this raw state.

That notion alone worried me. If she really wanted to and understood her powers well enough, I had no doubt she could incinerate everything around her. I could contain her at that level but not forever. Hell. I'm not sure anything could except maybe Gray or another True Heir. Gray was more likely to kill everything *alongside* Vegas instead of stopping her though. Their extreme power levels was one of the reasons that sorceresses were no longer created.

"Shut up," she growled with frustration struggling as her eyes grew so dark they were nearly black. Her power was roaring to life.

There we go.

"I'm going to kill you once I break out."

Was it wrong that I found her aggression hot?

I stepped up into her space and nailed my coffin. "If only you were strong enough."

I hit the pavement with her explosive energy's final release as I rolled onto my shoulder and sprang up with amusement. I felt instant relief that she was able to force me away and it made me feel as though I wasn't as dangerous to her well being. My shadows slunk back as I looked over a furious and fucking stunning Vegas. I was so distracted by the woman in front of me that I didn't see her move to tackle me.

VEGAS

"Screw you!" I collided with his muscular body like a rocket at the exact moment his shadows collapsed around us. I felt his form fade and I let out a string of curses as I hit the grass at full force. He was gone and my mouth tasted like fucking dirt.

All right. I may have deserved that for attempting to attack him. Then again, he was a total fucking anatgonizer.

"Where the fuck did he go?" I hissed, turning around.

Byron, now leaning against the doorframe with an entertained expression, snorted and pointed to the other side of the patio. I found the orange eyed mage sitting casually in a patio chair, his leg crossed at the ankle over his knee and lips twisted into a smile. At first I was angry but then my body stilled as a new feeling flooded me.

Holy crap.

Something flared inside of me, Kodiak must have felt it because he looked up from where he was a few feet away. My lips peeled back and a predatory, almost feral instinct flashed through me as Edwin's eyes widened in realization. Without attempting to stop myself, I shot across the patio impulsively seeking my target.

"Oh, fuck," Cosimo spoke from where he was near Byron.

This time, Edwin and I collided completely as I tackled him with my full body weight, his body twisting to cradle me as the world flashed dark. A smooth dark substance washed over my skin and ice prickled my spine for a millisecond before my eyes snapped open. I grunted as my back hit something cold and hard.

"What the heck?!" I exclaimed as Edwin looked down at me, his knee wedged comfortably between my legs and his arms braced on either side of me. I looked away and nearly passed out from shock.

We were on the roof.

Specifically, on the edge of the roof, the stone trim against my spine, and my one leg hanging off as if to remind me that Edwin was keeping me from rolling off to my death. Actually, I probably wouldn't die considering my healing powers. Huh. It would be hard to have sex if I had broken bones wouldn't it?

"Now," he spoke in a serious voice that was nearly seductive., "Are we going to talk about what you are so frustrated over?"

I found myself looking back at him and away from the dizzyingly high height.

You.

I swallowed and felt my fire start to burn through my center. I looked away and spoke. "Nothing, I mean it is something. I am just fucking frustrated, dude."

Dude? Come on, Vegas.

His chest rumbled as he gripped my chin lightly forcing me to look up at him, his massive frame gracefully held over me as the gray skies cast us in a foggy light. I could see his eyes were lighter for some reason. Almost relieved. I hated how much I liked that look on him. It made me happy.

"Maybe I can start," he suggested, his voice husky as he swallowed. "I'm sorry for keeping a bit of distance, *dolcezza*."

My face blushed at his correct assumption. I was such a pussy. He continued with a thoughtful look as his fingers strung through my hair gently. "Byron didn't have as many memories of you because of his age, but I was nearly ten when you left."

Emotions that hadn't belonged to me for years were back and I felt that loss. Or maybe it was our emotional bond. Either way, it sucked.

"You were very real to me." He traced my lips with a finger. "My entire world. Then you were gone. And the more time that passed, the more I began to think of you as an ideal or concept. I went nearly sixteen years without seeing you more than from afar."

"So, is this not what you expected?" I voiced my tone steelier than I expected considering the pain that lanced through me at the concept of him being disappointed.

His eyes darkened as he let out a low sound that was totally sexy and distracting. "Vegas, it is far better than what I could have ever expected."

Why had I been trying to attack this amazing man again?
I nearly rolled my eyes at myself.

"So, what is the problem?" I asked, my voice shaky. Not from nerves though, no this was more because of my ridiculous libido that, at this point, honestly probably had its own brain and heart beat. The thing did whatever the fuck it wanted.

"The problem," he grunted softly, "is that I'm concerned I'll fuck it up, somehow, some way, and I know losing you again would break me. You have and always will be my entire world, Vegas. I never want you to regret having me in your life."

I grabbed his shirt and brought his lips down on mine to stop his rambling. Also, to hide my tearing up at his sweet words. My concerns that had been growing, were disappearing. Now, if we could only get my sexual frustration sated. Although, I really had no hope in that considering Deci had fucked me *literally into* the next day and I was still turned on.

Edwin groaned into my mouth as the scent of red wine and smoky cigars drifted through my senses. Those damn shadows wrapped along my legs playfully in cool wisps. I squeaked as the cool smoky texture ran up my leg and caused my skin to break out in shivers. Shit, what else could he do with these shadows? I needed to know.

My fire jumped eagerly to play with them but I tried to restrain myself, not wanting our first time together to be on a fucking roof. I let out a small soft sound as he pressed into my center, against my training clothes, allowing me to feel just how hard he was. The roof wasn't sounding terrible honestly.

I pulled back short of breath as I whispered my response against his sculpted soft lips. "Edwin, you are very real to me. You are not a concept or ideal. You are not some fantasy.

So, don't treat me like one. I need you to be here with me, if you are serious about us -"

My nerves caused me to stop. He knew it because his eyes turned amber with heat as he searched my expression before leaning closer to take my lips. I sighed into it as the pace turned from impatient and hot to devouring. I gasped as his power shimmered and rubbed against mine, like two exotic wild animals that wanted to mate. I wasn't positive what was happening but it felt like my power was growing stronger with every passing moment. Edwin's training had blasted it to the surface impatiently. I could literally feel the fire right underneath my fingertips as I kissed him back, a searing heat building in my chest.

"I love you," he whispered as my brain blanked, my body roaring into a heated frenzy. My magic was jumping around like a fucking puppy.

He loved me?

Edwin loved me.

My magic wanted to claim him, especially since he had essentially offered himself to us. I moved my fingers and Edwin looked at my hand as I lifted it in awe.

Holy fuck.

"Edwin," I spoke breathlessly, my fingertips dancing with blue flames. I wasn't breathless because of the flames though, no this was all because of his words. Those were the real magic.

"Not yet," he whispered, holding my hand and examining it before meeting my eyes. "When you say them, I want you to mean it. Speaking those words to me will never be a casual affair, Vegas. You own me. Completely. If you say those words back to me, it means you are giving yourself to me as well. I don't think you are ready for that."

My eyes prickled with tears and something about my

emotions seemed to soothe him. Had he been nervous? The bastard said the most unexpected, horribly beautiful things. He should never be nervous about it. I nodded and took a shaky breath as he offered me a dangerous smile. Stupid fireworks exploded in my stomach.

Sorry, not fireworks. Bombs. Motherfucking bombs.

Edwin loved me.

Oh, my god. I needed to get myself together, I was acting like a preteen girl with her first crush.

The man in question gently grasped my hand and sat back, rolling both of us to sit on the far more stable and flat element of the roof. I tucked my legs underneath me as he sat across, his one leg propped up while he examined the flames flickering across my finger tips. Blue. Orange. Red. White. Black. Purple. Again and again in random timing. They contrasted the hazy mist that surrounded us like a soft white fluffy blanket.

Instead of focusing on the flames though, I was captivated by how young Edwin looked right now. In this moment, the nearly winter winds ruffling his dark hair and his eyes lit up with curiosity he could have easily been any other university student. But, no. The guy was a doctor. A special forces commander mage doctor. Oh! No, sorry wrong again. A special forces commander mage doctor AND prince.

That didn't make me feel like shit about my resume or anything. I've got fire.

I focused back on the flames and they jumped slightly gaining power as smaller ones licked the back of my hand and traced around my wrist in a smooth pattern. I had always thought of fire as rough and edged but these flames were smooth and controlled.

"Why are they different colors?" I asked quietly.

"Blue is hellfire," he whispered quietly. "I have never seen the black, white, or purple, though. Orange seems like your standard elemental weapon along with red."

Silence took over as my flames began to dance on top of my hand. I may have been hallucinating but the bitch looked like a ballerina. Then the oddest thing happened. I looked up at the small sound of worry Edwin made and realized his shadows were gathering as if watching the show.

Honestly, it was sort of creepy but in the best way possible.

"Woah," I mumbled as his shadows hesitantly twirled up in front of my flames and circled like a snake. My magic, the sassy bitch, didn't seem concerned in the least and instead expanded out to briefly skim Edwin's magic. I felt awe crash over me as the two, like predatory creatures, rubbed against one another in a soft affectionate way.

"Edwin," I whispered meeting his dark eyes, "this is some crazy shit."

He simply hummed his response and gently pulled his magic back, a wisp of darkness lingering as my magic shifted back into a luxurious slow moving pattern. I had the distinct impression my magic was put out her playmate had been taken away.

"Throw it," Edwin encouraged with fascination looking up.

I was confused for a moment before I focused on my hand and imagined a small red ball of fire. Yes, make a fireball Vegas. Listen to the crazy man who thought inciting anger and violence would be a good training technique. It had worked though. Plus, I needed a distraction from the extremely intimate moment we'd just had. See? Emotions before several cups of coffee never ended well! Specifically, this time it ended in my throwing fireballs. I drew my arm back, facing the backyard, and aimed towards the farthest I could see.

I grinned at my perfect aim.

Except, the minute it left my hand I saw someone leave the back of the house right into the line of fire. Without a second thought, I ran.

Now, I would love to tell you I knew what happened next. How a university student, very unathletic one at that, jumped three stories down from the roof and tackled a warm hard body before the fire destroyed them. I would never know. I covered the person as the tree behind us burst into bright red flames. Oops.

"Kitty?" Booker chuckled from underneath me. "Not that I don't love you on top of me, because I do. A lot. But what the hell just happened?"

I scowled at the nickname and pointed to my left. Booker's soft gray eyes went huge and if he wasn't so masculine I would nearly call them puppy dog eyes.

Wait. Wait just a fucking moment.

"If you are going to call me 'kitty,'" I crossed my arms on his chest looking down at him nose to nose, the fire growing larger behind us. "I'm going to call you 'puppy.'"

Booker's laugh was amazing, deep and very authentic, as he rolled us in one move away from the fire. He caged me and looked down at my lips momentarily. "Deal."

I grinned and grabbed his shirt pulling him to meet my lips. Kissing Booker was always so damn fun. That sounded weird but it's true, he had a light air to him and as his tongue swept into my mouth I felt as though we weren't even on Earth. He groaned into our kiss as my nails dug into his shoulder just slightly, his hips pressing into me and making me wish that we were very much not outside on the cold, hard ground. The velvet soft touch of his lips had me arching into his body urging him to...

Icy water hit the back of Booker's head and instantly soaked both of us.

I immediately snapped my eyes to the side as Decimus focused his water back up to the large burning tree. "Sorry, princess. I haven't mastered my magic completely."

The bastard looked so fucking proud of himself.

Booker grunted as I rolled him over and swiftly tackled Decimus to the ground. He laughed and fell with me, the ground shaking as earth began to shift underneath us with our mounting tension. "God damn it, Deci."

The grass curled around my wrists as Decimus pinned me by the hips and chuckled. "Well, now I've found an even better way to tie you up."

I was momentarily distracted because his eyes were so light they nearly looked gold. It was beautiful.

I growled playfully as I let my power seep out, burning the grass I was pinned to.

"Crap," I swore as both of us froze in our movements at the sound of a cough. A pair of beautiful dark leather shoes were in my vision and the weight of someone's amusement played on our bond. Both of us looked up to find Edwin watching us with an amused grin.

When had the bastard changed clothes?

Instead of letting it go, he crouched down and scowled at me as if the two of us were misbehaving children. "You're very violent lately, Vegas."

He did remember he had just said he loved me, right? Why am I not surprised he's acting like a magical asshat again? I should light his nice suit on fire. Maybe set all of them on fire.

Edwin let out a deep rolling chuckle at my thoughts.

I narrowed my eyes and he chuckled putting his hands up in mock surrender. "As I mentioned, it's not surprising with all the power coursing through you. *But* you should be prepared to be a tad more emotional, frustrated, aggressive... and possibly possessive. Especially now."

Decimus grinned. "I'm going to love this."

"Really, Edwin?" My brow crinkled in mock amusement. "Me? More emotional and intense? When did you realize that? Was it when I attacked you or got into a fight last night?"

His eyes flashed. "That sarcasm, Vegas, is going to get you in trouble."

Decimus chuckled. "Don't worry, princess. I'm sure it will be the fun kind of trouble. The one that ends in being tied up or spanked."

I groaned as Edwin grunted, clearly distracted now.

"The point of my informative statement," Edwin continued as Decimus rolled onto his side and trailed a hand along my stomach and ribs. Mind you I was still held captive by grass.

"Is that we are going to the Horde and I can not predict everyone's actions there as well as our team's here at home," he stated softly. My breathing stilled at the phrase "home."

It felt like home.

Decimus's eyes widened at the words as his head tilted in thought and Edwin's ears turned pink.

I mean it was our home now. It was just, no one had ever said it out loud.

"I love that," I whispered as my eyes prickled with tears.

"Fuck," Decimus grunted helping me sit up and releasing me. "Edwin, dude, don't make her sentimental. You just said she's emotional! Now you are making her cry and shit. Bandit may actually kill you. He hates Vegas crying more than anything."

Edwin winced and paled. "Sorry, *dolcezza*."

"No!" I exclaimed while tears dripped down my cheeks. "This is fucking ridiculous, I need to get this shit under control." My lips curled into a smile as I nearly started laughing.

"What's ridiculous?" Our heads snapped towards a grassy plot of land that now shimmered with three different powerful figures.

"Gray?"

Well, that wasn't a good sign.

7

VEGAS

"Taylor," Gray drawled while lounging back into our plush formal sitting room couch, "this was not a wasted trip! We had a mini vacation and now we are perfectly refreshed to kill Mario. Plus, how would we have known they were planning on returning anyway?"

Gray had come with Taylor and Adyen to warn us that King Mario may make more aggressive moves towards her allies.

You don't say!

Since I had been spotted with her last at the coronation ball when they had attacked, she stated her wish, read command, for us to return to the Horde. Apparently, there had been some recent attacks and despite her cool façade, I could tell that she was very concerned.

Currently, I sat amused and holding a warm mug of tea as the two of them bickered. Adyen sat next to Gray, his arm stretched around her in a possessive hold that tucked her body into his massive build. I took a sip of my tea as my boys and I waited for her to continue, all of us sweaty from working out. It was a stark contrast to Taylor and Adyen, who wore black jeans and sweaters, and Gray in her expensive tailored dress and heels.

Edwin spoke, breaking their bickering. "Your Majesty, we do actually have some news that we've been meaning to tell you."

My eyebrows hitched high. Was he about to drop the bomb that Gray and I were sisters? However, the minute he spoke my chest relaxed a bit. I felt as though I needed to be the one who told her that. It seemed intimate and private, especially considering her mother had been murdered.

"Vegas's stalker," Edwin began, realizing he had just summarized our problem a week ago in the Horde, "has been using a human at the local campus as a puppet to get past any magical barriers we've constructed for safety."

Gray's tri-colored eyes darkened as all amusement fell from her face. "How do you know that?"

I spoke, my voice soft and tired. "On Thursday we were at a party and the man, who we assumed to be a local drug dealer, confronted me. I am not entirely positive how I could tell but it became obvious to me that Gabriel, the human physically in front of me, wasn't my actual stalker. There was no way that type of power was consistently contained within his body on a daily basis."

Taylor frowned, tilting his head in a predatory movement. "You could tell that without any interaction?"

Uh. Fuck. No. Ignore me. I'm not powerful like that.

I nearly said "only since our bonding occurred," but knew that would lead to questions as well.

"Yes. Only since I received my tattoo," I explained.

See? That wasn't technically lying.

"That night Gabriel spoke to us and announced his true identity and how he had come to find me."

This was some intense rhetorical acrobatics, trying not to lie and also not revealing too much.

"Who is he?" Gray growled her body tensing.

"Victor, Mario's son. The True Heir of the Dark Fae," Byron stated softly.

For a solid moment, I thought that Gray's power may lash out. A massive clap of thunder sounded outside as rain began to pour down in sheets causing Deci to frown. Then she took a deep calming breath and adjusted the dark outfit that she wore while obviously thinking something through. God, the woman literally looked like a queen. Even on her vacation. I was officially jealous.

"You are leaving tomorrow," she demanded softly and met my gaze with a hint of sorrow. "I am so sorry for bringing this burden on you, Vegas."

Oh, shit.

I shook my head. "I think he was watching me long before we met."

She didn't look like she believed me. I felt the urge to expose my truth to her but Edwin squeezed my shoulder. Gray's eyes tracked his movement and Adyen placed a kiss on her own shoulder. I had seen the scars there at her coronation. The idea bought pain to me. The familiar bond flaring to life between us.

"Come see me when you arrive," she commanded softly. I stood and nodded as she hugged me in a tight embrace. I could see the concern on her face and I realized that she might feel that same connection I do. Or was I imagining family affection?

That was totally possible.

"Baby girl," Taylor drawled breaking the tension. "Can we stop in New York and see one of the shows where the humans sing and dance like little puppets?"

Adyen snorted as he rolled his eyes. "It was good to see all of you."

Then Gray and her men left. It was a black twist of energy and the portal shut. I shook my head because just like Tamara and her men, they just bulldozed into our lives and we just had to adapt. I somehow didn't find myself minding all that much.

In fact, it made me feel as though our lives weren't nearly as crazy.

My brow furrowed as I thought about how I would tell Gray our secret. I had to be careful because this wasn't just about us. No, this was about her deceased mother as well. I didn't want to keep it longer than I should but something told me to keep it to myself for a bit. I usually trusted my instincts. I would know the moment.

"Tamara and her men have already left Earth realm," Byron confided softly.

Tamara and her men had been rather helpful in regulating the area, however, the stalker had been silent until the other night. I was starting to notice his odd absences of communication. I felt like it was about more than just his decision to wait. There was something I was missing about this guy, something bigger than what we already understood.

Yeah, Vegas. That's how crazy people work.

I stood, placing my tea down, as I walked towards the stairs with a bath in mind. I could hear my boys talking and no one stopped me from slipping away. I needed a moment to think and instinctively they knew that. My power was a soft simmer under my skin right now, but unlike how it was before the fight between Edwin and me, I knew I could call it forth if I needed to.

My bathroom was luxurious but the tile was slightly

chilled from the dark weather outside. I looked down at the gardens, thick and lush even in the late fall season. My chest relaxed at the thought of going to the Horde tomorrow. I wanted my boys safe.

I peeled off my clothes and started the bath. I bet I could keep the water hot consistently without refilling. Now, that? That is a useful fucking power.

I added some lavender soap and slipped into the tub, realizing I hadn't locked the door. Oh, well. Honestly, if someone came in I would be relieved. Both Edwin and Grover had worked me up today and now I just felt tense and tired.

My eyes fell shut as my head tilted back. I smiled thinking about Edwin's antagonistic nature. The magical asshat needed to stay out of my fantastic fucking dreams. I couldn't blame him though. It was pretty dirty and fell right in line with Grover's teasing. I groaned as the dream flashed through my mind again.

Weren't you supposed to forget dreams?

The dream had begun with me. Alone. My ability to see was limited by the three flickering fireplaces that danced on all three sides of me. I assumed from the soft heat behind me that there was one on the back wall as well. I panicked at first, wondering if I was in a nightmare since my hands were strung above me and my feet barely touched the cold marble floors.

I realized very quickly that it was not a nightmare, but the soft silk ties should have clued me in sooner.

"Vegas," Kodiak had growled into my ear as his pine scent wrapped around me like his tanned muscular arms. Despite the opulent atmosphere, I felt as though I was in the presence of a wild animal. The vibrations of energy were so strong that I could almost feel phantom hands and mouths, pulling and tasting me. His wolf was clawing at the surface of his skin

wanting to claim me. I knew it was only a matter of time before he shifted.

"Kodi?" I whispered in a pant as his warm palms ran down my ribs to pull my ass against him. The silk ties swung back as my body arched to cause a very masculine groan to emit from his throat as he teased my neck with his teeth.

"You've been very bad," he chided in a tone that seared through my center as his hard, thick cock rested against my ass.

"No, I haven't," my dream self denied as he chuckled softly.

"Now, don't lie, beautiful," Blue whispered from right in front of me, causing my head to snap towards him as Kodiak began to rock his hard length against my bare wetness. I let out a whimper as Blue nipped at my bottom lip, refusing to offer me more than that.

"What did I -- do?" My breathing stopped on a cry as Kodiak slid into me. I tilted my head back only to find that Decimus was deep inside of me instead with one of his terribly sexy smirks. Oh, sweet christ.

"Walking around how you have? Teasing us?" He tilted his head as his hand wrapped around the front of my neck. He began to slowly slide in and out of me, my toes curling as a moan escaped my lips without permission.

Booker's soft chuckle sounded as he took Blue's place, his teasing touches gone, as velvet eyes turned nearly to an inky black. "Now that is a beautiful fucking sound."

I cried out as he leaned in to kiss me, his tongue playful against my lips, never giving me full access.

"Almost as beautiful as..." Decimus' voice faded to Grover's. His muscular body fit against my back as he slammed into me in a demanding way that was so different from Deci's teasing slow pace. I cried out as my head fell back. A cool silver lip ring pressed against my breast as someone's teeth began to tug on my nipple.

Cosimo's bright eyes sparkled with desire as Grover held me in place, fucking me hard and deep.

"Cosimo," I whispered as he began to kiss down my stomach and Grover's lips pressed against my neck, halting his movements. It left me a panting, hormonal mess.

"Sugar," Rocket whispered as Grover disappeared. Cosimo bit down on my hip gently as he continued to worship the front of my body. I desperately wanted to know what his lip ring would feel like against the heated skin between my legs.

"Rocket?" I whispered softly as he tilted my head up. Cosimo was gone then and it was just Rocket as he stepped into my space, his hands running up my long arms as a deep growl echoed. I needed him inside of me, the loss of Grover making me needy. He walked around the front of me, his skin golden and bare, as he watched me with a dark, intense expression.

In a swift movement, he lifted my legs and separated them before he pressed into me causing my head to snap back in pleasure as he fucked me with deep intense strokes.

"Ve," Bandit kissed my neck gently as his familiar length lined up with my ass. I whimpered as Rocket chuckled near my lips.

"Don't be nervous," Rocket whispered as my world blasted with pleasure.

"Bandit!" I screamed as he filled my small ass in one deep movement. Rocket hummed a sound of approval that turned deeper as they began to both rock into my hanging body. Oh, fuck. I could feel my entire body shaking but it didn't seem to matter to them in the least.

I had a very serious moment of wondering how that damn silk rope was hanging on.

"Trouble," Bandit's voice faded into Byron. The man who was filling my ass in a completely new way as his teeth sunk into my throat. I couldn't do anything but scream out my pleasure as the

two of them destroyed and consumed me completely causing my body to go limp.

I searched out for the last of my bonded. I was unsurprised to find a pair of orange eyes peering at me as the other two disappeared and two large hands removed the ropes from my wrist. Edwin lifted me easily, my legs wrapped around his waist, as circles of flames began to expand out around us. I could see each of my boys in the room watching as Edwin's shadows brushed against my skin.

"Dolcezza," Edwin whispered as he lined himself up with my center. "Wake up."

I scowled at the thought of his words ending my dream. How did my subconscious listen to his dominance when I didn't? Goddamn it. I had wanted to see where that was going.

Oh, my god.

My eyes snapped open with realization. The nerve! I mean I wasn't surprised, but still. He had been in my fucking dreams. Like actually in my dreams. I almost smiled because he was such a dirty bastard, but I would have to act upset about it later. Or have him make it up to me? That sounded more fun.

"Ve," Bandit's deep husky voice brushed into my ear as I jumped slightly. His deceptively soft chuckle sounded dangerous to me and that turned me on.

Because I'm normal like that.

"Yes?" I recovered with a smile, tilting my head back. "Do you need something?"

Who is glad they left the bathroom door unlocked? This girl!

His spring green eyes darkened as a low sound came from his throat. "I need a lot of things, Vegas."

"Well," I turned over so that I was leaning on the edge of

the tub, nose to nose with him but covered by soap and bubbles, "then you should take what you want."

Please, take what you want.

It didn't help that I was super turned on from my dream again. Bandit made a low sound in his throat as he reached out to brush my lip gently. I shivered as he sat back and pulled forward the stool from the vanity, resting his forearms on his knees with a wicked glint in his eyes.

Oh, no.

"If you insist," he smirked just a bit. "I want you to tell me what you were dreaming about last night. I want to know what Edwin was teasing you about and what you were just thinking about. I want to know it all and I want to see you come for me while talking about it."

Oh, yes. Because I was so good at dirty talk and being seductive.

I blushed at his direct command and took a shaky breath. It never ceased to surprise me just how dominant Bandit could be when the two of us were alone. It was startling and so ridiculously hot.

"Bandit," I whispered as he rose a challenging brow. My power sparked and I found my hand traveling across my chest down to where I knew I was wet.

"Other hand playing with your nipple," he commanded softly, his body relaxed against the counter as he watched me with unabashed heat. His long fingers tapped a smooth pattern on the marble counter as he relaxed his arms out. I whimpered as my eyes fluttered at the heat of this entire situation. I felt my toes curl as he leaned forward and spoke. "Now, Ve, tell me about your dream."

"It's a lot to recall." My brain was like fucking mush as I drew my slickness over my clit and pulled my nipple just slightly.

"Start at the top," he encouraged with slight amusement in his eyes at my nervousness. Fucker loved this. My hands paused.

"Keep going or I'll have Kodi punish you," he drawled softly as I considered letting him call Kodi up here. Instead, I followed his orders and my powers shimmered in excitement.

"It was dark," I whispered as he wrapped a strand of my hair around his ringed finger. I loved the dark jewelry Bandit wore, mostly earrings, but today he had cold metal rings that contrasted my hot flesh. I wanted those rings on my skin.

"Where were you?" he asked as my eyes closed.

"I was in a marble room with a fireplace in it," I whispered, "my hands tied up by bindings attached to the ceiling."

A low rumble echoed through Bandit's chest as I felt my orgasm growing closer, the bubbles disappearing and leaving my body exposed to his gaze.

"Then what?" he bit down on my ear as I jumped at his hand working down my leg.

I felt my eyes flash open as I met his gaze inches away. "Then each of you…"

His name echoed on my lips as his finger slipped into my tightness. Fuck. I arched back as his mouth took my nipple. My mouth was open but no words could come out.

"Each of us did what?" he demanded as my body became so tight with pleasure that my vision grew spotty. I could feel his power washing over me and the longer that I was exposed to it, the more I grew addicted to it. Electricity, almost painful, washed through me as my magic wrapped around his enthusiastically.

"I won't let you come unless you answer," he spoke softly in a low throaty tone. "And then I won't fuck you, Ve."

I would fucking tell him alright, "Each of you fucked me..."

It was a whisper that ended in a cry as he slid into me and I exploded on his length, my body leaving the warm water. I had no idea how he did it but one moment I was in the tub and the next he was pressing me into the vanity as water dripped from my body in the warmth of the steamy room. His pounding pace demanded more from me as I tugged his shirt forward, realizing he was practically still dressed.

I barely had a chance to get used to his size before he was holding my hands above my head and fucking me into the marble counter and mirror. I cried out as my head fell back and his other hand gripped my waist so hard that I hoped his hand print would be permanently etched into my skin.

"So, fucking perfect," he groaned as I felt my body tense for another orgasm.

"Please, Bandit," I cried out.

"Rub your little clit, Ve," he growled against my lips, releasing my hands. "Come on my cock for me so that I can finish inside of you."

I felt my chest break open as our connection crackled, the mirror shattering behind us as I cried out in ecstasy. Somehow sex had gotten even better with magic. I cried his name like a chant as he pressed us into the broken mirror, his hands cut on the glass and bleeding but protecting me from most of the damage. It didn't stop him and he reached his climax after I came almost three more times.

"Fuck," he hissed out while consuming my mouth during his release, triggering my final. I felt him bite down on my lip and the taste of blood passed between us like a toxic potion. He finally stilled inside of me completely and our release pressed between us.

Oh, my.

Bandit rumbled against my neck and picked me up in his arms, as if I weighed nothing, to take us towards the shower. I was shaking and all I could do was look at the man in front of me. Intoxicated. I was completely intoxicated by this man.

"Keep looking at me like that and we will break this entire bathroom."

"Sorry," I whispered.

Not sorry at all.

I watched as he stripped from his clothes and stepped into the hot water. He grinned knowingly as he helped wash my arms and back, glass falling to the floor. I noticed his hands were already healing far faster than they should.

"Bandit?" I asked quietly reaching a hand up to his face. "Why are you healing so fast?"

His body paused as he met my gaze slowly. "I don't know, Ve."

Edwin thinks it is something related to my family.

I jumped at the mental connection as my eyes rounded. I went to respond and he placed a finger on my lips.

I'm not ready for everyone to start looking into why I'm different yet.

I could hear the tightness even in his mental connection. I frowned thinking through his fast healing ability and our connection that occurred even before his magic was activated. I was in deep thought as he continued to rinse my body off.

As the shower turned off, I shivered as he wrapped me in a towel. I believed Bandit. There was something different about him and I should have clued into it far earlier. Then again, I hadn't even realized I wasn't human. So, yeah. I wasn't all that disappointed in myself.

"Stop overthinking," he whispered as I turned to face him, my eyes tracing his wet silver hair and then down to his lips. I raised up on my toes to kiss him deeply as he groaned and led me towards the door. I looked back at my bathroom and he snorted at my mouth popping open.

"We always leave rooms looking like a murder scene," I mumbled.

Bandit and I laughed as we walked back into the bedroom, finding Lucida sitting in my room with humor etched into her face. I blushed as she scowled at Bandit's towel wrapped form. He chuckled and kissed my nose, leaving the room and me in a towel. My best friend stood and peeked into the bathroom as her eyes widened.

"Dude, Vegas," she chuckled. "Were you trying to fuck *into* the mirror?"

I blushed. "Our magic has increased...well, everything."

Her eyes lit up, amused. "Oh, that's it! That's sealed it! Miranda?!"

It was around two in the afternoon, so I was very curious on why the two of them were here to begin with. I hoped it was for the reason I thought. I slipped a robe over my shoulders and closed it before tugging my towel off and hanging it on a small hook. Skills.

I know. Another awesome badass skill to add to my résumé

"What's up, baby," Miranda asked in a sing-songy voice. Then she saw the bathroom.

"Look at what sex could be like," she shook Miranda by her shoulders. "Who knows what our sex life could transform into! Honey, we have to!"

Miranda smirked. "That's why we are here, Lucida. You don't have to convince me anymore."

My eyes snapped to both of them. "You are coming with me?"

Lucida bowed dramatically and motioned to Miranda and herself. "Introducing your two new mages. Fabulous and Beautiful."

I snickered as Miranda rolled her eyes.

"Wait, so why are you in here?" I narrowed my eyes at Lucida.

She grinned dangerously. "We are going shopping for the trip, specifically for shit that they won't have in the Horde."

I groaned. I shook my head and motioned them out. "All right, all right. Then I need to get ready."

Both girls left the room and my heart squeezed happily. Now, I wouldn't have to lose any family. I tugged on a comfortable cotton skirt and a hoodie, not particularly feeling anything tight like the leather outfits I knew were coming. Maybe, I could convince Gray to pick new uniforms. Preferably ones that had stretchy material. Not spandex though because I'm not a superhero.

Although, if I saw that, it would be cool as hell.

"Baby," Kodiak called as I brushed out my wet hair and tied it into a braid. His forest green eyes sparkled as he looked over my body with a sense of possessiveness.

"What?" I asked softly feeling almost shy. I had no idea how I consistently fluctuated between sex goddess and being shy around these boys.

"Nothing." He grasped my hand and drew me from the bedroom. I followed after as we walked through the house, the shadows moving in a pattern that I knew wasn't natural. The bastard had eyes on me always. I narrowed my eyes at them, promising retribution for his sexy invasion of my dream.

The bastard had it coming.

"Where are we going?" I asked curiously as Kodi helped me up into his massive truck. Lucida and Miranda were talking enthusiastically in the back as Kodiak turned on some music before answering.

"Prepare yourself," he sighed. "We are going to the mall."

Oh, no.

I could hear Lucida's list and I put my head back as Kodi grasped my hand.

Why were we going to the mall?!

It had everything. Everything was bad because it meant Luci would need to go into each and every store. The woman had no control and a girlfriend that loved shopping as well. I squeezed my grizzly bear's hand. As he released it, he wrapped the massive rough paw around my thigh. I liked this car a lot I realized as I examined the interior and the shiny black paint that covered the part in front of me on the hood.

I bit my lip smiling. Did Kodi and Blue forget about my punishment? Because I earned that shit.

"No one leaves the mall unless we are together," Kodiak stated before shifting the car into park. Without any promises both girls got out and bounded towards their destination. I really had nothing I wanted to shop for.

I did however want to be entertained.

Now, what better way was there to entertain myself than to mess with Kodi?

My sassy smile grew.

"Baby," Kodi growled dangerously. "I will turn that ass cherry red if you leave my side."

His wolf howled underneath his skin and damn if I

wasn't planning to coax him out. See? This was why I was with crazy men! I liked them crazy. Or maybe I made them crazy? Kodi had lost all finesse in his actions. Now, it was just raw primal actions. I mean how did you tell a wolf to stop being territorial? My magic did a little cha-cha and winked, as if his change was all her doing. Additionally, it seemed our recovery time was shortening because she was ready to go. Again.

As we walked into the mall, the warmth from the heating hit me and warmed my skin. A delicious plan formed in my head. I completely blamed my magic for what I had decided I'd do next.

8

VEGAS

J had never sprinted so fast in my life and I couldn't help the smile that stretched across my face as the boys moved out of my way. I was through the house and onto the back patio as I heard his footsteps behind me. I placed a bit more effort into my sprint and reached the forest line, turning to face my very worked up and overprotective lover.

"Kodi," I warned him with a grin as I stepped back. I nearly tripped in the thick forested area and his dark green eyes tracked my movements calmly before finding my gaze in a predatory fashion.

Now, you are probably wondering how I got into this position, right? Well, we can thank my apparently decent seduction skills, a lot of dressing room teasing to waste time, and my ending stunt to successfully push his buttons.

"The way I reason it," Kodiak's voice was smooth like honey, "you put yourself into danger, baby. So, now I need to punish you. That's not even including the little dressing room stunt you pulled in the lingerie section."

What? A girl couldn't try on sexy nighties for her boyfriend?

It was also convenient since our family Amex, of which we now each had a copy, made all of the extra help scatter. It left us essentially alone and if it hadn't been for the cameras and one attendant outside of the fitting area, he probably would have fucked me senseless. Also, I may have teased him a bit, knowing he wouldn't pull anything because he was far too possessive to let anyone see or hear me like that.

Desire flooded my entire body at his words as I continued to walk backwards trying to hide my excitement. "I didn't do it on purpose."

I totally did.

In fact, I also sprinted through the house afterwards knowing he'd follow me. Track me. Now I was going to be punished. Oops.

Sorry, not sorry.

"You didn't leave the store on purpose right after I told you not to?" he asked with unmasked humor as he began to push up the sleeves of his Henley.

Oh, dear christ! Forearm porn alert! Also, why was his slight intimidation turning me on? Oh, man, I should probably look into that later.

Although, honestly, there were a lot more pressing kinks I could and should focus on first.

"Nope," I grinned as I made my way onto smoother land. Kodiak knew exactly what game I was playing at. Yes. I, Vegas, was literally poking the bear. Well, wolf. Come on, like you wouldn't? He told me to stay in the store or else he would spank me. Of course, I left the fucking store.

"Don't." He "tsked" as I grinned.

Then, I ran.

I let out a gasp as he tackled and rolled us so that I was

locked on top of him, my pelvis against his own. A slight moan came out of my mouth as he chuckled and rolled us to pin me to the forest floor.

"Is this what you wanted, baby?" He nipped at my lower lip in a sharp movement. "For me to fuck you on the forest floor as your punishment?"

My whimper and head nod made him grin. Fuck it. I wasn't good at keeping secrets so why not just admit it, right? He looked down at me and sat up, stradling my much smaller body as he ran a large hand across my breasts. I began to wiggle as he hummed his approval at my nipples growing harder. I felt myself arching up into him as he continued to lightly play with my body in a teasing manner that was nearly torturous.

He seemed to be contemplating what he'd do next.

"Such a good girl," he commended softly before humming. "Are you getting all wet for me?"

I didn't have a chance to answer as he swiftly turned me so that I was on all fours, my ass directly against his groin. Suddenly, wearing a skirt despite the chill was a fucking fantastic idea.

I tried to hold still as he pressed his massive erection against my ass and ran his nose against the delicate skin on the back of my neck. His hand wrapped around my hair as he tugged it back, rough but not painful.

"Is this what you wanted, Vegas?" he asked in a raw, gravelly voice filled with heat. "Is this what you needed?"

"Yes," I panted, my tone nearly begging as he dragged a rough palm up the back of my thigh before flipping my skirt. It exposed my bare bottom and I shivered at the exposed cold chill in the air. With a simple tug, he snapped my lace panties and my gasp had him chuckling softly. I didn't for a minute believe he was being casual about this.

No. This had been building for a bit and he had reached the end of my teasing.

"I can't give you want you want, though," he ran a hot finger along my spine as he pushed up my hoodie. "What you did was bad. So, instead I'm going to take what I want and then maybe, just maybe, you can have yours."

My skin broke out into shivers. Oh, good. I am positive I will like what he wants anyway. Also, can we just give a round of applause to the orgasm express? I mean it's like someone snapped a rubber band and out flowed sex. I am so perfectly in love with the idea of avoiding our responsibilites and fucking all the time. In fact, I may suggest the concept to Edwin.

The sound of his sharp slap against my ass drew an unfiltered moan came from my throat.

He hummed in a low tone and locked his hand more firmly in my hair. He spoke deceptively soft. "You like being bent over? You like being spanked and then fucked on the ground like the bad girl you are?"

Oh, holy shit, yes. I was a bad girl for him.

"Yes!" I hissed as he hit my ass again. I whimpered as he smoothed back over it gently. A chill of nervousness and excitement threaded through me as the sound of his belt coming undone echoed around us. I squirmed as he hit my ass again in a different place, and drew one finger along my wetness.

"You like being punished," he stated with approval. "Is that why you make me worry, Vegas? Do you want me to punish you more often?"

"Maybe," I admitted as another slap hit my ass. This one was harder and my skin broke out into shivers that flushed my entire body with heat.

His breath was hot against my ear. "All you have to do is ask, baby."

Then I felt the leather of his belt wrap around my legs to effectively pin them together. I looked back and a glint of darkness lit up Kodiak's eyes as he looked over the bind. I swear to the fucking gods if I didn't trust him with my safety I would worry about that predatory darkness inside of him. Instead, I pressed my ass up against him, eliciting another slap. The pain felt so fucking good, which was something I never thought I'd say.

I think it was because it wasn't a lot of pain but just enough to contrast the immense pleasure I knew was to come. It was fascinating, the small yet complete difference between him and Decimus. With Decimus it was all about controlling me but Kodiak wanted to punish me. I was so about both it wasn't even funny anymore.

"You need to stop putting yourself in danger," he spoke while leaning over me, his hand rough on my bare waist. "If you don't, I won't fuck you."

Oh, that was bad. I didn't like that at all.

"I promise," I whimpered as his hand began to gently strum my clit from under us. I wanted to push my legs apart but couldn't so instead I just continued to push my ass out as if I was a fucking animal in heat. He groaned as he unzipped his jeans and his massive - oh, christ - hot rod pressed between the globes of my ass.

I had a moment of considerable concern that he wouldn't fit.

"I don't believe you," he growled against my skin as his body tensed slightly. "I don't think you fully comprehend how obsessed I am with your safety, Vegas. How much it consumes me."

My eyes met his as I looked back over my shoulder and realized he was right. I had always thought of it as a game between us and before all of this it had been. Now, there was real authentic danger. There was also something very dark aligned with his obsession with my safety. The tone changed in a hushed second as those eyes darkened and he moved closer, so that we were practically nose to nose. I was practically trembling from excitement and a myriad of other messy emotions.

"Baby," he whispered his larger body eclipsing mine, "you don't make a fucking move without me knowing. You can't get away from me, Vegas, I won't let you."

Now, that should have bothered me, right? Except I think I'd realized a long time ago the extent to his madness. It didn't change how I felt about him and there was a small part of me that was thrilled at the intensity he displayed in how he felt about me.

I swallowed at his declaration as he gently stroked my necklace with possession as his eyes traveled there in consideration. "You know, I've always liked this necklace on you, Vegas. It reminds people that you're ours. That you're mine. Mine to protect. Mine to love."

I should have been shocked at his admission but then again, hadn't I always felt like it was a small piece of Kodiak around my neck? I just hadn't realized how territorial of a move it had been. He was right, though.

I was his.

I belonged to each of the boys and all of them as a whole. I could feel an overwhelming sense of love and affection fill me.

"When I tell you to do something for your safety, baby," he whispered, grasping my jaw lightly. "I need you to fucking listen to me before I land myself in fucking prison. Because that is where I go, Vegas. Everytime something even slightly bad happens to you I feel like commiting fucking murder. I need you safe for my fucking sanity, baby girl."

I could see the real pain and stress it caused him. I nodded without speaking as I saw the darkness leave his eyes and be replaced with a molten heat. I gasped as he kissed me and pressed into my heated center just a mere inch. He began to strum my clit again as he continued to sink deeper and deeper. I couldn't adjust or move. I had to just take him. All of him.

Fuck, it felt so good. My magic was thrilled, knowing that one of our bonded was close. She seemed on a hell bent mission to get everyone as close to us as soon as possible. I wondered if she knew something I didn't. That worried me.

"I'm going to give you what you want, Vegas," he whispered against my lips, "but I'm going to do it exactly how I want it."

I nodded as he pulled back only to ram into me fully. I cried out his name as the leather from his belt bit into my legs and his partly pulled down jeans roughed up my sore ass. Still, once he was seated there he let out a savage snarl that had me pushing back into him with encouragement. My hands curled into the dirt underneath me and a sense of euphoria filled me from being out of control. He was in charge here and I was completely okay with that.

Completely okay with letting go and living in this moment.

My gasp of relief was unreal as his pace became punishing and savage. Kodiak had that deadly lethal strength that came with his size. He was quiet though and moved with an ease that could only be expected from a true predator. I swear to god if this was my punishment, I'm going to be fucking up a lot. I'd find other ways besides messing with my safety though. I didn't want to actually worry him, I just liked messing with him. Mostly because I'd wanted this.

When I felt his teeth bite into the back of my neck, I cried out as his animal let out a growl that surrounded us and came from deep within his chest.

"Fuck, Vegas," he snarled against my neck. "You're such a good girl, taking me like this."

I felt my arms give out as an orgasm blasted through my center and made my entire body flash with heat. Kodiak caught me and kept me plastered to his chest as that belt came off of my legs with an easy movement. He continued to pound into me from behind and all I could do was cry out his name as pleasure broke over my skin again and again.

"I love you," he groaned out as I arched my back with a whimper between moans.

I barely got out a breathy "love you" before he was pressing my back down so that I was ass up and exposed to him. He let out a lengthy strand of curses as his pace slowed just slightly. He ground against me as I whimpered, his dick filling me to the point that a pleasurable sharp pain filled my body. He was so fucking deep.

"That's it," he cooed in a soft voice. "Take what I give you, baby. Such a good girl, taking all of me in your tight little pussy."

I would have never guessed Kodiak would have been such a dirty talker and I am *sooooo* glad he was. His deep baritone and the weight of him pressed against me felt fucking fantastic.

"Faster," I whimpered out my demand as he smacked my ass making me jolt against him.

"Greedy," he purred but quickened his pace. I cried out his name and within minutes my orgasm rippled through my center yet again and across my skin as my hands heated up. Kodiak went harder as he bit out a curse and roared my name before he found his release inside me. That connection of *other*, as it had with the three other men, snapped into place as another orgasm hit me like a Mack truck. I could feel both of us panting as he held me to his chest and I tried to rationalize what the hell just happened.

"Are your legs okay?" he asked softly. I could hear the very real concern there.

I looked down at them seeing that the belt had made them slightly red in a thick strip. I turned and nodded with a blush tinting my cheeks. "Absolutely okay."

Honestly, even if I wasn't and my legs hurt I wouldn't tell him because it was so grossly outweighed by the pleasure coursing through me. In a quick movement, Kodi was dressed and I was lifted into his lap so that I was pressed into his massive warm muscles. I sighed as the scent of pine overtook me and the warmth of his body relaxed me, making me feel safe. His large arm was wrapped around my center as he kept my sheltered in his body heat.

The forest was lively today. Or maybe I could just hear better because everything seemed excited and awake despite it being late afternoon. I did notice a distinct lack of animals near us and I think we could blame Kodi's wolf for that.

"Are you okay, baby?" He whispered softly tilting my chin up so that I could watch the wind ruffle his chocolate brown waves. The soft sweetness in his eyes had me nearly blushing even after what we had just done.

"Better," I whispered softly as he fingered my necklace lightly. I took the time to let my heart rate slow as he helped me get dressed, my body sore but satisfied. For now. Maybe, I needed all ten men because of this crazy magic sex drive?

"Hey, Kodi?" I asked curiously as he pulled me tighter

against him, standing to walk. My skirt and hoodie fell into place comfortably.

"Yeah?" I could see him looking up at the weather and occasionally at the redness of my legs. He genuinely looked worried and I loved that. I also found the dynamic fucking funny that he was worried about the redness he caused. Can we say confusing?

Very Kodi-ish.

"I like you punishing me," I rolled my bottom lip with my teeth at my shy admission. "Have you always been into... Well, I mean..."

"Just you," he whispered, meeting my eyes with his serious gaze. I noticed he wasn't wearing his glasses today and I had a feeling that he wasn't going to need them as his powers grew. I wondered if he had noticed the change. I noticed he'd been wearing them less and less.

"Oh," I blushed feeling my chest relax. I liked what we shared. It was ours.

He pressed a kiss to my temple. "You will let me know if I ever go too far, right? I worry, with my wolf being so present that I could end up taking it too far. He likes the idea of making you submit nearly as much as I like the idea of punishing you. So a bit too much."

"How so?" I asked as the house came into view. The mist of rain from earlier was back and we moved quickly to get to the house.

Kodi grunted and shook his hair a bit. "I don't know how to explain it without sounding like a control freak."

I smiled and clasped his chin pausing a moment. "Honey, I sort of know you're a control freak."

His ears heated slightly as I grinned at his slight embarrassment. He pressed his lips to the shell of my ear and spoke words that heated my center. "I like being able to control your pain, Vegas. I have no idea how to navigate this new world safely and it makes me feel better to control the one thing that I worry about you dealing with the most. Well, that and I like seeing my handprints on your ass."

Wow, now that is a way I've never thought about it before.

My black little heart squeezed with affection at his sweet yet totally fucked up notion. I curled into him and pressed a kiss to his cheek. He chuckled and shook his head at my acceptance.

"You know I'm probably certifiable, right?" he muttered almost to himself.

I shrugged and looked up at him. "Seems like the thing to be right now."

His laugh echoed deep in his chest and I was so distracted that I didn't even notice that Blue was standing in the doorway of our home.

"Have a good hike?" Blue offered a dimpled grin. Cheeky Blue, very cheeky.

"The best," I yawned and curled further into Kodiak as he walked in the direction of the kitchen.

"Well, beautiful," Blue caged me once Kodiak set me on the counter and started making lunch. It didn't surprise me that he wanted to feed me right after sex. I wasn't complaining. My appetite had totally come back swinging after our visit to the Horde.

"Yes?" I asked as he petted the red mark on my legs from Kodi's belt. I watched his lips twitch before meeting my eyes with questions. When I didn't speak he continued.

"We are leaving tonight on the private jet," he mumbled tracing my collarbone.

I nodded. "All right. Well, I'll need to shower and get dressed."

Kodiak turned around and scowled as I offered him a

sassy smile. He pushed a plate towards me and sat at the island watching me silently, waiting patiently for me to eat what he made. His wolf was right under the surface and I had a feeling that all it would take was a bit of push and boom! He would be out to play for real. My power loved that. She had loved him letting it out a few moments ago and now wanted to meet the creature that resided in his magic.

She was, as I was learning, an antagonistic bitch.

"Don't shower," he rumbled looking like a massive grumpy puppy. "You smell like me."

Blue started shaking with silent laughter as I hit his chest playfully. I took a bite of the sandwich he made. "Kodi, you know I can't go to the hangar looking like this. I have dirt all over me."

"It's true," Blue sounded amused. "We are using the actual airport today."

My wolf's eyes narrowed on me before he got up and walked from the room looking like he was on a mission. I cocked my head and Blue smiled. "My bet is that he makes you wear something of his or he scents some of your clothes."

He was totally right.

I was lost in thought for a moment and jumped slightly as Blue ran his nose against my collar bone again. I shivered as he tightened his hands on my hips and looked up at me with a darkening gaze. It was hungry but not just in a lustful way. No, this was something more.

"What?" I asked softly.

"You smell good," he mumbled as his hand stroked from my waist to my hip again and again.

I tilted my head. "You mean my blood smells good?"

Blue's dimples popped out. "Exactly, beautiful."

"I'm surprised you haven't tried to bite me yet," I goaded, thinking about Byron and my frustration with him not biting me again recently. I shouldn't ever challenge a psychopath, though.

"Is that so?" Blue moved forward in a predatory movement that had me jumpy. I was nose to nose with him. I fought the urge to lick his dimples and kiss the sexy bastard.

Lick his dimples? Who the fuck am I even anymore?

They were sexy dimples though. Dangerous, sexy dimples.

"I didn't mean right now!" I scrambled to slip under his arm as I looked back at him. His expression was amused but his eyes were still dark.

"Now that I know you're okay with it," he drawled with a lazy smile, "I'll try not to disappoint."

I felt a shiver go through me as I shook my head and walked backwards towards the door. "Nope. I didn't say I was okay with it, Blue. More than that, we don't have time for that today."

I was totally more than okay with it.

"I'll give you until we are on the jet, then I'm locking you in that back bedroom and playing with you until you pass out," he whispered as my nipples tightened.

Oh, man, come on. Now I'm all turned on again... Maybe, I needed to become a nun or something. That would be a hoot.

"Vegas?" Cosimo's exotic cologne enticed me closer to him as Blue winked and pretended to finish my sandwich. I turned and looked up into my playful Spaniard's crystalline eyes that were fairly light today.

"What's up," I tugged his hand as Blue chuckled. I was totally going to hide from him. Not because I didn't want him to bite me. Oh, I did. I just liked the chase. I was feeling super feisty today.

"Lucida was packing and she said she wanted to talk to you." He smoothed my back but there was an odd look in his eyes. I was about to ask about it but the minute we neared my bedroom, Luci pulled me in with impressive strength.

"What the fuck, dude?" I muttered as she slammed and locked the door. "What is going on with you?"

My eyes trailed back to the door because I could practically feel Cosimo's concern and I didn't like that. Lucida tugged on my arm again. Her eyes were bright and concerned as she pointed towards a box of tampons that I kept with my other cosmetics, it was clear she had been packing my stuff as well as theirs. I frowned.

What was her problem? It was a box of motherfucking tampons.

"They haven't been opened," she stated, her brow creasing.

Maybe she was having a psychotic break? Where was Miranda right now? She would know how to handle this. I should talk to her with slow and measured phrases.

Fuck it.

"So?" I drawled.

"We bought those six weeks ago right after your last period," she stated looking pale. "Please tell me you've had your period since then."

Everything inside of me froze like an icy day in January.

My mind reversed as I went back about a month ago to Halloween and then another week and a half to when I'd finished my last period. I had gotten my shot, which I had every three months, right before that. So, *why* hadn't I gotten my period?

I met Lucida's gaze as my walls snapped into place with a

lock and key before I imploded. My knees nearly broke but my sister grasped my arm and tugged me to her gently.

No. No. No.

Now was so not the time for this. Not that an unplanned pregnancy ever had a fucking time... but right now? Uh. No. We were saving the world and being badasses, we didn't have time or the secure life for a baby, a literal small life that completely depended on you. Oh, shit.

"That's impossible," I whispered softly, my voice thick with emotion.

Lucida frowned and nodded. "Maybe your cycle is messed up because of all this magic bullshit? That is totally possible, right?"

I swallowed hard as I looked out my bedroom window. The door opened as Miranda's perfume scented the air. She locked it once more as she tossed a white bag on the bed that Lucida broke open. My heart sped up as the reality of the situation hit into me, knocking my breath away. My brain was foggy with panic and I focused instead on keeping the boys out. I didn't want Edwin or any of them to know until I had confirmation on the results.

"Here," Miranda said, handing me a box of tests. I felt tears well in my eyes. If I was pregnant, I was totally going to fucking chop off some dicks. That sucked because I loved the dicks that would be responsible. I also had a moment of extreme thankfulness because of my two friends and Luci's fantastic memory. I clearly was fucking gone in the head if I hadn't realized my complete lack of a period.

Maybe I needed a personal assistant. Although, I doubt they'd keep track of shit like this for me. I suppose you never know.

Another knock on the door came and I knew who it was.

"Ve," Bandit spoke, his voice far more tense than usual. "Let me in."

"Just a minute," I said loud enough that my voice cracked. "Luci and Miranda are changing and I'm about to hop in the shower."

They shoved me into the bathroom where I closed the door, locking it before placing my head against the door. I took a deep breath and took out one of the tests. The box was a blue and pink color, standard, and contained three tests. I laid out one and paced the room before finally deciding to woman up and do it.

Have you ever had that moment when you need to pee and you just can't because you're nervous? Yeah, it sucks. Also, this door locking thing was becoming a habit. I wasn't a fan.

When I had finally put the test on the counter, I set a timer and sunk to the ground. I'd always loved this bathroom but right now it felt oddly like purgatory. My nails tapped on the cold tile as I rolled my head against my knees trying not to be sick. The nerves alone were making me miserable but more so that rolling flame inside of me was reacting defensively.

I tried to breath through this. Why was this bothering me so much?

Because it was unplanned. Because it wasn't safe with the dangerous life we led. Because a child is a super big deal. Because of magic. I had to ignore the voices on the other side of the door. I could hear them growing but I was afraid to search the bond to see what they knew. I didn't want my panic slipping through. I also knew I didn't have much time before they'd just break down the door.

This was so fucked up.

"*Dolcezza*," Edwin's soft voice appeared next to me as he

materialized through a set of shadows and frowned at my position on the floor. I felt very small and young. I felt like none of my power mattered or even magic in general. Right now, I was very much twenty-one year old Vegas who may or may not have gotten knocked up.

The worst part? If it wasn't for our life right now - the blood, stalkers, and potential war - this could have been a good moment. Unplanned, but a reason to celebrate. I loved the concept of creating something with the person or, in my case, people I loved. But right now? With how our life was right now, it felt like a cruel twist of fate.

I couldn't imagine anything worse than not feeling as though I could protect an innocent life. An innocent life that I had created. One that I was sure would become my entire world. I had to stop thinking. I closed my eyes.

"Hey," I whispered softly.

"You cut off our connection, well with everyone. What is going... *oh*."

Yeah. Oh.

I sat with my head on my knees as he went silent. I took a deep breath and when I felt him slide under me so that I was on his lap, I relaxed a bit. I partly wanted to open the door and bring my other boys in but I figured I would just start crying. My body was cold and I knew that I was barely hanging on right now.

I wasn't upset. I was scared. I honestly didn't know how we would handle this. You couldn't exactly postpone a war, right?

"Vegas," Edwin tipped my chin so I had to meet his eyes. "No matter what, this is going to be fine. It's unexpected, sure, but it's not something that we haven't talked about."

Freaking magic sperm.

The timer went off and both our heads snapped up, I

looked toward it and Edwin flicked his hand so that it landed in my palm. Thank god for modern pregnancy tests. My hand uncurled from the small plastic object to reveal a blue set of words.

Not pregnant.

My walls fell down as I was filled with slight disappointment and a good amount of relief. I knew right now would be a very dangerous time to be pregnant. Edwin kissed my temple lightly as a knock sounded on the door. He was holding me like I was glass right now and I hated it.

"Is it wrong that I'm disappointed a bit?" Edwin whispered in an odd voice as if he was confusing himself.

Join the club buddy.

I swallowed because a small part of me agreed. He spoke quietly in my ear. "I would still like to do some tests to make sure that everything is okay. With all the changes your body is going through, I've been a tad concerned about how it would affect you."

My head nodded without my permission as the knocking grew louder.

I gripped the pregnancy test and placed it on the counter, looking at my face in the mirror with adrenaline rushing through my system. Also, when the fuck had the mirror been fixed? Magic. I blamed magic for the inconsistencies that existed in my life. It was a fantastic catch all.

"Vegas?" Edwin asked quietly as I blinked.

I pressed my lips together, "I need a minute, Edwin."

His lips brushed my temple as his shadows kissed my skin in a soft farewell. I could still hear the knocking and voices, someone speaking louder than the others. I couldn't focus on it though and I wish I was lying when I said that my vision was blurring with hot tears. I could feel the adrenaline dissipating as exhaustion hit me.

My knees broke as I felt my hands hit the tile and my breathing got rough. This was so fucking typical. I would have a panic attack about this despite everything else I'd been through. It had been a long fucking two days. First, my Thanksgiving got taken over by asshole Victor and creepy Levi. Then I got into a fist fight only to bail my boyfriend out of jail followed by fantastic sex. Then I got my ass kicked in training by Grover before Edwin unleashed my magic and dropped the "I love you" bomb. Don't forget Gray's drop-in and Bandit destroying my bathroom mirror. All finished by Kodiak and I creating our bond and a fucking pregnancy scare.

I just needed a moment to not be in my own head. A break of some kind.

The fire inside me began crackling like a dangerous siren pulling forth an odd energy that had me shifting back from reality. I gasped as the entity inside of me took over, as if understanding that I couldn't handle this right now. I felt my tears dry as her energy filled me with strength. I guess I really was taking a vacation for one. I was a tad bummed it was in my head and not Bora Bora but oh well.

I pushed my odd disappointment from my mind. I wouldn't think about the odd loss I felt. The loss of not being able to have a normal life or opportunities. If there was no magic, war, or stalkers, this could have been a good thing. Yet, the first thing I'd been filled with was fear and a sense of pure panic.

I had no control in my life anymore. I wanted it back. Needed it.

My fingers warmed against the tiles as that odd black flame began to flicker against the white surface. I closed my eyes as an odd sensation overtook me. My legs straightened to standing as my eyes flashed black in the mirror my hair glinting in an odd obsidian and silver pattern. What the fuck was going on with me?

I raised a hand to the mirror and it began to warp under the heat.

The pattern was beautiful and the silver material pooled over my palms and onto the counter. I didn't even flinch when the door was all but kicked down. I wasn't listening, not truly. Silence echoed behind me and my figure swayed as the force within me, the obnoxious bitch, finally broke free without constraints.

Well, I guess I'd hit the end of the line. Now I didn't even have the option to be in control. There was some relief in that. I could just sit back.

Appearing for her first solo performance, we have Vegas's magic!

"Fuck," I hissed as my voice grew different in texture.

"Do not touch her!" Byron's voice was sharp through the bond. Out loud and mental.

"Ve?" Bandit asked his body right behind me, in a sharp and unnaturally fast movement, as his vibrant eyes met my own. I met his gaze and I turned towards the door. Byron gave me a wide berth as Kodiak made an upset sound.

"Kodiak," Byron snapped, "unless you want to be incinerated, keep your fucking hands off her."

I ignored them hearing Cosimo speak. "Is that a pregnancy test?"

That was going to be a problem later.

Blue was frozen in the doorway to the hall and as I stepped forward, I saw the hesitancy to step back. Unfortunately, my power didn't care and didn't like to back down to anyone unless she was in the mood. My black flames licked the floor in a predatory movement that forced him back with the threat of burning him alive. His eyes were dark as I walked past Decimus and Grover.

Decimus's eyes were alight with something responding to the fire surrounding me but he stayed silent. Grover tilted his head and his hand twitched as if to touch me. I continued down the stairs as if I was sleepwalking. Booker kept his distance but his eyes were capturing everything with fascination and a bit of fear.

Then there was Rocket.

Rocket whose eyes were nearly as dark as mine stood at the bottom of the stairs. His creature was right under the surface, for the first time since he had become a mage, and his body began moving backwards as I floated towards him to turn down the hallway and step outside on the patio. I wasn't sure why the pregnancy possibility had triggered my powers but I had to assume it was due to the extreme nature of my emotional swing.

Good to know. I just needed to not freak out ever. Easy peasy.

"Dolcezza," Edwin warned as I followed Rocket, his eyes a deep silver pool like the melted mirror upstairs. I was entranced by him. I couldn't look away from him and couldn't stop to care that we were walking across the cold wet estate grounds in bare feet. My black fire lit the ground around me as my skin shivered with pure magic. Realization hit me as my magic grinned happily. I knew what type of fire this was and I think Rocket did as well.

"What the fuck is going on?" Someone snapped from behind me.

"She had a pregnancy scare, apparently," Cosimo murmured quietly.

"Her power surged forward to protect her from extreme

emotions that would have probably blown up the house," Edwin explained.

Rocket's sculpted jaw was tight and I had no idea if he could hear them. I wasn't positive if I was even hearing them correctly. My eyes adjusted to the light as the two of us traveled through the thick forested edge of the property that would lead into uncharted territory. This wasn't the same way we'd traveled before and I found myself nearing a small clearing that smelled of earth and death. I wasn't positive how I knew that.

"Sugar," Rocket spoke softly and his hand reached out to me. I grasped it and my flames circled up his arm but he didn't appear harmed. His power was so cold. So naked and raw. It reminded me of bones dug up from the ground.

"Stop them, Edwin," Byron demanded urgently.

"It doesn't work like that," Edwin growled in a low and tight voice.

As we reached the clearing, the sky cracked with thunder as my flames spread out around Rocket and I like a comfortable barrier. His hand came around my waist as I let my hands trail up his massive arms and tan neck. Everywhere my hands touched, dark flames left patterns that almost looked like tattoos on his skin. He groaned as his forehead pressed to mine. I knew exactly what my power wanted and as I dove into him just a bit, I felt it.

"Shit," he hissed quietly as I tugged. My flames, black and almost fathomless in nature, roared to life as a crack in the earth turned the clearing quiet. My eyes fluttered shut as Rocket took control of his power.

And did he ever.

If you had told me that I was going to be fucking subjected to the living dead on this fantastic afternoon, I wouldn't have believed you. Honestly, I could have guessed we'd be training today and I could have possibly predicted Gray would show up. But this? No, this was different.

I stayed still in Rocket's tight embrace as hands in a bone white texture gripped my ankles. They only pulled on us to free themselves from the earth. I moaned as Rocket's lips met mine in the center of this unmarked and clearly very old burial site. Boston had so much thick and deep history that it wasn't very surprising. Despite his hot burning lips and mint scent, neither of us could ignore the moldy earth scent surrounding us, or the slight scent of decaying flesh.

So, I was starting to understand why necromancers got a bad rep. Especially if they were connected to someone like me. I could feel the dead around us and as my eyes fluttered open, I found his metallic gaze peering into mine. I could feel my power receding slightly but I felt different. Not as I had with Edwin. Not frustrated and playful.

No. I felt powerful.

I barely flinched as my flames moved to a low simmer and revealed the twenty skeletons we had raised throughout the clearing, contained and staring at the two of us with empty sockets. My men were standing facing the low simmering circle and all I could pay attention to was Rocket's nibble on my ear and the power washing over my skin from him. My magic was still circulating through me, but it almost felt as though the two of us had come to an agreement. A merger of sorts. Also, Rocket was totally turning me on but my power didn't think it was the time for fantastic sex.

Bitch. Now she is getting picky?

"Beautiful?" Blue asked quietly. Both of us looked at him with curiosity. Edwin stepped forward, drawing the gaze of all twenty-two of us, if you included the skeletons.

"This is fucked up," Decimus stated bluntly.

Yes, well said. But how sexy is it that Rocket is so powerful? Like, damn. I was bathing in his raw power like a stressed out mom of six at a day spa. Scratch that. A stressed out mom of twenty. Ha! Get it? Because of the skeletons?

"Rocket," Edwin's voice was sharp and contained an absurd amount of power. It didn't break my ring of flames and my magic had a dark smile on her lips.

Good. He wasn't more powerful than us.

"Yes?" Rocket asked quietly, his voice normal as his nose skimmed my throat and a throaty sound broke from him. I could feel a low vibration that his vicious magic, almost animal like, created under his skin.

"You need to put them back and separate from her, I don't want you to get into the cross hairs of this," Edwin warned and a low growl echoed through the area.

It was from me.

Classy Vegas. Growling at your boyfriend.

Wait, was he my boyfriend? Questions for later.

"Do not touch him," I snarled softly as my arm reached up to cup his jaw and encourage his soft kisses on my neck.

"Vegas," Edwin snapped and looked far more angry now. I liked that.

"What?" I asked amused.

What the fuck was he going to do about it?

My magic obviously had something in mind because she was acting as though she was getting exactly what she wanted.

His eyes flickered before he spoke. "Is this how you are going to react every time you can't handle something emotionally?"

I wasn't positive what reaction he was looking for. I shivered as my power exploded back to life and something darker crawled out. My head hurt from the whiplash. I broke from Rocket as he groaned and my black flames gathered at my feet, leaving the bodies to his designs. My sights were set on the orange eyed mage whose expression had now shut down. I could see the slight apprehension though.

He should be scared.

"Do not tell me how to react." A voice I didn't recognize hissed from my lips. A jolt of something passed over Edwin's face as Byron spoke something in that damn language I didn't understand. This time though, I felt as though if I focused on it I could begin to understand better. I could feel the clearing emptying and somehow I knew Rocket had let go of the bodies and put them back. I was curious how he had been able to do that.

"You need to snap out of it, Vegas," Edwin spoke, his body frozen as I drew closer, my flames wrapping around us in a circle. His dark shadows wrapped tight against him like a coiled snake.

"I don't need to do anything," I stated quietly. "I don't take orders from you."

My predatory instincts cued into the darkness rising in Edwin.

Playtime.

I think I'd come to the conclusion that our magic was a slightly older, darker power that existed within us. The Edwin and Vegas that grew up together weren't here right now. No, I was backseat to the show that was my power and the more that I goaded him, the more his control broke. It was probably a bad idea to let the primordial powers out to play, right?

In the back of my own head I began popping popcorn and leaning forward in interest. It really was terribly inappropriate, wasn't it?

"Someone needs to keep you contained," he murmured,

his eyes nearly black. I purred at the aggression under his skin. Fuck, I loved this. It was messed up but he was so scary right now, somehow looking larger than ever.

"And you are that person?" I asked in a throaty voice.

"Little girl, I've always been that person," his voice growing rougher as he stepped forward and my power flared around us. I could feel his dark, icy power rubbing against my skin as desire clashed with fury. It was intoxicating.

"Don't start something you aren't prepared to finish," I murmured quietly as his shadows seeped out to break my barrier. I wasn't giving it up, though.

"You have one chance to calm yourself down," he explained, his voice growing deceptively soft. "If you don't, I'm going to have to take control, Vegas. You won't like that."

My smile grew as I spoke the words to kick off what could possibly be a terrible decision.

"Do your worst."

9

GROVER

"*F*uck."

My eyes widened as the two of them clashed together. Byron grunted as a sonic wave of power pushed most of us back behind the tree line. I couldn't believe what I was seeing. Even putting aside that Vegas had thought she was pregnant for a moment, this? This wasn't normal. This type of power shouldn't be possible.

Vegas's entire body was lit with a now red hot heat that was in direct contrast to Edwin's pitch black shadows that surrounded them. I didn't want to get close with her like this. Rocket's unconscious body over Kodiak's shoulder in a fireman hold proved that. It didn't surprise me that our angel was more powerful than us. But this?

I just didn't know how to handle this.

Edwin's power was scary. I mean his entire body was bathed in shadows as the skies darkened to nearly black above and their bodies clashed together. I honestly didn't think his attempt to get her under control was working. Then again it was hard to tell. He was like a shadow himself, moving in and out of visualization as the ground iced near his movements. I grunted as her red flames fought against him.

I could barely track them. One minute they were on the ground, her pinning him and next he was slamming her into a tree to hold her still. I barely recognized the two people in front of us. I could almost feel the unnaturalness of their powers. They were lethal and dangerous. They were different people. Or maybe creatures was a better term. They were absolute chaos together and I couldn't believe these were the same two that had argued about Christmas decor.

Well. Sort of. I nearly chuckled at the concept of them fighting about Christmas decor in this type of situation.

Kodiak growled as they slammed onto the ground, the grass bursting into flames of orange. The thunder crashed in the skies and hid the sound of their collision. I was hypnotized by the insanity of what should only be seen in movies.

"Stop," Byron's eyes flashed dangerously at Kodi. "She is perfectly fine. In fact, the only person in any fucking danger is Edwin."

That was hard to believe.

As in the Horde, Edwin had seemed to undergo a change as his hair tips turned orange and his entire upper body lit up with runes. Vegas had changed as well but it wasn't the crimson and sapphire highlights as before. No, her hair was silver as usual but flickers of red and orange flashed across it as if it couldn't decide what it wanted to be yet. I wondered if it had to do with the fire she was using. What type of fire was this even?

Bandit stepped up next to me and I looked at him to see his expression turning thoughtful, intense, and far too dark for my liking. I had a feeling he was attempting to make a decision and I opened my mouth to speak.

"Bandit," Byron warned as my silver-haired brother ignored him. I think it was then that I realized how little I knew about those around us. How much the game had changed. Byron cursed as Bandit stepped through the barrier without any concern.

"How is that fucking possible?" Decimus asked as Byron went silent, his face paling. We could all feel the barrier pushing us out, not allowing for any movement.

"I have no idea," he muttered looking horrified if not shocked.

Bandit walked forward with a casual slow gait. The darkness in his eyes had me concerned but he didn't flinch as they crashed to the floor right near his feet. Instead, he crouched down as both of them froze and met his gaze with animalistic glares. Edwin was breathing slightly hard but looked far more controlled than the heated furious gaze of Vegas's eyes.

It was clear Edwin could hold his own against her, but Bandit did the simplest thing and ended all of it. With all of the calm in the world, he reached forward through the flames and shadows to touch her temple with his thumb. His other hand rested right at her sternum over the vertical tattoo of our markings. My own silver masque tattoo tingled in response. Vegas froze, her body quieting as he moved his lips causing Edwin's eyes to widen.

Then she was down.

Unconscious.

The flames died instantly as Edwin's power rubber-banded back to him. I grunted at the impact that shook the ground. I briefly wondered how many bodies were under there, but figured now was not the time to consider that. I could, however, feel the natural minerals and metals throughout the entire property. Everything from the coin four feet away to the large picture frame that held a safe behind it filled with human weapons. It made sense now, my obsession with weapons.

"Holy shit," Booker spoke my thoughts exactly.

Blue stepped forward into the clearing as Edwin met his gaze before looking back at Bandit. Our silver-haired brother simply picked up Vegas and brushed her hair back from her flushed face. He turned and walked towards us with a nearly bored expression on his face.

Silence descended as he met my gaze and then the others.

"Kodiak could you get some water and meet me upstairs?" he asked as I jolted at his tone. His voice was dark and commanding. Decimus's jaw dropped we watched him walk past and towards the estate.

"Edwin?" Cosimo asked as the mage joined us looking pale as Byron offered him a back pat.

He looked as though he were a million miles away as he spoke softly to all of us. "We need to leave for the Horde now. Be ready to go as soon as she wakes up."

Everyone began to leave the clearing as I stayed back a bit with Blue. My brother was unusually quiet as I met his concerned gaze. Something was very different about Bandit.

What the fuck was going on with our family?

10

VEGAS

I imagined that this was what it felt like to be sore from working out. Now, I will never be one hundred percent sure of that because I don't workout and didn't plan too much. Still, I felt fucking terrible. What in the heck was wrong with me?

Then the memories came flooding back and I felt as though I would cry. I didn't want to open my eyes. I didn't want to see the damage I'd done. I'm sorry not the damage *I* had done, the damage *we* had done. The bitch inside my head laughed as if my conclusion was fucking funny.

Yes, Vegas. Now there really are people inside your head.

I was starting to understand why Edwin was so fucking mad.

"Dolcezza," Edwin spoke against my ear. "I need you to wake up."

"No. You probably hate me. Why don't you hate me?" I whispered into the pillow my face was pressed against. I could feel the affection rolling off him and it made me want to punch him.

"How can I hate a part of me?" he murmured causing me to smile. Crazy fucking bastard.

I looked up and he met my gaze as the evening cloudy skies pierced through the windows. I could feel the other boys around the house as well as the two girls. I groaned remembering the past two hours. My skin felt alight with a buzz I didn't understand and my head felt awful, like I had just been hit over the head with magic. Oh, wait, that wasn't a fucking metaphor. I frowned trying to remember how our fight ended. Edwin was waiting for me to talk and as I slowly turned my head, I found his bright orange eyes sparkling with amusement.

"Your magic is an asshole," I accused. "An antagonistic asshole."

His lip twitched. "Me, antagonistic? I think that award should go to the woman who not only released Rocket's necromancer powers but also summoned soul fire."

Glad we were all on the same page about the black flames then.

My chest contracted as if my magic was rolling her eyes. I put up a middle finger as he wrapped an arm around me and pulled me into his chest. I didn't even try to *not* cuddle into him as he groaned at my leg that hooked around his waist. He could deal with it.

You wanna cuddle? I'll cuddle the shit out of you.

Then I saw it.

"What the fuck?" I muttered looking at my hand.

So for the record, I love tattoos but I had never wanted to be the one with hand tattoos in the room. I blinked and then frowned at the thin, albeit beautiful, runes decorating my fingers and hands. They had a vine like appearance to them but instead of containing a rose at the end, it was a silver flame. Honestly, they were pretty fucking cool but I was starting to look a lot like some weird Cochella chick.

You know who you are and you know that it is some cultural appropriation bullshit.

"You should see Rocket," he grinned.

I shot up and grunted, my head hurting and spinning. "Where is he?"

"In this room," he answered, "but Vegas we need to talk about what happened."

I was gone.

I felt a tad bad but honestly I was too focused on making sure Rocket wasn't hurt that the requested conversation would have to take a back seat. I felt selfish. Why had I let my power make me so selfish? I could have hurt him. Fuck. I could have hurt all of them. All because I couldn't handle a goddamn pregnancy scare. To be fair that really was a crazy fucking situation after a long forty-eight hours.

Was it, though? I was actively having sex. I mean it's not exactly a secret how babies are made.

"Rocket?" I flung open the door as I blew right past several of my boys and crawled right into the bed. Rocket grunted as he dragged me under the covers while keeping his eyes closed. I could feel the exhaustion on his end. It was so odd to see him so relaxed and exhausted. His blonde hair was messy and dark circles lined his eyes. He wore only a pair of boxers.

Thank you divine entities.

Instead of trying to keep track of the conversation around me, I leaned against his tanned chest and let him nuzzle my neck and hair. I would normally worry about it turning into a fuck fest but both of us were very tired. I sighed happily as I spotted a pattern on his neck.

Holy crap on a shit stick.

"Did I do this?" I whispered as he squinted one silver eyes open. Our heads were both tucked under the blankets comfortably and I was very glad that I got to place my hands on his bare chest.

"I always wanted more tattoos," his lips quirked.

Liar.

"I'm so sorry, Rocket," I spoke muffled into his chest. "If I'd hurt you..."

"Sugar," he drawled softly tilting my head back and brushing his thumb across my cheek bone. "Besides exhaustion, I feel great. I feel like all that power was finally released and is now at a normal level."

I could relate to that. Plus, the tattoos were sexy and made my magic smile with a possessive glint. Now, that is just all sorts of messed up because she was me. I mean it felt like two different entities but at the end of the day she was the magic from which I was made. I shook my head and took a deep breath. He tucked my head under his chin, allowing both of us to relax for just a moment before I faced what I knew was out there.

"Princess," Decimus announced from somewhere in the room. "You can't hide under there all day. We need to talk about what just happened and the fucking pregnancy test in your room."

So blunt.

"Dude!" It sounded like Grover hit his shoulder. My power bubbled under my skin but stayed dormant. I groaned as I flipped the blanket up causing Rocket to make a discontented sound. I went up on my elbows and lifted my brows.

"What about it?" I narrowed my eyes.

"Were you going to tell us you thought you were pregnant?" Blue looked genuinely upset.

Ah, shit.

They weren't even mad. No, instead, they all looked freakin' sad. Like puppies. Rocket must have finally heard what they were talking about because he cursed and turned my head gently. His eyes darkened but he looked back at the others before I responded.

"Luci had literally just brought it up to me," I muttered, embarrassed for not thinking of it myself. "I didn't even fucking notice, but the last time I'd had my period was six weeks ago."

"Shit," Cosimo murmured looking concerned. Now, some women would have probably felt awkward talking about their period in a room full of men and to that I have two comments. One, they are grown men and if they want to have sex and risk pregnancy, then they can deal with learning about periods. Not that I had ever had any of my boys act like that but you know me, can't waste an opportunity on social commentary.

Secondly, these boys had been going to the store for me for years. Years, folks. I nearly smiled thinking about how they had come back from the store with a red velvet cake, prosecco, and a heating pad last year when I'd had terrible cramps. Like tear worthy. Sweet boys. Sweet, smart boys.

"I'm not though," I offered a smile that hid my tiny bit of disappointment. The boys didn't even attempt to do the same. Especially Rocket who muttered something that sounded like "trying harder."

Booker watched me with a curious look as if he could feel my disappointment and Byron just seemed genuinely lost as to what to say. I don't think he'd ever thought about our future like that. He lived very much in the moment.

"Where's Kodi?" I asked quietly.

Edwin laughed from the doorway. "He's downstairs."

"Why?" I frowned as Byron grunted and stood.

"He shifted because he was concerned."

"Concerned my ass," Booker muttered. "The man had a full blown panic attack."

"Shifted?" I frowned as Blue flashed me an amused smile. My magic clapped and did a tiny twirl. Apparently, she had gotten what she wanted. What that was, I had no idea.

All I could imagine was Oprah's voice: *You get magic! And you get magic!*

"Come see," Edwin spoke and I attempted to stand up.

"Where is Bandit?"

The room stilled completely as everyone looked in different directions to avoid my gaze.

"I'm right here, Ve," Bandit's voice was low and different than before. Edwin didn't say anything as I slipped past him to Bandit, his eyes a vibrant shade of lime green that almost seemed fluorescent. His body was relaxed but his power seemed to be shifting restlessly under his skin. It felt contained and agitated like an electrical build up.

"Hey," I frowned slightly. "Are you okay?"

His smile was small as he nodded. "Yeah. Let's go see Kodi. He's worried."

I felt like there was something I wasn't understanding.

"Oh, my god!" Luci practically tackled me. "Can we say 'bad bitch?' Dude, I heard you totally kicked ass!"

I grinned and Miranda laughed as she pulled my best friend away and Luci continued to talk. My focus though, as I came down the stairs, was on a massive chocolate colored wolf. A massive chocolate colored wolf that was undeniably not a grizzly bear. Alright, now I'd have to give up the comparison.

"Kodi?" I choked out as I reached the bottom of the

stairs and came face to snout with a massive, as in as big as me, wolf with deep green eyes.

"Careful," Byron muttered but I reached forward as the wolf snorted at Byron. I smiled at his dismissive attitude as the wolf nudged my throat and trailed his wet nose on my skin. My skin broke out in shivers as I reached my hands up to thread through his dark thick fur. I realized that I had completely bared my neck to him without thinking, didn't that mean something in wolf nonverbal cues? A soft noise began as I curled against the wolf slightly, causing me to feel very sleepy. It felt like it was tuning a piece of my soul, sparking it so that the two of us were on the same frequency. Our connection buzzed with pleasure. Since earlier today, I could feel it like I could feel the other four.

"Is he fucking purring?" Decimus sputtered.

Kodi let out a low rumble, almost growling, as everyone went silent. I yawned and pulled back, kissing his nose. "Come on, Kodi, shift back."

"Uh, Vegas..." someone began.

Oh, man. Did he ever.

I inhaled with surprise as the wolf body in front of me began to snap out of place and a familiar man returned. Naked.

"Oh, christ," I mumbled as Kodi flashed me a cocky but dirty smirk. I mean we'd had sex but that was fast and dirty. This was him, completely naked.

"Ah!" Luci screeched before bounding up the stairs. "So gross."

So not gross.

Kodiak wrapped his massive hands around my waist and pulled me against him as I sighed. I couldn't even find it in me to squeak at the size of his erection. My hands, elegant and small, smoothed against his massive tan chest in a rhythmic pattern.

"So," Edwin coughed with hidden amusement through our bond. "If we aren't too busy, I'd like to talk about putting you on a different type of birth control."

Instantly, different sounds of protest erupted as I rolled my eyes. I looked back at Edwin and nodded knowing that the boys were just being silly. Kodiak, in one move, had me up in his arms as we walked towards my bedroom up the stairs.

"Shower time," Kodiak muttered as I tried to not grind myself against him. Wasn't this my second one today? I had fucked in the dirt and been touched by skeletons so I suppose I needed it. What I really needed was sleep.

"I thought you didn't want me 'washing your scent off?'" I teased as his eyes flashed dark and a rumble sounded courtesy of his wolf.

"I don't," he muttered, his voice graveled and rough. "But for right now a sweater will have to do. I don't want anyone at the airport smelling sex on you. I'd have to kill them."

So territorial.

The warm water felt fantastic on my skin as I leaned back into Kodiak's hard body. Despite his obvious excitement, he seemed fairly content as his hand skimmed my chest and down to my hips. I let my body go limp and relaxed as he continued to trail over everything with a simple loving touch.

"Kitty?" Booker's voice called out.

"Puppy?" I quipped as his soft laugh echoed from outside the shower.

"What in the fuck are you calling one another?" Kodiak asked with a lazy smile and a curious brow raise.

"He's my puppy," I teased. "And I'm your kitty, right, Booker?"

"Fucking hell," Kodiak muttered. Booker peeked his head in as I blushed slightly at how exposed I was, his soft velvet eyes tracing over my body and wet hair Kodiak washed with lazy movements. I needed more sleep clearly, my eyes nearly shut.

"I left out clothes for you," Booker muttered lightly as his eyes looked over my body in a greedy fashion.

"Clothes sound boring." I kept my eyes locked on him.

"What sounds more interesting?" Kodiak asked with a deep chuckle as his fingers tweaked my nipple and caused a small yelp in surprise.

"Being naked," I mumbled as the shower water turned off and Kodiak ushered me out into Booker's arms. He kissed the top of my head and strode out as Booker picked me up with ease and led me into the bedroom. I think the boys forgot I could walk sometimes.

"You are so beautiful," Booker murmured softly and began to dry me off with a soft white towel. He was so obviously turned on yet he took the time to make sure I was completely dried and began to brush out my hair while I wrapped myself in a soft robe. The raging sense of lust that plagued me as of late was momentarily replaced by soft love and affection for my artist.

"I was worried about you earlier," he whispered, his eyes melting into a softness I loved.

"*The Night of the Living Dead* moment?" I murmured.

He grinned with a dark chuckle. "No, that doesn't surprise me, really."

His handsome features shifted to become nearly sad. "I was actually talking about the pregnancy test, kitty."

"I would have told..."

"Would it be that bad having kids with us?" he asked softly and suddenly. My mouth popped open as I turned to look up at him with confusion.

That bad? What the heck?

"Is that what you think?" I asked standing up to kneel on the vanity stool to be closer to eye level with him while grasping his shoulders. "That I was upset because I don't want to have kids with you all?"

He shrugged, scowling.

I lifted a hand to his jaw. "Booker, I swear that wasn't a thought in my head. I mean sure, it would be really fucking crazy, but my biggest concern? The biggest concern was the fact that our lives have been extremely dangerous not to mention violent as of late. I would never want to risk our baby..."

I was cut off by a deep kiss as his hands delved possessively into my hair. My heart beat rapidly as I clutched his soft shirt to encourage him even closer. I breathed in the scent of fresh laundry and paint that floated off his warm golden skin.

"Good," he grinned, "because I should probably warn you that you are about to face a battle about this birth control thing."

I rolled my eyes, scoffing while containing my amusement. "It's not a battle if I've already decided that it is happening."

It was a fucking battle.

My legs were crossed in the bed, the soft lined leggings and massive sweater from Kodi keeping my figure warm as I attempted to bat away every fucking rheotrical attempt at persuasion. I couldn't believe I was cold when I hadn't been for so long. Although, everything felt cold compared to my fire from earlier but I had a lot of warm bodies to keep me cozy. All of which were placed somewhere throughout the room.

"Boys," I sighed with exhaustion. "I am not saying we can't have kids but this is getting crazy. We are in the middle of a massive transition. Now is not the time to have kids! How am I the rational one about this? I hate being rational."

Edwin was oddly quiet as everyone else voiced different levels of disagreements. Cosimo, being the best at compromising, sat behind me while waves of grumpiness rolled off him. The worst? Rocket, Kodiak, and Blue who looked positively put out and upset at the concept. *All* of them reeked of possessiveness and caveman like attitudes.

Typical, I would get stuck with a group of twenty-two year old nesters.

"Dolcezza," Edwin drew my attention back as I looked at where my magical asshat was kneeling in front of me. We were still at eye level with one another which I totally found sexy because, you know, apparently tallness was still a turn on for me. You would think I'd get over it.

"Yes?," I offered with a challenging look.

I swear to the gods...

"I am totally fine putting this spell on if you are really sure." I heard the slight plea in his voice as my mouth popped open. "Or, and just consider this, you could let nature take its course."

Yes, because I am sure having a sexual relationship with ten people wouldn't increase those odds.

"Oh, my gods!" I nearly yelled and poked his chest, eliciting a rumble from his magic. "You are supposed to be the reasonable one! You and Byron, who has been noticeably turned against me as well. I can not handle this caveman shit. Put the spell on now, Edwin. If I find out you somehow accidentally messed up this one hundred percent proof birth control spell, I will kill you."

Byron chuckled softly as Blue offered him a grin. All these bastards were in cahoots with one another.

"I mean it. I am officially tabling this conversation until later. You can't just tell a woman you want her to have your baby, I mean shit we haven't even talked about marriage!"

I fucked up. I knew I'd fucked up.

The room stilled as something ignited in Blue's eyes and a few boys exchanged glances but stayed perfectly quiet. Somehow, I was far more nervous they weren't arguing. My eyes searched each of their faces as I tried to dissect the emotions there.

Nope. Better not.

"Fine," Edwin smiled with an amused glint. I didn't trust it.

"I'll have Gray check your work," I warned, his eyes flashing dark at my challenge.

A cold shiver elicited a gasp from me as he pressed two fingers into the center of my sternum and began speaking softly in that language I was unfamiliar with. I wondered briefly how he had learned so much more than just his specific magic type. For example, how did glamouring work? Or this birth control spell? I clearly had a large gap in knowledge that I couldn't help but want to fix. My eyes closed as the spell tightened around my core and a small whimper pushed out. It didn't hurt exactly but it felt odd.

"Just let me know if you ever want the spell removed," Edwin stated softly.

I shook my head frustrated and drawled sarcastically. "Yes, yes, I know. Mission Knock-Vegas-Up will have to wait until another time though, boys. We have a war to win."

FIRE & SMOKE

I had no idea if we would win, but it seemed to motivate everyone to get up.

"This is fucking ridiculous," Lucida laughed from the door as Miranda chuckled. It seemed the two of them found my situation hilarious.

"Watch it," I threw out. "Until you have your magic, I can kick your butt."

Luci snorted and tossed up the middle finger. "Even with magic you wouldn't be able to kick my ass. Now, if you had focused more on self defense…"

I let out a low growl but was interrupted by Byron. "It is nearly six. We need to leave for the airport, now."

My body fell back as I groaned and Cosimo pulled me into him so that his head rested against my beating heart. The slight scowl on his handsome face while looking at me made me smile because I knew it had to do with my expression. The man mirrored my smile as I let out a soft laugh. My eyes traced over his tan beautiful face and the piercings I loved.

"That's sort of creepy," Byron noted curiously.

We both shot him a look as he chuckled and put his hands up in mock surrender. I was barely paying attention to the loud conversation in the room but to Byron's authentic smile and Cosimo's body heat instead.

"Hey, Byron," I purred, feeling amused.

"Yes, Trouble?" he replied narrowing his eyes with cautious amusement.

"Is there any way," I started as Cosimo nuzzled my neck, "that we could drive my totally awesome car to the airport?"

The deep comfortable laugh that sounded from him made me smile. "Sure, I will just have someone pick it up and deliver it back here. But I get to drive because of the weather."

"Aye, aye," I cheered with a mock salute.

I ushered Cosimo to a standing position and the lazy cat-like man just lightly nipped my shoulder and I groaned at the spark of hot desire. My feet barely touched the ground before Edwin wrapped his arms around my waist and lifted me. My heart gave a small thrill because he never just casually picked me up. I took full advantage of it and clung to him like a baby koala.

"How are you feeling?" he asked curiously as everyone began filing out.

I mindlessly ran my fingers through his hair while thinking about his question. "Honestly?"

"No, not honestly," he mocked.

"Ass," I narrowed my eyes and tugged a piece of thick hair.

"Yes, you have a fantastic ass," he retorted as I flashed him a coy grin.

"Yeah?" I smirked then sighed dramatically. "See, I just don't know if I believe you, Edwin. I mean, are you *even* attracted to me?"

Conveniently, no one was left to save me from my antagonistic words. Bastards.

"Edwin!" I gasped as the mage pushed me against the wall so that I was caged between it and his hard body. My legs were wrapped tightly around his waist and his hard length pressed between us, encouraging me to rock just slightly. I knew my sexual frustration with him would boil over eventually!

He let out a soft low sound as his forehead pressed against mine. "Sorry, Vegas, but we don't allow nonsense comments in this household."

"Bullshit!" I gasped in mock indignation. "All anyone ever says around here is a bunch of nonsense!"

Edwin chuckled as his massive hands squeezed my ass. "I disagree and I can't figure out for the life of me why you would ask me something so nonsensical!"

"Because you haven't kissed me!" I blurted out my truth. "At least, not like before. You keep pulling away physically and I thought after we talked that maybe it would change."

The mage's eyes darkened just slightly as a heat simmered there. "I'm sorry, *dolcezza*. I am, well, attracted seems like a meek word for it. But admitting my affection is far easier than showing it to you. I don't want to overwhelm you and I'm not sure I have a ton of control to be honest."

I yanked him forward to meld my lips to his in an unbreakable seal. I was finding that Edwin and I had rather split personalities, though because one minute we were joking and the next I wanted to fight or fuck his brains out. He let out a low growl into my mouth, so unlike him, and began to consume me as my body heated under his icy power.

"Fuck," he murmured against my lips. "You're going to kill me, Vegas."

"At least it will be a good death," I teased in a breathless pant.

A small smirk tilted on his lips. "Oh, it will be good, all right."

He ground into me as my head tilted back. I could feel his shadows rolling over my body as they became almost tangible, grabbing and caressing my warm skin with a cool touch. I gasped as he grinned against my pulse.

"I promise that you and I will have a lot of fun together, love," he whispered softly before his eyes met mine. Slowly, he slid me down against his hard frame until his shadows covered me from head to toe, his massive body eclipsing any light from my room. The wall behind me was hard but everything else felt like a cool comfortable blanket.

"Now?" I asked with an innocent and sly smirk.

He grinned and shook his head. "Let's get to the Horde. Your safety is far more important to me."

"Always worrying about me," I muttered.

He chuckled and swept me up into his arms in a bridal lift. "You're completely right. I should be far more focused on that delectable ass and fucking you into the wall, shouldn't I?"

My face went bright red. "Edwin!"

His silent chuckle rumbled against me as he carried me out of the room. "Don't ever doubt how attracted I am to you, Vegas. Everything has its timing and you, my sweetness, try my patience in that timing every moment of the day."

I crossed my legs over one another as he carried me down the stairs. "Is that because you find me sexy?"

He scoffed at my eyelash bat. "That is a small singular word to describe how I feel about you."

I bit my lip. "Why don't you show me instead of describing, then?"

He shook his head as he looked down at my lips. "Keep biting that lip and I'll punish you."

"Jealous?" I goaded. "You could be the one biting it."

He cursed as he tightened his grip on me. Byron was at the door outside the garage as Edwin placed me down onto the floor, his erection pressing against my stomach.

"You look flustered," Byron cackled at his brother. "Can't handle a flirty Vegas?"

Edwin tossed him a scowl and kissed the top of my head before stalking off, his shadows hesitating before following him. I smirked.

They liked me better.

"Come on, Trouble," Byron tugged my hand as I offered him a bright smile. His shy smile returned as the two of us walked hand in hand toward my car. I tugged on my boots before I slipped into the passenger door he held open.

"I love this car," I whispered as he tossed me a handsome smile and turned it on. The low purr made me shiver.

"If you get turned on by cars, I'm going to have to keep you forever," Byron muttered as I let out a sharp laugh. I could hear the truth and slight insecurity in his words.

"Yeah?" I leaned close to him over the center console. "Well, I do find cars pretty sexy."

I really didn't, but with Byron? Yeah, I fucking did.

I couldn't lie. My body was fairly sore from the events of the past forty eight hours. I had been training muscles I promised I'd never use and been having fantastic sex that used every single muscle I did want to use. However, despite these two facts, I offered Byron a coy smile and awaited his response.

"Yeah, Trouble?" he chuckled while merging onto the highway. "It seems you've found a lot of things sexy lately."

Ass.

I scoffed. "Are you blaming me for having a high sex drive?"

He shook his head. "Blaming? No. Distracting? Yes."

My lips pursed. "I don't know."

I remembered the grudge that I'd been fostering after he ran off last time he bit me. I mean, I was allowed to be a tad bitter about that, right?

His warm lava eyes stared at me in question before a devious grin took over his face. "Is that so?"

I blinked innocently, my lashes fluttering. "What?"

"Are you mad at me? Do you feel as though I've neglected you?" he teased, his eyes sharpening in a dangerous fashion as they snapped down to my neck. I felt my heart beat faster. I could never keep track of Byron's attitude. Sometimes flirty and other times dark. I sort of loved it. It didn't escape my notice that the faint outline of his silver bite on my skin warmed under his gaze.

Also, I really hope he was assuming and couldn't read my mind.

"Maybe," I teased while tilting my head with interest. "I guess there is only one way to make it up to me."

The airport, Logan International, had a separate set of gates and parking for the private charter flights. I could see that the Ivanov jet taxiing but it was farther away, making me realize we would have a small wait. I wasn't focused on that or the rainy cold weather. No, instead, I was focused on the dangerous blood mage whose aura was sparking with lust and excitement. He parked my car with a flick of the wrist and turned to face me. I almost blushed because despite the obvious desire there was a soft affection in his eyes paired with something deeper like true happiness.

My car wasn't very large and Byron was massive. Like, huge. So I felt, despite our distance, that he was taking up all of my air. I wanted to offer him even more than that.

"Do you know the game you are playing at, Trouble?" he whispered, his voice thick and husky. "I can assure you that my lack of attention hasn't been out of desire but rather control."

Ugh!

I tossed my hands up and groaned. "I'm so tired of control! I don't need others to have control for me. I'm perfectly capable of exercising it when necessary!"

In the next moment, so fast that my head spun, I was pulled from the car and tossed over his shoulder. We were stalking up the stairs towards the private airport lounge as the heating from the building warmed my damp hair. I offered security a wave as they chuckled letting us through, clearly not bothering to check our identification. Pays to be a prince, right?

I tried to wiggle down and Byron tsked before smoothing a hand over my leg. "No, no, no. You didn't want control so now you don't get any."

"Byron," Kodiak demanded. "Put her down. I don't want her like that in public."

"Buzz kill," Byron muttered as I let out a strangled laugh. He slid me down his massive muscular body so that I could offer him a teasing look and wiggle that elicited a groan.

"So sorry, Golden," I grinned, backing up from the suited man with messy hair and intense eyes. Those eyes tracked my movements before a dark shadow shimmered behind his eyes, my magic grinning like a fool. She wanted to pull out his power.

"*Dolcezza*, you probably shouldn't encourage him or move away."

I didn't listen. Instead, I turned smiling and bulldozed right into Blue's cinnamon scent. I gasped as he lifted me up swiftly and Byron appeared right behind me against my back.

"Why, hello," I chuckled as Byron kissed my neck and Blue narrowed his eyes at my playful expression.

"Now, beautiful," Blue spoke in a low soft voice. "What did I say about the plane again?"

Oh, good, I was hoping he wouldn't forget.

"Hm. Oh, yes! That you were going to *attempt* to bite me," I quipped as Byron captured my chin with his strong fingers and looked at Blue with amusement.

"Is that so?" Byron gauged in his husky voice.

"Has she been teasing you as well?" Blue asked with an uncanny amount of perception.

"Torturing," Byrob corrected.

"Of course," Blue huffed.

"Boys," Edwin's voice was harsh as he motioned with his head towards the far wall. We all looked that way to find the other guests of the private sector staring at us. Gaping really. Well, some staring and some leering. None of it good.

Oh, man.

I turned tomato red as I slipped down between them and moved to hide away from the large number of suited men staring at us in open shock. Hah. They were shocked by the three of us? Try the eleven of us!

"What the fuck are you looking at?" Byron snarled in his commanding scary voice as all of them looked away. Blue, without any dimpled smile, offered a narrow stare that even put me on edge. It was clear that we'd been isolated, the eleven of us, for a bit too long. I'd completely forgotten how humans were about polyamorous relationships. I didn't feel nearly as confident standing up to billionaires as I did with college assholes.

"I'll be right back," I chirped feeling embarrassed as I speed walked towards the women's washroom. I could hear Luci jogging after me and I let out a dramatic sigh as she tumbled into the beautiful marble bathroom after me.

"People are such assholes," she muttered and scowled.

I grunted as I tried to take deep breaths and fan my face "I can't wait to get to the Horde. I don't like thinking about how 'unusual' we are here. I can practically taste the judgement."

"Right!" Lucida exclaimed, smiling. "Like, don't get me wrong. It's a big change, but also do you know how nice it will to not be judged for being homosexual or being an interracial couple? I'd always found that particularly frustrating, just because I'm Hispanic doesn't mean I love Miranda any differently than a white woman would. I mean now I just have to worry about being judged because I wasn't born with magic. After this human nonsense I can deal with any shit."

I grinned and hit her shoulder. "Look at you! You're a natural already!" Really though. I'd been far more freaked out than she was at first. Then again, I also had far less information from the magical asshats to base my decisions and choices on.

She preened and flipped her blue hair. "What can I say? I'm fabulous."

Miranda peered in and offered me a sympathetic smile. "Honey, can you come grab coffee with me? We have to go into the main part of the airport and I would rather not go alone."

"Absolutely. Want anything?" Lucida asked me. I shook my head as the two of them left, leaving me to my slight embarrassment. I scoffed at the stupid stuck-up humans in the other room. I didn't find anything wrong with the way I loved these men, so why did they? I blushed because I was totally falling for the Ivanov brothers.

Who was I kidding? I had nose dived off the cliff. I was so screwed.

I jumped as the bathroom door opened. With a quick turn I faced who I expected to be one of the boys, Miranda, or Lucida. It was none of them and my magic snarled inside of me, pacing like a predator wanting to escape.

"What the fuck are you doing in here?! Get out!" I hissed feeling shocked that any man would just walk into a women's bathroom. Especially a human male. Ew. I watched as his dark eyes looked over me with leering and hungry appraisal. I cringed as he narrowed his eyes.

"Don't like what you see, sweetheart?"

He locked the door and leaned against it. He wasn't a massive man but still larger than me. Unlike before, when my magic was only accessible at the thought of others in trouble, my magic was ready and sizzling.

"Get out," I demanded as I kept my face stern. I refused to admit that this really freaked me out. I lived most of my life sheltered from moments like this and while it made me furious, it also made me sad that a man would consider this acceptable behavior.

"Why?" he asked walking forward, "How am I any different than your boyfriends out there?"

Where the fuck do I start?

"First," I snapped in a lethal voice, "I don't know who the fuck you are. Second, I don't answer to you so fuck off. Third, you're disgusting if you thought this was a solid idea. Now, leave me alone, you freak."

His steps took him forward and for just a moment my PTSD hit hard. I tried to not think about the man who'd killed Vivi. I tried to not think about the demon I'd burned alive while he laid on top of me dying. I tried to not think about Nathan. No. Instead, I focused on keeping out of this creep's reach so that I didn't kill him. I really didn't want to see a headline regarding a man burned alive inside Logan International Airport.

"Come on," he needled moving closer. "Sluts like you love this shit. Maybe you just want someone to take control."

Instead of answering, I let my flame spark defensively around me and I could feel my eyes darken as a dark rumble broke from my throat. Oh.

Well, that was a bit animalistic, don't you think, Vegas? You just growled at someone essentially.

The man's eyes widened as he stepped back slightly looking afraid. "What... what was that?"

"Leave," I whispered, feeling furious and disgusted.

"Angel!" a charming voice called from outside as my lips tilted up.

"Grover," I called out, never taking my eyes off the man. "There is a crazy creep in here! He's locked the doors. A bit of help unlocking..."

Now, I really thought he was just going to unlock the door. Apparently, his powers had a different plan because the metal door flew forward so fast that I had to duck as the man slammed face forward into the tile floor. Yikes. That's not very sanitary. I moved myself to the side to distance myself from him even more.

"What the fuck?" the man stuttered as Grover walked in and grabbed the back of his collar while standing over his body.

"Worst mistake you've ever made, dude," he muttered while tugging him up so he nearly choked. A familiar set of footsteps sounded to reveal Blue. His sharp eyes took stock of the situation and the balding man in Grover's grip, as something feral worked its way through his expression. A dark sound that produced chills of desire and a teeny bit of fear rolled through the air. He smoothed it out a second later, offered me a smile sans dimples, and spoke.

"Did he touch you, beautiful?"

Bye bye, Creepy Motherfucker.

"I would be burning my own skin off," I muttered and landed a kick at the guy's leg in passing. Now, why did that feel so good?

"Would you mind getting Edwin for me?" Blue asked his

hand, smoothing over my shoulder lightly. I kissed his cheek, nodding, and walked out of the bathroom as my power wavered around me. Honestly, I was probably putting off some serious vibes but it seemed to scare any of the other men watching me.

All their heads turned down and I grinned. Human men looked rather shrimpy, at least these guys. I flounced up to Edwin and tugged his hand so that he looked at me. I could see the crease on his forehead and it was clear he'd been distracted enough to not hear what'd happened in the bathroom.

"So," I clasped my hands in front of me. "Some creep just locked me in the bathroom and tried to insinuate that I'd have sex with him because since I was with multiple men. He suggested I must be a slut. I may have freaked him out a tad because my powers went all 'fuck you dude.' Then Grover, the sweetheart, blasted the door in and Blue is now asking for you because he probably wants to know just how far he can go in punishing the bastard or killing him."

Silence.

Edwin let out a low primal growl and stalked towards the bathroom. Kodi, my protective wolf scooped me up as if inspecting me for injuries before rubbing my neck and nuzzling my hair. This was totally a weird wolfy scent thing, wasn't it? I was distracted so I missed the livid expressions on Decimus and Byron's faces. Bandit, my silent, maybe sociopathic, sweetie, began to softly play with my fingers between his own. His eyes continued to focus on where the other boys had gone. Booker, his sketch pad forgotten, narrowed his eyes at the men behind us before moving to stand so he blocked us from their line of sight. Cosimo, his expression concerned, faced Kodi and I as he seemed to be searching my face. Rocket, looking tired, stood up and yawned. He stretched those lean muscles and offered me a dangerous smile, making my heartbeat speed up, as he kissed my cheek and followed after the other boys. I totally blushed at the cute gesture. A fleeting thought occurred to me.

I hope that man wasn't some important billionaire or some shit.

"I have to be honest," I murmured quietly. "I'm fucking exahusted."

I was happy to see that the plane had pulled in, but right now? I just wanted to curl up and have fantastic sex.

Sleep! I mean sleep. Fantastic sleeping sex. Sex sleeping. Sex. Aw, crap. I really just wanted to have more sex.

All right. I admit it. My magic is turning me into a nymphomaniac. I haven't heard any complaints though, have you? Is it really addiction if the people who love you are supporting it?

Yes, Vegas. Yes, it is.

My body was suddenly pulled from Kodiak as I jumped at Byron's unexpected gesture. I clung onto him as he buried his head into my neck and stalked toward the jet. I could feel the intensity of his energy underneath the surface and at first I was concerned, before I realized how turned on I was. I could feel the aggression rolling off of him and I wondered if it was because they hadn't been able to kill the guy. If he was anything like Blue, that was exactly it. I couldn't smell blood on him and I briefly wondered how those teeth would feel if used for harm and not pleasure.

"Byron?" I whispered as he muttered a curse, pushing towards the back of the jet, before kicking open the private quarters. I bounced on the bed, letting out a squeak. Blue's charming laugh echoed as he slipped into the room and locked the door.

"Beautiful," Blue's husky voice lilted. "I do apologize, but Edwin didn't allow us to kill him."

Shit. Now I knew why they were all worked up.

BLUE

Vegas's pulse picked up as Byron tugged off his jacket and my eyes wandered over the expensive cream and black interior of the bedroom. I could feel rage pumping through my veins and I tried to take a breath, trusting Byron far more than myself right now. He was used to the aggression and bloodlust. My lips peeled back and my skin began to prickle at just the thought of killing the fucker that tried to touch my beautiful Vegas.

I shook my violent thoughts and kicked off my shoes, crawling forward onto the bed as I tracked Vegas's quick pulse. It reminded me of a hummingbird's wings. As of late, it had been quicker than normal but I knew this increased speed was also due to the excitement and glossy lust in her eyes. As my body eclipsed hers, I felt better. I wanted her under me and protected. I also wanted to pierce her perfect smooth soft skin. Ever since she'd given me the green light to taste her, I had decided I wouldn't ask twice. Byron slid behind her so that she was cradled against his chest and pinned between the two of us.

I ran my nose along her skin as she sighed in a breathy, almost needy, whine. If there was something more possessive than taking in the actual blood that kept her alive, I'd be all ears. I didn't think there was an alternative, however, and I could see that Byron felt the same way. After our connection was sealed into place it became far easier to monitor the group because I could get a sense of where and how the other men felt. It wasn't like Vegas's connection but it aided in making us closer. Right now? I could feel his blood lust and excitement, our girl shivering from the combined energy pressing against her. I'm sure that if we thought her afraid, unable to feel and smell her desire spreading through her veins like speed, we'd pull back.

Honestly, if I tried to pull back now she might hurt me. Our girl was becoming a feisty, vicious little warrior. And here I thought she couldn't get sexier.

"So beautiful," I murmured tilting her jaw and flicking my tongue against her warm skin.

"Blue," she sighed softly as I held myself above her. Byron took his time but began to slowly move her hair into one, silky twist that kissed the back of her neck. As his lips grazed her skin she jumped and something flared in her eyes.

"Both of you?" she whispered, her breathing quickening.

"Is that what you want, Trouble?" Byron asked as she tilted her neck. My hand smoothed over her soft silky skin as my dick, somehow, became impossibly harder. I wanted to bury myself in her. Right now. I tried to find some small shred of patience.

"Yes," she whimpered as her flame began to grow in a soft kindling pattern. I had no idea how I could feel her power so well but it was just a natural instinct.

"Vegas," I captured her chin to make sure her purple eyes met mine. "Are you positive?"

Her head bobbed as a devious smile filled my face. Byron muttered a curse as her power rippled across her skin and those purple eyes darkened to an amethyst color. I watched Byron kiss down her neck before his sharp teeth pierced her flesh. I found myself enrapt with the bright flush filling her face and the soft sound that escaped her rubied lips had me groaning. I inhaled the scent of her smoky blood as a drop escaped.

My tongue met it as Vegas shivered and grasped my shirt, pulling me closer.

The scent of her blood in the air was like the sweetest scent on earth. As my lips trailed to the other side, I breathed in the soft midnight rain scent that drifted from her skin. I could die happy with her scent around me. Without permission, my teeth broke her flesh and pleasure rocked me straight to my core as my dick began to fight the tightness of my pants. Byron had told me the first bite would leave a silver mark and I was glad I'd picked such a viewable place. I wanted my mark on her.

I groaned against her skin because she tasted far better than anything I'd ever experienced. I let the smoky taste seep into my entire system as a small whimper came from her soft red lips as she began to roll her hips between the two of us. I honestly think I could come from this alone.

"Please," she cried softly. Byron chuckled but pulled away. I took a deep breath as I pulled back meeting her eyes. I could feel true shock radiating through me at the pure love that filled me and filled our bond. I'd always loved Vegas but this was something else. This was something more pure than human emotions. It wasn't possible to describe it.

There was a moment where the three of us paused as if the realization of our connection had us taking a breath. Then without warning, lust so violent that I nearly buckled, coursed through me. Byron tugged off her sweater as I practically shredded her leggings, not bothering to save her panties or the bra Byron tossed to the side. Vegas's skin shimmered under the dark lights as her nipples grew tighter and her head fell back against Byron's shoulder. Her body trembled with need and I felt my control snap into place, knowing I needed it to ensure she felt fantastic. I wanted this experience ingrained her fucking psyche.

"Lean her back," I demanded with a growl as Byron bit down again and pulled her against him so that she was laid out and completely exposed to me. Was it wrong that the predator side of me was thrilled at how she was exposed to me in such a submissive way? I wanted to devour her like a lion would its prey. I groaned as I began to kiss her soft smooth legs. I let her peel off my shirt but didn't stop the kisses until I found the exact soft flesh I'd been looking for. I bit down on the soft flesh of her thigh, claiming her, as she shot off the bed in a cry of pleasure.

Relief shot through our connection as I realized, with a masculine satisfaction, that she had just climaxed. I groaned at the feel of her hands pulling my hair as I ran my nose along the apex of her thigh, breathing in her desire. Her climax had made her impossibly wetter and my mouth watered at the thought of tasting her mixed with the blood on my lips.

I looked up at her, noticing that Byron was light marking places of her body as blood began to drip down in intoxicating patterns he licked as they fell. I groaned as I ran a finger along her soaked slit and she let out a loud moan.

"Does this turn you on, beautiful?" I asked, my voice confident as she hissed out at Byron's fingers trailing and teasing her breasts. Shit. I was starting to understand why Bandit liked watching.

"You know," she gasped and whimpered with closed eyes, "it does. Damn it. Blue, please."

I chuckled and let my tongue trail along her slit as Byron bit, her voice raw and calling out both our names. I practically came from the taste of her silky warmth against my mouth. My hands tightened on her thighs as I began to lick her sweetness. She squirmed against my mouth and tongue.

"Blue," Byron grated before lifting her sweet, tight ass off his lap. "We've got to move her or else I'm going to end up coming and I want to be buried in her fuckable mouth before I do that."

Vegas let out a cry of near distress as I moved away but I quickly sucked on her clit with a light graze of teeth before flipping her around. I fucking loved seeing her on all fours and I wrapped my hands in her hair as she braced herself slightly over Byron.

Goddamn. I loved this woman.

I could feel her excitement and curiosity. I was suddenly thankful there were ten of us because I wasn't positive that a single one of us would be able to keep up with her sex drive. I gently bit her back leaving a mark and letting the blood pool and trail down her spine. I couldn't help but spread it out along her skin, smearing its perfect white texture with crimson. My teeth nearly hurt from the tension I held in my body.

"Trouble," Byron's voice was sharp as he tilted her head up and pressed a thumb to her plush lips. "I want these wrapped around me. Can you do that for me?"

"Yes!" Her answer ended in a cry as I pressed right into her, my pants barely undone as my cock sank into her heavenly warmth. Byron cursed as she leaned forward to unbuckle his pants and brought her mouth around him.

I grasped her hips in a bruising hold as red marks began to appear and her mouth dipped up and down on Byron. I could feel my body tensing and I could barely push through her as she tightened around me. This was heaven. The sounds of the three of us were fucking erotic as hell.

"Blue," she gasped as she gagged on Byron. His eyes shut

as he gripped her hair in a tight hold, one I'd normally hate but I was far too focused on the way those silver strands were becoming darkened on the tips with blood. My tongue teased along her spine as I tasted blood and sweat on her skin. My pace quickened as I caused her to cry around Byron. I loved Vegas this way, completely naked and wild, between any two of us. Or more. Fuck it. As long as she felt good. I tightened my grip as I began to fuck her harder, sending sounds throughout the room that matched the smell of sex.

"Fuck her mouth is so perfect" Byron muttered through gritted teeth as her sexy head bobbed up and down and her back arched. I ground my jaw as I forced myself to not come yet. I continued to demand her pleasure as I strummed her clit and she moaned around Byron.

"Do you like this, beautiful?" I whispered. "Do you like being between us?"

She nodded as I continued to grind into her. Fuck, she was so perfect. I also felt my aggression and worry abating. She was safe between the two of us and that made me feel far better than any physical release. A sense of possession ripped through me as I bit down on the soft part of her upper back and she cried out.

She shouted something incoherent as I continued to slam into her ruthlessly. Byron's hands tightened as he grasped her face gently while fucking her mouth until climax. Vegas moaned as I reached my climax, my movements faster than humanly possible. My thumb pressed right against her tight little ass while I bit down leaving another mark on her spine. Blood poured and stained the cream colored silk sheets that were turning more red by the moment.

"Fuck!" she cried out. Her sounds had me coming. I

groaned as I slammed into her and filled her, my head falling against her spine as I continued to spill into her. Fucking shit. Despite my exahustion, I totally licked up the blood from her shoulder like some feral fucking animal. There was a lot of blood around us. Normally, I'd be worried about blood loss because it was *a lot of blood*. As it stood, her bites were healing rapidly. Almost too fast. I wanted to leave more of a mark. Silence echoed through the bedroom as we all collapsed against one another.

Her head rested on Byron's chest as he breathed roughly, blood dripping down his mouth and shirt. I'm sure I looked no fucking better with my pants barely pulled up and half-collapsed over Vegas. Goddamn did I want to keep her here though. Safe. If she was between us she couldn't get hurt.

"Beautiful," I murmured, "that was hot as fuck."

"Thank you, thank you," she teased her eyes half closed. "I'm here all day."

Byron chuckled. "Well, in that case…"

A knock on the door had all of us groaning. I rolled to the side but tugged a blanket up over Vegas's half-naked form. I met Edwin's amused expression as he looked at all the blood on the bed and her sated expression, her sleepy eyes light and happy.

"You know," Edwin spoke with amusement, "I really hate to interrupt the fun as usual. But we are about to take off."

"We're going to be in here," Byron muttered and tugged the two of them under the blanket fully. I offered a head nod to Edwin before crawling into the other side. Her back was pressed to Byron so that I could have her head against my chest. The smell of blood made me feel content as I thought about how a piece of her was embedded in my fucking body now.

"Beautiful?" I asked quietly.

"Yeah?" she whispered, her eyes sleepy. I knew her well enough to know that she was nearly passed out. Barely conscious.

"I love you," I murmured.

"I love you both," she drawled with a yawn. "So much."

Byron stiffened as his eyebrows went up and eyes colored with shock. I could feel the surprise radiating through him at her words. I realized he probably hadn't assumed how Vegas felt. At least not fully. That was how it was with Vegas though. Once she loved you, there was no going back.

"She's never said it to you?" I asked curiously.

Byron met my gaze and shook his head looking rather lost. "No."

"She means it," I noted softly. "She may not remember saying it, what with the excessive blood loss and all. But she means it. Vegas never says anything she doesn't mean."

He nodded wordlessly and put his forehead against her shoulder in thought. I looked up at the ceiling and took a deep breath, feeling a bit better after not being able to fucking kill that piece of shit earlier. I mean he probably won't be walking anywhere soon, but still. He deserved more.

My mind flashed over the past twenty-four hours as I shook my head. It had been a crazy fucking day and we had a lot more questions than answers. One of my main concerns right now being Bandit. I thought I knew that kid like the back of my hand but I was starting to think there was something far larger at play regarding his place in this world. Putting aside all of the other issues we were facing, namely with this stalker, I wasn't positive that we were making the right move going to the Horde.

Wasn't that closer to Victor?

I supposed Gray would be a level of protection that Earth didn't have but I had no means of gauging what this guy was possible of. I held in a snarl and a small sick smile at what I would do the minute I got my hands on the fucker.

My hands skimmed over Vegas's smooth, naked waist as I thought back towards the pregnancy test. I didn't feel remorse for the dark, animalistic part of me that wanted her to get knocked up. It was wrong, right? That I wanted to tie her to me in anyway possible? Still. I didn't care. I wanted her to be ours forever and besides marriage, something I planned on solving soon, that was the other for sure way. At least, that was what the more primal part of my mind was telling me. I think I knew that she would never leave us...but just in case.

With a sigh, I glanced at Byron and noted that the Ivanov brothers and I needed to talk. My eyes fell shut into the first real sleep this week. Vegas's blood was on my lips as I entered into the dream sphere.

11

VEGAS

"*Oh... little flame,*" *a soft menacing voice sang. It echoed around the dark caged room as my eyes snapped open. I briefly wondered if this cage was his sadistic creation or here to keep me protected. I hoped for the latter.*

"Kitty," Booker whispered wrapping his arms around me, their warmth keeping me anchored. I met his velvet eyes as sudden fear overrode comfort. Why was he here?

"Booker," I clasped his face while turning into him. "You need to leave. Now!"

He shook his head, his eyes darkening, as he slowly looked behind me. I felt my eyes widen at his expression. I'd seen a lot of expressions on Booker's face over the years, from joy to shy smiles. This anger though? This fury? It was liquid velvet magic wrapping around us in the form of thick orbs of ink. I felt my hands fidget in an attempt to reach out and touch them. I knew they'd welcome me.

"He drew himself into your dream," Victor's voice chided. "Smart boy. Very smart."

"Let her go," Booker hissed in recognition of my mental

imprisonment. His voice had a deeper, darker edge that nearly reminded me of Rocket.

"She's mine," Victor purred while pacing outside the cage. His swirling robes were the only sign of this movement. The rest of him was hidden by shadows. "I will let her wake up when I want. Besides, I know she wants to know what I have to tell her. Don't you, little flame?"

I turned back towards the cage bars as Booker wrapped himself around me, his ink kissing my skin as he rested his lips on my silver bite marks. I figured they would have healed fairly fast considering the fantastic sex, but this was quicker than I'd even expected. I tried to not think about such wonderful memories amidst the horror of the current scenario.

Victor, nearly as if he could read my mind, let out a low growl. "Soon, girl, you won't think of anyone else but me."

I snarled as my power sparked under his command. "I'm not afraid of you, so say your fucking piece and let us go."

"Good," he whispered as a pale hand wrapped around the bars. "I don't need you to be afraid of me. My father on the other hand? Well, I think you will find that Gray's kingdom is hard-pressed for time with their upcoming battle. You should be very afraid of what he will do. Of who he will hurt."

"Explain." I tried to not let the panic overwhelm me. He was just doing what he knew best. He was simply playing on my weakness. My weakness that I'd thought I had been striving to fix.

"I mean that yesterday there was an attack on their northern border," he stated softly. "I give it only a few days until my father commands his entire army south."

"Why are you telling us this?" Booker asked softly, his magic soothing my fear and keeping my warmth trapped around us so this place didn't leech it out of me. I knew instinctively that it

would. After a time, it would blow out my flame. Victor would destroy my flame.

"I am warning Vegas! Not any of you. I am telling her because she has a choice to make. A choice I warned her about. I can stop him my little flame, stop the massacre that will occur while he chooses to extract Gray quietly. All I require is you. It can be as peaceful as walking across the landlines..."

"No," Booker warned softly. I squeezed his hand.

I had figured that when I reached this point in time, I would have done the predictable thing but that didn't seem like the right answer. While my instincts were towards self-sacrifice, I also knew that could do more harm than good. I didn't trust that they wouldn't still attack. I didn't trust that throwing myself on the proverbial grenade would solve anything. After all, he was admitting that Gray would still be in danger. My power purred in agreement and seemed happy to be able to distinguish a self-sacrifice worth making and one that was pure folly.

Side note? Fuck you, King Mario. I couldn't wait to see Gray kill the bastard.

"I am far more useful fighting with them then giving myself over to a man's word I don't trust. I would be used as leverage predictably and I won't be playing this game with you. Now. I would very much like to wake up."

My scream was loud as the floor underneath us began to splinter and break apart. Booker grunted as his magic exploded from orbs into massive ink splotches that kept the surrounding rubble from hurting us. I tried to not look at the ink splotches because right now was not the time to make a weird comparison to the Rorschach test. I felt my head squeeze painfully as the floor finally gave out and the cage walls collapsed in. A roar of fury I'd mistaken for an earthquake broke through the ink barrier and caused a snarl to leave my lips.

"Hang on, Kitty," Booker whispered as we were plunged into complete darkness.

"Puppy?" I whispered my voice softer after minutes of sitting in silence. Our warm bodies were pressed together and I could feel the cold attempting to affect us. I tried to not listen to the odd sounds around us, but my hearing was overcompensating for my lack of sight. My breathing turned rough as Booker's heart began to beat rapidly against my back. My power was trying to spark but it was just so cold.

So cold.

Then a sound began to play. A light tune that would have been pretty if it wasn't for the broken keys and static. Like an old-timey piano tune through a 1940s radio. I felt my breath still as my hearing began to reach out, no longer okay with being in the dark. I barely knew what we were standing on nor what was around us. We chose not to move. I prayed the creepy music would go away.

Not a lucky day for me clearly.

"Whatever happens," Booker whispered nearly inaudibly, *"do not let go of me. Something broke the connection between his pull on us and our place within the real world."*

Solid. Good. Limbo. I like it.

"Ve," a soft voice whispered from somewhere in front of me. I refused to answer.

"Ve?" It spoke again as I jumped. The music was closer this time and I began to shake as Booker wrapped me protectively in his ink. It felt like a shield.

"Booky?" A woman's voice spoke in a cheery tone. *"Booky? Mama's been looking for you all day!"*

The man behind me froze. I gathered the voice was Booker's mother. The one that had abandoned him.

"Ve!" A voice screamed in my ear. I refused to break as both of us fought to remain silent. A chill had broken across my entire

body and my heart was beating so loud I was worried it would break from my chest.

"Booky!" The saccharine sweet voice sounded again, this time closer. The music shuddered to a stop. A slower, more desperate and sketchy tune, like some twisted carnival midway, began that made the air around us rumble. I could feel Booker's chin over my head as we began to feel the air squeeze at us. Whatever it was, it wanted through our barriers.

When all of the music and voices suddenly shut off, I knew we were in trouble.

Our rough breathing was the only audible sound. I closed my eyes because it truly didn't change anything. Booker's paint scent comforted me but I couldn't let my body relax. When a loud sound echoed, like a steel door closing, both of us snapped ours heads behind us. Instinctively.

"Fuck!"

I crashed into Booker as we fell backwards onto a rough rock surface. All at once, several things occurred. My mouth opened in a soundless scream as the individual who'd caused such shock peered down at us. Individual? Creature? No. This was a mirrored face. A portrait? It was shadowed and a pair of empty eyes and expressionless features looked down at us. Seemingly not attached to a body and pure white in color. No pupils, nostrils. Almost like an unfinished sketch.

The second we hit the ground my flames roared to life and Booker grunted in pain at the power rocking through him. His ink held, though, and my eyes widened at the sudden chaos around us. I paused as both of us looked around the illuminated room, somehow no longer focused on the phantom mirror.

"What are they?" he whispered in horror.

I had no idea.

"Ve!" One of them screeched as the white, scaled creatures

crawled towards us. They were long and skinny, like snakes but with human hands and purple eyes. Holy shit!

"Booky!" Another crawled forward as hundreds surrounded us on the black obsidian rock on which we were sprawled. The room was a massive cave-like structure. Silver liquid surrounded us, housing the serpentine creatures.

"Vegasssss," another one gave a sibilant hiss. "Where is Vivi? What happened to poor Vivi, Vegas?"

My magic seethed at the pain rocking through me as Booker's ink pulsed. I leaned back against him as I looked around, knowing the only thing stopping these creatures was Booker's ability to use his magic so well. Was it because we were in the dreamscape? Or had he somehow advanced further than I realized?

"What is that?" he asked in my ear. All the creatures shrieked. My eyes spied a dark ball of energy that rose from the silver and caused the horrible white scaly animals to jump back into the liquid. I was relieved but stood cautiously with Booker. Had we jumped from the frying pan into the fire?

"If this is the fucking 'white light' that everyone talks about, I'm asking for a refund," I mumbled as Booker, despite the situation, chuckled. We watched as the black light mutated into a lilac color and shifted into a humanoid form.

This was some Glinda from the Wizard of Oz shit. If this woman asked me if I was a good or bad witch, I might lose it. Scratch that. I would lose it. One hundred percent.

"Is that..." Booker began, but I had already had the same thought. Gray?

No. It wasn't. Not exactly. I swallowed as the figure's feet touched the lake and walked up the rocky surface. My eyes followed her onyx colored hair, trailing along the silver surface, as she kept her dark eyes on the two of us. I tried to not freak out, my chest heaving, as my fire sparked and I positioned myself in front of Booker.

FIRE & SMOKE

"Ve," she called. The woman's voice was flute-like.

The wind rushed out of my system as if my magic recognized the woman.

"Who are you?" I demanded softly. "Where the fuck are we?"

She tilted her head while keeping a polite distance. The woman wore a silver gown that was nearly iridescent. It nearly looked painted on. When she spoke my mouth popped open in true surprise.

"I am your creator," she whispered reaching a hand forward through the ink as it welcomed her. She laced her hand with mine. "And her mother."

My ears turned bright red. I'd just cussed in front of a queen. I shrugged.

Wouldn't be the first time. But, hold the goddamn phone. Gray's mother?

"You are the previous queen?"

Just needed to make fucking sure.

She smiled and looked at Booker without answering. "I see you found one of your ten?"

"All of them, actually," I blurted breathlessly. A million questions flooded my brain.

"So, you created me? Why? How are you here? Where the hell are we?" My thoughts were a rambled mess.

Her long finger silenced my lips and she spoke sincerely. "I don't have much time before your men try to awaken both of you and I am already fighting against a very angry Dark Fae prince. Unlike my natural child, you hold a piece of my power inside of yourself and that allows us to stay connected despite my energy's passage out of this realm. It is because of this that I need you to warn others of what is to come."

"The war?" I asked quietly.

Her eyes softened. "So much more than that, dear child. You were born not just to be a weapon in Gray's battles but to serve *the entire realm. As the only sorceress created in thousands of years, you have the ability to affect so much. Change so much and not just in the Horde. It is up to you to harness that power. Where Gray was meant to lead the Horde into the next generation of power and peace, you were meant to change the Fae lands for good."*

Oh. Well. Then. No fucking pressure, lady. I would get some vacation time first, right? Right?!

"I think my power is broken," I whispered, ignoring the internal hiss. "I can't seem to get complete control of it. I feel like every time I get emotional..."

"There will be mistakes," she interrupted gently. *"But you have to remember, Ve, that you are magic. It isn't a switch. It is a part of your very essence and all you need to do is embrace it."*

"Okay," I accepted. I think I'd known that. We had already begun bonding far more than simply a few days ago.

"Plus," she touched my cheek before stepping back, *"the sooner you release your powers, the easier your men will find control over theirs."*

Yes. Please tack on the responsibility.

"Thank you," I added as she smiled at me and then Booker.

Before she left I spoke clearly, "Wait! What is this place? What were those? And the weird face?"

The woman's eyes lit with mischief, *"this? This is the dream realm and there are many creatures that live within it. This is the place that nightmares grow up. This is the place you should fear the most sweet girl."* Her silver light followed her as the darkness closed around us again. This time, however, the large creepy creatures didn't return.

Trippy... just trippy as hell.

"Please, tell me that was real," Booker whispered.

"There are two of us. We can't both be crazy right?"

Then the yelling began. I cringed as familiar voices began to *echo around us and Booker grunted out a curse. I clung to him as the room began to shake and my chest imploded with tension.*

This was going to hurt.

VEGAS

I wasn't positive when I first became conscious. I could hear yelling and my entire body screamed with pain as the faint smell of blood filled the air. Reality seemed to flicker and when a warm healing power washed over me I cringed. I was so cold that I felt my toes would fall right off. My mouth opened to speak but instead a scream filtered out.

Then everything went black. Until now.

"*Mi tesoro,*" a soft warm voice whispered against my face. "I need you to wake up."

"I promise she's alright," Booker stated, his voice thick. "She's just has been through a lot."

"Did that really happen?" Cosimo asked. "You drawing yourself into her dream? Gray's mom? It sounds so unbelievable."

"Almost as unbelievable as you being able to heal the damage our bodies suffered from being ripped through dimensions? Yeah. I know how it sounds," Booker muttered.

"Your ink saved both of your asses, it could have been far worse Booker," Cosimo's accent grew thicker with concern and sadness.

I shivered as my eyes began to flutter open. Instantly my nose was assaulted with the soft scent of a land that was home yet so new to me. It was so fucking comforting. My jaw clenched as I sat up and met a pair of soft velvet eyes and Cosimo's concerned diamond ones.

"Shit," I muttered looking around my bedroom. We were

in the Horde. Hadn't it been Saturday night when I'd passed out?

"You've been out for nearly two days," Cosimo answered my question. Somehow. I exhaled as Booker adjusted my blanket and both men angled closer to me, watching and waiting for me to say something. Anything. It was then that I caught sight of the massive dark wolf at the bottom of the bed. He was tense but sleeping.

Poor Kodiak. I shook my head knowing that until my powers and theirs were under control, his anxiety and emotions would cause him to shift.

"Everyone else finally went to bed after Blue and Edwin threatened them." Booker motioned to two figures stretched across some couches near the fireplace. "What that threat was, I still don't know."

I smiled. Silly boys. I studied each of them and resisted the urge to snap a photo. It was clear the two of them had been in deep conversation based on the amber liquid left in crystal glasses on a near by table. Edwin was spread out with his head back and legs spread. Blue had tossed his feet up on the table, his back against Edwin's shoulder. It was so cute.

"Kodi," I whispered. His huge, shaggy head popped up and I smiled softly as he let out a soft low whine. My hand reached out and he nuzzled his nose into it before jumping off the bed. He disappeared into the bathroom and I knew he'd be out soon.

"How are you feeling?" Cosimo asked with a soft kiss drawing me back into the comfort of the bed.

"Exhausted," I whispered as Booker hummed and both of them drew me tighter between them. Then Kodi walked out in his basketball shorts and bare chest, his eyes dark and jaw tense. I put my hands out and after grabbing another blanket, he crawled forward between my legs and wrapped his arms around my waist. Tonight I craved the feel of his slightly shadowed facial hair on my smooth stomach. He didn't disappoint.

"Are you sleeping in here?" I asked Booker because Cosimo was already dozing off as he slung a leg over Kodi's muscular back. I loved my pile of puppies.

My artist looked hesitant for a moment. I knew he had physicality issues, but I needed him. He seemed to sense it because he tugged off his shirt and began undoing his hair from a tight braid. I gave him a sleepy smile as he wrapped an arm around my shoulder so I was nestled snugly between the three of them. I know it was terrible timing but in some ways this felt like a victory. Booker was sleeping in the same bed as us. He was relaxed against me and felt safe.

"Vegas?" Kodi asked softly as I peered down at him.

"Yeah?" I asked softly.

"Thank you for telling him no," he whispered, his eyes darkening as I realized Booker had told them everything that had happened. I offered Kodi a real smile.

"I can't help my lack of preservation but there is no point to it if it won't keep all of you safe." I mussed his hair. "That wouldn't have been useful at all."

Kodi nodded and Booker chuckled softly but kept his eyes closed. "Well, it did something useful alright."

"What's that?"

"I think you will find everyone is far more amped up about all of this than before. If Gray hadn't been planning on a war, one would have found the Dark Fae anyway."

My laugh was authentic as I closed my eyes. *My boys aggressive? Violent? War like?*

Never.

12

VEGAS

*S*leep eluded me despite my body's aching need for it. I think I'd just reached a point where there was so much on my mind that my body wouldn't settle until it was handled. I gave up as dawn broke through the hazy warm bedroom window. It was completely dark in the room, on the predicted Monday morning, except for the gray light. The curtains, thick and heavy, made it seem intimate and the soft sounds of breathing from my boys were like the sweetest sonnet.

I took a deep breath and refocused myself on the day.

I crawled out of bed and left the room to find a shower that wouldn't wake everyone up. I wanted them to sleep. They needed to sleep. My clothing was tucked under my arm as I smiled softly in reaction to the shadows twisting around my ankles like a cat.

Maybe I needed a fucking pet.

Without knocking, I slipped into the closest bedroom I found. Rocket's room. I was nearly soundless but Rocket still squinted open an eye as I nodded towards the shower. He curled a tan finger at me as I crept towards the bed.

"Sugar," his voice was rough as he sat up, pulling me close enough that his lips were on my temple. "You scared me yesterday. You and Booker both."

My throat tightened as I reached for his face. "I'm sorry." I also was sorry because despite his serious words, my eyes continued to flicker down to his shirtless ripped torso. I nearly groaned at *my* fire tattoos on his skin. I wanted to trace each and every line with my tongue... and I'm turned on again.

He shook his head and pulled me into a tight hug. "No need to apologize. Ever. I just can't lose either of you, Vegas. It would break me."

Fuck. I knew just how much it took for him to say that. His stern face was so earnest and vulnerable. Not uncomfortable but very emotional. I could watch him every day for a year and he would never portray as much emotion as he was in this moment. I kissed his power, a raw force, with my flames as his lip curled up in a sexy, cute way. I echoed the kiss with a slight lip brush.

"I love you," I whispered softly.

He hummed and brushed a finger across my bottom lip. "I hope you know how much I love you. How much I need you."

My body shivered as he chuckled and lifted me to stand. "Go on now. You have a shower to take. I can't imagine you feel very clean after dealing with everything yesterday. Plus, Booker mentioned some scaly white creatures."

I scowled. "Don't remind me, but on that note, can't I just stay in bed with you?"

"Later," he flashed me a smile and nodded towards the door. I turned to find Edwin standing there with dark eyes and a tense posture, fully dressed in a suit.

Oh, man. Someone wasn't coping well.

"Meet me in the gardens?" he asked his voice wavering but still commanding.

"Let me shower and I'll be right down," I offered softly. He nodded and walked away. I let out a slow breath. I could just feel the tension in the house. It was very clear that they were very well aware of what happened and my only question was how in the hell would I tell Gray. I figured I would tell her when I saw her, but then I also had no idea how I would even broach that topic.

Hey, so I know we totally are besties but - fun fact! We are actually sisters! I'm also made of magic for your humble weapon use and apparently, your mom, who appeared to me in a dreamscape, believes I can change the entire Fae realm. Pretty cool, right?'

I shook my head as I began to cleanse my body from the previous travel. Streams of dried blood fell to the tile in light pink rivulets that caused a shiver to ripple across my skin. I closed my eyes and let my fingers linger over my healed bite marks as I thought back to how Byron tasted and the way Blue's teeth felt piercing my skin. I wanted their mouths on me again. Good news? I was officially living out my fantasy of having vampire boyfriends. Also, I had clearly slept through the loopy part of blood loss.

My hair was growing thicker and I found myself nearly annoyed with it for the first time in forever. I scrubbed it and once done, I hopped out of the shower and looked at my soaking wet locks. If only I had a way to instant dry. I smiled and realized if I tried this I would either burn my hair and skin off or it would work.

Instead of using flames I focused on heating my skin up just slightly, not unlike how I'd burned Gabriel to let go of me at the party. I grinned as the water evaporated off my skin on command and my hair began to dry into a smooth healthy wave of silver. Even my bangs curled underneath correctly. Christ. These were the perks of magic! Right fucking here. My lips were colored dark today and my eyes a deeper purple than before.

I frowned, who the hell had carried me through the portal? What was even going on anymore?

I slipped on a soft red dress. I know. Unusual, but it fit the medieval vibe of the Horde fairly well. It was made of comfortable, likely expensive material. It hung off the shoulders with long loose sleeves and pulled in at the waist only to float back out. It was warm and comfortable. I slipped a small pair of hard-soled slippers with little fluffy fronts.

Yep. Cute little slippers.

Fuck the system. I would not wear shoes.

My light footsteps carried me downstairs as I followed the shadows towards the French doors and massive patio. Unlike Boston, the Horde still maintained a massive amount of fall foliage and the garden was blooming with seasonal red, orange, and black flowers. My head tilted at the sight of all the unnatural plant life. Well, unnatural to Earth.

I knelt down as my fingers traced the edges of a black rose. It's petals opened underneath my fingers in response. I breathed in their light scent and opened my eyes to find Edwin, standing at the pathway looking nearly lost. Lost and somewhat heartbroken, which made no sense.

I shivered as a memory slammed into me from nowhere.

"Ve!" Edwin called out as Byron kept a hand over my mouth from laughing. I was bouncing on my toes, my soft purple dress matching Byron's jacket.

"Sh," Byron whispered, his smile contagious. "We can't let him win this time."

"If you don't come out, I'm going to send my shadows out," Edwin teased, his voice charming as always, making me feel

completely enthralled with his presence. Edwin didn't know but I wanted his shadows to come out and play. My flames loved them like they loved Byron. He was my sun and Edwin my moon.

Byron tugged my hand as an icy chill ran over us, the fall skies darkening, as the game started and a thrill of excitement passed through me. I pointed for Byron to break off from me and he hugged me before sprinting off, my light footsteps avoiding the leaves and the grass burning ever so slightly against my bare feet.

I didn't have control over my powers like he did. Then again, Nicholas said he was special. My powers were unusual and he always said my magic had a life of its own. I knew he didn't mean it as an insult but it made me want to be like Edwin. When my moon had offered to help me control my flames with his shadows, I'd instantly accepted. There wasn't anything I didn't trust him with.

"Ve," Edwin's voice rang out. "I know you are nearby."

I jumped over a large bush and ran into the rose garden, the fall weather bringing black roses and a tug of joy in my stomach. My lips were hurting from smiling and when I finally fell to the ground amongst the roses on all sides, I couldn't help but giggle. I knew he'd find me.

"Gotcha!" Edwin chuckled as he tugged me up from the ground and I let out a squeak of laughter.

"Unfair!" I called out in a sad voice as he held me close. "The shadows were watching me."

Edwin's orange eyes warmed as he smoothed my hair. "Always, Ve, always."

Then he chuckled as one of his shadows wrapped around a rose and plucked it, without thorns, and rested the black-petaled plant in my small hand.

"These are my favorite," I told him earnestly as he began to lead me towards the large manor.

"I know," he offered softly while holding my other hand. "That's why they will always be here, no matter what."

"You promise?" I whispered as he simply squeezed my hand.

"Ve!" Byron laughed coming up on my other side. "You let him catch you?"

"His shadows saw me," I complained with a pout. "But look!"

Byron saw the flower and nodded as if he liked it as well, making my heart squeeze. He was always so nice and I knew, even when he didn't like something, that he would try to find it interesting for me. When Nicholas called all three of us to dinner, I kept the rose right next to me on the table. I wasn't afraid of it dying because I knew Edwin would always make sure there were more.

"Vegas?" Edwin's voice was soft and husky as my eyes opened to find that I was sitting on a stone bench on his lap in the middle of the rose garden. The very one from my memory. I felt my ears heat as I buried my head into the curve of his neck.

I sighed as his massive hand cupped the back of my head. I spoke in a teasing tone. "I still think I should have won that round of hide and seek."

Edwin's eyebrows went up as an authentic beautiful laugh broke through his lips. "You remember that day?"

I nodded and curled closer to him. "They are slowly returning. Small things like the rose gardens. I can't imagine what it was like growing up here. Can you tell me about it? What happened after I left?"

Edwin's eyes seemed to grow softer as a set of footsteps sounded, alerting me to Byron's presence. The massive man lifted a nearby patio chair and set it so that he could face us before lifting my feet into his lap. He smirked at my little slippers.

"You want to know more about us growing up?" Edwin

sighed with a distant look that wasn't sad but more thoughtful. "I mean, it was a far easier life than either of us would have had earthbound at our age. Our parents are fully caught up in ruling their home country but due to the promise we showed as mages in the Horde, Nicholas became our mentor and parent. They had other children so they barely …"

"You have siblings?" I jumped as Edwin kissed me softly to shut me up.

Bastard.

His lips smirked at that.

"When you came along a few months later, after my fifth birthday, the three of us were placed here for the following five years. It was amazing. I mean truly. It was those memories that got me through our time on the East Coast and with my parents."

"And Maria," Byron chuckled. "Maria was the best fake mom someone could ask for. Our real mother, bless her soul, is a terrible person."

"Byron!" I hit his arm playfully.

He offered me a bright smile. "No, really, Trouble. She hates everyone."

"No pressure if I ever meet them!" I exclaimed.

Edwin grinned. "What are they going to say? I'm the fucking heir and Byron is their golden child despite his attitude towards it. Now the polyamourous concept may make a few people uncomfortable when we get married…"

I put my hands over my ears as Byron squeezed my foot.

"Oh, no you don't! I hate when all of you joke around."

"It's not a joke," Edwin cemented before continuing on a little more relaxed. "Anyway, after we parted ways I had eyes on you as we formed the Red Masques and aided in the discovery and relocation of our other eight."

"Edwin was very tempted to show up randomly," Byron chuckled. "He left a few shadows with you more often than not."

"That is so sweet," I offered a shy smile.

Edwin rolled his eyes. "Obsessive. Sweet. It's a fine line."

"What is obsessive," Byron pointed out, "was when you saw she had written several papers on Edgar Allen Poe and named our entire organization after her favorite piece."

Oh, my gods.

"Really?!" I squeaked. Talk about flattering!

Edwin's ears heated as Byron massaged my foot causing me to groan internally. "He was very insistent. I would say it was pretty damn romantic if I hadn't had to hear his damn pacing back and forth over every tiny symbolic decision. I'm surprised that office still exists."

"As if you are so innocent," he chirped at his brother, "Really though, Vegas, he is right. I wanted to be part of your life in any way possible and Byron was completely on board so don't let him fool you."

Byron scowled as I just relished in how entertaining and amazing these men were. My throat tightened as I thought about how I wished, how I needed, for life to continue like this. I wanted the threat gone so that all eleven of us, thirteen if you counted my best friend and Miranda, to live in peace. God, I was totally acting like a nester.

"Where are Lucida and Miranda?" I asked softly with sudden realization.

Byron perked up. "Sleeping, I believe. They are going to get their tattoos today. As well, Gray would like to meet with you for some type of uniform fitting."

I nibbled my lip gently as Edwin hummed and stopped me with his thumb. "I need to tell her about what is going on. I just don't know how or when."

Edwin nodded looking very tired. "What happened last night was very upsetting."

Understatement.

With a deep breath I nodded. "Well, it's a new day and if he is right, we have about two or three days until Mario arrives. I can at least tell her that. I just have no idea how to explain how I know."

"I told Palo," Byron noted confidently. "He understands the sensitivity of the situation. He said he will make a note of it as a source of information."

"Thank you," I squeezed my sun's shoulder as my moon nuzzled my neck.

Goddamn it. I couldn't deny it. They were mine. I wasn't letting them go.

The fall air was crisp and I could feel the energy of the Horde building. It felt more savage than it had less than a week before. I frowned slightly as I slipped away from them and pressed my hand to the earth, letting the energy swirl around me and making my body surge with heat. This was the land that I'd been born from and as I thought about my creator, I realized that I could feel her energy inside of me. She was right. I was a part of her.

I'd never considered myself particularly in tune with nature but I could feel it here. I could feel the pulse of the Horde's life and essence transforming and growing with each moment of the day. The center of that power and change was the castle. Somehow I knew that Gray was causing the land to flourish and it was truly authentically amazing to experience.

It was fascinating everything I was learning about my magic in such a short time. I knew that was a good thing because it seemed to help my boys. More than that, I was starting to feel as though I was stepping into the role that had always been meant for me. It felt right.

I wish there was some way to show how much they meant to me. I knew I had the one tattoo and my hand markings but those felt predestined. I wanted something of my own. An idea hit me as my lips pressed together.

"Byron?" I asked softly looking up at the blood mage. "I can go with Miranda and Luci, right? I want to be there for the tattoo."

He tilted his head to the side and nodded looking at the dawn sky. "Actually that's a good idea. They should probably be waking up soon as it is. Gray wanted to have an early afternoon meeting."

"What are you doing today?" I looked back at Edwin. His eyes had been on my lips and they moved up as he offered me a cheeky smile. Now why did I feel like he was thinking dirty things? I narrowed my eyes as he grinned more.

Then he groaned and put his head down. "Today? Today, I need to go to the Red Masques headquarters. Possibly even the academy if I feel like we don't have enough teams to handle this. Hopefully, Victor was exaggerating because I would really like to get a few training sessions with our full team before Mario decides to attempt another attack."

I swallowed nervously as my eyes shot down. "Are there a lot of them? The Red Masques?"

Byron squeezed my hand. "Don't worry about that, Ve. Your magic isn't comparable to theirs."

That wasn't exactly what I was worried about. Well, in a way I was, but it was more that we would be behind in all of this magic shit. I started to respond but the back door swung open. I nearly chuckled at the sight of Lucida barrelling down the path like a kid on Christmas. Her clothing was casual, more than normal, and she wasn't wearing makeup.

"Finally!" she exclaimed, jumping up and down. "Good to know you are alive, Ve! Now, let's go! I want to do this magic thingy! Even Miranda is up."

Holy crap, my ears.

"Coffee," I demanded as both boys released me and we began to walk side by side, the three of us listening to Lucida's excitement. Honestly, it was pretty cute. When Miranda offered me a large mug of coffee I smiled in a thankful way.

Edwin kissed my lips in a surprising brush as the four of us stood near the door. I felt bad about not saying goodbye to the boys but I knew I'd see them in a few hours. He must have sensed my hesitation.

"I will let them know where you are before I leave."

I mouthed thanks as my best friend dragged me off the estate. Bitch better not spill my coffee by accident.

VEGAS

It was nearly an hour later that we were sitting at a very familiar table. I was on Byron's lap as his nose trailed my skin and a soft rumble of comfort came from his chest. Laurena, Athen's and Neo's mother and now Mage Representative, began preparing the blood ink. I cringed as she handed Byron a small knife and she offered me a sympathetic look.

Lucida and Miranda were silent and wide eyed. I'd never seen them so quiet and she was looking at Laurena as if she was Queen of the Fucking Universe. Just wait until she meets Gray. Without hesitation, I took the knife from his hand, the stone bowl underneath us. I cupped his massive hand and brought it down to his palm.

I didn't want him ever taking a knife to his own skin again.

Those warm eyes grew darker as the moment became oddly intimate, the knife pressing into his flesh as I made a quick cut. The scent of blood permeated the air and you could hear it dripping into the stone surface. Without looking away he slid the bowl towards the other three who were talking in low tones. I automatically took the white cloth bandage nearby and wrapped his hand gently, knowing he would only need it for an hour. When I finished, I looked back up and found an indecipherable expression on his face, filled with confusion and intensity.

It looked like he had something to say but when he looked up behind me, he frowned. I stood up and tugged him so that we were walking from the small cottage's back patio to face a thick lush garden. I could smell Laurena mixing the potion and I kissed Byron's palm as he held me close, his big body wrapped around mine.

A light, cold dewy rain fell around us, creating a misty vision of the scenery and making us feel almost as if we were alone. I could see the dampness in his messy blonde hair and I ran a hand through it just to feel the silky white texture. A sensation in my chest that had nothing to do with magic began building.

I knew damn well what it was and something about this morning had cemented it.

"What were you thinking about in there?" I asked softly with my eyes meeting his. For the first time ever his eyes were a rich brown filled with streaks of gold and green. I wondered briefly if that would have been his eye color if he hadn't been a mage.

"You," he answered, his voice thick with emotion.

He spoke again in a low nearly pained voice. "Why did you take the knife from me?"

Oh.

My ears heated slightly. "I don't ever want you taking a knife to yourself. Ever."

Silence permeated the area for just a moment. He seemed shocked by my answer and then overwhelmed, his face growing pale almost. I smoothed his jaw, reaching way up, as a flash of determination flipped through his eyes hard enough to give me whiplash. His large arms reached behind me to pick me up so that my butt was seated comfortably on his crossed arms. I liked being eye level with him.

"Why would you do that?" he asked in a barely audible voice.

Why would I do that?

Because I didn't want him to hurt himself? Because it represented an action that brought him harm and self-doubt? Because I didn't want him to associate magic with pain anymore? Because...

Well, shit.

"Because I love you."

For just a moment everything from the dewy rain around us to the noise inside seemed to pause. Then Byron's lips melded into mine like a hot wax seal. I inhaled sharply as he kissed me in such an intense and hungry way I practically clawed at his clothes for more. My entire body broke into a heated shiver that had him breaking away with eyes that bled into a bright red. They spoke to his magic's reaction to my words. Even his hair seemed to be lightening, as if his glamour was no longer holding. I could faintly see that his tattoos had broken through and I wondered if it was purposeful or if he hadn't realized it had happened.

"I love you, Ve," he whispered his emotions a whirlwind

on his beautiful tanned face. My heart squeezed as I shivered at his soft, almost pained whisper. His arms squeezed around me as the two of us pressed our foreheads together while our breathing became nearly synced.

"I love you so much," he choked and then made a low sound in the back of his throat. "I didn't think... I had no idea you could feel or did feel the same about me."

"Of course I love you. You're my sun." I whispered, offering him all my emotions. I wasn't lying. Byron was my sun and Edwin my moon.

Unshed tears began to build as he swallowed and squeezed me tighter. He offered a tight laugh, "Hate to tell you, Trouble, but I don't have much of a sunny disposition."

I didn't have the words to explain that his emotions fueled my own like the sun offered life. I didn't have the words to explain that he made me feel, good and bad. Intense and relaxed. He was like a cup that was constantly overflowing with emotions and reactions. A quality that seemed to light a fire under my ass and made me feel just a tad bit intense about everything. I offered him a slight smile and peppered his face with kisses. He was my sun and he could fucking deal with it. His glorious full smile that broke out made me wonder if he knew what I was thinking.

"I hate to interrupt," Miranda's voice sounded from the door as we both looked over. Literally everyone was always 'hating to interrupt.' I just didn't believe them. Her face was pink and she looked very sorry. Why did people continue to apologize if they were going to interrupt anyways?

"You okay?" Byron asked his voice thick as my own. I nodded and he offered me a bright smile and walked with me through the door and back to the seat we had inhabited before. I refused to move from his lap despite my concern that we may break the chair. Laurena offered me an understanding smile while Lucida wiggled her eyebrows.

Crazy bitch.

"All right," the ink mage started. "Who would like to go first?"

"Me!" Miranda stated as I noticed Lucida paling just slightly. I could tell she was a tad nervous and I understood that completely. It was a scary concept.

"What would you like your tattoo to look like? The rune will be hidden within it," she explained as Miranda sat in the chair across from her.

"Could you do a morning glory?" she asked pulling up her sleeve to expose tattoos. Holy crap, had I ever seen her without long sleeves? Maybe not that arm? She had an entire sleeve of flowers with only a few places not filled.

Laurena nodded and I closed my eyes, knowing when the stone needle hit her skin as magic blew through the room. I could instantly feel the difference in connection compared to the boys but her magic still spoke to me as most people's did. It seemed almost natural for me. I could smell the earth mixed with the soft patter of rain on leaves. It was akin to the rainforest.

"Elemental!" Laurena cheered with a happy expression as Miranda's eyes popped open. The blue was more green than before. The ink mage continued. "Specifically with an earth affinity, I believe."

"I agree," I stated softly as Miranda hopped up and squeezed Lucida's shoulder. My best friend shot me a nervous look and I smiled at her. She could do this. She was a total badass.

I think I knew what she was before the needle touched her skin. I wasn't surprised when the same earthy scent filled me with the undertone of animal noises exploding

FIRE & SMOKE

through the area. I could almost feel the jaguar underneath her skin as she paced restlessly and let out a deafening roar that had me jumping in my seat.

Here kitty, kitty... I was starting to believe that I was not a cat person.

"Holy crap!" Lucida explained looking down at the sleek black cat that was wrapping around her golden arm. Laurena smiled.

"Sometimes, I like to let the magic lead me," she explained and sat back. "Now, how do both of you feel?"

"Tired," Miranda yawned as thunder cracked outside.

"I imagine it will be a few days until you feel your normal," she stood up and walked towards the counter, where she began cleaning up.

"Wait!" I jumped up as Laurena raised her brows. I then turned back to Byron and offered him a smile. "Golden, do you mind waiting outside with the girls?"

He tilted his head and chuckled. "Sure, but we need to go to that meeting with Gray."

"When do we need to go to get to the castle?" I asked Byron.

"Within the hour," he stated but stood up walking towards the garden.

"Can they come with?" I pointed towards Miranda and Lucida. They both looked like eager children and Byron nodded signalling they follow him out. He was probably going to brief them on what to say and what not to say around Gray regarding our secret.

"Okay," I turned back to Laurena as she sat down and I pulled up my hair. "I was wondering if you could give me another tattoo? I have the silver bonded one and the pattern on my hands but I was hoping to do something along my upper back, down the spine."

I may have started on my path to becoming a tattoo addict. Was that a thing?

"What were you thinking?" She rose a dark brow.

"A quote. It can be small but I want it down my spine," I spoke quietly.

"Here," she pushed me a piece of paper. "Write it down because some of us have far too good of hearing."

I chuckled at her reference to my mage outside. I began writing as she aided loosening the back of my dress so that my entire spine would be exposed. I had asked her if she needed me to lay down but she just laughed and moved my hair to one side. I imagined she would write my tattoo from the top down. My hand began to write out my favorite piece from the Masque of the Red Death.

There are chords in the hearts of the most reckless which cannot be touched without emotion.

I closed my eyes as she began working and my heart squeezed in affection, thinking about how much I had grown to love these boys. Even my handsome and crazy magical asshats. We were an insane bunch, I mean truly mad. Yet, I saw the good in these men every single day and moment would not go by in our many years together that I wouldn't appreciate them. Despite my concern over King Mario's war, I tried to trust Bandit's word.

He didn't see us dying.

I had no idea how loose that interpretation was but I had to believe that we would not only survive this but that it would barely be a bump in the road. My breath hissed out as the magic from the tattoo, consistent of Byron's blood, surged through me. I could feel the hot flames of my magic roar to life in response and the bitch began to do a happy jig inside my head.

Yes. Yes. I know. You're happy.

"All right," Laurena spoke while wiping the skin with a cool cloth. "May I suggest changing? I have a backless dress. I'm not worried about the ink but the skin may be a tad tender for a few hours."

Or I could just have bomb ass sex to heal it.

I nodded and took the dark purple dress she offered. It was the perfect length and a tad big in the bust area but I was able to adjust it so that my back was exposed to the open air, my hair braided over my shoulder, and my slippers on. I took the bag she gave me and offered her a hug, leaving through the back door.

"Oh, thank god," Lucida complained dramatically. "The two of them are talking about *Dungeons and Dragons.*"

I chuckled and glanced over at an excited Miranda and interested Byron. "Golden, you play?"

He looked at me in mock horror lifting a hand to his chest. "I am not just a pretty face, Trouble. I'm offended."

I rolled my eyes as we walked towards the street. The girls were in front of us as I pointed toward the castle. Byron walked next to me until he looked at me with a frown. "Why the outfit change?"

Instead of answering I just hopped ahead so that he could see my back. I heard the inhale of breath as he caught up to me, lifting me up so he could see it better while walking. It was impressive but he was totally manhandling me. Which I shouldn't find sexy...

I'm sorry but he can totally just toss me around wherever he wants and instead he's super sweet. I mean, that is just some fucking perfect shit there. Hypothetically though, if he wanted to toss me around more I wouldn't mind. Especially in bed.

"Ve," he grinned offering me an amused look. "You may make Edwin cry with that."

I let him put me down as we kept pace with the girls. "You really think so?"

He chuckled and tossed me a look. "I know so. Whether he does it in front of you, we will see, but the guy is a total romantic. I mean there aren't a lot of men who would name their massive special forces organization in response to a poem that a woman in their life liked."

My cheeks heated as we approached the massive large gates. I had no response because the bastard was right. It was super fucking romantic. The guards let us through without question looking terrified of Byron which was a bit sexy. I couldn't deny that.

"Where did she say to meet them?" I asked curiously as Lucida tugged at my hand looking a tad overwhelmed. I smiled at my sister as Miranda smoothed over her back, her rational way of thinking having allowed her to already process all of it. Luci was a bit more like me. Noticed a lot and could be easily overwhelmed by it.

"Byron," a deep voice stated as all of us found Adyen, the massive giant dragon dude, standing in the hall waiting for us most likely.

"Adyen," Byron offered a smile as they exchanged one of those weird man handshakes.

"Hello," I chirped as Adyen offered me an amused look and then frowned at the other two women, probably worried and overprotective of Gray.

"This is my sister Lucida and her girlfriend Miranda," I informed him as he nodded.

"Well," he chuckled. "I'm certain Gray will love having more women to dress up."

"Huh?" I asked as Lucida and Miranda whispered behind me.

He shook his head as we walked. "The woman has been

playing around with materials all day. She is attempting to create leather uniforms for women. She's making, and these are her words, 'Henry the 8th Chic.'"

I snorted as we climbed a spiral staircase and I heard her voice.

"Marabella!" Gray whined. "You have to wear one, even if you don't fight. We will all be matching and it will be totally kickass. Look at Esme! She looks like, badass. Bobby, doesn't she look like a badass?"

We pushed through the door and heads turned our way. I barely had time to examine the massive circular stone room with its myriad of materials in different colors, before Gray was hugging me.

"You're here!" she exclaimed her dark hair whipping around like a snake. "Now you can help me explain why we need all of the women to wear a badass uniform."

A devious grin slipped on my face. "I actually have two more people for you to dress, Gray this is my sister Lucida and her girlfriend Miranda."

Gray's eyes lit up as she moved at an inhuman speed to gather both of them in a group hug. "Any friend of Vegas is my friend. It is so wonderful to meet you, now come, come. We have work to do."

This was the Gray whirlwind.

"Baby," Athens drawled from where he sat near Adyen. "You're going to give yourself a heart attack with how excited you are."

Gray ignored him and began to pull out materials as a woman with stunning dark hair, littered golden streaks in her curls, approached me. She offered me a smile as the scent of feline shifter surrounded me. I could see that Byron was talking to Rhodes and Palo. The demon's eyes were on Marabella who was attempting to calm Gray down and pick up all of the discarded material. Taylor and Neo were sitting on the other side of the room playing some odd game. It was a familiar and homey scene that just so happened to contain some of the most powerful creatures in the Horde.

"I'm Esme," the dark haired woman spoke confidently, her eyes warm as she reached out a hand.

"Vegas," I smiled as another man approached behind her. I noticed his eyes kept straying towards Marabella and the expression on Palo's face made me realize he noticed. It wasn't exactly an angry expression but just unbalanced, like he was trying to figure him out.

Was it wrong that I loved how soap opera-ish this was?

"This is Bobby," Esme explained as I looked over the large tanned man with golden hair and happy eyes. He tilted his head to the side and the action briefly reminded me of a dog, like a golden retriever or something.

I needed a pet clearly.

"Nice to meet you." I met his hand as he offered a smile.

"Vegas!" Gray exclaimed. "Come help me, Lucida is saying she won't wear dark colors."

I nearly busted out laughing but just walked over. Somehow I knew this was going to be a very long afternoon. It didn't stop the warmth and affection from spreading through me like a wildfire.

Family was chosen, not just blood and it felt like our family was growing.

13

VEGAS

It was nearly four in the afternoon when we returned from our uniform design fitting. We hadn't gotten much actually accomplished. However, I had been very entertained and it had given me the opportunity to spend time with Byron away from everyone. As well, Gray had seemed like she really needed the relief of spending time with friends.

I could see the tension that her men carried and despite her cheeriness, it was clear from the dark circles under her eyes that she was anything but relaxed. It was in part why it had been so easy to entertain her attempts to dress us up in a myriad of different materials when we all knew damn well we'd end up wearing something most likely made of leather.

It was nearly a half an hour ago when I'd run out of steam but Lucida and Miranda had chosen to stay. I think they were enjoying spending time with Esme and Marabella and they had mentioned showing them around. I wanted my sister and her partner to be happy here so I was very happy to give them the green light to stay.

Not that they were waiting for my permission...

I was now up in my room having just taken a shower before sitting down onto my large bed to brush out my hair. I briefly wondered if I should get my haircut but I figured that would kill Blue on the inside, so I would put it off for now. Eventually this shit would need to be cut. I couldn't have hair to my ankles now could I?

Byron had mentioned that Cosimo, Bandit, and Booker were somewhere at home, but that everyone else had chosen to go with Edwin to the Red Masques meeting. I had a feeling that it wasn't as innocent as wanting to "spend time together." No. If I knew my competitive and aggressive boys, they most likely wanted to know who they would be working with. I cringed thinking about how overprotective they would probably be when we started working with other teams.

The blood mage had gone to join them and I'd briefly said hi to both Bandit and Booker. I wish I could have told you what those boys were up to but when I found them in the study, they had instantly moved away from the desk and some obvious sketches that were laid out. I hadn't pushed it because neither of them seemed scared or angry, so I figured it was a good surprise they were working on.

With an obvious yet sweet dismissal, I'd found myself searching for Cosimo but failing. I figured that this was a sign I should take the time to relax. So I would. Once I finished brushing my hair I grabbed a large book to the right of my bed on a small nightstand.

Simplistic Magic for Children

I nearly snorted because I knew Edwin had put this here for two reasons. The first being a very real interest in my magical education. The other was a total jab and an antagonistic attempt to get me all heated up.

I'd show him simplistic fucking magic.

Unfortunately, I clearly was not in the academic mood because within five minutes my eyes began to close. I placed the book to the side and sighed. How bad would a nap be? Maybe just a cat nap?

Except that didn't seem to work either because no shorter than twenty minutes I was in that odd state of not sleeping, but not quite awake. When a sensation crawled up my spine associated with one of my boys, I didn't bother opening my eyes. My body felt like jello and my skin was flushed and warm from my shower. As the evening sun started to hit my skin I turned on my back to let the soothing light travel across my skin.

Somehow, I must have dozed off at some point because the next sensation I felt was a gentle kiss placed on my ankle. My magic, a low flame, began to build as my body began to wake up from its small cat nap, very much renewed. Not just mentally but also sexually. I shivered under the warm touch as a pair of rough, long fingers began to massage my foot gently, causing an absolutely unavoidable moan to leave my mouth. Cosimo's deep, yet soft chuckle gave way to his accented voice that was like a warm mediterrean breeze running over my body.

"*Mi tesoro,*" he whispered kissing the other ankle. "Do you tempt us on purpose?"

I opened one eye to find us very much alone and his crystalline eyes dancing with amusement and a whole lot of heat. I let a small smirk crawl onto my lips. "How am I tempting you?"

A low soft sound came from the back of his throat as he crawled forward to lay between my legs, his head tilted so that his chin rested on my barely covered thigh. Suddenly, this very light robe seemed annoying and not necessary. I should take it off.

Yes, Vegas. The comfortability of your robe is why you want to take it off.

A lazy relaxed smile broke onto his beautiful face as if he could read my thoughts. His hand began to draw patterns on my opposite thigh. At his touch, my breath caught and my hand found its way to his soft silky hair. His smile grew as my skin broke out in hot chills.

Hadn't I told him I like him between my legs? Bastard listens to everything.

"You always look angelic sleeping, but to come upstairs to your tight sexy body spread out nearly naked? It's hardly fair," he complained, his eyes trailing along my body up to where my face was no doubt flushed.

"You, poor baby," I teased with a coy smile. A surge of confidence broke through me as it usually did with Cosimo. I licked my lip in an involuntary gesture. "Are you suffering?"

Because I was.

Instead of answering, he bit down on my thigh playfully and caused me to whimper. "I am. You will have to make it up to me."

I let out a soft breathy laugh. "And how would I do that?"

"Let me taste you, Vegas," he whispered, playing with the hem of my robe. "It will ease the suffering. I promise."

As if I would say no to that!

I hummed as if I was undecided but he only grinned as if he knew exactly what I was doing. I fucking loved that he was asking because somehow that was even hot. This man was just sexy. It was that simple. His words made me feel as though I was in complete control, which was something I was finding that I needed right now.

"Please?" He began to smooth his full rough palm over my skin.

Instead of answering, I let my thighs open as he let out a low nearly pained sound. I gasped as his hands gripped my hips and he crawled up my body just a bit more. My mouth opened in a soft sound as Cosimo began to trail small love bites along my inner thigh towards my wet heat, before moving to the other side. Fuck. I was practically squirming before his lips or tongue even tasted me.

"Cosimo," I was now nearly whining. "Please."

He groaned as his tongue pressed against me and into me, causing my body to arch off the bed in harmony with crying out his name softly. I let out a breathy gasp as he began to devour me, his tongue a finely tuned instrument out of this fucking world.

Holy guacamole.

How had I been missing out on this all these years?! I could feel everything in my body twisting and turning as my nipples grew tight and hard, the robe I wore essentially falling apart to leave my body bare. His large hands moved to cup my ass as he lifted me up to his mouth in a hold just tight enough I couldn't move from his grasp. There was nothing to do but accept the treatment of his tongue and damn if I didn't fucking love that.

My hands pulled at his silky hair as he let out a sexy sound between a moan and something more primal. I could feel him increasing his speed as I began to tremble against him, the wave of pleasure building inside of me. I couldn't help but move against him with my own roll of the hips, hoping to reach the moment he was offering because fuck if this wasn't the fastest I'd ever come. It didn't help that the sexy lip ring I'd been wanting to tug on for nearly a month now was pressed right against my wetness in a cool almost dangerous sting. My clit was practically pulsating with need and I felt like I was going to pass out from how turned on I was at the moment.

His mouth was magic. Magic, folks.

"Use me, Vegas," he whispered against my skin. "Use me to make yourself come."

"Fuck," I gasped as he gently bit down and pleasure exploded up my spine and into the rest of my body. My climax only continued its momentum as I gripped his hair harder and I realized he was going to make me come whether I wanted to or not. I very, very, very much wanted to. The build up was so intense that the small lightning bolts of pleasure had my eyes tearing up as my words became incomprehensible.

I think somewhere between him slipping two fingers into me and humming against my clit, I burst into a million star particles. Hot liquid heat flooded my body as I felt my eyes fluttering shut.

Wow.

"You taste so good," he groaned while continuing to gently lap up my release. I could see the tension in his body though and I knew he was suffering. I very much wanted to return the favor after trying it with Byron and I had imagined a million times what Cosimo would taste like. I was about done imagining it.

"I bet you taste better," I sat up as his eyes went wide and I met him in the center of the bed. While he wasn't exactly clothed, in just sweat pants, I was completely naked. I didn't mind though and my orgasmic high had me acting confident. I kissed him with an erotic flick of the tongue before pushing him back into where I had just been.

"Vegas," he rasped out with molten heat turning his eyes darker. "You don't... *Mierda!*"

I had already peeled down his sweats and took him in my mouth at that last declaration. Now, I would like to state that this was in fact only my second blow job, ever. I know. Poor him, right? I had no fucking idea what I was doing but apparently it was fucking working because he cursed in Spanish as I worked my mouth around his tan, rigidly smooth cock.

I really needed to take time to appreciate each of my boys' dicks. They were pretty great. *I guess I'd need to see ALL of them first. Poor me.* I grinned at that thought.

"Fuck," he groaned as I went even deeper like the girl I had seen on the few videos I had gotten away with watching. Remember I lived with eight boys so there was no privacy. Although, I had experienced some really fun walk-ins before with the guys.

Cosimo's reactions gave me the confidence I needed to bob my head up and down enthusiastically as his breathing became erratic. I noticed that when I did a slight swirl of my tongue, Cosimo practically shot off the bed and I pat myself metaphorically on the back for being intuitive. It was different giving a blow job without Blue pounding into me from behind. I could actually take my time to savor and enjoy his taste. My body shivered under the hot demand of his body as he began to pump in and out of my mouth while holding my head in a gentle yet direct way.

"Vegas," he rasped out in a near plea as his hands grasped my hair tightly. "I'm going to come."

"Good," I managed before I took him completely. He groaned out a long strand of Spanish curse words before his cum shot down the back of my throat. I could feel his breathing slow as I swallowed it down and looked up at him from under my lashes. The salty after taste had me getting turned on again but this time it was subdued from that fan-freaking-tastic orgasm. Cosimo was still semi-hard as I pulled away and offered him a coy smile.

"You," he sat up dragging my hips forward so I was laying on top of him naked. "You are a fucking siren, sent to kill me."

I nuzzled his chest and rained small kisses. "So I'm guessing I did a good job? That was only my second one ever."

Before I knew it Cosimo had rolled us and had me pinned below him, his crystalline eyes nearly arctic with intensity. "Really?"

My lips twitched at the undercurrent of possessiveness that all my boys seemed to have. Maybe it was a magic thing? I licked my lips in a subconscious reaction to wanting to play with his sexy lip ring. "Yes, because my dating life has been very 'happening' these past few years."

He offered me an affectionate look mixed with amusement at my comment before kissing my lips gently. "I love you, Vegas, really so much...and not just because you give amazing head."

I barked out a laugh while offering him a flirty smile. "I would say you're the perfect one. I could get used to waking up like that."

"Yeah? You know I'd never deny you anything."

I wiggled my eyebrows at the lightness in his eyes. "Anything, huh?"

He offered me a smoldering look. "Anything."

A cough had both of us looking towards the door, my naked body only covered by Cosimo's own half naked body and now pulled up sweatpants. Booker stood with red ears and amusement playing on his face.

"You know, Puppy," I drawled with amusement. "If you keep walking in, I might start inviting you to join."

Instead of Booker looking surprised his eyes twinkled and he offered me a devious grin. Oh, my! That's what he wanted! I opened my mouth to say something but Bandit appeared behind him looking curious but also very relaxed. I liked this look on my boys.

"We came up here to tell you that dinner is ready," Bandit explained.

"Or we could have dinner up here," Booker offered in a small underhanded comment. I couldn't help but smile at that and promised myself that next time I would do just as I promised.

Cosimo ignored him as he jumped up and pulled on a shirt, walking past Bandit. I tied my robe and fluffed out my hair before going towards my closet. Pulling on a massive sweater and leggings with cute GOT socks.

"I like those," Bandit nodded towards the socks as I pointed my feet to show them off. Booker chuckled and pulled my hand as the three of us headed downstairs, voices raising to let me know that the other boys were home...with friends.

"So," Booker drawled. "The boys may have invited another team back for dinner."

My eyes widened as I felt anxiety hit me, right as we entered into the kitchen. Thanks for the fucking warning, bud. My boys looked over as several sets of new eyes flashed over to me and my ears turned red. God, talk about awkward. Any chance that a team of supernatural individuals with extended senses, *didn't* hear Cosimo and I? The man in question winked at me with a cocky grin. He had known! I would kill him.

"Uh," I spoke before clearing my voice. "Hi, there."

"Is that her?" a man asked. He was nearly as big as Adyen.

Kodiak grunted as Edwin spoke. "Yes, this is Vegas. She's ours."

I narrowed my eyes because he totally could have phrased that more professionally. Instead of focusing on the super cool magic men in the room, like six or seven of them, I let Kodiak wrap his arms around me as I pressed my nose to his pine scent. Rocket lingered near by as well, his face blank of any lightness that he exhibited around me. Instead, he looked fairly scary.

If this was how the boys were acting around a team I assumed to be "friendly" then I wouldn't want to be the other guys. The other men all offered me greetings. I responded but kept my voice soft as I began to watch the room to see what exactly was going on here. After they resumed their conversation, Edwin motioned for me to come over. I tucked myself into his side as Blue stood to the other playing with my hand splayed on the counter. My eyes narrowed as he traced over my ring finger with his own, the tattooed V very noticeable. I didn't like the devious look in his eyes. I wish I could tell you what everyone else was talking about but a lot like Tamara's men, I was feeling a tad overwhelmed with the amount of power.

There was one man, the big one with dark hair and searing silver eyes, whose magic felt almost like Kodiak's wolf. The man next to him was far more colorful, his hair a crimson and eyes lime green, but for the life of me I could not tell you what species he was. Frankly, he had a bit of an unhinged look so I didn't have the balls to ask. Off to the right were two men talking amongst themselves. The first one that looked nearly angelic was a demon, I believed, and the other had rose colored hair which contrasted his alchemy magic. The amount of magic in the air was intoxicating and fascinating. I slid my eyes over to the two men talking to Edwin as well. One was leaner and slightly shorter but the power rolling off him was extremely intense. I could say nearly the same about the man next to him that smelled like a demon but also a mage. How was that possible? Questions for later! The seventh one? I couldn't tell what he was. I'd yet to come across it.

"What are you?" I asked before I could stop myself. Edwin let out a small bark of laughter as the man snapped his gaze towards me, his eyes a bright fuschia but growing darker. He didn't look like the other men, he was taller and had extended ears just slightly. His magic felt natural but there was a tinge of something darker.

"I'm Fae," he said, tilting his head curiously. I wondered if his hair, dark with bright pink ends, was natural or dyed.

"No, you're not," I frowned at his lie. "Unless I haven't met all the different types of Fae that exist. You aren't dark, nor light, and you aren't anything I've met in the Horde so far. Your magic and your appearance are slightly different than everyone else's. So, what are you?"

"What is she?" the man asked Edwin as his team mates began to offer amused looks.

"None of your business," Byron stated softly drawing my attention as I flashed him a smile. He smirked and I was happy to find that Edwin and Byron were still acting normal even around the people that they commanded.

"All right," the man sighed in a tired tone. "Do I have to answer?"

Edwin looked down at me and his eyes sparkled, dipping to my lips and then back. "No, you don't have to, but if you don't I will tell her because she will most likely be upset. Then if she is upset I will be in a terrible mood at training tomorrow which means that all of you would suffer because of that choice."

"Tell her," one of his team mates scowled. The animalistic one.

I frowned and offered the man a look. I could tell he really didn't want to. So, instead I spoke up. "It's fine actually, if you really don't want to tell me that's your secret. I just wanted to know because I'm still learning about everything."

The man's eyes softened momentarily as Edwin chuckled, all of his team members offering him a weird look. The man met Edwin's gaze and shook his head. "Damn it, Edwin."

"I didn't do anything," he grinned like a kid on Christmas. "You're the one with guilt issues. The woman said you don't have to tell her if you don't want to."

"But," he groaned, "that look! That is unfair."

"What look?" I peeked at Blue who offered me a sweet smile.

"The look!" the man exclaimed as all of my men chuckled.

"I'm really lost right now," I frowned. "Listen, if you don't want to tell me, I get it..."

"Elf!" he announced, throwing his head back. "I'm an Elf."

Silence.

I began smiling. "So, are we talking like Lord of the Rings or Will Ferrel here?"

"Oh, Maker!" The man threw up his arms storming from the room as everyone else cracked up. I smiled feeling rather funny honestly. Plus, I knew he'd be back. Bandit was making homemade fettuccine alfredo. No one would miss that.

14

ROCKET

I didn't find it particularly surprising that I couldn't sleep. No. I was awake for more time than asleep in my life. That was in part because of my father. He was the main reason I couldn't sleep tonight. Unbeknownst to most of my brothers and Vegas, my inability to express physicality well had nothing to do with men and very much to do with specifically my father. It was why I didn't normally join Vegas's bed at night. As a child, I'd learned to stay up because if not my father would sneak up on me while I was sleeping. Whether he was drunk or sober, if I slept he would begin to hit me and if I was awake he'd search the house until he found me. By then I'd braced myself enough to handle the blows.

Never to my face. Always solid punches and kicks. Never any weapons.

So, yeah. It wasn't surprising that I couldn't sleep tonight because change always disrupted my ability to act normal and Vegas releasing my powers was a massive change. Even now my powers were like a raw force under my skin wanting to crawl over the ground and pull on any previous vessels of energy. I closed my eyes and my magic attempted to compromise by prompting me upstairs to where Vegas was sleeping.

I didn't trust what I would do if I slid into bed with her. Not right now at least considering I was as likely to feel like crying or flinching than I was to fuck her. It was extremely irritating.

Instead, I sat with my back against the half wall with my legs stretched out on the stairs of the back patio. The Horde's moon was very interesting, with almost a secondary shadow or moon painted in a violet hue. I watched it momentarily, not recognizing any of the stars before looking at the garden before me. Despite the change, I was thrilled at the prospect of living here permanently because there was so much knowledge to be gained in this new realm. The surrounding forest was dark and there was a slight breeze that carried the songs of a pub near the edge of the kingdom. If I had to assume it was soldiers celebrating before whatever the fuck was going to happen with King Mario.

"Rocket?" I almost jumped as my head tilted to find an ashen Vegas. I immediately frowned and stood up wanting to understand why she looked so pale.

"What's wrong?" I asked softly and she simply gripped her sweater tighter walking towards me while watching the space around us as if she expected something to change.

Instead of answering she buried her head against my chest and I didn't flinch at her easy contact. My arms wrapped around her in a protective gesture. Her heartbeat was fast against my chest and I could feel the vibrant life radiating off her. My magic allowed me, I'd found, to recognize how much "life" someone had. It was odd and would have been uncomfortable if I really cared about others outside of my family. As it stood, I didn't.

Vegas didn't feel like the normal life energy that even most mages had. It made sense that she had been made from magic because her entire energy force was a brightly lit pure source of magic. It was a stunning visual that made me see why Booker enjoyed aesthetic art efforts.

That was Vegas though. She made me want to do irrational things. Made me want to make irrational choice. Made me want to give myself to her completely.

"Sugar," I whispered against her forehead. I needed to focus on why she was so still in my arms. I needed to focus on why she seemed so cold. Why her hands were trembling against my chest. Her breathing was tight and I could hear her little heart pattering.

"Vegas," I pulled back and tilted her head up gently. Her purple eyes were clouded in fear and yet were still hazy from sleeping. It was almost as if she'd never woken up.

"Rocket," she whispered her bottom lashes clouding with tears.

"Vegas," my voice became sharper. "What is going on?"

Her soft hands cupped my face and she looked so pained. "It was a dream."

"A dream?" My chest relaxed but only marginally. The caw of a crow sang through the night air as a wind swept over us causing her hair to shift gently as I rubbed her shoulders. I was worried that she was cold out here. Something I would have never thought of if it hadn't been in reference to her.

Her breathing sped up and her eyes glazed over. "It has to be a dream, just a dream right? Dreams can't come true Rocket, right?"

I could feel her anxiety so I lifted her into my arms, her legs going around my waist as I sat down on a stone bench, keeping her tight against me. I wasn't good at emotions and seeing her cry made me feel awful. I could feel my chest tightening and panic began to threaten my own sense of stability. I forced myself to calm down and instead cupped her jaw.

"Tell me about the dream," I whispered in a calm voice.

"I can't say it," she choked. "I can't make it more real than it feels."

Shit.

"Can you show me? Like you did with Edwin?"

Her eyes snapped up as her eyes filled with relief as she nodded also maniacally. I settled her comfortably as I asked. "How do we do this?"

Her breathing was slowing and she put her head on my chest. "I'm going to remember it and I need you to just close your eyes. If you don't start seeing anything after a few seconds, let me know."

That didn't end up being a problem.

A flicker of heat shot from the center of my chest and up my neck into my head. Instantly, her vision was transmitted, except instead of it just being her I was somehow with her. I didn't think she could see me though. I was simply an observer. It didn't feel like that though.

I was about to open my mouth because the dream appeared to be fairly normal. We were standing in a forested area, according to the surroundings in the Horde, and she was looking in the distance. There was a small frown on her perfect face.

As she began to walk forward I realized the earth was saturated with water, or what I assumed to be considering the dampness in the air. Except, despite the lighting, I could see her dress becoming darker on the edges in a hue that looked nearly black. The only sound was the night air pushing through the trees and a light thunder in the distance.

I had no idea where she was going but it became clear to me that something was scaring her. Even in the dream she began to shake her hands trembling. My eyes were focused on her so when she let out a small cry, my head immediately darted to our surroundings. I felt my brow furrow as I realized we'd reached a hill that she stood at the crest of, her dress darkened at the edges as she began to cry about what was over that hill. Her form was highlighted by the moon and on either side of her were willow trees that seemed to be reaching for her. I stepped up cautiously as she began to shake and cry in earnest.

I didn't risk reaching out and touching her despite my need.

Then I saw her reason for her distress.

Holy fuck.

As far as the eye could see was nothing but decimation. The entire vista, a field that faced a larger border, was littered with bodies and brightly lit fires amid the chaos. Horses lay on their sides bleeding out while letting out pained calls. I could hear voices of fallen allies calling, asking for help, some of them using her name. The stench of blood and decay was in the air, thick and heavy, as she took a shuddering breath and walked forward.

I could hear the crush of bones underneath our feet and the squelch of wet blood. She clearly didn't notice it because her pace picked up and she nearly sprinted. I had to jog and when I'd reached where she fell to the ground, I instantly regretted it. I knelt down next to her and stared into my own face.

Except I was dead.

I was starting to realize why she'd woken up. Then I

noticed she was crawling around with sobs as all ten of our bodies appeared, some clearly dead and others seriously injured. It was disturbing, no doubt but something felt off causing me to look around.

Then I saw it.

"Motherfucker," I spit out at the memory.

Now, I had no idea what this guy looked like so I could be wrong but I didn't think so. Instead there was a man standing in the distance with a small smile on his face. My brow twisted just slightly because he looked so similar to Bandit.

I wasn't joking. This man looked like Bandit's brother or something. He was taller and had darker eyes, but they were bright enough to see from a distance. I wanted to tell her to look but I was far too focused on the possession on this man's face. I stood and walked towards him noticing there was something very wrong with him.

Health wise.

Life wise.

Despite his outward health, it was like he was filled with a sick, unhealthy power. If my knowledge on my powers was even decent I'd say that this man was dying. How was that possible though? I was a few feet away absorbing everything I could about the man when the dream ended.

A gasp sounded from Vegas as she began to shake slightly but was absent of tears this time. Before speaking, I took a deep breath and grounded myself in the present. When I opened my eyes she was looking at me with a lot of pain and a bit of curiosity.

"Sugar," I whispered. "I want to tell you something but you need to promise me you are going to keep calm. Becoming angry about this won't help."

"What?" she frowned.

"When I was in your dream, I saw him."

Her head tilted and when realization hit her nostrils flared in furious anger. I wrapped my arms around her as he attempted to breath and not burn everything down most likely.

"Continue," she begged.

"When you see him, which hopefully you won't, I need you to be prepared. He looks like Bandit. In fact, if I didn't know better I'd say they were related. Although with everything lately I suppose it's possible. He is taller and has darker eyes but the resemblance is there. There is also more. He's sick and not just in a fucked up way. He's physically sick, it's very odd."

"Rocket," she shook my shoulders gently. "You are rambling."

I looked at her and nodded. "The point is that I think he created the dream to scare you into giving up. He looked like he was enjoying everything about what was occurring and in no way looked part of the actual dream."

Her head bobbed in understanding and I could see the anger there.

"Bandit said he didn't see any of us dying. I should trust him on that."

"We should see if he has had any visions about this situation," I noted to myself.

The two of us sat in silence for a bit, processing everything.

"You scared me," I admitted.

She nuzzled my neck in apology. "I'm sorry, why were you up? I was worried that after the dream something was going on."

I considered not saying anything. Or saying that I was tired. Instead, I spoke the exact truth. "I have issues sleeping whenever we go through a big change. My father," I closed my eyes, "he used to take me by surprise while I was sleeping. When I was awake I could predict the pain, but not if he surprised me."

Her entire body stilled as a pained shadow crossed her eyes. I instantly felt terrible. Instead of speaking though she wrapped her arms around me and kissed my jaw, causing a low rumble to echo through my chest.

"Rocket," she whispered, "thank you for telling me that."

"I will always tell you something if you ask," I hesitated. "It may just take more time on my own."

"I know." She squeezed me tighter and I absorbed her affection.

I could feel the heaviness of the situation leaving and a small smile crawled onto my face at an idea. Her body was tense as I stood up and I looked at her small feet, glad to see she was wearing shoes and comfortable clothing.

"Can you let Edwin I need to tell him something?" I asked, setting her down.

"Sure," she nodded her eyes glazing over, "hold on."

I looked behind her as the French doors opened and Edwin walked out looking very awake. I chuckled to myself knowing the man hadn't been sleeping either.

"What's going on?" he asked looking at the two of us.

"I have something to update you on," I continued. "We need some space away from here, though. Is it safe for me to take her to the pub nearby?"

"You can hear that?" Edwin asked, amused.

I nodded and he looked at Vegas, clearly seeing the same thing I was. He looked up at the house and I followed the noise he was hearing as Blue, Decimus, and Kodiak walked out. I actually smiled this time. They really couldn't sleep without her, like it was a serious attachment. I noticed that all of them were looking at Vegas with concern but I just shook my head.

"Sure," Edwin spoke, "what about you three?"

"What about us?" Kodiak grunted scooping up Vegas easily.

"We are going to the pub. Rocket has some new information and I think all of us need some air," He stated clearly referring to our little sugar.

"Sure," Blue flashed a smile and looked at Vegas. "I'm glad you're dressed so... comfortably."

She stuck out her tongue knowing he was commenting on her covered modest clothing. I did as well so I couldn't say shit. Decimus groaned at her little pink tongue and cursed walking towards the front of the estate. I grinned as we began walking towards the pub.

My eyes caught Vegas's gaze from where she looked at me over Kodiak's shoulder. Except this time there was no longer fear there. No instead there was heat. She offered me a wink before tucking her head back into Kodi's neck. I shook my head.

She was playing a little game but she didn't realize that I was done playing around.

I hoped she was ready for that.

VEGAS

It was a pleasant surprise when Rocket had suggested going out for some fresh air. Lord knows I needed it between my fury about Victor's presence in my dream and the true heartbreak I'd faced because of it. However, fresh air wasn't exactly how I would describe this.

The pub had real stone walls and the entire building reminded me of something out of, well, *Lord of the Rings*. In fact, I could see the elf and his teammates somewhere two tables down. The most surprising fact had nothing to do with the worn wood floors and smell of ale. Which yes, if you wanted to know, tastes far different than beer. No, the most surprising fact was the interactions I observed in an entire bar filled with SE guards and the Red Masques. It was an interesting relationship and similar to observing Airmen and a Special Operations unit relaxing together.

Shit. How did I become Special Operations?

Because you're the Baskin-Robbins of fire, Vegas. Thirty-one flavors.

It didn't escape my notice that besides the woman working behind the bar, I was the only female here. I knew Gray was frustrated with the aged notions that existed in the Horde and I couldn't disagree. Who has a military any more consistent of all men? When I'd asked Edwin why he didn't create more teams with females, he stated that their parents never enrolled them at the academy. Nor would they put them in training for the Supernature Enforcement at thirteen. Apparently, that was where Gray's True Heir guard had trained.

Despite the massive male presence, my boys didn't seem very concerned and I knew that mainly had to do with Edwin. Bastard was scary. Even now, in a relaxed setting, with his sleeves rolled up, he had a dangerous air to him. Now that is totally possible because the conversation he and Blue were having wasn't exactly normal. I blamed Cain in part, who'd shown up because he wanted to update them and also told me in his deadpan voice that Tamara says "Love you!"

Yes. That was as funny as it sounds.

So, they were being violent as usual. Kodiak was drinking and keeping watch on everything around him while also looking through a tablet Edwin had handed him. Apparently, Edwin expected all of us to learn shit. Didn't the magical asshat know it was holiday break?

I smirked as Edwin narrowed his eyes at me with an amused tilt to his kissable mouth.

Decimus was talking to someone he'd obviously met earlier and having a fairly in-depth conversation from the looks of it. I didn't miss how his eyes continued to dart towards me though. Then there was Rocket who was sitting right across from me and, despite his watchfulness, found it in his time to pin me with intense stares. Normally, the probing stares would make me nervous. Right now? Well, after tonight and what he told me, I just wanted to be closer to him.

Physically.

Preferably naked.

I grinned as I realized how "in public" we were and how the mass of people socializing would feel if I played with Rocket. As I've said, I have always made sure to never tease Rocket because we were a tad explosive.

Unsurprisingly, I felt a tad irresponsible tonight. I stretched out my foot and nudged his gently.

He took a sip of his beer. "Yes, Sugar?"

I loved his accent.

"Just wanted to know if you'd come to the bar with me to get a drink," I drawled and offered a sweet smile. "I don't want to go alone."

"Good," Kodiak stated as I shot him a look. The man was ruining my flirt game.

Rocket chuckled softly and offered me a playful gaze, knowing exactly what I was doing. Then again he had drunk a bit more than usual so he could just be tipsy. Tipsy Rocket was very affectionate and my confirmation came as he decided to wrap his arm around me as we walked toward the bar, nibbling the shell of my ear and causing me to jump - much to his amusement.

"What can I get you?" the male bartender asked as I crossed my arms over the bar and Rocket braced his hands on either side of me from behind. It was a protective enough stance that men on either side of him turned their bodies away. My lip twitched at that. Even in Horde standards Rocket was scary it seemed.

"What's good?" I asked as the man slid me a list of different options and pointed out a few. The entire time I was moving I made sure to not be discreet about my teasing. Instead, much to Rocket's pain, I pressed my ass right back into him and I could feel his already semi-hard excitement grow more. My toes curled in anticipation.

Choo. Choo. Orgasm train...tickets, please!

"I will have two of those," I pointed towards one that apparently had a vanilla aftertaste. As he left, I let my smile grow. Rocket's lips finding my ears.

"Careful, Vegas," he chided with amusement. "You don't know what you're asking for. I have no qualms about bending you over right here in public. In fact, I love the idea of showing people just how *mine* you are."

I tilted my head back and his hand gently touched my hair, his nostrils flaring slightly at our position. He could totally fuck me like this and I'd be a happy camper. "I think I know exactly what I'm asking for."

"Hold them for us," Rocket snapped as the bartender returned with our drinks. Rocket's eyes filled with something dark and heated. The bartender chuckled as Rocket spun me towards the side of the room where the back hall led to a door. I was practically jogging to keep up with his pace and I went to say something snarky as we exited into an empty back patio.

Except my mouth was suddenly very busy.

"Fuck," I whispered against his lips as the man let out a rumble from his chest and his kisses grew more intense. I could tell Rocket was pretty close to unraveling and in true Vegas style I very much wanted to poke the bear.

I mean, come on, I'd never teased the guy. I had to give it a try!

There was something so primal and raw about Rocket, from his magic to the way he interacted with others. I had no idea why I thought I would have been safe in a public space. As he pulled away, his eyes hard and heated, he pinned me against the wall with his hips as my head fell back to look up at him. I could see the tension pulsating through his muscular arms as he lifted one to my lip and drew a thumb across it in a soft yet seductive pattern, in contrast to his energy. I shivered as he grasped my jaw in a firm hold.

"I'm not going to play this game with you Vegas." He unzipped the neck of my oversized sweater and exposing my neck to the open air. "Instead I'll just fuck you. Hard and good, exactly how you've been asking for it. Isn't that right, Sugar?"

I felt everything tighten at his husky rough southern accent as his teeth scraped against my jaw causing a moan to tumble out. I bit my lip to hold it in but instead squeezed his shoulders to allow him to feel just how affected I was.

"I don't ask for things I don't want," I whispered boldly.

His eyes turned liquid as he let his hands travel underneath my sweater causing my skin to heat. I could see my chest rising and falling as he easily cupped my breasts and growled at how hard my nipples grew under the lacy material.

"I should deny you. Make you wait until I can make love to you in a bed at home."

"Later," I whispered in a rushed voice. "We always have time for that later."

"Do you like the idea of me claiming you right outside the bar? Where anyone could walk out? Where anyone could hear your moans and know who you belong to?" he whispered tersely as I let out a small whimper.

"Yes," I admitted as a dangerous look crossed his face before he pressed an almost sweet kiss to my lips, deep and loving. I shivered as he turned me and pressed me against the stone wall, just like we'd been in the bar. My fingers reached to grasp a stone as he buried his head against my neck.

His hands made a seductive and smooth pattern down my ribs and to my leggings. I could feel the primal magic inside of him making him tense and I wanted him to let it out, but the damn man wanted to prolong this and I wasn't about to say no to more time with him.

"You're positive?" he asked, sounding almost unsure.

I looked back at him. "I love you Rocket. I'm positive."

That feral glint entered his eyes as he kissed me in that savage way and peeled down my leggings just underneath my ass before pressing my back with his large hand so it arched. I let my head fall back as he pulled up my sweater and groaned at whatever he was seeing. Good to know he liked it.

I jumped as I felt a bite to my right ass cheek as he chuckled softly his long thick digit playing lightly with my already very wet slit.

"I'm not sure I'll be able to control myself once I start," he admitted.

"I don't want you to," I confessed and it seemed to be the answer he was looking for.

"Rocket!" I cried out as he filled me with his entire length in one solid push. How had he even gotten undressed? I didn't even care as my breathing became rough and he bit down on my shoulder just holding his deep hard length inside of me, so long and thick I'd thought I'd pass out. My core clenched and tried to adjust to his size.

"You feel so fuckin' good, Sugar," he drawled as he pulled back and then slammed back into me causing me to moan at the thick deep feeling. His hand wrapped around my hair and I completely relaxed my body allowing him to position me.

I barely had time to enjoy the sensation of his slow pulses, before he started fucking me. I do mean fucking. I cried out as he began to pound into me with a nearly athletic and supernatural pace, his timing and stroke perfect. I could feel him hitting parts of me that I knew would leave me sore for days. I could have tried to monitor my volume but I found myself not giving a fuck.

Let them hear how much I loved his touch.

"Fuck, fuck, fuck," I hissed as he grunted and pressed me into the wall so my chest was nearly flat against it. My cries were echoing because of the stone and he was nearly shaking with the energy under his skin that damn raw primal magic meeting mine in recognition.

Quicker than any of the others, I felt that connection snap into place as if our magic was saying "about fucking time." I barely had time to appreciate it before his movements became even more ruthless his goal clearly to drill me into the fucking wall or knock it down. I officially gave my body up to Rocket when he wrapped one of his hands around my neck from the back.

It wasn't a tight hold but it was damn sure possessive.

"Oh, shit," he growled against my neck. "Sugar, you're going to make me come from those sweet noises."

I couldn't help it though and the way my legs were pressed together had friction building so that I could feel my climax coming. My breathing was erratic and Rocket's was as well, causing my nipples to harden despite being pressed against the stone through lace.

"I want you to come, Vegas," he demanded. "I want you to explode on my cock while I fill you so full of come it spills out. Can you do that for me, Sugar? Will you let me come inside of you?"

That would be a yes.

"Yes!" I cried out as a mini climax had me squeezing him tighter. His tight muscles were flexing underneath me as he worked my body like he knew it better than me. It was totally possible. He did know a lot about the human body.

My climax came out of nowhere and I was swept away by it, my magic lighting a wildfire in me as his magic fueled it. Everything inside of me became heightened as he demanded my pleasure and had me screaming out his name as he did exactly as he promised by filling me up with his cum. My eyes rolled back as I let my body go slack against his, that massive tanned body the only thing keeping me up right now.

For just a moment the two of us were frozen as he refused to leave me. I refused to ask him to. I let my head rest back on his chest and despite the sounds from the pub it was oddly intimate. The cool wind brushed past us and he shielded me easily before pulling out. I offered him a smile as he rolled up my leggings and adjusted himself, pulling me back into his arms.

I nearly purred as his lips traced my jaw and he nuzzled my neck. That animalistic energy was gone for the moment and instead, in its place, was a very affectionate and sort of cuddly Rocket. I inhaled his clean scent mixed with mint, wanting to rub myself all over him in an attempt to get closer. I wanted his scent on me.

His hand delicately drew up my spine. "Is this a new tattoo?"

I nodded and shot him a smile. "It's from…"

"*The Masque of the Red Death*. It's beautiful."

My heart shone with his words and I shivered appreciatively.

I had no idea how long the two of us simply stood out there with his arms wrapped around me caging my body to the wall with his much bigger one. Long enough that I actually began to get sleepy. Long enough that when the door opened, I knew it was Kodiak being worried about us.

"Is she sleeping?" he asked curiously.

Rocket brushed my hair back and I snuggled closer. For sake of argument, yes I was sleeping. Let's go with that. I didn't really feel like using my body or mind right now. My magic agreed and the bitch did a luxurious stretch before curling up on her side… with Rocket's magic behind her? And Kodiak's wolf?

All right, all right. I liked that shit.

I clearly was drunk because my imagination was creating some pretty cool shit.

"Let's head back," Rocket suggested lifting me up so I was wrapped around him like a tree monkey. Kodiak must have gone to tell the others because I suddenly felt his energy leave.

"I love you," Rocket whispered against my temple. I opened my eyes and offered him a sleepy smile as a light flapping sound, like wings echoed around us. My eyebrows rose as a stunning obsidian butterfly circled us with an ease, landing right on Rocket's shoulder.

He frowned. "I've never seen one like that."

"It's stunning," I whispered and then smiled back at him. "I love you too, by the way."

He pressed his lips to the middle of my brow. "When all of this blows over, I want to explore this place. Actually see how different it is from Earth."

I fluttered my eyelashes with a coy grin. "Want company?'

He flashed a smile. "I just assumed you would be coming."

Why did that sound like it had a double meaning?

He hummed his approval as Blue, Edwin, Decimus, and Kodiak walked from the pub towards us looking fairly drunk. Well, more so the first and a bit the second. I was glad in this moment that Rocket had already told them about everything going on because Blue had no attention while drinking.

"Beautiful," Blue sang while scaring away the butterfly.

"Blue," I scowled, "you scared away my butterfly."

Edwin spoke softly and tucked my hair behind my ear. "We can get you more."

I looked up to where it had flown away, I'm just not sure another one would do. My lips pressed together as I tucked my head in Rocket's neck and shoulders, relaxing. The boys' voices were like soft lullabies in my ear.

I wasn't exactly positive when I'd fallen asleep but I had.

15

VEGAS

I stood at the front of the room feeling completely out of place and slightly intimidated. I kept a cool exterior but I would have been far more comfortable standing next to Gray's throne than with my boys here. I know, surprising. Edwin was talking but I could barely hear him, although I always loved his voice, I could feel the eyes of the entire room on me. Nearly all male.

I'd never understood how famous celebrities were comfortable with so many eyes on them. That was what Byron and Edwin were in a sense, but maybe not celebrities. Just very important people and due to my association I was considered very important. I'm positive Edwin would have said it had to do with my difference in magic and how that was what made me special. Jokes on him. I didn't want to be special.

Just a simple woman wanting some mashed potatoes and wine.

I was still bitter about Thanksgiving.

Kodiak was upset at all the attention send our way, his chest rumbling every so often and I was tucked between

Byron and him. I was technically standing on my own but they felt very close. Or maybe I was just really warm? I didn't think it was that but you never know.

When Edwin dismissed everyone to spread throughout the massive training gym, I refused to move and waited for the magical asshat to come get me. I was being a total little bitch right now but I felt super awkward. Even my boys, albeit only a few feet away, were preparing to go through combat exercises. Some more than others. While they had the ability to because of their natural athleticism, Bandit and Cosimo didn't really fight. Although when they did, it really showcased how skilled they were. Bandit reminded me of air being so light and agile on his feet and Cosimo smooth and nearly entertained, like a predator playing with its food. I had heard Edwin mention that he only needed them training for the first hour and then they could go do whatever it was to focus on their powers.

Wait... *the first hour?* Ah. Shit this is going to suck.

"Dolcezza," Edwin spoke softly. "What's wrong?"

I breathed in and met his brilliant eyes. "I'm just feeling a bit overwhelmed. I have no combat experience or fighting. Shit, Edwin. I haven't seen a gym in... really, ever. Except for maybe at the university's campus tour."

His sculpted lips broke into a grin. "You don't need experience. Remember your body is hard-wired to run on instinct. Similar to how Her Majesty is built. You react naturally to things in a way others would have to be taught."

"How?" I frowned.

"Come." He nodded towards the center front of the room.

My figure was clothed in all black with sneakers and my hair braided. I refused. Refused to wear leather today. That was for when I felt fabulous, and only then. Today was not a fabulous day. Although I couldn't say that completely because my entire body was deliciously sore from Rocket and that made the day pretty great.

"I'm either going to need to goad you into acting or you will need to make the first move," Edwin admitted and I shook my head.

"That won't work, Edwin, and it really won't work during the battle," I smirked. "As much as I love our fights."

He looked contemplative and simply stepped back. "All right, attack me first then."

I closed my eyes and my magic opened one eye giving me an annoyed look before simmering to life. The minute she saw that Edwin was the person I was supposed to attack she sat back down and shot me an incredulous expression.

Yes, Vegas. Imagine your power as a persona to deal with the crazy.

I've officially lost it.

"It won't work Edwin," I groaned. "My magic is annoyed that I would want to attack you."

He chuckled and raised a finger. "One, you need to work on trying to meld you two together."

Probably won't happen. She's a bitch.

"Two, what is the difference between now and on the patio?"

"You're not being an ass," I chirped as a few of the men, not my boys, snapped their heads over. I almost rolled my eyes at their horror stricken faces. Byron seemed to find it all fucking amusing. Then again his amusement could have nothing to do with our conversation and everything to do with how scared everyone seemed to be of him. Little did they know Golden was *my* vampire, who liked to cuddle and often went out of his way to purchase tacos for me.

Really though, in the past week the man had come

home with tacos three times. I was seriously falling for him. He was hot. A vampire. And gave me tacos. I mean. Come. On.

Edwin just chuckled and walked forward tilting my chin up gently. I narrowed my eyes. "Edwin you're not helping me seem very badass right now."

His orange eyes flashed and I realized that the man had let down his glamour, so had Byron though. Both of them covered in runes that seemed very popular with mages.

"Would it help to go against someone else?" he asked gently. I looped my arms around his neck as his shadows seeped out to twirl up my ankles playfully. I was momentarily distracted letting out a laugh as he chuckled kissing my forehead. Then I considered his question.

I looked around at the entire room and realized that everyone was staring. Something about what Edwin was doing was freaking them out. His head snapped around and he let out a low rumble, "If you aren't doing combat training then you have time to do spellcasting, don't you? Turn the fuck around."

I've never seen heads snap away so fast. Apparently spellcasting sucked? His shadows were wrapped tightly around me in a defensive and rather comforting way. My gaze found his again as that wicked sexy glint appeared once more.

"Now, what do you say?"

I frowned. "What type of power will asshole McGee have?"

"Heir power," he spoke softly.

"Well, what the heck am I supposed to do then? My options consist of Gray's brother Silas or Gray herself!"

"Vegas!" a light voice sang as Edwin's eyebrows rose and I turned to find Gray waltzing in as if she owned the place.

She probably did, right? I was so happy to see her as she pulled me into a hug that I hadn't realized the entire room had gone silent, bowing at the waist. Her guardsmen stood watching us with amused expressions.

"Stand up!" Gray ordered and flashed the room a savage grin.

I almost chuckled at the nervous energy. I stepped back and spoke. "Are you training with us?"

"I figured it's better than training with a bunch of men that won't actually fight me." She shot a scowl at Neo in particular who just grinned. It was sort of a scary smile.

"You may face the same problem here," Edwin admitted.

Gray, who I now realized was dressed in leather, smiled at me. "No I won't, because Vegas is going to fight me."

My fire perked up and I for a minute assumed that she wouldn't want to fight the creature she was supposed to protect. Then the oddest thing happened, similar to when we first met. My power rose up and hers did as well, my mind creating a friendly competition between the two as if they were... sisters.

Shit. I really needed to talk to Gray about all of this.

"Let's do it." I bit my lip holding back my authentic excitement.

I hadn't realized that people had cleared the edges of the mats until I looked around, going far to the right in order to face Gray. I could tell, don't ask me how, that Gray's power was rising up as a different shade of shadows brushed over her face and my flame reacted easily. In fact, my power seemed to be getting a fucking boost from being around hers. It wasn't cold and icy like Edwin's magic. Hers was smoky, like how a campfire smells once the flames die down.

"Shit," someone muttered behind me as my body lit up red and orange flames, my fingertips and hair showing the shade the most. I could see my skin rippling in an orange almost metallic shade.

"Oh," Gray cooed, "I need to know how you do that. You are an enigma, my dear friend."

You have no idea.

Then Edwin stepped up and a barrier that hadn't been there before surrounded the crowd on either side, like a wall of black shadows. They moved swiftly and everyone stepped out of the way. I looked over to see that Neo had aided in handling the other half of the circle. Something told me they were worried about our power hurting others.

Now, that's just silly. And accurate.

"I've never sparred before," I admitted as she took a step closer, her movements turning lethal as my magic began to rise up to handle my physical body.

"It's instinctual," she replied. "At least for me. You have to just react."

"React to what?" I spoke too soon because I barely caught sight of her barrelling towards me before I braced for impact. But then nothing happened and I realized my body had moved. I mean really moved, like several feet away causing a true smile of delight to light up Gray's face. I couldn't help but get excited as well and I moved forward as the predator within me made an appearance once again.

I think that was the moment our battle began in earnest.

I bent lower as her ashes and smoky raw power tried to lash out at me, concealing her physical form until she was nearly on top of me. I rolled out of the way and shot out a burst of fire that tugged at her ankle and had her nearly falling. She was able to break away from the energy, barely.

"Never sparred, my ass," she chided and jumped over my next attack, grasping my shoulders as I instinctively attempted to fling her off. Instead, we both tumbled to the ground. Our powers fluctuated between dominance as ash and fire exploded throughout the ring. I could no longer tell the difference between the smoke and the wall of shadows containing us.

I rolled away and stood up bracing for another attack. Instead, noticing she was a millisecond late in standing up, I attacked first only to have her hit me in the sternum.

Fucking shit.

This continued for quite some time and I realized with joy that I was truly matching Gray. Almost mirroring her and it seemed that the more she showed me from combat and her power, I was able to harness and absorb. I felt like my physical body was growing with capabilities I didn't think were possible. This was a fantastic confidence boost I hadn't even realized I had needed.

"Vegas," she was out of breath, as was I. My body was in so much fucking pain but she continued. "How the fuck are you matching me?"

This was the moment to tell her.

My back hit the mat as I kicked at her, my hands gripping her hair as fire exploded around us and I broke away. The two of us laying on the mat and panted.

"Gray," I groaned trying to drag my ass up. "I can barely fucking move right now, but there is something you should know."

Her eyes looked interested and unsurprised as if she'd figured I'd been keeping something to myself. I opened my mouth to speak when the barrier fell like a sheet of glass. What the fuck?

"Gray," Rhodes barked urgently. "There has been another attack on the North border."

It seemed the entire room was frozen staring at us in horror and shock. We did look a bit messy, didn't we?

Covered in sweat, ashes, and my skin sparking with fire. I was so close to rolling over and just sleeping. However, the minute Gray heard his announcement she rose and met her men's gazes. Then she snapped her head towards Edwin.

"Be ready tomorrow," she spoke to Edwin although everyone could hear her loud and clear. "I have a feeling this is his last small attack."

With a shoulder squeeze in farewell, Gray and her men were gone. I laid there exhausted and worried as Byron and Edwin dismissed the men with orders. My eyes closed as fear spiked through me, what if it wasn't a dream he'd created? What if it was more?

"Dolcezza," Edwin spoke softly, his voice raspy. "Are you okay?"

I muttered a curse and opened one eye. "Okay is very subjective, Edwin. Am I alive? Am I exhausted? Am I super badass for matching her? Yes. Yes. Yes."

He let out a booming laugh and helped me up easily. Blue approached, looking rather happy with a hint of pride. "Beautiful, you're a total badass."

"Thanks, honey," I smiled. "Now please carry me because my legs are totally about to give out."

I groaned dramatically as I was scooped up and we began walking out of the building, my men talking in hushed yet enthusiastic voices about the practice. I noticed the sun was far lower than it was when we arrived. I frowned.

"How long were we in there?"

"You spared for nearly three hours."

"What? No fucking way," I muttered, "I need a nap."

"As long as you're awake for tomorrow, seems Gray believes that Mario will attack."

I would be the one to sleep in on the day of an important war. Typical.

I REALLY COULDN'T TELL you how I had gotten home because I continued to doze off. I thought I would be out for the count but it seemed that after my nap, my fire was still wanting to train. The problem? It was nearly midnight and most of my boys were sleeping. After last night my sleep schedule was fairly messed up though.

For the first time ever, I walked into a gym and I turned on the music. It was very loud and I was glad that it was a soundproof room. With amusement I approached a punching bag, knowing it would aid in stress relief but not knowing the first thing on how to punch.

Except it seemed my body did.

When I pulled back my hand and fingers adjusted as I landed a soft test punch on the bag, perfectly done. Fuck this was awesome.

So for the first time ever I had an amazing gym workout. My only gym workout and man were the standards set high. Due to falling asleep I had taken a very quick shower, not messing with my hair, before coming down here. I would need to do far more after this because I could see streaks of ash in places I missed. My hands continued to punch the bag with repetitive and strong motions, causing my knuckles to actually bleed a bit. Something that only added to my badass nature of course.

I was totally going to nag Lucida about this.

I frowned momentarily because I hadn't seen her all day but relaxed feeling her presence within the house. So, as the music increased its steady tempo, I increased my speed.

Eventually, I just took off my shirt and I was left in a sports bra and my shorts. My braids were falling out but I just continued feeling my muscles, eventually after what felt like an hour, scream for relief.

It was about then that the music shut off and my breathing was the only sound in the room. My eyes snapped to Booker who stood in the doorway watching me with a curious expression. I couldn't see his eyes but his posture was comfortable.

"Hey," I offered him a smile. "Why aren't you sleeping, Puppy?"

He walked across the room. "I could ask you the same thing, Kitty."

A playful smile flashed onto my face. "Just testing out how badass I can be."

Instead of answering, he turned me around and his hand found my slightly sweaty back. I had barely broken a sweat and that was saying something.

"When did you get this?"

My tattoo!

"Yesterday with Lucida and Miranda," I grinned as he nodded and kissed my shoulder.

"It's beautiful. I want to give you one."

"Right now?" I turned back into him smiling.

He shook his head laughing. "No, when I give you a tattoo I want it to be something special."

"Everything you draw is special," I admitted as my flame became a comfortable simmer.

A coy smile broke onto his lips that had my body tightening. "Yeah?"

"Well, maybe I should draw on your body often, then," He admitted stepping forward as I laughed and continued to back up.

"I only have so much space," I quipped.

He tilted his head. "Maybe I should scope out more of that space. See what I'm working with exactly."

"Now, Booker," I chided. "That just sounds like you're trying to get me naked."

"You would be right," he finally admitted, caging me against the gym's large window that looked out at the moonlit patio. His inky power broke across my skin and I felt my lips crook because I could almost feel the change in our magic.

"Booker," I gasped as he nipped at my collar bone. All playfulness from before began to disappear as desire spiraled through me and had me sinking closer and closer to him.

"Yes?" he teased. His hands, usually paint stained, were so large they spanned my ribs. I groaned at the contact as my hands gripped his massive arms. How did I forget how muscular he was? My body had a light sheen of sweat on it and it only enhanced the lust growing inside of me rapidly.

I could feel my core clench and my adrenaline swiftly changed to need.

"I need you," I whispered as my head fell back at the touch of his fingers against the soft material of my sports bra. He made a low sound as my nipples tightened against his touch and a breathy sigh pulled from my throat.

"Eyes, Vegas," he whispered and my head snapped up.

"Now, what do you need me to do?" he asked curiously with humor as I began to squirm against him. The bastard was playing with me.

"I need *you*," I emphasized feeling a blush crawl up my neck and chest. I loved when the boys talked dirty but I didn't have any experience in that field.

Booker shook his head and tugged on my lip in a

teasing manner. "Sorry, Kitty, but I'm going to need more than that. After all I am right here. So you have me, technically."

I let out a pathetic sound as I whispered. "Please, Booker, I need you inside of me."

The bastard bit his lip as those soft eyes turned into stormy pools. "Inside of you where, Kitty? Your mouth?"

"No," I groaned as his fingers trailed up my ribs and pushed up the sports bra.

"Where, then?" he asked playfully while taking his sweet time rolling the material up and off of my chest. I gasped as his heated hands brushed across my tight nipples. My thighs kept shifting together and, as if he noticed, his dark pant leg parted them with a devious grin.

"Inside me," I hissed out far too turned on to be embarrassed anymore. "I want you buried inside my pussy. I want to be able to slide up and down on your cock."

Oh, sweet god. I felt my face flame. Who was I?

Booker groaned and pressed into me, his erection hard as I began to greedily take off his shirt. "I love seeing your sweet pretty mouth form those fucking filthy words, Kitty."

Totally worth it.

His shirt fell to the floor then and a whiny moan came from my throat. Remember when I said Booker hid his body under his designer clothes? Well, right now I was being treated to a sight that would be ingrained in my mind forever. Tanned perfect abs. I mean perfect. How does someone get grooves like that? All my boys were fit but this was intense. He winked at my perusal as I greedily took in his massive shoulders and trim hip that led to a pair of tight pants.

Shit.

He caged me against the cool window in complete view

FIRE & SMOKE

of anyone walking by. I was glad it was nighttime. He groaned into my skin. "You are a fucking vision, Vegas."

My breath caught at the sincerity of his tone, right as his teeth closed down around the soft underside of my breast. He licked it gently and continued his path to my nipple as he knelt before me. My smaller hands found a place inside of his thick blonde hair. A surge of confidence rushed through me and I realized it was because of Booker, he made me feel confident about myself. Not that the other boys didn't but it was a different dynamic.

"Tell me what you need," he whispered against the center of my chest as I leaned back into the cool window. "Tell me how you want it?"

"*Any* way," I instantly responded as he began to roll down my spandex. "I just want you Booker. I need you."

His nose trailed down my core as he let out a low small growl that was very unlike him. I gasped as he shoved my shorts down the rest of the way and left me bare.

"Kitty," he looked up at me slowly. "Are you wet? If I slide my finger down there, will you soak my fingers? I bet you will."

He groaned at the thought. "Christ. You tasted so fucking amazing last time. I need it again. Do you want my tongue on your wet little pussy, Vegas?"

Fuck, yes, when you say it like that!

I squirmed as I panted out a "yes."

I squeaked as Booker lifted me up, his massive hands on my ass and brought my center to his mouth. Holy shit. I wasn't even worried about falling either because he had such a sturdy grip on me, nothing puppy-ish about him right now.

"Booker," I moaned as his hot tongue began to plunge into me. My toes curled as I began to push my heat against him just a bit more, his low masculine groan causing me to nearly climax right there.

"You taste like fucking ambrosia," he whispered as he circled my clit with a gentle motion before biting it. I jumped as he chuckled and did it again, the contrast had me crying out his name as my body fluctuated between sweet and rough. I could feel the orgasm coming but I needed him deep inside me, I could feel the absence and it was only making me more needy. My skin which had only been slightly flushed before felt hot all over.

"I want to come when you're buried inside of me," I said breathlessly as his eyes shot up to me with a seductive sense of triumph. Alrighty, maybe dirty talk wasn't that hard.

"Your wish is my command," he teased as he stood up and had my body slide down so that my bare spine and ass were pressed against the glass with my legs wrapped loosely around him. I whimpered as he dropped his pants and boxers, his large member already in my grasp as he murmured my name through a groan.

"Please." I wasn't opposed to begging.

He pressed closer his forehead to mine as he moved his hard member against my clit slowly, causing desire to spiral without entering me.

"Vegas," he whispered against my lips. "Please don't give me something and then take it back. I can't live life without you after loving you like this. I need to know you won't leave. Please, Vegas."

His voice was so raw with pain so my words spilled instantly from my lips. "Booker, I will never leave you. I promise. You aren't the only one who wouldn't be able to live. I need you Booker."

His eyes met mine, pulling back, because he knew I didn't mean sex. I really did need Booker. He was the playful spark of light in the dark. He was my artist and I was his muse. He was the man in my life that blushed and then convinced me to talk filthy to him in bed. No. I needed Booker for more than he would ever realize.

"Say it again," he demanded knowing those words meant more to him than "I love you." The intensity in his eyes made me feel dizzy. I couldn't see anything besides him. I couldn't feel anything besides him.

"I love you," I whispered, "and I need you...fuck!" The punctuated ending erupted as he slid home and caused me to cry out. My legs squeezed against him as he let out a low masculine sound and buried his head in my neck. I had to admit. I was a bit sore because let's face it I'd been having sex a lot. Yet the sting of pain was momentary before pleasure began to make my body relaxed.

"I love you so much," he hissed out before sliding out and slamming back into me, my legs shaking as he forced my hands above my head. The only thing holding me to the wall was his hips and the steady motion of him impaling me.

"Oh," I moaned as he hit a spot that caused white hot pleasure to shoot up my spine.

"There we go," he cooed before kissing me with strength and passion. "I need you to come as many times as possible before I even think about finishing. Then again, this feels so fucking amazing that I may just stay in here. Would you like that, Vegas? I could just leave myself buried inside of you all day."

"Yes," I moaned at his hot words.

I let out a breathy sound as he pushed into me again with a hard yet slow paced thrust. He spoke in a rough voice. "Can you come for me like that, baby? I want to pound into you but I need you to promise that you will give me all your pleasure. When we are together like this, it's all mine. Can you do that?"

Oh, shit, that was by far the most possessive thing I'd ever heard him say.

"Yes."

I clearly hadn't realized what I was asking for. I let out a scream as he began pounding into me and reaching that white hot point, again and again. I could feel my first climax building and I did what he asked. I let myself go as I gripped onto him, his fingers biting into my ass.

"Booker!" I cried out as I squeezed him and he just continued his demanding fast pace that had my legs shaking. My orgasm slammed into me like a fucking freight train and I screamed, my vision blacking out and a white hot heat began spreading throughout my limbs like molten lava.

"Another one," he demanded as my hands moved into his messy hair. I could feel the sweat forming on my skin as the two of us slid together again and again. I had never understood the term, bouncing on someone's dick, as much as I did now. I was being so fucking loud I was worried Kodi would think something was wrong.

Thank the gods for sound proof walls.

The second orgasm threw my head back as Booker did his damned best to fuse us together and form my tightness to his dick in a perfect mold. The man had the fucking stamina of a race horse, shit. I was shaking like a woman possessed as he continued and I could feel the glass window behind us fogging up as sweat dripped off my skin and his in a dewy layer.

"Booker. Shit. I can't," I cried out in response as he chuckled in a strained voice. I had lost track of time or the fucking universe Was I even alive right now?

No, no, no. This was heaven.

"Yes you fucking can," he purred while licking my damp neck. "I won't come inside you or at all until I get at least another one."

No. No. I wanted him to come. I loved it when my boys came because that meant our connection grew and flourished.

Holy shit.

Those words resonated with me and I realized that was just how sex healed me. It fueled our bond. The more I had sex with my boys the closer I felt, obviously emotionally, but also magically. I would have thought more on the concept if I could focus at all right now.

My vision was at best shaky as I let my body go and any help I'd been giving in holding myself up faded. He had my pinned to the wall as he fucked me mercilessly. I wanted to come so bad but I couldn't.

I just couldn't, it was too much.

Then he moaned into my neck and rubbed my clit, sending a fresh scream and orgasm through my body. My head fell forward against his neck as he ground against me. Tears of pleasure fell from my eyes as he began to demand more out of my body than I thought possible. I was almost worried that the window behind us would shatter, but I am not sure that would make either of us stop.

"Such a good fucking kitty cat," he gritted. "Now tell me where you want me to finish."

"In me," I said breathlessly. I worked for his orgasm with my own. I know weird, right? I deserved it. My magic demanded it.

"Fuck," he groaned as he quickened and somehow grew impossibly larger inside of me. I gasped as he slammed into me one last time, hitting the window behind me, and moaned out his release in a rough nearly guttural sound.

I loved seeing him come undone. It was a fucking masterpiece of pleasure.

He was whispering soft loving words in my ear but I couldn't distinguish them. How could someone process words when they were in a euphoric state? A heavenly high? I felt out of control and completely amazing. Fuck. I could barely see and I was trembling from head to toe. Sweat covered both of us and I could feel his muscles shaking slightly from either adrenaline or emotions.

My tear-stained cheek pressed against his neck as Booker tried to collect himself. Everything in my body was sore and I felt as though I'd run a fucking marathon.

Not that I would ever actually know how that felt.

I pulled back and grasped his face. Those hooded gray eyes were filled with a sated light and his arms were slick with sweat as he wrapped me closer so that I was like ivy.

"Let's go upstairs, my little muse," he whispered carrying me to what I hoped was a shower. I nuzzled against his neck and sighed a few minutes later as warm water began to cascade down our bodies. He started to set me down and my shaky legs had me grasping him in concern.

"Don't worry," he whispered softly. "I've got you. I've always got you, Vegas."

He did. My head fell back against his chest as his skilled hands began to massage my skin with soft lilac smelling soap. I felt like I was in a near trance, like I couldn't take care of myself so I needed him to do so. I had never felt so truly dependent and I realized that the after effects of sex with Booker meant that I would truly need to rely on him.

As in I would fall the fuck over without him.

"Holy shit," I finally murmured. Sex with all of my boys was drastically different and fucking sexy in their own way but not comparable. This took the cake for the most unexpected. I wasn't even sure what to call how I felt right now. My body sung as if it had been abused with pleasure.

Was that a thing?

God. I wasn't positive how I was going to survive this orgasm express with the intensity of the other boys and this. I mean, shit.

"You are so beautiful," he murmured and began to whisper sweet things against my skin as the two of us soaked in the hot water. After a while my eyes opened and I realized I was tucked into bed with Booker next to me, his eyes trained on his sketch pad that he had open. It was clear form the very early dawn light filtering through the window that I'd slept and I felt fucking fantastic.

"Hey," I whispered.

"Kitty," he greeted with a playful smirk.

"We should really do this more often, Booker," a familiar baritone noted casually. "I don't think I've ever seen her this docile or well rested and evidence would suggest that it was because of us."

I let out a low sound and turned toward Rocket, his eyes sparkling with something almost playful. I smiled because I was between the two of them.

"You want me docile, Rocket?" I teased as Booker pulled up against my back and nuzzled my damp hair.

Rocket grinned as his eyes shone. "No, Sugar, although you do look very peaceful which must be doing wonders for your body with the flood of..."

He started talking science shit. I pulled him closer as he chuckled and the three of us lay wrapped up in one another. This was how I was always meant to be. This right here. God, I loved them, which I echoed easily. Booker's breathing was calming and his arm was stretched behind me all the way across to where Rocket laid. My necromancer had his arms locked around my waist and his head resting on my chest. It was perfect.

Booker and Rocket were slightly different than my other boys. Sometimes I felt as though they were in their own world and I loved I was part of it. I suppose I sometimes felt that way with Byron and Edwin. I wasn't positive how long we laid there before a knock sounded on the door.

Edwin opened it and the three of us offered him a sleepy look that made him smile. I could feel that the energy of the house and the Horde was shifting. It was so early and Edwin didn't have to tell me why he was here. I tucked my robe around me and stood up, Rocket and Booker both started the process of getting out of bed. I totally checked out their muscular butts and cute boxers.

"Leather?" I asked with a small attempt at humor.

Edwin brushed my chin gently, "Yes, they were dropped off early this morning. Gray was right. The attack last night just drew attention to Mario's army that the scouts saw traveling towards us. We need to be ready within the hour."

I met his gaze and nodded feeling a weird sensation brush over my body, as if I knew something was about to change. I had experienced this several times but today it was particularly strong.

"Show me where my uniform is?" I asked quietly.

Edwin nodded and tugged on my hand leading me towards his office. It looked like several of the uniforms had already been picked up which meant half my boys were already up. Edwin leaned against his desk and handed me a folded length of material and nodded towards a side door that I knew led to his bedroom and bathroom.

I took my time getting ready, somehow knowing he'd wait for me. I hoped that my boys wouldn't be too weird about me fighting in today's battle. I snorted pulling up the dark material along my legs. Of course they would.

The uniform was different this time. It was real armor and mine was exceptionally lightweight and moveable, making me know it had no metal on it. It briefly reminded me of the tough skin of a snake or rhino. There were natural patterns on it like snake skin but it was thick and dark like a rhino's skin. It was a full pant and the top had long sleeves with a high neck that left only my hands and face visible. I would need help with lacing up the back but for now I just laced up the boots that were light weight and had room for several weapons against each side. I didn't bother calling Blue in to help with my hair, instead I pulled it back into a tight braid and pinned it up so that it was completely out of the way, even my bangs.

"Edwin," I called out as he appeared in the doorway only a moment later.

"Dolcezza," he commented with approval. "That looks great on you."

"Good," I grinned. "Now help me with the back."

I turned towards the counter and gripped it as I put my head down slightly, waiting for him to tie up the leather crossings in the back. Except he didn't approach me for the longest few seconds and when I turned I nearly swore. He was standing right fucking there and his eyes were on my spine with absolutely intensity.

Near rapture.

"Edwin?" I asked softly, almost worried. It was odd because Edwin still surprised me often fluctuating between intensity and madness.

"When did you get this?" he asked in a voice so soft I barely heard it.

"The other day when I went with Lucida and Miranda..." I trailed off not being able to tell exactly how he felt about it.

His eyes were nearly black when he looked up at me, his hand lightly skimming my spine as he turned me so I was pressed into the counter. I didn't move in part because the energy rolling off him was so intense and the other part... well, that was because he had such a tight grip on me that I couldn't move. His magic seemed to be present and struggling with Edwin for control as his shadows wrapped around my ankles and legs protectively. My magic, the lazy bitch, rolled to her side propped up and rose a brow in confusion. Then he said the craziest shit I've ever heard.

"Don't come with today, stay here. Stay here until we get back," he whispered, his jaw tight as he stared down at me. I felt as though he could see everything, above and below the surface. Those massive hands cupped my jaw gently as a look of profound concern, sadness, and affection filtered through his eyes.

I opened my mouth and he silenced it with a kiss that had me shivering. He pulled back and his hands, tense on either side of me now, were shaking with tension. His voice was a harsh whisper. "I know you will go anyway, so I need you to promise me something, Vegas."

My head was nodding before I'd thought about it.

"If you think for even a moment that you are in danger of being caught or killed, you don't stick around to see what happens. You get the fuck out of there. I don't care who is involved. Promise me that you will keep yourself safe."

I couldn't lie to Edwin.

"I will do my damned best to keep myself safe," I said in a rough voice, "but I won't run away from the people I love if they are being hurt Edwin. Ever. I won't do it."

I saw resignation in his eyes and something far more

dangerous as he nodded and began to lace up the back while still facing me. Impressive, I know.

"I love you, dolcezza," he whispered against my forehead once he was done.

I went to tell him what I felt but he placed a thumb on my lips "Don't say it out loud. Please. I'm barely hanging on right now. If you say it I may lock you up and not give you a choice on the matter."

He was being honest, I could tell.

A knock on the door had both of us turning to find Bandit standing in the doorway. His eyes were a far lighter shade today, nearly electric and Edwin offered him a look I didn't really understand. Both of them were in thicker armor but it fit their bodies. He kissed my head and passed, leaving Bandit looking at me with an odd and almost concerned look.

"What's wrong?" I whispered.

Bandit walked closer and wrapped his arms around my neck and pulled me flat against him. His words scared me. "I can't see anything about today, Ve. No deaths on either side. There is something blocking me."

My body broke out in chills as I processed his words. When I pulled back my hands found their way to smooth over his chest. "You still see us alive though, right? We don't die in the long run?"

He nods and frowns. "It doesn't mean others won't die. It doesn't mean someone won't get hurt. I don't know how any of this works. For all I know, my lack of visions regarding our deaths could mean nothing."

"I have to believe it does," I whispered.

His eyes closed for a moment before he pinned me with a look. "I heard that creepy bastard looks like me."

I shook my head. "He might have similar features, but

trust me his similarities won't stop me from kicking the bastard's ass."

Those eyes flashed dangerously. "I want him dead, Vegas. Somehow, some way."

My lips twisted as I offered a mini head bow. "One dead Dark Fae Heir on it's way, sir."

Bandit let out a real laugh as he pulled me from the bathroom. I could hear everyone downstairs and a larger movement outside. I passed the window and my eyes widened realizing the whole of the Red Masques were outside in formation. An exciting thrill had my magic standing up finally.

The bitch knew a battle was coming and she shimmied into armor and war paint.

As soon as I stepped down onto the main floor, Kodiak was there and his eyes were darker than usual today. He didn't need to say anything to express his concern. I pressed a kiss to his cheek and continued walking forward. Decimus and Grover both offered me looks that were a bit lost and I knew they were probably feeling a bit overwhelmed with all of this. I squeezed both of their shoulders and stepped outside as Cosimo and Booker looked over. I felt far better knowing they would be at the base camp along with Bandit. Bandit because the representative didn't want to lose their only time mage and Cosimo and Booker because healing and ink rune abilities were in demand during battles.

Rocket stood slightly behind Edwin, Blue, and Byron. His metallic gray eyes met mine and I couldn't help the small flicker of black fire that flashed across my skin. His power was right under the surface and I could feel my power awakening all of my boys' energy. I heard a few of them adjust slightly as they muttered curses. My fire roared to life as I stepped up next to Blue.

"Beautiful." He offered me an exciting look that filled his denim blue eyes. I squeezed his hand as Byron pressed a kiss to my temple.

"Are we ready?" Edwin asked, his eyes nearly black as his icy power expanded. I could see myself in his obsidian eyes. I was surprised to find that my lilac eyes were black and my hair shimmering with different shades.

This was so not the time to look like a rainbow.

"Shall we?" Byron led me towards a space between units. Edwin was shouting commands and Blue stood on the other side of me as my boys filled in between us, similar to how we'd been at the party earlier last week.

Shit. Was that only a few days ago?

As we began to move towards the northern district, I tried to shut down my more emotional side. It was a futile event and the more I embraced it the stronger my powers seemed to emerge. I muttered a curse under my breath. I was glad I hadn't made that damned promise.

All I knew for sure was that my boys were making it out of this alive.

I could fucking guarantee that.

16

BANDIT

I'd always considered myself a fairly imaginative person. Well, at least I'd read a good amount of fantasy elements that would have led me to believe I'd know what a battle like this would have looked like. I really had no fucking clue, though, because this was nothing like the movies.

My eyes trailed over the entire massive field that faced the north wall, a hazy mist filling the space in the early morning light. My skin crawled with energy and I felt frustrated at my magic which had gone completely silent. I didn't think any of my family would die, but a bit of a heads up on injuries would have been nice.

It was odd seeing the same men that I'd grown up with in a position like this. The representatives and myself were placed in an advisory base camp that overlooked the entire scene coupled with a contingency of archers. My enhanced vision allowed me to see the mass quantities of SE guard and the Red Masque members. It reminded me briefly of a large pyramid with the Red Masques on the outside lines and the middle filled with soldiers.

Edwin and the rest of our team were split on either side of Queen Gray and her True Heir Guard. All of which caused my head to hurt because of the massive pull of power. I mean, shit, it would have been scary if anything actually scared me. Well, one thing did.

That one thing was standing right next to Gray.

Although, this was a different version of Ve. I would almost claim that this side was more natural to her in some ways but I could tell it was shocking to some of my brothers. I didn't blame them. She had been intimidating while battling with Gray and even now I could see her flames flashing across her skin like scales.

It really wasn't the time to be getting turned on, but that didn't stop me. It didn't seem anything stopped me from getting a fucking hard on regarding Vegas. Even now the feel of her skin under my hands was like some embedded pattern on my subconscious.

"Don't worry about them," Laurena spoke. "They are prepared."

I looked at her and examined her kind smile before speaking. "I'm not worried."

She tilted her head. "You seem worried. I can feel it in your energy."

My brow dipped. Was I worried? That was very unlike me.

"Maybe," I admitted. "I'll admit that I am frustrated with not being able to see anything helpful."

"Bandit," she drew my attention. "You just received your powers. Don't be too hard on yourself."

Yeah, that didn't cut it for me.

I nodded and my mind went back to the situation at hand. There was a darkness roaming under my skin and it was hungry for blood, particularly Victor's blood. My nostrils flared just at the thought of him hurting Ve. He was going to die. Whether I did it or she did, one of us would be killing him. I didn't need my magic to know that.

A scout ran up the stairs of the base camp and began to talk rapidly in that damn language I needed to learn. Everyone looked towards the northern borders. It was a forested natural land barrier and currently it was growing in size with Fae in black and green. I noticed they weren't running but walking.

"Maybe they want to negotiate?" one of the representatives spoke.

I snorted. No. That wasn't it.

My entire body froze as a familiar energy source entered the presumed barrier. Except it wasn't Victor's magic. It was an older man on a white horse that matched his silver hair perfectly. My eyes widened looking at the man approaching our front lines.

For the first time ever, I felt truly taken off guard.

I could feel the shock radiating through our family bond and I was realizing very quickly why exactly Victor looked so much like me. I hoped I was wrong but something told me that the man approaching Queen Gray was related to me.

And I didn't mean a distant cousin.

I went to say something to Laurena when a shock of pain pulsed through my brain causing me to let out a curse. My knees broke as mind numbing pain seared my body like acid burning away at my skin. My fingers gripped blindly at the floor as my eyes closed.

I had never passed out in my life and I'd been through a lot of pain.

There was no doubt that I was about to pass out and right before the blackness consumed me, my power roared to life in defense. White static noise filled my vision and ears as a picture flashed before my eyes, warning me of what to come. My magic pulsed out and I could feel the shock wave moving across the army.

I went to speak but it was far too late for that.

VEGAS

"Holy fuck." I heard Decimus refer to the man riding towards us on a horse as white as Gray's was black. The power radiating off him was intense but the shocking part had nothing to do with that and everything to do with the resemblance he bore to Bandit.

There was only one way that was possible and none of us had the time to consider that right now.

However, the threat of Bandit being taken from me, even if unreasonable, had my power turning to an extreme searing melting temperature. All around me my men's powers jumped to life and it was so intense that Gray looked at me momentarily. I kept my focus on what was ahead of us. I wanted to explain to her what she was feeling because the woman knew something was up. I felt guilty as each moment passed without telling her.

Her main focus and attention was on something entirely different.

I could feel her fury rolling through our very light connection. She hated the man in front of us and I couldn't blame her...but I could join her. After meeting my creator, it was very clear that this asshole deserved to die. So he would. I could do that for my new friend.

"This isn't right," I murmured.

A pulse of power rolled over everyone, even Mario, that was from the back of the camp. Bandit. I looked back and felt static crackle in the air causing everyone to shiver. Mario's expression turned dark but before anyone could say anything, it was gone.

Silent.

If my connection with Bandit wasn't still present I would be terrified of what happened to him.

Gray shook with fury as she took a deep breath. A coldness seemed to invade her body. She spoke softly. "I would agree with that."

"Gray," Rhodes spoke tightly. "There were troops attempting to come from the east border but we've intercepted them with the men already stationed there."

She nodded and offered him a slight shoulder squeeze, never looking away. Their army was large but I had to admit I was feeling fairly good about the odds. Which was exactly why Mario's amused smile bothered me. The concern over the odd power surge was missing. I looked up at Gray and her nostrils flared as if she was attempting to grasp what the cause of his humor was.

There was silence as they paused nearly fifty yards away, both armies coming to a stand still. I breathed out as the air around me misted because of my body temperature. The cold ground was still under my feet but the surge of power from my boys was nothing like I'd ever felt before. I had no doubt that they were capable of aiding in this victory.

Would it be a neat and practiced event? Gods, no.

Would there be extra bloodshed for fun? Absolutely.

Would I be making inappropriate jokes through most of it? Yep.

Mario nodded towards the center as he approached, as a sign of goodwill no doubt, and Gray encouraged her horse forward. I was momentarily distracted by how badass she was and how fucking crazy this situation was. Her entire suit was silver and her hair was pulled back so that her crown sat prominently on her head. Rhodes stepped up next to me along with Neo, both of them tense as though they were ready to intercept at a moments notice. If I hadn't been in my own power bubble, I'd be blown away by their intense levels of energy.

I couldn't hear what Mario and Gray were saying to one another but based off her intense emotions, it clearly wasn't good. I hated the smile on his face and I realized after just a moment that something was terribly odd about their conversation. It was like there was no point to it...

"Guys," I spoke quietly but rushed. "He's distracting her."

Rhodes looked at me. "It's possible that he doesn't know that we've captured the east border."

Neo shook his head. "She's right, this is something different."

The next few moments seemed to occur in slow motion. I know. That is stereotypical, right? Except it truly felt that way. My head snapped up as a sensation hit me like a freight train.

No sooner had he said the words than time rippled past me in slow motion. My flame roared up inside of me defensively, hitting me like a truck as a massive roar ripped through the dawn. Before I rationalized what it was, my hands flung out as my skin burst with searing heat and a low snarl broke over my lips.

A sonic boom broke out of my chest and just as it had been with Tamara's men, it shot out in all different directions in a searing breath of power. The power flashed a black mirrored surface as the dragon's flames hit it.

It would have burnt everyone. It would have killed everyone.

I felt pleasure spike through me at absorbing the impact

of the dragon's flames. Cool. Good to know I can get off on fire and fighting. Always an interesting development.

My power snapped back as chaos rained down on the area around us. The skies filled with multiple dark shaded dragons as Adyen broke through the air while shifting. His form massive and much larger than the Dark Fae's dragons. I noticed several other gold-colored dragons and briefly wondered if there was a relation. I didn't have time to do that though because on the ground Mario's army collided with ours as the two opposing sides clashed like aggressive waves. I narrowly avoided swords that swept towards me as my body defended itself instinctively.

My gaze whipped to my boys and the rest of Gray's army. I calculated that we were approximately the same in size but that size was nearly incomprehensible. The two armies were only distinguishable by the colors of each uniform. My gaze filled with green and black as a massive man swept me aside with the hit of a club. Who the fuck uses one of those?

I grunted as my hands lit up with blue flames and my power twirled to life, smiling at the anger rising in me. I began to throw them at the fuckers in small direct hits. It seemed as though hellfire, my blue flames, were effective because the intended targets burst into flames instantly.

In the distance, my hearing picked up on my boys as I was able to catch just how well they were doing. Blue, in true fashion, was covered in nearly as much blood as Byron as the two psychos seemed to work together in order to kill as many soldiers as possible. It was sort of sexy but I tried to ignore that because now was not the time.

"Watch out, princess," Decimus grunted as I rolled to the side and a vine, massive and dark in coloring, shot out to grasp two men that had moved towards me with supernatural speed. It was hard to keep track of just how fast everyone was moving and I felt my eyebrows go up as the men disappeared into a sinkhole. That was cool as fuck.

"Catch!" Grover called out as I turned and grasped a lightweight black sword in my hand. Instantly, my blue flames transferred from my hands onto the sword.

"Grover," I grinned as I met someone's blade theirs melting with ease. "This is fucking amazing."

Also, can we just talk about what a badass I am. It reminded me of killing the demon in Las Vegas. I loved that. I loved it because I didn't feel helpless. I sort of felt like Gray. Gray, who was causing a massive explosion of ash and cold ice. My magic was urging me to go back to Gray but as someone slammed into me, I swept my sword right into their stomach. He cried out and blood sprayed onto me but not as much as I expected because it cauterized the wound.

"Vegas," Edwin sung with enjoyment as the eccentric fucker flashed me a smile. His icy power kissed mine as he ran right past me and instantly killed those who passed him, the liquefaction of their organs obvious from the dark liquid falling from every orifice.

"You are all enjoying this way too much," I muttered as a snarl broke through behind me and Kodiak's energy surrounded me. I jumped up as his lean dark body darted forward and I turned just in time to miss a hit to the face. Another club? Wait, was that a flogger?

A raw earthy scent crawled over me as I turned into Rocket. His eyes flashed dark as his powers flared to life and my black soul flames licked his skin. Someone slammed into him from behind but turned to ash right as they hit into us. A knife slipped from Rocket's boots as he threw it directly behind me and hit someone square in the chest.

"Holy fuck!" Heat flashed over my skin. "You are so getting laid for that."

Rocket let out a bark of laughter as I slipped under his arms and brought my sword up to arch into someone in front of me. I briefly saw a flash of blue eyes and my heart hurt. It hurt because I knew I was killing someone that was being forced into this situation. Mario didn't strike me as a very understanding king.

The guilt was gone then as the same figure attempted to stab me in the same movement. All right, fucker. You deserve to die. I rolled beneath another massive man and began to sprint forward with a speed I didn't realize was possible. I found myself moving towards the storm that was Gray as lightning flashed in the sky that struck several of the hundreds of men in her vicinity.

So fucking cool.

I let out a cry as the earth buckled underneath me and I was thrown back. My head snapped back as a massive creature let out a terrifying roar. I snarled. Fucking dragons, man. Instead of attacking though, the creature did something so much worse. In less than a moment we were surrounded by flames in a tight circle and as his head dipped down I heard my savage power purr in excitement. The flames weren't harmful to me but no one else would be able to reach us.

Us... as in Victor and me.

Yes. Victor. The man who walked with an agile, almost easy gait along the dragon's scaly neck before letting his feet hit the ground. Despite the quietness of the sound, I heard it because the rest of the battle silenced within our circle. I'm sure it was still going on but I couldn't focus on anything else but the fucker in front of me.

My skin broke out in shivers as I fought to bury my fear deep down inside of me. It wasn't too hard. I couldn't be scared at this moment because I was so furious. Furious at this bastard I planned on killing. My chin shot up as he finally met my gaze.

Fuck, did he look like Bandit though.

"Little flame," he flashed me a cruel smile. As his power wrapped around the circle I could feel the sickness that Rocket had noticed. The acidic energy rolled across my power and began to pierce my skin like small needles. I refused to fucking react, though.

Victor's dark green eyes, nearly black with a fluorescent green around his pupil, narrowed as he stepped closer to me. His head tilted in a predatory dip and I tried to focus on his magic rather than the massive size difference between us. Victor was massive, nearly 6'6", if I had to guess, and his icy white hair was braided back to highlight his lean face.

All right, now I felt bad about my *Lord of the Rings* joke before. This. This was very Lord of the Rings-ish. I mean the man was wearing a hunting ensemble with a bow and arrow. It was a cool look if the man wasn't so fucking crazy.

I had to keep noting the difference between the two of them. Victor and Bandit. Bandit and Victor. My Bandit was tall but around 6'4 and his muscles were leaner but more defined. My Bandit didn't smirk like that. My Bandit was the one that had been my best friend since I was ten. Bandit was mine and Victor fucking sucked for looking like him. I knew that was irrational.

"I have to say," I drawled because I clearly liked playing around with death. "You aren't nearly as scary as the games you craft. I'm authentically disappointed."

A small smile tilted his lips as he put out a hand in a peaceful gesture. "The last thing I want to do is scare you, Vegas. Now, come on. We don't have all day and I don't want you around this bloodshed."

My mouth popped open as I nearly sputtered. Was this a fucking joke? Was this guy real?

"What the hell do you not get about me NOT being interested in you?" I snarled. "Are you delusional?"

A flash of feral anger crossed his features as he stalked forward, causing me to back around the edge of the circle away from him. I could have crossed but I knew it wouldn't change anything. No, the only thing that would change this would be fighting back and I just wasn't prepared to attack yet.

"Little flame!" he yelled with fury. "I don't want to hurt you. Come here, now."

I smirked and realized my time for delay was up. "That's fucking unfortunate."

Over his shoulder, I could see the group of soldiers attacking Gray double in size. I knew she could probably handle it but my magic knew that it was meant to be fighting by her side. It also may have had something to do with my men being around the same area. I flashed through our connection and I was happy to find that they were still healthy. Bandit, though, seemed tense. He probably had seen Senior Crazy and Son.

"Why is that unfortunate?" Victor asked moving forward as I let my body choose which flame it wanted to fuck with today. Turns out she was in a bad fucking mood.

"Cuz' I really want to hurt you," I hissed as my hand shot out to press against his chest as I forced soul fire into him. I figured it wouldn't kill him but when his growl ripped through the air, I realized I may have fucked up. He really had been holding back.

A wave of sickness hit me as I narrowly avoided his power. It was like a green wave of acid reaching for me. He chuckled darkly and offered me a determined look.

"Now, sweetheart, you're going to have to be punished for that little stunt."

In a movement so fast he didn't expect it, I jumped over the dragon fire and turned preparing to brace for another attack. Except this time the fucker was faster and hit my sternum before landing another punch to my face. Asshole. I threw my body weight back and flipped in the air, ignoring whoever called my name. I wasn't really in control of myself anymore and I took a backseat as my magic took center stage. Victor and I began to exchange blows and despite his strength I began to feel far more confident than I'd even felt sparring with Gray. I think it had to do with the fact that I hated this fucking guy.

"So talented," he quipped softly. "A true prize. Much more than I expected."

He was so close behind me that I had to duck and my hands heated to burn him. I was suddenly missing that sword. I had no idea where it was but most likely somewhere by that massive dragon. I grunted as the fire burnt his flesh and exposed bone with a nasty smell. Luckily, it only lasted a horrible moment before his skin regenerated. Talk about a useful skill.

Guess I would have to be able to do this more often than I assumed.

"Maybe you should adjust your fucking expectations," I snapped.

"So naïve," he chuckled as I watched his power collapse around him in a movement so fast, I barely had time to prepare for his reappearing act. I rolled down and pulled out two black smooth knives and wedged them right into his groin. He let out a howl of pain that had me smiling because I'd genuinely surprised the bastard.

My victory was short lived though.

Gray's sudden grunt of pain and fury through our connection had me sprinting towards her. It left my back open for attack and if it hadn't been for Edwin, turning me away from the acidic shot of magic, I would have paid for it. He pushed past me and let out his icy black energy in a disastrous effect.

Sucks to be you, Vic.

"Having fun?" Gray asked in a laugh that sounded pained. She continued to move like a storm that was killing all of the men around her. Something was off though and I realized that her magic felt weak. Almost drained. My head snapped to Mario who was very obviously playing fucking games. A low sound broke through my chest as the man's eyes met mine with smug amusement.

Oh. My magic was livid.

"Something like that," I ground out. I felt a whole new defensive power roar to life and light me up. One that had nothing to do with myself and everything with the fury I felt towards Mario's attack on Gray. The bastard was sitting watching this play out like it was a fucking soap opera.

It wasn't just her either. No, as I looked around my skin began to boil at the bloodshed that was occurring. My dream flashed through my head and determination slammed into me. What sealed it for me though? My boys. Their faces were covered in blood and while they were alive, I could feel the exhaustion through their bond. Was it possible Mario was pulling on everyone?

How had things turned bad so fast? I cursed because I'd clearly been distracted by Victor.

This wasn't my kingdom but it was my home. A home I hadn't even remembered but felt instinctively alive inside of me. I could feel the energy of the land rise up to support me as it recognized my acceptance of my origin. I wanted Mario

FIRE & SMOKE

dead and not just because of Gray or my boys. No. I wanted him dead because the fucker was trying to hurt this land and the people who thrived in it.

I'd never felt so determined before.

"Holy fuck," someone shouted as my body launched forward and an intensity like never before filled me. Fury rolled through me as my hands lit up with purple flames.

Flames that whispered words of vengeance.

I'd always believed that emotion could harm your ability to focus. So, of course magic had to be different. The more I felt, the less confused I became and the more alive. My magic rolled its way up from my toes all the way to my hair as I reached him. Mario seemingly surprised, dismounted from his horse and attempted to shoot his dark acidic power at me. Like a lightning bolt. It didn't stop or hurt me though. Instead I sped up and, right on impact, someone screamed my name.

Except, instead of rolling to the ground I was airborne and Mario's scream had me realizing this was all me. I had never been one for heights but I found myself soaring through the air as my back arched and I carried the fucker upwards. My purple flames began to burn him slowly, almost in torture, as he began to tremble and shake. I could feel when he stopped pulling on others because he started to use all his power to fight me.

It wasn't working.

"End this," I demanded, holding him up by his collar. I was impressed by my strength and wondered if it had to do with the wings.

Wait. What?

Holy what the actual fuck.

My head shot to either side as I realized that my ability to fly came from two brilliant flame-like wings that shifted through a beautiful pattern of purple and black. Dude. I can't even. I would need to focus on this way more later...

"Never," he snarled as I tightened my grip.

"I will kill you," I whispered. "Call them off or I will end you, Mario."

I nearly didn't recognize my voice and realized my magic had turned it into an almost textured tone. I saw his mouth move as he whispered "fuck you" so, I let him go. His screams made me smile and I found myself thinking that I may not be all that different from Blue. I caught the bastard king twenty yards down. He grunted as I grabbed the back of his armor and swung him around to face me.

"Now," I demanded sharply.

Something flashed in his eyes though and I ducked just a minute late, one of his dragon's hitting into me from the side before grasping him in his talons. I followed down, diving towards him, while letting out a blue explosion of fire on some of the Dark Fae soldiers. I landed and stalked towards where the king had been dropped, only to find myself freezing.

A simple sound had everything paused. My breathing caught.

No.

Just no.

Victor flashed me a smile as he stood over Kodiak's wolf form. I felt panic hit my chest and my magic silenced for just a moment, her indecision between helping Gray and saving Kodiak fighting for dominance. I ignored her and stepped forward, before crying out as someone gripped my hair. Before I could do anything, Blue had them on the ground and had ripped out their throat.

With his teeth.

Well, that answers that.

"Don't touch her fucking hair," he muttered. I would have found it funny if it wasn't for another howl of pain.

Shit.

Without thinking I stalked forward, my black flames lighting up next to my blue in a defensive manner. Victor had a brilliant grin on his face and as I grew closer I realized that Kodi was being held down by his power. Oh, shit. I was so about to break a bunch of promises.

What was I supposed to do though, let him have Kodiak? To kill Kodiak? Ask Gray to aid me while she continues to massacre her way through the hundred soldiers trying to take her land? No. This was my battle. I felt some of my boys, namely Edwin, attempt to reach me but I threw up a barrier of flames that even he couldn't reach. The Dark Fae prince's smile lessened slightly as he realized what I was doing exactly. In another surge of power, he forced Kodiak's shift. His special uniform clothed him but there were acidic holes and my lips peeled back at the sight of the profuse blood and injuries scarring him.

"Kodi," I whispered as I ignored the prince and dragon. The calls from outside the circle didn't matter. I brushed his dark matted hair, wet with blood, as I let a cold fury settle over me. I wasn't happy about what I was about to do but it may be just the way to rid myself of Victor.

"Baby," he groaned. "Don't you fucking dare."

"I'll kill him," Victor drawled nearly sounding bored.

I had no doubt he meant it.

"Vegas," Kodiak growled as blood dripped down from his nose. "Go. Now."

"No," I whispered as I fully knelt down and Victor's power released softly to hover around the two of us equally. I knew it could clamp on painfully in a moment's notice. He had no need to worry, though, I wouldn't kill him here. I would kill him when no one was around to suffer the consequences of my choices.

"You promised," Kodiak demanded, his eyes wide and filled with pain. I leaned his head into my lap as tears threatened. Emotion kissed my cold fury.

"You can punish me later," I murmured as he let out a soft angry rumble. There was a wound in his stomach that was pooling with blood. He was going to die.

"Time to say goodbye, little flame," Victor announced.

"Can I have a minute?" I asked softly, my chest vibrating like boiling water.

Victor didn't say anything but he didn't stop me from placing my forehead against Kodiak's as his hands gripped my forearms. Gods. This was my fault. I had gotten distracted. I had tried to fight a battle that wasn't fully mine. If I had fought Victor then Kodiak would have never tried to fight him in the first place.

"Baby," his voice cracked as tears welled up, "please don't go."

My magic slowed like molten liquid and before I knew it, a white flame sealed over Kodiak's massive body. His injuries began to slowly heal. So, that was what that was for. Victor moved and I knew he would kill him instantly if I pulled anything. I pressed my lips against Kodiak's gently as I felt our bond strengthen. My chest tattoo burned gently.

"I'll find you," he managed in a soft pained breath. It made me know that this was the right choice. I wasn't about to let him die.

How ironic and cruel life could be. I had no doubt that my choice here would have long lasting effects and it was the cherry on top that it was Kodiak of all people. He would beat himself up over this. Still. He would be alive.

"I know," I murmured gently. "You always know where I am. I have no doubt that you will find me."

"Time is up," Victor stated harshly.

"I love you," I stated softly as the cold spread back through me in response to shutting down my emotions. Victor grabbed my hair and caused a groan to pull from my lips as he dragged me towards the dragon. Kodiak, barely moving, offered me a broken look as I offered a soft smile from the prison of Victor's power.

He would try to find me.

I didn't want it to get to that though.

I would get out. I would get out on my own.

My powers went silent with his wrapped around me. I hated that. I hated that I couldn't fight back right now. As the black flames fell my boys seemed to realize what exactly was going on. Emotions so intense, I had to block them out, hit our bond.

Blue's eyes met mine, turning black against the red blood covering him, as a blankness took hold of his expression causing tears to well up in my eyes. I wasn't sad though. I was furious. How dare Victor make my boys feel like this. My hearing was muted but I could see Decimus turn from where he was using his magic to effectively root people to the ground. His concentration was lost and I nearly yelled in warning as men broke away to attack him, luckily Grover kept his wits enough to keep him alive. His eyes filled with so much pain that I felt my chest break. I refused to cry out as Victor effectively dragged my body up the dragon and tossed me on my stomach, my hands gripping the creature.

Byron began running towards us and I watched as Victor threw out a shield causing my blood mage to nearly get knocked on his ass. Rocket must have heard the impact because he turned from killing someone to lock eyes with me as a silver mist began to form around him. He watched me void of emotions as pain rushed through our bond, making me feel sick. I barely missed that the dead around him began to rise, from both sides, as they seemed to await orders from Rocket. The man couldn't seem to tear his eyes away from me though.

I really hoped Mario knew how to deal with zombies.

I almost laughed at the small sense of pride that filled me. I knew the boys would win this and I felt as though I was doing my part by removing one major threat. He was only here for one reason after all. Plus, it would be easy to kill him away from anyone I would worry about.

I just needed him isolated.

When a pull of energy shot through me, Edwin's black eyes met mine as a look of pure horror and fury crossed his features. As the dragon took off, Victor pressed my neck down in a tight hold as my breathing turned into a pant. My magic was completely pinned inside of me and I realized this was the danger of a Heir and why Gray and I had been so well matched. It pissed me off because this douche wasn't even a True Heir. He didn't deserve to one up me.

As we soared through the air, I felt an icy tendril of power pull at the dragon. Victor just laughed, flying higher. I met Gray's eyes that were black as she held Mario in her grasp. The king appeared to be dying. Thank fuck.

As we passed the once constructed base camp, I saw Cosimo, Bandit, and Booker fighting and attempting to aid in keeping the counsel members safe. They weren't sitting idly by though and I was proud to see how strong everyone was being. I couldn't meet my boys' expressions but Bandit's energy was so dark that I forced myself to meet the spring green gaze. I sent out a soft pulse of affection through our bond as he whispered softly in response.

I realized that somehow his power had broken through and Victor seemed to notice. I tried to distract him by struggling. I had an instinctive feeling that Bandit's powers needed to be kept secret for now. Victor leaned against my ear and whispered cruel sharp words.

"Time to go home, little flame." He tugged on my ear and bile rose in my throat.

I briefly remembered when I told Booker I'd kill this fucker. I planned on completing that. The next time they saw Victor he would be dead and I would be the one standing over him.

His blood on my hands.

II

THE DARK FAE

17

KODIAK

"Shift."

The demand made me furious and that was the first rational thought I'd had in the three weeks we'd been traveling. I let out a low growl as the surrounding camp stilled. I knew I was a scary motherfucker and my wolf was proud of that. I let out a deep, pained sound that turned from a whine to a grunt as I fell directly onto my face. The ground in our camp was frozen and with it came a light snow.

I didn't want to think about any of this.

I didn't want to think.

Shortly after demolishing the Dark Fae army, we realized that a small unit had made it out and were returning back to the kingdom. I'd shifted immediately for tracking purposes and despite our extended travels I hadn't turned back until today. Until Edwin had demanded it and, god, that made me furious. I closed my eyes as my lashes brushed the white snow that laid on the ground.

Vegas loved snow.

Fuck.

"I'm really tired of all this shit," Edwin spoke in a dark tone as I went up on my fists, his power receding as he tossed me a pair of pants. I refused to verbally respond because my voice was choked from the raw pain echoing in my chest. God, it hurt so much. So much more than it had as an animal. In my wolf form I felt nothing.

In this form I felt guilt. So much terrible guilt. I couldn't even see in front of me. So much that I couldn't even think about why. Why I felt so guilty. Why she was gone. I couldn't go there. Not today. I couldn't. Not until I had her in my arms.

Not until I had found her.

Even in human form my tracking was fantastic and I had aided in our travel towards the Dark Fae lands. It had been my singular focus. There had been no military resistance as we crossed their border. Their military was depleted and Edwin suspected they had bunkered down in the main castle. So that was where we were headed.

Except now I was in so much pain I could barely focus on tracking her.

I needed to, though.

God, why did it hurt so much? There was more than just the guilt. My skin felt overheated and my head was pounding. My wolf was whining in my head and I felt as though I was losing consciousness. What was going on?

Edwin had dark circles under his eyes and his face was hollow. He looked as awful as I felt. The animal part of me wanted to shift back so that I could seek her out. I didn't need her necklace or arm tracker to find her. That damn scent, lilac and midnight rain, was ingrained in my subconscious. I could find her anywhere. I wanted to move faster than these fucking soliders would. I wanted to reach Victor and Mario tonight. I wanted to tear into their flesh and devour them whole.

I wanted them to suffer as much as I was suffering.

I wanted them to feel the pain I felt.

I wanted them to feel the loss I felt.

I wanted to kill them. I'd never experienced this level of bloodlust.

I faced Edwin and offered him a blank look. I could see Blue walking towards us and his face was void of emotions, completely. Our entire connection had been shut down and until today I hadn't realized the extent of it. I knew they had tried to connect mentally with Vegas but nothing had happened, no response from her for three weeks. I let out a deep breath and shook my head to clear my dark thoughts.

I could only meet Edwin's eyes though. I didn't look at Blue.

I didn't want to see the blame.

It was my fault she was gone.

Absolutely gone.

This was my fault. I caused this.

My thoughts were disrupted by an electric shock that went through me. I let out a low pained sound as my skin broke out into cold shivers at the thought of her alone. At the thought of her being tortured.... being hurt... being touched by him. By them.

I felt nauseous tension break through my throat. I began to shake. I wanted to shift. I was furious. I was guilty. I was sad. I wish this was just a panic attack. Red spotted my vision. My wolf was trying to tell me something but my brain didn't get it. It didn't understand the message.

Maybe I had officially lost it.

Overwhelming panic and anxiety rooted through me as I

nearly passed out from trying to stop the shift. He would only force me to change back. I knew I needed to stay in human form. I was more helpful when I could actually communicate.

"What the fuck is going on with you?" Blue snarled as my wolf let out a low, violent sound. I could hear everyone around us trying to act like they weren't staring at the obvious tension occuring.

Edwin frowned as his brows pulled together and realization dawned on his face. Of what? I had no idea. I closed my eyes. I couldn't stop the chant that started in my head.

Vegas.

Vegas.

You did this. She is gone because of you.

My Vegas.

My baby girl.

I could see her wide determined eyes that were a light lilac when filled with tears. She peered down at me with so much love. So much love before sacrificing herself. I let out a low and angry growl that almost sounded pained. I was supposed to be finding her and I hadn't. We weren't moving fast enough, I was a failure.

She had said she wouldn't leave.

That she wouldn't give herself over.

She did it to save your life.

My wolf was whispering in my head. I knew he was right. I knew that I would have done the same for her. But, god. Why did she have to go? I loved her so fucking much it hurt.

"He's going through withdrawal," Edwin muttered in near shock. "I need to ask Adyen or Rhodes. I can't confirm it because it is essentially unheard of even when you are a naturalistic mage and have an animal counterpart, but I think he is going through mate withdrawal."

The world went silent with that one word.

Mate?

Mate.

Holy shit. Mate.

Vegas's beautiful voice hit my ears from the day of the battle. As I began to shake and my sight blurred, I heard a familiar voice. He was talking to Edwin and I began to let out a shaky breath. God. I knew nothing would make sense until I found her.

I needed her.

"You need to open the connection back up," Adyen snapped at Edwin.

"Why?" Edwin whispered his voice rough. I knew we all wanted to hide our pain.

"He needs something to stabilize him," Rhodes explained. "It should work. When they formed the mating bond they traditionally should have spent most of their time together until his animal calmed down. The fact that he even has a mate is mind blowing because unless you have shifter blood, it doesn't happen. I can only assume the strength level has to do with the larger connection between the group of you."

"The connection you have yet to explain," Adyen muttered.

"Not the time," Blue hissed.

"Just make it stop," I nearly puked.

Without another word the bond was opened up. I grunted as pain flooded through me. Not just pain though. I felt everything. Insanity. Fear. Possessiveness. Darkness. Pain. Fury. So much anger. At the base of it though?

At the base of it, there was something familiar.

The soft scent of midnight rain filled my lungs as the ten of us connected with ease, despite the pain. Lilac had my wolf letting out a soft whine as we both calmed. The nausea disappeared and my eyes began to clear. I could breathe and as I pulled in a breath of fresh air, I realized that my guilt was being replaced with determination.

I stood up as I met Blue's eyes.

Blue who had been my best friend and brother since I found my family. His eyes were dark but he offered me an understanding look before squeezing my shoulder. I hadn't realized how worried he'd been and something about that resonated in me.

I'd always been worried about Vegas's safety and well being.

I knew there was more to it than that now. I had to worry about the whole family. I tried to center myself and knew that was what Vegas would want. She would want me to watch out for our family. My wolf let out a small sound at the idea of being assigned a protector in her mind.

One day we would have a real family I'd need to watch out for.

Our own children.

I suppose this was a better time to start than ever.

My voice was rough as I looked up at the dawn, letting my senses expand out. "We can be there in less than a week if we leave now and stop less at night."

I'm coming for you baby girl.

BOOKER

My skull felt as though it was going to explode. I could even imagine what it would look like against these tent walls. I could also ask Sheriff to paint me a picture since the bastard refused to leave me alone. Originally, we had all been thrilled that Tamara and her men had shown up to the battle field despite being late. I know. Who is late to a war, right? Apparently they had gotten into an argument about what she was wearing and it delayed them for six hours.

Yeah. That is just as ridiculous as it sounds.

As it stood though, Sheriff now wouldn't leave me alone and he continued to ask me for things that he knew I couldn't give. Like my first sketch I'd ever drawn which was no doubt buried underneath years of trash somewhere in the United States. I tried to pay him no mind because I had no idea what the fuck I would say to him.

"Alright," Sheriff bargained from the chair across the room, "I want your first ink drawing."

Was this asshole for real? I dropped the pencil I was working with and stared at the ink across from me. The ink that would allow me to make anything essentially real.

My lips twisted.

I wished that I could make Vegas appear.

That thought turned over in my head as I felt the realization hit me. Why couldn't I draw a way to her? Couldn't it be as easy as drawing a door? Or maybe there was a spell for locating her.

Despite the cold, I sprinted towards Edwin and Byron's tent not even bothering to call out. Sheriff was making enough noise as it was. When I entered the tent, I wasn't surprised to find the first already up with his gaze fixated on a glowing candle. The second was a bit more depressing. I could practically see Byron spiraling and while I wasn't one hundred percent positive, I felt as though that was a dangerous thing. It wasn't like I could ignore the scars on his arms.

"Booker?" Edwin looked at me curiously.

"Is it possible to draw, with ink obviously, a doorway to reach her?"

I didn't bother with niceties.

The mage tilted his head to the side and then shook his head making my heart sink. "I don't think so because the Dark Fae would have wards stopping that. Plus, portal traveling can get very... messy if you haven't done it before."

My hand found a way through my thick hair, "Yeah. That makes sense. My only other idea was asking if there was a locator spell."

Edwin stood up as a wave of recognition crossed his features. Byron seemed confused. "Edwin, what are you doing?"

The man had a lot of fucking books and he was now inside of a case sorting through some of them. I realized that Byron had joined him as he finally reached the one he'd been looking for. It was black and had a green leather lining.

"What is that?" I murmured.

"This," Edwin looked authentically happy for the first time in weeks, "is the entire blueprint, hand drawn by an ink mage, of the Dark Fae castle. It is about one hundred years old but things around here don't change much anyway."

"So what can it do?" I tilted my head not getting it.

"We need something of Vegas's," he suggested as Byron began by grabbing two candles and setting them on the floor, seeming to know what exactly Edwin was planning.

"I don't think I brought anything," I frowned.

"I did," Kodiak stated, walking through the tent looking wide awake despite the dark circles. "It isn't much but it should do."

He handed over a soft purple scarf that I recognized her normal winter wear. I wondered where the hell he'd kept that while shifted. As Blue joined us, I had my answer.

Shit. I understood why they brought it. I bet it smelled like midnight rain and lilacs.

"Byron, can you go get Rhodes and Adyen? They will want to be part of this," Edwin was still setting up.

"Part of what?" I asked again.

Bandit stepped through the tent as Rhodes and Adyen joined. Thank fuck this thing was so massive. Blue wore a puzzled expression, but no one commented on how Bandit just seemed to know everything. No one would question him right now as it was, fucker is scary. As in far scarier than normal and totally because Vegas wasn't around to regulate his brand of fucked up.

"We," Edwin stated, "or should I say you are going to summon Vegas and use your dreamscape ability to get past the wards. I will be able to track where you are going since I'll be the anchor here and then we can use the map to distinguish exactly where she is in the castle. It's not much but it is more than we have right now."

"I've tried the dreamscape…"

"Not like this," Edwin's eyes glinted as I sat across from him. "I am going to ground you here in this real world but I need you to focus on her. Try to push past the wards that are going to try and block you."

I nodded. God, how I wanted to see her. Even if it was in a dream.

My eyes closed as I felt his power circulate through the room like icy pins. My hands gripped her scarf and I brought Vegas's beautiful face to mind. I could hear Edwin speaking in a language I didn't understand and my magic wavered. Everytime I felt close to her bond something stopped me. I was concerned. Then I was pissed.

So, I barrelled right through it.

My feet touched the ground as I looked around at the stone hallway, the torches dying down and metal bars lining the wall. I looked to the left and right before feeling myself tugged towards the first. I jogged towards the long corridor and continued to examine each empty cell.

I had a terrible feeling about this.

I passed a heavily guarded cell and focused on the form curled up in the corner. My heart hurt assuming it was Vegas or Gray. It wasn't though. A pair of white diamond eyes met mine as wings fluttered around the tiny form on the ground. Holy shit whoever this was could see me.

"Down the corridor," *She spoke, her voice soft and pained.*

"How long have you been down here?" *I asked feeling odd talking in this realm.*

Her laugh was sharp and sad, "Does it matter? Just remember when you storm the castle, there are many of us locked up down here. Try to not let the place burn before we are rescued."

I nodded and she turned away into the shadows. I felt a tug on my power so I hurried down the way towards what I hoped was Vegas.

"Gray?" *a voice whispered.*

Vegas.

"I know," *Gray muttered,* "I don't think it's a bad thing, it feels like familiar energy."

Fury burned through me as I came upon the scene in front of me. Vegas couldn't see me but I could fucking see her. She was alive. Gray was alive. Barely.

Fucking shit.

Every protective bone in my body rose up and I wanted to rip her from those chains. I wanted to take her home and keep her safe so she never had to think or experience this again.

"Got it," Edwin stated as my eyes opened to find him marking a place on the fourth level of the cells. I shook with fury and didn't even have the ability to ask how I had done that since neither girl was sleeping. Maybe it was a dimensional thing?

"They are both alive," I whispered as everyone seemed to murmur about that.

"How is she?" Kodiak asked softly.

"Alive," I muttered. For now. We needed to get there soon. I wasn't sure how long they would last.

I continued, "But, we have a problem."

"What?" Edwin demanded.

"They aren't the only ones down there."

COSIMO

There was nothing worse than being surrounded by people suffering. I saw it all. I saw the way Rocket removed himself from the group. How Kodiak seemed to barely hold his human form. How Grover continued to keep near me because Decimus was unable to make conversation without yelling. How Blue snarled at everyone and that dimpled grin had turned to a full psychotic break. How Edwin seemed to be cold and distant. How Byron drank more and had started several fights. How Booker was no longer drawing. How Bandit was scaring the absolute shit out of me. The man sat in the same place every single night, staring out into the frosted dark distance. I could barely tell he was breathing. How I hadn't spoken much because I was so overwhelmed by the amount going on around me. I saw all of it. None of these were things I could heal physically.

It didn't help that I was exhausted from healing so many.

Queen Gray had been taken when Mario had gotten her guard down for a singular moment. She had been taken and I watched as Gray's men began to dismantle. Adyen was going through something like Rhodes that I didn't understand. Something about having a mate. It was what was hurting Kodiak so much. I had been happy to see him turn back into human form. Now, though, he was very amped up. I had nearly gotten into another fight with him today but kept my mouth shut because I knew he was suffering.

We would be there soon and then it would be fine.

Taylor was sitting across from me as he drank from a cup of ale, the fire flickering in his eyes as he watched Bandit with curiosity. I couldn't tell how he felt though. I couldn't tell because he was nearly as expressionless as Bandit. My eyes trailed to Neo and Athens, the massive twins. Both of them were silent though and while one was expressing a lot of pain the other was blank. I could feel all of their power and I felt like I was about to explode.

I stood up with sudden movements and stalked away from the fire.

"Wait up!" Grover called out as I stalked into the bare, forested landscape. I was breathing roughly and the further I removed myself from the camp, the better.

"Dude," Grover jerked my shoulder back.

My frustration bubbled over and before I knew it, I had him slammed to the ground with my arm at his throat. My brother's dark eyes were only filled with concern, though, and I instantly felt terrible for hurting him. I shook my head and fell to the snowy ground next to me. Both of us let our breathing regulate.

"I'm sorry," I muttered softly.

"I get it," he sighed. "I feel completely useless."

I nodded in thought as I looked at the dark skies and watched as flurries began to fall gently. Vegas loved snow. I loved Vegas.

This was so fucked.

"I'm glad Kodi shifted back," Grover pointed out.

I nodded. "It's good. Really good. Hopefully after finding her, he won't feel as guilty."

"I think we all feel like that," he whispered and I nodded.

I had felt fucking stupid standing to the side as my brother's stood on the front lines. At the same time, I had helped so many injuries that my guilt was partially absolved. Could I have helped Vegas, though? Could I have helped Kodi?

I shook my head as Grover patted my arm and sat up.

"Why did you leave camp?"

My mouth parted as I spoke. "I can't handle it. It's overwhelming. Usually it is easy to just focus on Vegas but without her here..."

Grover nodded in understanding.

"We're going to get her back," he stated softly, his jaw tense. It was odd because out of all of us, it seemed he was able to rationalize it the best. He was filled with absolute belief that we would get her back without any doubt. I wished I could have that certainty.

"We have to," I whispered softly finally sitting up and putting my arms on my knees with my head down.

"I think Vegas is the last person we need to worry about," he admitted with sudden vigor, "She's stronger than any of us and she knew exactly what she was doing when she made that choice. The people we need to worry about are in the camp. Our brothers who can't seem to even utter a word to anyone or each other without breaking into a fight."

He was right.

"So what do we do?" I asked, helping him up as we both stood.

Grover offered me a smile and nodded towards the

campground. "Let's get these bastards together. I think it is time for a family meeting."

For the first time in weeks I smiled.

He was right, a family meeting was exactly what the fuck we needed.

18

VEGAS

"Good morning!"

That goddamn voice. Gray muttered a curse from the cell next to me as my eyes found her. My lips pressed together as that cold fury grew and grew. You would think being so in tune with fire that I'd have a boiling temperature. This didn't feel hot though. This felt calculated, cynical, and lethal.

Victor's time was coming and the man didn't realize that every single day it grew closer.

I had attempted to keep count on how long we'd been in these godforsaken cells. I believed we were going on week four now? It didn't surprise me that no one had come for us yet, it had taken several hours by dragon alone and that wasn't counting the complicated landscape that the Dark Fae lands possessed. Honestly, though, I was okay with them taking their time. It made it easier for me to focus on killing Victor and I don't want to brag but we'd actually maintained ourselves fairly well.

I could feel the cold air leaking into the small little window that was more like a vent in the high corner of the other side of the room. Whenever it rained, water would rush through here and pool in our corner.

Now, you are probably wondering how the two of us fuckheads got here. Well, the overall answer is different than as to why we are in this specific cell. Once Victor had captured me, I'd been pinned under his power until he tossed me into this holding cell. I think his initial concept had been to keep me there while he organized our "marriage" quarters.

Jokes on you fucker. He didn't realize that I loved motherfucking dungeon cells now.

Whose fault is that?

Gray on the other hand had been captured by Mario during what I'd gathered had been a brief second before he drained her fucking power. When she'd been put into the cell next to mine I'd been livid but also relieved to know she was alive. After several attempts on Victor and Mario's part to wrap their power around ours, they had failed to move us from the cell. Why? My magic was fucking pissed and while being chained in our cages, it was quick to defend both Gray and I. So, while King Mario had survived and Victor had captured me, neither of us could be physically touched and it was so fucking funny to watch them.

They were an antsy pair.

So, nearly four weeks later I hung with my arms above my head in cold chains that didn't allow me to break free with my magic, but didn't inhibit the actual use of it. My armor, from the battle, was soaked and my body chilled despite my internal temperature. Gray looked nearly as bad and there was a sadness in her eyes as if something had truly broken her heart before she was taken. I could only assume that love would put that in someone's eyes.

I didn't ask though because I was so not in the consoling mood.

As it stood, my emotional capacity was limited so I focused on keeping Gray safe.

Unlike my chains, her magic was actually muted and she was essentially human. I could only assume that was because they had no idea what I was but knew how to handle her.

I winced as an open wound on my wrist began to sting. I thought I'd understood pain. In some respects at least, but never physical pain. The boys had made sure of that. While Victor himself couldn't hurt me, he had sent in several soldiers who in their attempt would end up burnt to cinders. My cell was littered with bones and ashes from the flames that had consumed the men who dared to enter my cage.

Or lair.

Honestly, I was starting to feel pretty badass.

After day six though, they'd stopped entering Gray's cell because I'd made their suffering even worse by burning them alive slowly. For hours. Healing and then killing. Healing and killing.

I was pissed they'd stopped bringing us food, though.

My eyes scanned over the remnants of the many lives I'd taken and I once again found myself completely and utterly unaffected. I was affected by the vocal tone of Victor's voice though. It gave me insight on the type of day we would have. See, I was super duper lucky.

Not only did I have a murderous stalker with a fetish for blood and bones, but he also had two distinct personalities! There was Victor the depressive sick mage and the Victor that was stoic and rather sadistic. Both were in "love" with me and they took care to randomly switch each morning so that I could experience both equally. After week two I'd gotten it down.

"Little flame," he sang and offered me a sad look. "Won't you come out and play with me?"

I snorted because fuck him. However, I had to admit in my dehydrated state he looked a bit too much like Bandit. Just a bit. My fists curled inwards as I spoke calmly. "Victor, honey, if you get these chains off me we can have all the fun you want."

Gray laughed softly, her dark hair matted as her weight shifted in the pooled rainwater where her leg was chained to a center spoke. I wondered why they had us in two different binds but it didn't really matter. My arms were going to hurt like a bitch after this.

"Really?" he asked sincerely a look of affection passing over his features.

Gross.

"Absolutely," I whispered, my flames boiling under my skin.

"Victor!" Mario snapped his voice furious. "Back away."

Victor flinched and it was pretty easy to see where this multi-personality had derived from. I had no idea what this fucker did to his son but the man's magic was sick and twisted. It felt cancerous or diseased.

"Fuck off," Gray hissed her smoky power trapped inside of her like a bottle. I tugged on my chains but they refused to move. It made me feel better to try everyday, though.

Even if I did break out, I couldn't exactly leave Gray.

"Don't be so distraught," Mario chided gently as he began pacing the long cell room in front of us. Victor kept his eyes on me but leaned back against the stone wall, clearly afraid of us father today. Shit. I just knew if I could get the motherfucker alone, I could get our freedom.

"Hard to be in a good mood right now, asshole," Gray hissed gently, her power hissing in the containment of the binds that kept her prisoner.

"Well," he stopped and focused on us, "we have good news then. Both of you will be attending a wedding tonight."

Oh. This was going to be bad.

"Whose wedding?" Gray snarled her teeth sharper than normal.

"Little Gray," Mario sighed. "Do you remember when you watched me murder your bastard of a father and rape your mother?"

Gray flinched just slightly as her breathing increased.

"Of course you do!" He chuckled, his robes dark and sweeping. I blinked to clear the vision of Bandit from my head.

"Anyway," he smiled and walked forward. "You see, that day I was attempting to arrange for your marriage to Victor. I found that you were betrothed to the Light Fae prince. Of course, I was furious, so I killed them. Now, frankly, you are far too strong to keep around so once I have taken the Horde, I plan on killing you. So, my son will be marrying your little sorceress and hope that is enough of a help to control your band of misfits."

Fantastic.

Now, you are probably going "Oh, fuck. Vegas, you totally didn't tell Gray that and now he just threw out that you're a sorceress."

Except, four weeks in captivity had led to us talking a lot. Gray laughed at Mario's disappointment in a lack of reaction. Seriously? Is he an actual child?

Before I asked the important question, my brain blanked

as the memory of our conversation flashed right across my vision.

"This fucking sucks."

I snorted as my head rolled to the side so that I could see Gray's frustrated face. I was going to offer my joint complaint but then I realized there was something more to speak on. It was the middle of the night and I'd killed one man today. No one else would be coming tonight.

"Gray," I mumbled. "I have something to tell you. Something that I know Mario will bring up whether I want him to or not."

"I know," she whispered softly and looked at me with understanding.

"I grew up in the Horde."

Her eyes widened as I swallowed.

"I was created by Nicholas, an alchemy mage, a sorceress upon creation around twenty-one years ago. One of the only ones currently alive. I was unaware of this, of course, until the night or your coronation but I'll get to that. You see, my initial hesitancy came from the fact that the person who ordered my creation was... your mother."

Silence echoed through the space as I met Gray's eyes. I feared disbelief but instead there was pain and intense curiosity.

"She wanted to create something or someone that would be able to be a weapon for you. Someone so powerful that they could match you. But not just that. When your mother created me I became attached to her so even in her death she was able to contact me... informing me that I have a larger purpose within the Fae lands."

"You talked to her?" Gray sputtered.

I sighed. "Yeah, I should have explained that better. When we were taken into the dreamscape by Victor, your mother saved Booker and me from some creepy white scaly creatures. She appeared. Your mother said that I had a larger purpose and that message you got from Palo? The advice? It was from here. She seemed to be right. This was much larger than I could have ever expected."

"*Our mother,*" she whispered.

My head turned "What?"

"*Our mother.*" *She looked at me softly.* "*She created me and created you. We are sisters. Right? It's why we have such a strong connection.*"

"*I was built to be a weapon,*" *I mumbled.*

"*No.*" *She shook her head.* "*It sounds like you are much more than that. Go on, though.*"

I nodded as warmth filled me. "I was sent away from the Horde when you disappeared. I grew up with both Byron and Edwin, living at their residence with Nicholas. He sent us to Earth Realm for our safety and I was placed in a foster care safe house with a human who understood the delicate situation. The Ivanov brothers began to gather my circle of ten and I ended up growing up with them."

"*Circle of ten?*" *she whispered.*

"*They keep me grounded and protected.*"

Her head nodded slowly. "*Why are you telling me this? Besides Mario?*"

"*You mentioned that you felt bad about bringing me into this,*" *I whispered.* "*And I need you to understand that this would have happened whether or not you and I met.*"

"*What?*"

"*Mario had sent Victor over to find me, knowing that I was a sorceress. Unfortunately, the bastard got all creepy and before I knew it, Edwin had announced we had magic and shit.*"

Gray whistled after a moment. "*Well, shit. That explains why you are so strong.*"

"*I'm sorry I didn't tell you sooner, I just needed to work through it... I needed to understand it,*" *I spoke softly.*

"Hey," Gray assured. *"Don't worry about it. It's not like I have told you everything about my life."*

"But this could have affected your decisions," I mumbled as my eyes closed, tired.

"Vegas," she demanded my attention, *"Knowing this only makes me happier I've met you. We are in this together and if anyone can get out of here, it will be us."*

Not if I had to marry Victor. I blinked and cleared my thoughts. "Why?"

Mario smiled. "When she dies, the power from her will either fill you or her death will drain both of you. Either way, it seems like a good compromise because either way you are in our control. My control."

"Father," Victor spoke in a low tone.

"Shut up!" He roared as his son flinched. "I am giving you what you fucking want."

"Well, if you're asking for my opinion, I'm not really a marriage type of girl," I muttered.

I totally was but not with Vic over here.

Victor looked alarmed. "I'll be a good husband."

One case of spousal homicide on it's way.

"How about you and I talk about this alone," I gambled as his eyes lit up. Unfortunately, I almost needed him to be the scary Victor and he was opposite of that tonight. The one that stood up to his father was nowhere in sight.

"Not now," Mario snapped and then flashed a smile at me. "I will send someone down to aid you in getting ready. After all, I'm sure your wedding day is important."

Then the king was gone and Victor left more slowly, a small smile on his lips.

Ew. Just ew.

"This is our moment to escape," Gray spoke, her voice rough as the livid expression on her face

I nodded in determination. "I know. Do you think we can do this?"

Gray's lips curled, "I think that if anyone can do this, it's us."

The door to the room banged open and a pair of guards came in holding two shaking women between their arms. My magic softened as both women, one pale with light hair and the other with a smooth dark complexion, began to cry.

Fuck. I wasn't sure how I felt about that. I couldn't kill them like the guards, they were innocents.

"Let's go, ladies." The guards shoved them into each cage with a bundle of whatever they had with them. Normally, the moment they were within reach they'd be dead but I couldn't do that to these women. Instead I offered the woman a soft smile and she stopped crying so much.

"I have to help you get dressed," she whispered, her skin ashen.

I wiggled my chains and she reached up, adjusting a pair that allowed me to stand while keeping my hands above my head. I groaned as she slipped a piece of metal onto my ankle before releasing my hands. Pain shot through my arms and shoulders as I let out a cry.

"Shut it, bitch," a guard chuckled. Gray was in the process of getting undressed and the guards leered at her barely covered body.

I closed my eyes as the woman began undoing my armor until I was in nothing but a pair of underwear and a bra. I shivered as the woman lifted a bottle of dark liquid.

"You have to take it. You will be drugged out for about six hours and your magic won't work," she stated softly and my breathing grew harsh. I nearly hit the bottle away but Gray made a noise and I looked up at the woman's large eyes.

What I saw there blew me away.

The tears and the fear were fake. I frowned as she winked at me and offered a bottle that I had a feeling didn't contain anything. My mouth opened as cherry syrup filled my mouth I swallowed and she unhooked the chain attached to my ankle strap, my power attempting to break out. I breathed in and tried to act like I had no magic. Clearly there was something bigger here at play.

"Chambers. Now," The guards hissed as the four of us walked by them. I nearly made it up the stairs before one of them pulled me back. God, I wanted to kill the fucker already.

But then they would know the potion didn't work.

"So much friendlier now," he grunted. "You didn't think we wouldn't want to play with you, did you?"

I cried out as he grasped my hair and knocked me to my knees. The other three women backed into a corner. I breathed out as I looked up at the man with a snarl. He only grinned and brought a knife up to where he held my hair in a tight twist.

"We wouldn't want this getting in the way, now would we?" He chuckled as one of his men grabbed my ass and caused me to cringe with disgust.

The door flew open but it was too late. Silver long strands of hair floated around me as Victor began shouting orders and slamming his own soldier into the wall. Ah, yes. This would be Victor Number Two. I felt arms on me but I couldn't think right. Instead my now shoulder length hair fell against my face as I looked over the mass of silver hair on the ground.

Oh, my god.

The fucker cut my hair off.

A dark smile broke onto my face. Blue was going to kill him.

"Vegas?" Gray whispered. "Are you okay?"

"Feel lighter already," I murmured with cold fury.

"My beloved," Victor grasped me in a hug that was commanding. "I'm so sorry."

I looked up at the serious Bandit look alike and patted his cheek. "That's okay, Victor."

His power wrapped around me and I detached quickly as my helper grasped my hand. My soon to be dead fiance looked annoyed but he waved us off as he turned to look at the other soldiers. He began yelling.

"Don't run yet," Gray's woman said in a serious tone. "We have people stationed everywhere but we want to deal the most damage so we have to do it at the ceremony. That is if we want to be free of these bastards."

"Who are you?" I whispered as they closed us into a dark room and lit a few candles, I could hear the bathwater running.

"Later," my girl answered. She pulled me into the bathroom and practically shoved me into the tub. Fuck, this felt good. I hadn't showered in weeks and we had been forced to use the washroom in this small steel bin.

Fuck my life.

Oddly, I trusted these women and when I found out her name was Giselle I began to view her as more of a person. There wasn't anything very memorable about her but she had a small tattoo on her cheekbone of a black butterfly. I frowned at it remembering the very real one I'd seen a bit ago. I closed my eyes as she massaged my shoulders for the fight to come and began to help me wash my hair and body. I even got to fucking shave, thank god.

"I am so sorry about your hair," she whispered as the tub

began refilling and I went back out to the main room. My back sunk into the fabric chair as my eyes closed.

My own reflection startled me.

The angular face I loved was thin, far too thin, and I had dark shadows everywhere. My lips were purple almost and my eyes black. I had short, shoulder length hair, and overgrown bangs. It was choppy and uneven. I sort of liked it. It felt right. Bold and intense like my new life. As Giselle began to twist my hair up off my face I began to think about my boys. Something I'd avoided.

Unfortunately, the minute I did my connection sparked up.

Oh, fuck. They were close.

My eyes snapped to the window and Giselle turned my head back offering me a warning shake. "All in good time. Remember, patience."

I swallowed as she offered me a glass of water and some light food, my body violently disturbed by the substance. I lifted a thin hand to my necklace and smiled. Kodi.

"We will be able to store some things in your dress but you will need to use your own powers," both women explained as we were dressed. Gray was placed in a brown woven material that made her growl. I had to admit it was ugly.

I was placed in a dress so thin I was positive you could see my new underwear and fresh bra through it. I had thanked Giselle for that. With ease I reached down into the boots they had provided me with in a light, knee high cream and placed a silver dining knife there. It would have to do.

A knock on the door had all of us jumping.

"Little flame," the stoic voice called. "Come out."

With a groan, I opened the door and came face to face

with Victor. My vision blurred and I thought it was Bandit, causing tears to threaten.

"Don't cry," he pulled me in close. "This is for the good."

Bastard was crazy.

"Shall we?" Giselle asked as Brenda, Gray's helper, nodded. We could do this.

19

VEGAS

I had imagined my wedding often but everytime it had been unique.

This took the unfortunate cake though.

The hall was filled with Dark Fae and the windows were open airing out the humid and sweaty hall. People were drinking and soldiers openly groped a few women serving ale. I groaned as the music started a cheery tune and the two helpful women disappeared into the crowd, leaving Gray and I alone.

"This is shit," she mumbled, grasping my hand.

The hall itself was beautiful with a gothic cathedral top and dark walls. The thick curtains and marble floor had me wondering what century we were in. My pale, sheer dress had a high, lacy neck and pooled around me hiding my boots. I shivered as men began to shout leering remarks.

"So glad that you could join us!" Mario chuckled as he stood looking very sober. "Everyone please welcome Queen Gray of the Horde and Vegas the Sorceress."

I sort of liked how that sounded.

As we began to walk forward my power snarled at me to

break free. I tried to reassure her that her moment in the spotlight was very soon.

"My son," Mario motioned him forward as the dark-eyed Victor stood awaiting me. Gray growled as Mario pulled her into his side and I stepped up to meet Victor on the same level.

Music began to grow louder as the lights dimmed. Someone began to speak in a haunting tone and I realized the magic level in the room was rising. Something about this felt terribly off. Victor had a concerned look on his face.

"Vic," I whispered, gaining his attention. "Don't do this. If you love me, don't do this."

I felt my eyes widen as his eyes lightened and a shy voice spoke. "I have to, little flame. He will kill you. He will kill me."

I moved forward, grasping his hand and pulling him close. "We can kill him."

Something overcame Victor and both façades swept aside, leaving a broken boy that looked very young. I felt tears pool in my eyes as dark acidic magic swept through the air.

"Mario!" Gray screamed. "You can't bond them."

I heard something hit the floor.

"I can't stop him," Victor whispered moving closer so that our lips were only inches apart. His voice resonated deeply. "Only you can."

What?

"How?" I demanded.

His eyes shone with sadness, "When the bond starts forming, you have to destroy my magic."

"You'll die," I whispered with a horror that shouldn't have been new to me. I didn't know how I knew that exactly. I hated Victor but what he was suggesting was selfless. The man may be deranged but it seemed his father was mostly to blame because at the center was a broken young man. He truly believed that he loved me enough to die for me.

He nodded and a wiser look flashed over his face. "The three of us are not meant for this world. We were split upon birth and our father fed the sickness. We would gladly sacrifice ourselves for you."

Like his three personalities? This was so fucked up. I could barely deal with two.

"Why are you doing this?" I demanded not believing him.

"Use hellfire," he muttered, his voice turning stoic as his eyes met mine.

His voice echoed darkly in three layers. "We told you little flame, we love you. We want you. But we can't have you. He will never let us have you. We can't kill you, so you must kill us."

I think I was losing it.

"Do you want that?" I whispered and felt pain lance my chest. He was a total creepy jerk, but shit.

"Yes," he said in a weak voice as the bond began to form.

I had a moment of doubt but then I felt pain through my connection with Gray and didn't hesitate. My wall snapped down and my magic flooded the entire room as glass shattered and flames roared to life. Screams sounded as familiar scents filled the air from a short distance.

They were coming.

A weight sagged in my arms, a very frail almost dehydrated version of Victor. I sunk to my knees with his skeletal frame as I lifted a hand to his chest. Those eyes watched me and I had to assume only the supernatural world was keeping him alive.

"Do it," he demanded in a whisper.

My eyes closed as hellfire encased us. I felt it spread through him as I intertwined healing and soul fire. He would die but hopefully wherever Fae ended up after death he'd be at peace. My body began to simmer to a low heat as I fell forward, bracing myself on my forearms. I looked to the side as I found my flames had blocked off the four of us and were attacking soldiers. There were also women, in all black, moving through the crowds with agile speed.

Was that Giselle?

"You deserve this," Gray growled as she grasped Mario's face and snapped his neck. Then she reached into his chest with her nails prying the skin apart before ripping out his heart. Tears streamed down her face but a smile of relief broke out only a moment later.

Dude.

My power receded and I quickly realized the battle was coming to an end. The women in black stood to either side but I couldn't focus on anything more than the door flying open.

They were here.

20

VEGAS

"You know," Gray muttered, dragging herself closer to me as chaos erupted, our wonderful Horde men realizing the enemy was dead. I didn't look up yet. I couldn't look up yet.

Instead, I picked up my sister. Yes, I know I have two and maybe even three if we count Miranda. It is fucking awesome! Anyway, her arm wrapped around me as I realized she had a large gash on her right side that was bleeding. We must have been a sight with me in a wedding dress covered in human ash and the length of the material soaking in the blood pooling from Mario's very dead corpse. Bastard deserved it.

"I didn't imagine your wedding this way," she signaled to the dress.

I snorted as the two of us made our way down the marble steps hanging to one another. "You imagined my wedding?"

She met my eyes. "Of course, once we became friends I started wondering just how one would pull off an eleven-person wedding. I have some great color ideas if you were wondering. None of them include the fucking bridesmaid dress I have on right now."

Yes, brown paper bag wasn't very "in" right now.

"If it wasn't for being queen, you could probably be in the fashion industry," I noted ignoring our audience as we neared closer. The room was silent except for the crackling of some remaining flames and our voices.

"You think so?" She laid a finger against her cheek in thought. "You know we could start our own fashion industry here, but it may be important to bring cars over first."

A cough sounded from one of the women in black. Both our heads tilted up as we found the women smiling, the soldiers looking wide-eyed, and our boys... well, that was a lot to unpack.

"What happened?" Rhodes barely managed as I tried to keep my emotions blank as they had been for the past month. Blank, because if not I'd cry. Blank, because I was one hug or sweet word from losing it.

Four weeks without my boys.

I can honestly say that is the longest I have ever gone without them.

Gray sighed and pulled me into a hug. "I'll go explain, go see your men before they rip you away from me and I have to kill them."

I squeezed her hand and walked slowly to come inches away from my men. I looked up as I sighed trying to process what exactly I would say.

"Vegas," Edwin spoke and something very small in my chest started cracking open. I tried to calm it down but it wasn't working. I closed my eyes.

"I'm fine," I whispered softly and then frowned. "You're actually here?"

Those pumpkin eyes melted into amber and I think my

body melted when he stepped close to me and spoke. His arms wrapped around me as I started shaking. "*Dolcezza*, I promise you are safe now."

Yeah, I lost it. Typical.

My sobs racked my body as Edwin picked me up, my boys circling around us as I felt soft hands against my bruised skin. I shivered and I was positive I looked like a total fucking mess, but Edwin continued to hold me and to soothe me in the bubble we had. I was so flipping tired and my arms hurt like a bitch. My magic was throwing me the middle finger while tossing me her vacation plans. Not giving me a choice. I was a hot mess. A total fucking hot mess.

"Edwin?" I whispered softly.

"Yes?"

"I love you."

I did. I loved all my boys but I wasn't about to wait another fucking minute to tell the bastard how I felt. I loved him. I loved him so fucking much I wanted to roll my eyes, at myself!

I think seeing Edwin's eyes water slightly tipped everyone over the edge. Before I knew it, I was being kissed hard by the orange eyed mage and the scent of cinnamon surrounded me. Blue's face was filled with pain and longing as he plastered my body to his.

"Beautiful," he spoke in a strangled voice, opening his mouth only to close it again.

I knew.

I knew the pain.

"I know," I whispered as I pressed my lips to his in a soft kiss. I nearly smiled as his fingers reached up to lightly touch my short choppy hair.

"What happened?" he murmured softly and met my gaze.

"This big ugly motherfucker cut off my hair. He and his buddies are probably still downstairs," I responded softly with a small smile. My magic offered me a devious wink. She knew exactly what I was doing.

"I sort of like it," he whispered before the predatory spark appeared. "But downstairs, you say? I am going to go kill them on principle."

I laughed and he flashed me that dimpled smile. There was the psycho I love.

"Is this a wedding dress?" Edwin asked softly tugging on the sheer material.

I didn't have time to respond before Cosimo's arms were locked at my hips and his forehead against my own. I felt tears well up again as he pulled away slightly and those intense eyes began raking my body. His magic kissed my skin and he lifted my wrists growing furious at the state of them.

Fuck. It looks really bad. I could see the raw skin and the way my hand tattoos seemed to be twisting very slightly to surround the area protectively.

Or I was hallucinating.

Totally possible.

"Everything heals," I murmured gently.

He nodded and looked behind me as the scent of bamboo made me smile. Grover's warm chocolate eyes examined my expression before he flashed me a charming smile.

"See?" he whispered, "I knew you'd kick ass. Aren't you glad we did that extra training?"

I barked out a laugh because despite looking worse for wear he was trying to make this situation lighter. My peacekeeper was still inspecting my injuries. I was worried about my boys though and even if I hadn't had a chance to look them over, it was clear they were run down.

My magic continued to wave a picture of Bora Bora in my face.

"Princess," Decimus's voice was raw as Cosimo stepped to the side and my dark knight invaded my space. Those hard dark eyes flashed over me as he muttered a curse.

"Don't ever do that again," he stated gruffly kissing my forehead while brushing through my short hair. "I... I wouldn't know what to do without you."

Grover and Cosimo both tried to not smile but I rubbed a hand across his slight cheek blush. I spoke softly. "I would give myself one hundred times over if it meant saving any of you."

Decimus eyes melted and pulled me from their arms. I wrapped my legs around him and basked in the soft energy that seemed to radiate from all sides. The scent of sea salt and the feel of calming waves against my skin. I could cry.

How often had I imagined this? I had spent hours thinking about them. My memory wasn't nearly as good as being held by them. Then again, I never thought it would.

"Trouble," Byron spoke softly behind me.

I had Deci set my feet down as I turned and immediately crushed the massive man into a hug. It was easy because he had already knelt down partially with one knee. He grunted and I began to snuggle his neck and chin. Immediately, the whirlwind mage began relaxing. Sometimes, I'd found, my overt affection calmed him more than words ever could.

"I love you," I murmured.

"You're my life," he said softly, his red eyes meeting my own. "Do you understand that? You are the start and finish, baby. You're everything."

FIRE & SMOKE

I nuzzled his face before I turned to face two gray eyed boys. One had hard eyes that matched his blank face, the other looked broken. God. I had left them. I mean I hadn't, but essentially I had.

Instead of saying anything I stepped up towards them and placed a hand on either of their chests gently. Rocket's heart was beating extremely fast and Booker opened his mouth to say something.

"I'm sorry," I whispered.

"Fuck that," Rocket whispered as his voice broke. I squeaked as the man yanked me against his hard body and melted my body with a searing kiss.

"Don't ever apologize for being brave, Kitty," Booker spoke from behind me. I felt safe and comforted between the two of them.

I cursed my libido because I knew it was waking up, my magic sighing luxuriously as she began to apply lipstick and dress in lingerie. This was not the time.

"I didn't want to leave," I mumbled softly.

"I know, Sugar," Rocket groaned softly and squeezed me tighter.

"How are your arms?" Booker whispered, massaging my shoulders gently. I breathed in his scent and that magic signature reminded me of being in my cell.

"How do you know about my arms?" I frowned.

He smiled softly before paling. "I was able to use the dreamscape ability to find your location. I saw you and Gray. Vegas, you should have never had to go through that."

"Later," I swallowed as Rocket's chest began to vibrate as his breathing increased.

I couldn't afford for Rocket to go nuclear right now, because he would.

"Vegas," Booker whispered as my eyes followed him. I

felt my heart melt because Kodi was leaning against the wall watching me with hooded eyes and an expression that broke my heart. I kissed both my boys cheeks gently as I walked as if I was approaching a wild animal.

His wolf tried to let out a whine from his throat and rush forward. He grimaced and held the wall tighter as if stopping himself. My hand came up and he began breathing rougher.

"Don't," he grunted.

Pain severed my heart as I stopped inches from him. "You don't want me to touch you?"

A low growl broke from how hard his teeth were clenched. I could see the guilt written all over his face and it made me mad that he was doing this to us right now. I wanted to punch and hug the fucker at the same time. My temper flared.

"Baby," he looked down at the floor as if the weight on his shoulders made it impossible to meet my gaze.

"Don't do this Kodi," I whispered fiercely and stepped forward so we were an inch apart. His body vibrated with tension as his arms flexed with constraint.

"I can't...you wouldn't have ever...I fucked up."

"Shut up."

His head snapped up as those eyes turned to green fire. My hand grasped his shirt as I pulled him closer. Now, honestly, he probably let me but it was pretty badass pulling a massive man like him and it working!

"Are you listening to me Kodi? Because I need to make sure you hear all of this."

He nodded but his eyes kept flashing to my hand, small and pale. Bruised like my wrist. I'm sure my face wasn't very pretty compared to the last time he saw me.

"I did not just spend a month in his fucking place for

you to act distant," I vibrated with anger. "Do not for a minute feel guilty when I know you would have done the same in that situation. I fucking love you, Kodiak. So I need you to listen well when I say that I do not blame you and never will."

"Vegas..."

"I don't blame you for my bruises or cuts. I don't blame you because that was my fucking choice. I chose to save you and do not degrade that by stepping away from me because you feel guilty. I won't fucking have it." I banged my fist softly against his chest.

The two of us were suspended for a singular moment and then he cracked. The massive man swept me up and buried his head in my neck. I almost smiled because he was practically fucking purring over here. See? My boys could be super fucking sweet.

His hand began to rub my back gently as he kissed my neck and collarbone. My chin and face. I could feel him growing hard but he didn't seem rushed. I knew he was putting his scent all over me and I brushed his hair gently because it seemed to relax him.

A small smile came to my lips that had him looking up. "What?"

"You know," I pressed a light ghost of a kiss to his lips. "I really should have listened to you better..."

Kodiak's eyes flashed up in an emerald fire as amusement and something a lot darker crawled across his expression. His large rough hand picked up my wrist as he gently kissed it but instead of backing away from my innuendo he made me want to screw here and now.

"That's true," he drew a thumb to my lips and let me slide down his body. I looked up at him as he shifted us so that the stone wall he nearly broke earlier was against my back. "That was bad of you, baby. Good girls wouldn't do that now, would they?"

"No, they wouldn't," I offered him a coy smile. "Guess I'm not good."

He groaned bringing his lips against my skin. "I suppose we will have to punish the bad out of you until you are my good girl again. How does that sound?"

Sign me up, please.

Now.

"I think," I breathed in roughly as he lifted a hand to tug gently on my necklace that rested in the hollow of my neck. I knew that he was still worked up but I was happy to help transfer some of that energy into this instead of guilt or anger.

"What do you think?" he whispered.

"I think both of you have an audience," Decimus spoke next to us as we both whipped our heads to the side. Kodiak let out an annoyed grunt and turned so that I was behind him, offering a glare that had everyone but our family turning to find something or someone to look at. It was pretty fucking funny.

"Plus," Deci snickered, "Kodi won't do shit, princess, until you gain back all of your weight, eat a million meals in front of him, and heal."

"Damn right," he muttered. "Throw a few more trackers on your sweet ass. I trust my wolf, but not that much."

I rolled my eyes as he narrowed his own. "You can't just go around hunting and stalking me, Kodi."

He totally could.

"Wrong baby," he grinned. "I'm pretty sure stalking is in the direct definition of being your mate."

Huh?

"Your face," Grover commented while eating an... apple? I would think about that later. "Is adorable angel."

"Mate?" I raised my eyebrows.

Kodiak nodded with an enthusiastic spark. "Yep, and guess what? I feel awful when you aren't around so for my sanity and health, you have to stay plastered to my side."

"You," I poked him, "you are a bit crazy."

"Aren't we all?" Edwin spoke from a few feet away. Good ass hearing.

Then I stilled as the scent of fresh cut grass had me stepping back into a warm body.

"Ve," Bandit's voice whispered against my skin.

I turned and met his gaze that was filled with a darkness that honestly scared me. I wasn't naïve and I'd seen the darkness in each of my boys but Bandit right now seemed dead. His eyes were black and his skin paler than normal. I noticed him rubbing his right pectoral as if it was hurting. I didn't see any injuries but something was very wrong.

"Bandit," I whispered, pressing right up into him and pulling his head down.

"I couldn't feel our connection," he mumbled softly as if he was falling down a dark hole.

"I know," I said gently. "But I'm here. I'm not going anywhere. He is dead."

The silver-haired mage wrapped his arms around my head and back so that I was completely intertwined with him. His magic greeted mine but the electricity seemed to be growing larger. I pulled back as he shook his head, my hand resting on his pectoral that was searing hot. I pulled gently on his shirt and gasped, a secondary moment before he sealed his lips over mine.

What is that?

Bandit's eyes darkened as he looked around the room thoughtfully as doubt creased his forehead.

I don't know. It appeared when we walked in.

It by the way? It was a massive dark tattoo that covered his right pectoral and seemed to reach out in all different directions. The shading was black with harsh geometric lines but in the center was a diamond shaped emerald. My magic was desperately trying to tell me something but I knew my time mage was trying to get his bearings about him.

We needed Edwin.

Then the beautiful man was there. Turning his back he looked at Bandit and with a nod from the time mage, I peeled down his shirt slightly.

I could have laughed at his expression.

"What is it?" I whispered.

Edwin swallowed and met Bandit's gaze. "I have no idea how that is possible."

"What if Victor wasn't? Would it be possible then?" Bandit frowned.

What were they talking about?

"Yes," Edwin hissed softly and ran a hand through his hair. "Fuck, that would be crazy and explain… Well, you."

Bandit authentically laughed as I frowned at both of them.

"Boys," I tugged both their hands. "Care to clue me in?"

"We would need more information," Edwin looked at the women dressed in black. "Maybe talk to the Obsidian Butterflies…"

The what? The man was mumbling. Freakin' lunatic.

"Edwin," I growled.

His eyes met mine as Bandit placed his chin over my head and grasped me as if I was being held captive. Edwin brushed a kiss to my forehead and what he whispered in my ear had my eyes popping open.

"So, what the hell does that mean?" I muttered.

Both of them were silent as I looked around the massive room all the way to the throne. Christ.

"Killed 'em!" Blue announced covered in blood and holding some hair in his hand. The fucker had given them a haircut.

I had to know was it before or after they died?

Blue offered me a wink. The man would kill me.

My body was exhausted but I refused to go to bed until I'd talked to everyone about what had happened. I wanted to wake up refreshed and new because I had a feeling something big was about to change. I bit my lip as I went to go talk to the last person.

The apprehension I had was two-fold. The first part was instinctual just like the feeling I'd had before stepping into the Horde. The second had to do with what Bandit and Edwin had insinuated.

Was it possible? Could Bandit be Mario's son? Victor's brother? If so, was he half-blooded or full-blooded? We didn't even know for sure that his mom was in fact his mother.

This was all kinds of messy.

The scariest part was that Edwin had only heard of that type of tattoo on one other person. Gray. Yet, instead of rushing to assumptions, because that one was a bit intense, he wanted to have Palo look at it.

I thought that after a goodnight's sleep everything would make far more sense.

My feet stopped as I found Grover sitting in my bedroom, his dark hair glinting from the fireplace light and those sweet eyes lit up with confidence. Goddamn prince charming. So perfect. He beckoned me forward and I easily found my way in between his legs as he wrapped his arms around my waist. His dark hair brushing my chest.

"I knew you would kick ass," he murmured and my chest clenched at his confidence in me. Out of all my boys, Grover had never faltered in believing that I was okay or that they would reach us. He had been strong. Despite being uncomfortable with magic at first, the man seemed to be accepting it easily into his life.

I offered a soft smile, smoothing his face. "So why the worried brow?"

Despite the smiles I could see the slight hesitancy in his face and I knew something was weighing on his mind. His eyes darkened slightly as his ears turned pink. "I'm not upset really, I just don't know how to ask for what I want right now. I tend to get tripped up on words with you, angel. I don't want to fuck it up."

I blushed at that. "I don't know about that, you're pretty damn charming."

Does everyone remember the dirty talking in the gym? Or the orgasm? Tripped up, my ass.

Yet, I believed him and felt like he wasn't trying to make this a casual moment or particularly light-hearted.

He gently pressed his lips to mine and spoke against them. "Vegas, I need you. I know this isn't the most romantic time and it's out of the blue, but I need to feel connected to you. Like you are paying attention to me. Like you want me as much as I want you. God I sound so fucking needy, don't I? I just tend to get like that with you. I want all of your time and attention even if that isn't possible."

His honest and bare admission as he blushed and rubbed his neck in a nervous gesture had me kissing the rambling out of him. I do mean kissing him with vigor as I pulled him by his dark uniform. It took very little time for the two of us to pull one another onto the bed so that we were entangled together, my ash covered ball gown against his battle worn leather armor.

Now if that didn't scream "prince charming" I don't know what did. What? Your fairytales didn't look like this?

"Oh!" I gasped as he smoothed his palms along my thighs, each wrapping around easily, as he pushed up the material to expose my body. His kisses tasted like fucking chocolate and I felt as though he was unwrapping me like a present.

"Angel," he groaned as he slowly unlaced my boots before kissing along each ankle and looking down at me with affection and adoration.

"Grover," I whispered as he tugged off his top and exposed his *holy shit* abs. I caught the drool but he shot me a teasing smile as he let his hands wander down his abs to where his thick cock pressed against his leather pants. I sent a mental prayer up to whoever the fuck blessed me with this. These beautiful men were mine.

Time seemed to slow for us, the languid and easy movements like melted chocolate against my skin. The room was warm and cozy with just the fireplace and light music playing from somewhere in the house. I had the distinct feeling that he planned on taking his time.

"I think I fell in love with you the very first day I saw you," he whispered softly, his smile easy and eyes filled with true happiness.

I blushed slightly because he was being all cute and shit. "Yeah?"

"Of course." He slid down the straps of my bra and began to peel the cotton material off to expose my breasts. I gasped as he kissed and pulled at the nipple with his teeth. My lust, which had been missing while in prison, came roaring to life. Obviously, my magic felt like she had some making up to do.

"You were," he whispered, kissing all my skin gently before continuing, "the most stunning, angelic little girl I'd ever met. I wanted to wrap you up and keep you safe even at that age. For the life of me, I could not believe how or why someone would have willingly given you up. I promised myself I would always be a good friend to you. Someone who deserved to be in your life and that you would love."

"You are that and so much more Grover," I whispered at his soft words. "I love you."

With an easy movement he peeled off his pants and I almost glared at my panties blocking our union. He offered me a cute grin and rocked against me, his hard, big member pressing against my clit. I let out a moan as he tugged with his teeth on my skin.

"Eyes on me," he whispered as I opened my eyes and stared into his liquid ones. I squirmed as he tugged down the only lace on my body with his teeth and I jumped at the sensation of him grazing my wetness.

"I need to taste you," he whispered before looking up, "but I won't stop if I do. Right now, I need to be buried inside of you. I need to know that we found you. That you are here. I need you, Vegas."

"You have me," I whispered as he lifted me onto his lap so I was facing him, my legs wrapped around. With impressive strength he lifted my hips and positioned me right above the tip of his cock my body trembling. His lips pressed against mine as he breathed in before sliding me down in an easy movement.

"Grover!" I gasped his name as he groaned in a guttural way.

Oh, my 'lanta, this felt good.

My eyes were caught on his gaze and we were nose to nose, connected in the most basic and elemental way. For just a moment, the two of us relished our connection growing like a beautiful blossoming flower. I knew this was only one side of Grover but something about this felt right. We'd had enough violence and aggression, this was romantic and filled with heat.

"I have to move," he whispered as I rolled my hips and we began a slow almost torturous pace. The metallic taste of his power had both of our bodies heating up as the room turned thick with desire and power. There was light sweat on both of our bodies as he rolled my hips again and again, my clit rubbed right against his tight muscular body. The entire time our faces were connected through a kiss or were a mere inch apart.

I gasped as he began to move quicker and my nails dug into his hair as he wrapped his massive hands under my ass. He began to lift me easily off his cock before sliding deep again. Each time he felt different and my head fell back as he sucked on the soft skin of my collarbone.

"Oh, shit," I whispered as he began to move deep inside of me causing my body to shake against his. I felt my body clamp down as a climax burst through me and he cursed at how tight I was. I began to move faster against him eager for that next climax and the one from him that would solidify our bond.

"Come on, princess, give him another one," a dark voice chimed in my ear as I gasped and Grover chuckled.

Decimus stood rubbing a palm over his rock hard erection as he offered me a heated look and Grover continued his deep pace.

"Angel," Grover grinned as a far more devious spark filled his gaze and brought my attention back. "I am going to turn you around."

I nodded as he easily turned me so that my ass was pressed against his hard abs and our sweet love making turned into a dirty reverse cowgirl experience. I cried out as our bond lit up and he began to pound into me while gripping my ass. I leaned forward and was essentially eye level with Decimus dick. Something he was loving.

My mouth popped open as I cried out.

"Shh," Grover grinned. "Keep making all that noise and Deci will have to stick something in your mouth to keep you occupied."

I moaned as my body tightened and a heated chill broke over me. Decimus grasped my shoulder length hair gently and tipped my chin up.

"I think she wants that," Decimus offered me a dangerous smirk as he unzipped his pants with one hand. I fell forward and grasped his forearms as Grover began to pound into me with a new pace. A pace that had me climaxing and shouting out his name just as something silky, hard, and hot pushed between my lips. I let my mouth open as I sucked on Decimus like he was my new favorite candy.

"Oh, fuck," Decimus grunted.

"How does her mouth feel?" Grover asked as he bit down gently on my spine as I shivered and he slowed his pace once again. This pattern was making me dizzy.

"Better than you could imagine," Decimus grasped my hair as he began to slide in and out of my mouth with vigor.

The pace was set and Grover began to fill me fully with each stroke. He stretched me and as I cried out I felt our climax snap the bond into place.

I felt dizzy like floating on a liquid surface as I heard distantly Grover roar out his release before filling me completely. Decimus stroked himself into my mouth before he released his salty perfect taste in my mouth and I swallowed it with ease. Oh, fucking shit.

"Oh, wow," I whispered softly as Grover lifted me gently as Decimus nodded and fell forward. I snuggled between them as the three of us laid there in a peaceful and comfortable peace.

"You know," Decimus chuckled, "I actually came here for something."

"What?" I tilted my head.

"I see why the delay occurred," a voice from the door said as amused orange eyes met mine.

"You wanna tell them?" Decimus asked as Edwin looked over my naked body before muttering under his breath. I barely covered myself with a light blanket and offered him a cheeky smile.

"Yes," Edwin sat down at the edge of the bed as Grover walked to the bathroom. I totally checked out his muscular butt.

"Earth to Vegas," Decimus teased as I jabbed his rib.

Edwin sighed and shook his head. "I blame myself for this entirely and I know they are doing it to prove a point, but the eleven of us have some unofficial business to attend to regarding the Red Masques."

Oh, no.

No.

No.

Absolutely not.

I need a motherfucking vacation.

"Edwin," I flopped over grabbing his waist, "we just defeated our enemies, don't we get a break? You're the boss and shit, please? Also, we have a few things we need to straighten out."

He kissed my cheek. "Yes. After the trials."

"What are the trials?!" I exclaimed as I felt my magic scowl. She wanted a sexy magic vacation.

Edwin tossed me a smile. "I designed them and you have to pass them in order to become part of our organization and go into the field. I knew I shouldn't have let my commanders meet all of you. They are far too curious and want to see you in action. So, we will need to do that before any of our 'Sexy vacation magic.'"

I frowned. "It's ' sexy magic vacation.' When the hell is this?"

The mage twisted his lips and stood up, backing away gently as I narrowed my eyes.

"Edwin?" I growled.

He grabbed the door handle and spoke. "We report right after Christmas."

I let out a frustrated sound as the mage ducked out of the room. That bastard. I threw myself back into bed as Grover smiled from the doorway. Decimus muttered curses as well. See? The grumpy bastard and I were on the same page.

"Come shower," Grover signaled.

"You coming?" I asked Decimus.

The bad boy opened a closed eye and shook his head. "I'm about to knock out, princess."

I sleepily walked over to Grover and we stepped into the shower. My head fell back and I ran my hands through my hair. I fucking loved having short hair. Although Blue continued to stare at it as if it was a foreign entity.

"I like this," Grover pulled gently on the hair that brushed my shoulder, "I was always afraid of hurting your hair because it was so long."

"Now," I smiled wiggling my brows, "you can toss me around everywhere."

He growled and bit my ear. "I plan to, angel. Also, don't think this changes my plans to fuck you everywhere and in front of the other men."

I shivered. "I wouldn't mind that."

He hit my ass as I yelped. He began to smooth bamboo body wash over me. I loved that smell. I gasped and pointed at him.

"You!"

"Me?" He chuckled while offering me a crooked smile. The fucker was so hot. His auburn hair a million wet directions and his muscular body sudsy. God damn it.

"You use my body wash," I declared dramatically.

He nodded and offered me a cheeky smile. "I like smelling it on my skin, it makes me think of you."

Oh. Well, then.

I blushed and rolled my eyes. "Fine, I suppose that's okay."

"I love you, agel." He yanked me into him.

"I love you, too."

EPILOGUE

BYRON

"This is bullshit," I stated easily as the four of us sat around Edwin's office. "We just got done with a fucking war, Edwin. They just got done with a war! Tell them to back off. Vegas needs to rest."

My brother shook his head. "They won't let it go and it looks bad on our part. Double standards and all."

"What about her health?" Kodiak demanded his eyes intense.

"She will go last," Edwin dictated. "Every day they will be testing one of us. I will explain the need for her to be last in the order."

Blue spoke then. "And what are we doing about the letter from those women?"

I shook my head and smiled. The Dark Fae had been hiding their very own group. An anti-government assassin group named the Obsidian Butterflies and they were very interested in Vegas. We had heard rumors and Edwin had met a supposed one once, but this was different. They were openly communicating. They were also interested in Bandit but for a much different reason. One we didn't know how to approach yet. I kept quiet about it for now."

"After the holidays," I offered.

All of us nodded and seemed to be lost in thought. I closed my eyes and felt a surge of thankfulness that Trouble made it home safe. I had a few moments where I considered that she wouldn't, that they may have fucked her up too far. Instead, she was alive and, despite looking bruised and far to thin, she was alive.

My body twitched, urging me to go upstairs.

"I can't believe that fucker tried to marry her to that piece of shit," Blue spoke softly, his eyes darkening.

I shook my head. "Yeah, I'd prefer to never see her in another wedding dress unless her cute self is walking down the aisle towards us."

The room seemed to still at my outspoken opinion but I didn't retract them. Instead, I met Blue and Kodiak's eyes. They seemed on the verge of wanting to say something.

Blue jumped in. "Regarding that, we need to talk to the two of you."

Edwin sat back and tilted his head as I waited patiently.

Kodiak spoke in a rough voice. "When we watched Vegas get hurt our sophomore year, we sat down and decided that we never wanted to lose her to another man. That we would rather share. At the time, we had no idea what that meant, but now. I mean now, shit, I just know that there is no one else for us."

I nodded.

"We want to make this permanent," Blue spoke softly, his voice filled with determination.

"What are you saying?" I asked.

"I'm asking," he stated. "I'm asking about how serious you are about your future with Vegas."

Silence met the question for the moment.

Edwin spoke, his eyes darkening slightly. I knew it was hard for him to deal with Blue's commands but my brother had the control to navigate it. Maker help us all if they ever get into a fight. "I have always been serious about my past, present, and future with Vegas. I don't plan on ever leaving her side again."

Blue looked at me. "And you?"

I smiled authentically. "What had I just said about the wedding dress again? I love Trouble and I always will. I'm in it for the long run."

Blue and Kodiak seemed to exhale and looked at each other. I watched as the blood mage pulled something from his pocket and held it out to both of us. My eyebrows rose as I looked at the image on the paper.

"When?" Edwin asked, his lips tilting up.

"Christmas morning," Blue announced as Kodiak nodded.

"Are we asking?" I asked softly.

Kodiak snorted with mirth. "I think it may be easier to just put it there ourselves."

She was going to lose it.

My eyes found the picture again as my heart squeezed. Yeah, this was the right move. I didn't want to move forward with our lives without making it very clear who our family was. I closed my eyes and breathed in the acceptance through our bond. I hadn't ever thought we would find something like this. Somewhere that we felt loved and accepted.

"We can make that happen," I nodded towards the illustration, "time frame wise."

Blue flashed a smile. "I was hoping you'd say that."

M. SINCLAIR

INTERNATIONAL & US BEST SELLER

M. Sinclair is a Chicago native, parent to 3 cats, and can be found writing almost every moment of the day. Despite being new to publishing, M. Sinclair has been writing for nearly 10 years now. Currently, in love with the Reverse Harem genre, she plans to publish an array of works that are considered romance, suspense, and horror within the year. M. Sinclair lives by the notion that there is enough room for all types of heroines in this world and being saved is as important as saving others. If you love fantasy romance, obsessive possessive alpha males, and tough FMCs, then M. Sinclair is for you!

Just remember to love cats... that's not negotiable.

ALSO BY M. SINCLAIR

Vengeance Series

#graysguards

Book 1 - Savages

Book 2 - Lunatics

Book 3 - Monsters

Book 4 - Psychos

Complete Series

The Red Masques Series

#vegasandherboys

Book 1 - Raven Blood

Book 2 - Ashes & Bones

Book 3 - Shadow Glass

Book 4 - Fire & Smoke

Book 5 - Dark King

Complete Series

Tears of the Siren Series

#lorcanslovers

Book 1 - Horror of Your Heart

Book 2 - Broken House

Book 3 - *Announced soon!*

The Dead and Not So Dead Trilogy

#narcshotties

Book 1 - Queen of the Dead

Book 2 - Tea Time with the Dead

Book 3 - *Announced soon!*

Descendant Series

#novasmages

Book 1 - Descendant of Chaos

Book 2 - Descendant of Blood

Book 3 - Descendant of Sin (*coming soon!*)

Reborn Series

#mayasmages

Book 1 - Reborn In Flames

Book 2 - Soaring in Flames

The Wronged Trilogy

#valentinasvigilanties

Book 1 - Wicked Blaze Correctional

Standalones

Peridot (Jewels Cafe Series)

Collaborations

Rebel Hearts Heists Duet (M. Sinclair & Melissa Adams)

Book 1 - Steal Me

Forbidden Fairytales (The Grim Sisters - M. Sinclair & CY Jones)

Book 1 - Stolen Hood

Book 2 - Knights of Sin

Book 3 - Deadly Games

Join our Group on Facebook The Grim Sisters Reading Group.

STALK ME... REALLY, I'M INTO IT

Instagram: msinclairwrites
    Facebook: Sinclair's Ravens (New content announced!)
    Twitter: @writes_sinclair

Printed in Great Britain
by Amazon